S0-AAE-998

FROM HELL TO HAVANA

Hoyt Barber

DISCARDED
MASSILLON PUBLIC LIBRARY

JUN 14 2007

MAIN
MASSILLON PUBLIC LIBRARY

Copyright © 2007, Hoyt Barber

All rights reserved. No part of this book may be used or reproduced in any manner whatsoever without the written permission of the Publisher.

Printed in the United States of America.

For information address:
Durban House Publishing Company, Inc.
7502 Greenville Avenue, Suite 500, Dallas, Texas 75231

Library of Congress Cataloging-in-Publication Data
Barber, Hoyt, 1955-

From Hell to Havana / Hoyt Barber

Library of Congress Control Number: 2006936088

p. cm.

ISBN 1-930754-92-2
First Edition

10 9 8 7 6 5 4 3 2 1

Visit our Web site at
http://www.durbanhouse.com

Dedicated to my father, Harry L. Barber.

And in memory of my friend of thirty years, Edward H. Kelly, founding publisher of *Millionaire Magazine*.

Special thanks to my editor, Paul Thayer, my literary agent, Kitty L. Kladstrup, and my publisher, Durban House, all of whom have enhanced my writing life.

This novel is a work of fiction. Names, characters, places and incidents are either the product of the author's imagination or are used fictitiously. Any resemblance to actual persons, living or dead, events or locales is entirely coincidental.

"May you live in interesting times."

—an old Chinese curse

Prologue

IF CHOU HWA AND HIS PASSENGERS WEREN'T KILLED FIRST, he knew they were about to change the world. He sat behind the wheel of his black Rolls-Royce on a quiet Hong Kong side street and stared into the predawn darkness, sweat coursing from his dark hairline to the bulge of his jowls. He hated this business, but he wouldn't show his guests that he was scared shitless, and felt half crazy waiting for his fourth and final passenger.

Until now he had had the distinctions of being the world's largest shipping magnate and the brother of Hong Kong's chief executive administrator. Important, yes. But he would gladly sacrifice his brother and their family honor for tonight's plan to succeed. That and only that would give his life meaning.

America had to go down, this time for good.

He listened to the soft conversation of his three passengers in the backseat. How could they sound so calm? And where the hell was Liu? Chou Hwa wanted to scream.

He started the ignition, punched on the AC, and squinted into the rearview mirror. General Fuk Yat Poon looked relaxed as he spoke quietly to Madame Lieng Huang. The general's girlfriend, Suzi Nahn, sat between them. Her short black dress shimmered in the scant light from a string of yellow lanterns hanging nearby, showing off her curves. The general's hand cupped her knee, and she laughed, a soft music.

Chou Hwa studied Madame Huang's aging face. The Dragon Lady. *You get the face you deserve,* he thought, remembering the old saying. She was tough, an international arms trader, masquerading in pink silk. An absurdly large ruby necklace rested on her bosom.

Sudden movement on the street grabbed Hwa's attention. Finally. Liu Zhengzhong hurried from the stone building, lugging a cardboard box filled with sensitive documents and computer disks. Hwa pushed the trunk release button, and the car shuddered when Liu dropped the box into the trunk. Hwa felt like singing, until nausea threatened to double him over.

The trunk lid thumped shut, and Liu slid quickly into the seat beside him.

"Where the hell were you?" asked Hwa.

Liu was a member of the mysterious Xinhua.

The rodent just gave him a brooding look.

Hwa fought down the bitter taste of bile at the back of his throat as he accelerated and blended into the sparse traffic of Nathan Road. Heart pounding, he directed the car toward Kwai Chung in Western Kowloon, the busiest port in the world.

No one said a word. He and the four others hadn't been together for six months, since they'd attended the festive annual spring reception for China's official press agency in Hong Kong. Recently the secretive Xinhua had changed its name to the Liaison Office of the Central People's Government in the Hong Kong Special Administrative Region. The move was intended to improve public relations, but everyone knew the group had been a front for the Communist Party in Hong Kong since the late 1940s. Xinhua had wielded an invisible but absolutely powerful hand in the government, business, and the media.

The silence became uncomfortable. Hwa glanced into his rearview mirror. General Fuk Yat Poon was watching him.

"Did the payment arrive?" the general asked.

He held the man's gaze in the mirror. "Yes. Confirmed two

days ago."

"Good. One less thing to think about."

Hwa looked back at the road, his thoughts doing acrobatics.

"I personally handled that transfer because of the delay," Suzi Nhan said. "Our Zurich bankers traced it to a London correspondent. They sat on the funds for no reason, didn't even offer an excuse."

"More cash for the bank's coffers," said Madame Huang. "Making interest. Sometimes the transfers can take weeks."

"Everyone else has been paid, General," Miss Nhan said.

Hwa guided the big car into a sweeping turn through the darkness of the nearly empty streets.

"When we get to your headquarters, Hwa," the general said, "we will double-check the inventory against our list and Lieng's to make sure we have everything. We must assemble the weapons quickly when they arrive in Havana."

"Do not worry, General," Madame Huang said. "That has been done. Everything is in order."

"I trust it is, Madame," the general said. "But we must be concerned about theft. Corruption is everywhere."

"True," she said.

"As soon as the shipment goes out tonight," the general said, "I will advise Castro."

Madame Huang nodded. Hwa knew she had assigned two technical advisors to the military. "I have added three more exotic weapons to the package at no extra charge," she told the general and smiled. "But you need our special advisors to ready them." She touched the general's arm. "Try them. You will want to buy more."

"You are a shrewd woman, Lieng," the general said, his face unreadable.

"We are all for the same cause, no?" She smiled again.

Her two advisors were spit in the wind compared to the general's hundred and ten men from the People's Liberation Army, ready to sail on a different ship. They were specialists in weapons, terrorism, and deployment. As far as Hwa could tell, Washington knew nothing.

"Tonight's shipment will give us the advantage." He patted his chest. "And Castro is in our pocket."

"When is the next shipment scheduled?" Miss Nahn asked.

"In ten days," Madame Huang said. "Everything has been set in motion. Many shipments will depart like clockwork in the next few months."

Miss Nahn said, "Won't someone notice a pattern?"

Hwa, surprised to hear the question from her, answered on behalf of his family's business. "The Happy Fortune freighters are registered in many tax-haven countries. Cayman Islands, Bermuda, Panama. You see? Insulation."

"Good," Madame Huang said, then chuckled grimly. "If we fail, Beijing will cut off our hands. Already the general has had a problem with them."

"If this goes smoothly," he said, ignoring her remark, "we will receive premier treatment. Otherwise . . ." He shrugged.

Again the group lapsed into silence.

Finally the general said, "But you are correct, Lieng. I do have a problem. I am caught between Taiwan and China, and now it is getting worse."

Suddenly Liu Zhengzhong turned to the general. "Beijing did not intimidate Taiwan very much, right? They keep moving farther away from us." When no one replied, he said, "Chen Shui-bian's election was terrible luck. He is too independent, too happy to do business with the United States."

The general nodded slowly. "It is a huge problem. Washington is using the situation to their advantage, of course. Their intelligence is limited in our country, thank the gods. But Taiwan's is excellent, and we know they are giving information to the U.S. Defense Intelligence Agency. Dangerous business. This forces our hand."

"I read in the *Sing Tao Daily,*" Miss Nahn said softly, "that the

U.S. may give weapons to Taiwan."

"Yes," said the general, looking at her, his hand still on her knee. "The Taiwanese want U.S. support. Washington has moved two aircraft carrier groups to the Taiwan Strait. Worse, they may sell them equipment to create a missile defense system."

Madame Huang grunted. "Our threats are useless against Taiwan." Her rubies glittered as she turned toward the general. "Our work, this move, may be the only thing that can neutralize Washington. It is brilliant, General. A bold move—by you, and by Beijing."

He nodded at her. "It was a big challenge to sell them. Beijing wants the western hemisphere shaky like this one, but they are cautious. If we don't get in there first, a rogue state might." He thumped his fist on his knee. "As it is, those fucking North Koreans have long-range missiles that can hit California. Ready to fly. Ours can only reach Hawaii. And the goddamned Arabs are ahead of us, and determined."

Madame Huang said, "But now, General, we will make our move."

Hwa slowed and searched the streets, watching for an important turn.

The general said, "Yes, and this moment is our best chance. The U.S. is vulnerable now and too slow in developing the Theatre Missile Defense shield. Only talk. Little progress." As he spoke, his voice rose. "Without our Cuba plan, we may never target the continental U.S. Internal problems would kill us first."

Hwa pulled the vehicle to a stop in a left-turn lane at a red light, and when the light changed he made the turn and accelerated. "Well, General, sir," he said, "I have developed a careful plan with your personnel. These shipments will go fast, and smoothly. And undetected, until Beijing decides to show their hand."

"Good," said the general. "That is what I want to hear."

"As for weapons, General," Madame Huang said, "I can supply all you want."

Hwa knew that the Dragon Lady was both fearless and ruthless. Now here she was, sitting in his back seat and conspiring with a general, no less!

Liu Zhengzhong sat quietly beside him, but Hwa thought his restless hands told another story. The little man was a nervous wreck, just as he was. Hwa knew that Liu was a communist, like everyone else. But he also knew that he was slightly cuckoo, obsessed with China's problems in the world. Liu's eyes shifted, giving him a haunted look that Hwa barely recognized. Hwa also knew that Liu thought the idea of backing Castro was pure suicide. But Liu was not a military strategist. He was only a journalist, and not a real one, at that. Hwa decided, to protect their mission, they would have to handle him with care.

He had started to feel more relaxed during the quiet progress through the city. But now a pair of headlights had settled in behind the Rolls, and his breath caught in his throat. His eyes throbbed at the sight of the dual shining orbs in the rearview mirror. Naturally a few other cars would be on the streets, even at this hour, but as he looked again he had the sick feeling that these lights had been behind him way too long, just hanging back there. Watching him.

"I'm taking a slight detour," he said.

"Detour?" The general sounded alarmed.

"Probably nothing," Hwa said, trying to sound calm. "A car has been following us. I don't know for how long."

Miss Nahn said, "Someone is always out at night."

"Mr. Hwa, turn left there," Madame Huang said, pointing. "We will lose him."

Hwa responded instantly and smoothly, as did his well-engineered British automobile.

Hwa accelerated along the dark, narrow street, checking his rearview mirror. The others also turned to look. The other car slowed, then nearly stopped on the main boulevard. It paused, then went on.

"We have a problem, Hwa." The general's voice was icy.

Liu snapped his head around. "Who are they?"

"Who knows?" the general said. "Keep going, Hwa. Get to headquarters. *Fast.*"

Hwa tromped the gas pedal.

"If someone is following us, we will soon know," the general said.

Hwa urged the Rolls toward a main artery that he knew would lead them directly to Kwai Chung. When they swept onto the wider road, he accelerated into the straightaway. Just then a car appeared at a side street on the left and tore out, tires squealing, and fell in behind them. A moment later a second car shot out of a street just ahead and spun to face them.

Hwa yanked the wheel and swerved wildly, barely controlling the heavy Rolls as it barreled past the car. He buried the pedal and surged forward. A glance in the rearview mirror confirmed his worst fear. Both cars were hot on their tail, and the headlights were gaining on him. "Damn them!" he said.

"General, I have a gift for you," Madame Huang said, her voice sounding calm and centered behind him. "I think this is a good time for gifts." She pulled a large, black, hard-shelled case onto her lap. "A special heat-seeking, handheld missile. Do you mind, General, if we use it now?"

"Holy Buddha!" whispered Liu.

"Why wait?" the general agreed.

Her face luminescent, Madame Huang opened the case and smoothly assembled the weapon as the chase cars closed the distance. She looked like a child at play. "Beautiful piece," she said. "Do you like your new toy?"

The general smiled and nodded. "I like it very much, Madame Huang."

She lowered her window and lifted the two-foot-long, tubular weapon with both hands. She leaned out, balanced the launcher on one shoulder, took aim, and fired.

The weapon flashed, and seconds later one of the cars ex-

ploded so thunderously that the Rolls shuddered with the shock-
wave. The fireball behind them careened drunkenly into parked
cars and exploded again. Hwa death-gripped the wheel and held
to his speeding course.

"Beautiful!" the general said.

"Unfortunately, sir," Madam Huang said, "I brought only
one."

Hwa peered into the mirror. The second vehicle slewed
around the blazing wreck and bore down on them with renewed
determination. He had to do something fast.

"Hang on!" he shouted. He cranked the wheel violently, fighting to keep the hurtling Rolls on course. The steel-belted radials
screamed in response, an octave lower than the shriek that issued
from Suzi Nahn's slender throat. Just when Hwa thought he was
winning the battle, the right front tire exploded, and he lost all control. He gave up just before the front wheels slammed over the
curb and launched them toward the base of a towering skyscraper.
The last thing his senses registered was just the first part of the
most horrible sound he had ever heard.

Moments later, the driver of the following car decelerated
with quick care and chirped to a stop near the wrecked Rolls. He
took in the horrific scene, his heart still racing, and fought to dis-
cipline his emotions.

"Listen," he said to his passenger. "We go in fast. Check the
status, grab evidence, and get the fuck out of here."

The other man nodded, and they opened their doors. They
stepped into the eerie scene, the only sounds a thin hiss from
somewhere and the hot tick of metal. The driver approached cau-
tiously, gun in hand, feeling dizzy and holding his breath, his partner close behind him. He peered with a sickening interest into the
smoldering vehicle and at the gruesome scene there. Nothing
moved.

"Hey!" His partner gestured him toward the trunk. The sprung lid revealed a single cardboard box.

"Grab it, and let's go." He glanced around. The street was dark and empty.

They hustled back to their car. His partner heaved the box into the back seat and jumped into the front next to him. They shut their doors quietly and sped away from the scene and into the welcome cover of the night.

1

Déjà Vu

CLIFF BLACKWELL STOOD ON THE BOW OF HIS YACHT, his twelve-gauge Webley and Scott shotgun raised to his shoulder, and aimed at a clay pigeon as it arced over the Mediterranean Sea across a cloudless early November sky. When the spinning disk floated into his sights, he squeezed the trigger, and it exploded into tiny fragments. He lowered the gun and smiled at Victoria.

"Great shot," she said. "How does that antique feel?"

"Wonderful." He took a deep breath of the sea air and gazed at the blurred coastline of the Riviera. He felt good. Lately his life had seemed nearly carefree. And at the moment he was enjoying the peace of being far enough from their berth in Monte Carlo to indulge in some shooting practice in the late morning sun. He liked the deep sense of privacy and freedom he felt on the open water. He smiled at Victoria and said, "Your turn."

A mobile telephone rang, startling him. He had spent many years with telephones, but recently he had gotten used to infrequent communication with the outside world.

Victoria grabbed the phone and passed it to him. He took a few steps down the deck to speak.

Victoria raised her own shotgun and shouted "Pull!" The clay bird spun aloft, and she followed it with her gun.

"Cliff?" The voice on the line was distinct, but sounded strangely disembodied. "Cliff, Grant Love here."

Cliff was relieved to hear the friendly voice. He covered the mouthpiece until Victoria had fired and the disk burst into shrapnel. She flashed him a big smile, and he gave her a thumbs-up.

He exchanged pleasantries with Grant, who was Victoria's father and who had become a good friend to him as well.

Grant said, "Cliff, I won't waste your time just now, but you need to come to Washington."

Cliff listened to dead air, suddenly feeling concerned. "Come to D.C.?"

"Yes, Cliff," said Grant. "For a meeting. It's important. You need to leave right away. I'll explain everything when I see you."

Cliff didn't know what to say. He leaned against the rail and squinted at the sleek profile of Victoria's cobalt blue Bell helicopter gleaming in the sun on its special helipad. "Grant, I need to know more."

"They just said it's a big deal. Something about a car accident in Hong Kong. Sensitive stuff."

"What?"

"I know. What can such a thing have to do with you?"

"Grant . . ."

"Don't worry, Cliff. They assured me that it's not about the past."

Cliff sighed heavily. "All right, Grant. You tell me to come, I'm coming."

"Good. The sooner, the better."

"I'll leave tomorrow. I'll fax you the details tonight."

"All right. Then I'll set the meeting for the following morning. Meantime, I'll get back to you about where and when to meet me."

"Okay, Grant. See you soon."

"Give my love to Vic. And don't worry."

Cliff rejoined Victoria, the conversation still playing in his mind. Suddenly everything looked unreal in the brassy sunlight. Victoria put down her shotgun and swept her golden mane back from her face.

"Good shooting, Vic. That was your father on the phone."

She looked surprised and worried. "Dad? How's he doing?"

"Good," said Cliff, feeling distracted.

"Short conversation. He didn't ask for me?"

"He sent his love, but he's a bit preoccupied. He received a call from the government."

"Oh?" Her eyes narrowed.

Cliff glanced at the crew member who had been working the clay pigeon launcher. "That's all for now, Peter," he said. "Tell the captain we'll need to return to port right away." He handed his shotgun to him. "And put this back in my collection, would you?"

When the young man was gone, Cliff gathered his thoughts and looked at Victoria. She regarded him steadily, worry clouding her eyes. He took her hand. "They want me to come to Washington, Vic. For a meeting."

"What kind of meeting?"

"Something important, according to your dad." He squeezed her hand. "Nothing about the past, they assured him."

She looked skeptical. "Oh, sure. You know it'll be trouble."

"I hope not. But what choice do I have? These guys can be persistent."

"I'm worried, Cliff." Her voice was barely audible, and her eyes had darkened.

He was worried, too, and that old feeling of tightness had returned to his chest. He tried to stay calm so he wouldn't scare Victoria even more. He fingered a lock of golden hair from her forehead. "I'm meeting them with your father in thirty-six hours. We'll know soon enough."

"Dammit, Cliff, I know it's going to be bad. I can feel it."

"Listen, Vic, don't let it get to you. We don't even know what they want. Yet."

She sighed. "I'll pack your bag. I just hope . . ." She looked away.

Cliff hugged her. "Take it easy, Vic. It's just a meeting. I'll be back soon."

The next morning, Cliff sat alone in the cabin of his Gulf-stream V jet, staring absently out the round window at the wide, blue skies over the Atlantic, already missing Victoria and his warm Mediterranean world. It was the second Monday of November, so he knew the weather in Washington would be cold. He thought about the meeting. What the hell did they want with him now? He had no more business with the feds, and no loose ends to discuss. Fifteen months had passed since he'd cut his deal with them, which had granted him total immunity from prosecution. If something needed to be discussed about that, he would have heard from them sooner.

The plexiglas reflected a thin image of his face. He figured he looked just like what he almost was at the moment, a man of forty-something, the picture of health and success, without a care in the world as he sat in comfort in his luxurious private jet. But the truth was much different now. What peace he had known was recent and brief, and now that seemed to be over. His left eyelid twitched.

A vivid scene flashed in his mind—the time when Larson was shot to death right in front of him. Alfred Larson. His former chief of security and his brother-in-law, but also an undercover NSA man. When they blew him away, the gunmen just said it was a matter of "national security." Granted, Larson was a prick, and he had to be stopped. The hit team had swept in by helicopter and landed on his yacht at the last minute and wasted no time. They had saved Cliff the trouble of shooting Larson himself. His nightmares about that scene had finally become less frequent, like the other bad dreams about that time, and he no longer spent nearly every waking minute thinking about those days.

In fact, the last fifteen months had been one of the most peaceful times in his life. For once he had felt a complete sense of freedom and almost no pressure. But Grant's call had brought it all back, front and center. He gazed again at the distant clouds.

Victoria Love had helped to see him through that bad time, and he had recently thought about asking her to marry him. They had sailed to Monte Carlo together to relax, and they were planning a world cruise. He felt good about the idea of marrying Vic. He had spent too many years alone after his first wife and son were killed in a car accident.

Victoria was beautiful and intelligent, compassionate and mentally strong, driven to succeed on her own terms, and a true risktaker. His kind of package. And she had been the best kind of friend during his troubles the year before, as had her father, Grant. She had been through a lot with him, more than most people would have taken on. But she might have doubts about committing herself to even more, and he couldn't blame her now.

Cliff's gut told him something big was brewing in Washington. He was anxious to see Grant and learn more. He felt good just knowing he'd be with him. But the throbbing pain in his temple was a warning. He'd be lucky to experience a moment's peace at all anytime soon. He might be lucky to *live* until his wedding day, much less plan the thing.

Just after dawn the following morning, CIA agent Donald Witherspoon met with his boss, Cecil Danforth, and his colleague John MacGregor at headquarters to debrief prior to Clifford Blackwell's arrival. Despite the early hour, Witherspoon was wide awake. Ever since his divorce a few years back, he had basically lived only for the job. And he liked his new assignment. Liked it a lot.. This meeting had potential, too. The three of them were a select team, chosen to spearhead this special project. They'd already put in long weeks. He was tired, sure, and he figured the others were, too. But he was up for the meeting with Blackwell.

The three men sat together with their usual familiarity in the typically bland office at CIA headquarters, Danforth at his mahogany desk and the other two seated in gray upholstered guest chairs in front of him. Each of them nursed a cup of coffee.

"Glad we have some time before this Blackwell shows up," said MacGregor. He coughed once, the gruff hack of a smoker. "I hear he's a savvy guy with too much money. Knows a few of our secrets."

"He's slick all right, John," Witherspoon said. "And he's well connected. But don't worry. We know a few of *his* secrets, too."

"Might be the man for the job," said MacGregor. "But do you think he'll do it?"

Witherspoon shrugged. "I dunno. But, remember, he's got a strong ally in Grant Love. The old man's been a go-between for us with Blackwell on some other sensitive stuff. This'll be the first time we deal with Blackwell directly."

Danforth nodded. "That's right. Rumor is, Love's company is merging with another advertising giant, and that'll make 'em the world's biggest. Let's handle Blackwell carefully, or else . . . Well, it could be embarrassing." He patted his pocket, looking for his smokes. "They threatened us with bad publicity once before, but fortunately that didn't happen."

"He's probably still sore from the last time," said MacGregor.

Witherspoon glanced at his lean colleague and silently admired the European cut of his olive suit. His brown eyes were alive this morning, shining with an inner light. "Why'd he ever want to do business with us?"

"I'm not sure," said Witherspoon, "but my background research on Blackwell turned up something pretty interesting."

"Like what?" asked MacGregor.

"His father was a gunrunner."

"Oh, yeah?"

"Doesn't fit this guy's profile, does it?" said Danforth.

"You're right," Witherspoon said. "The Blackwell family actually has a long history in the banking business."

"So how come his father's so colorful?" MacGregor said.

Witherspoon chuckled. "Well, his grandfather lost the family fortune. The whole estate went to the maid."

"You're shitting me," said MacGregor.

"Nope." Witherspoon smiled. "Not a penny trickled down to his dad."

"So," Danforth said, "Blackwell's father had to be a self-made man, so to speak."

Witherspoon nodded. "And so did Blackwell."

"Where'd the old man run the guns to?" MacGregor said.

Witherspoon grinned. "This part you'll love. Cuba."

"No kidding? When?"

"He was helping the anti-Batista underground in the late fifties."

Danforth said, "If this buccaneer spirit runs in the blood, we may be in luck."

"Blackwell's also an ex-Marine," Witherspoon said, "but maybe not typical."

"What do you know about his service record?" MacGregor asked.

"Stationed at Camp Pendleton, 1978 to 1980. Seems he chose the military over higher education, something about no funds for college. Joined the Marines instead. He went into business right after that."

"Four years active duty?" MacGregor asked.

"Just short of three," said Witherspoon. "Got caught by an accidental explosion during a training exercise. Shattered his knee."

"Honorable discharge?"

"Right, but he wasn't happy about it, I heard." Witherspoon

rubbed his temple in thought. "Another thing. I called the FBI because I know they've had a few run-ins with him. They put me on to a special agent out of Chicago. Sam Paradise. Apparently this guy's made a study of Blackwell. Claims he likes to curl up under a rock, wait for the right time to strike." He smiled.

Danforth said, "Did this Paradise guy tell you anything else?"

Witherspoon shrugged. "He just said they perceive him as a guy who lives for the kill, moneywise. A shark in financial waters."

Danforth retrieved his cigarettes. "Well, we've been over all the alternatives." He lit up, took a long draw, and leaned back in his chair. He wore his usual conservative dark blue suit, and his face was a roadmap of experience beneath a full head of wavy brown hair going gray. He carefully blew a lungful of smoke off to one side. "I think Blackwell's our best bet. And I think we can work with him."

"Operation Smoke-Out is way overdue," MacGregor said. "Castro doesn't even need a reason anymore. He fought hard to survive that last health scare, sure. But if the old bastard gets senile he may decide to push the button himself."

Witherspoon chuckled. "True. Convenient that the Chinese are trying to support him. Just what we needed, a good excuse to go back in there and kick his ass."

"The timing couldn't be better," said Danforth. He tapped his cigarette on an ashtray. "We've got lots of issues on the horizon, and we can't afford any delays because of a new president." He left the cigarette burning in the ashtray and quietly cracked his knuckles. "By the time the new chief gets up to speed, Cuba'll be armed with Chinese missiles pointed directly at us, gentlemen. If the president had any sense, we would be in DefCon Three already."

Witherspoon stood and stretched his tall frame as he paced slowly around the room. "The Chinese have been supporting other rogue states, too," he said. "Exporting weapons of mass destruction to their friends."

"True," MacGregor said, heading for the coffeepot. He

splashed a little too much into his cup and grabbed a stack of napkins. "China made a lot of progress under the previous administration. And how about those illegal Chinese contributions to the last presidential campaign? And the secrets the Chinese grabbed on all of our weapons systems? Then the cover-ups. Christ." He picked up his coffee cup. "Hell, we may as well have published the blueprints on the Internet."

Witherspoon grinned. He loved this stuff. "Be interesting to see what the new president does," he said.

Danforth joined Witherspoon at the window. He gave him a look that Witherspoon couldn't read. Danforth leaned on the sill and said, "We thought the situation between us, Taiwan, and China was something. But this is a real curve ball. We gotta move quick, or we'll have another Cuban Missile Crisis on our hands."

"Just what we need after that business in New York," MacGregor said.

Witherspoon returned to his chair and said, "So it's simple. We have to protect Taiwan and snuff Castro. And kill any more ideas in those tiny Chinese brains about Cuba, with or without Castro."

"We all know how bad things are now between China and Taiwan," Danforth said. "So it's critical to keep the flow of intelligence on China between Taiwan and the U.S."

MacGregor sat down too, coffee in hand. "China's always been pissed off about our support of Taiwan. That probably started this Cuba thing. That and the fact of our lame-duck president and the new guy coming in."

Danforth nodded. "And they even had the nerve to warn us." He reached for his cigarette, which had almost burned down. "Like with the little guys, China uses our military strength as an excuse to build long-range missiles." He took a last drag from his cigarette and stubbed it out.

Witherspoon said, "Yeah, the Chinese really want a missile that can carry nuclear, biological, or chemical warheads and reach the whole continental U.S., not just Hawaii."

"And we know that Cuba," Danforth said, "has developed advanced biological weapons technology and is likely exporting it to other terrorist states."

"Bad shit," Witherspoon said.

"Damn straight," Danforth said. "Cuba's military threat has been underplayed for a long time."

"And we know that Cuba could launch a limited biological warfare offensive against us right now," MacGregor said.

"Hell, developing weapons of mass destruction is the goal of all these hostile countries," Danforth said. "Look at the Iraqis, the Libyans, the Syrians, the Egyptians, the Sudanians, and the Iranians, all backed by the Russians. Next it'll be Pakistan and India. They already hate each other's guts. Greece and Turkey will probably haunt us, too."

MacGregor said, "Everybody wants a piece of our ass."

Danforth nodded. "Including all those international terrorists we're stalking right now. Not just our favorites like bin Laden and Abu Nidal, poor dead bastard, but hundreds more, just biding their time."

MacGregor stood up. "We've got to develop the National Missile Defense program." He rapped on the desktop and looked at Danforth. "You have an extra smoke?" He took the offered cigarette and held it between a thumb and finger. "But everyone's afraid we'll escalate the arms race, maybe start a nuclear war. But the race'll go on anyway. Only difference, we'll be more vulnerable."

"On the other hand," said Danforth, lighting up again, "we have our dear friend Fidel." He took a deep drag and exhaled, squinting through the smoke. "As you know, this agency has gone through a shitstorm thanks to our involvement with Castro. We've waited for this day for forty years. We can't blow it this time. If we do, I don't even want to imagine the fallout."

Witherspoon liked this kind of talk. Sure, it was partly re-hash, but hell, the three of them hardly ever got to hang out and shoot the shit. "By now Castro's probably heard that his shipment won't be arriving as scheduled," he said. "Poor baby. I just wish we knew if he's gotten any others. The Chinese don't know what we've learned, so they'll probably reorganize their efforts and try again."

He walked back to the window. The new day was all bleak sky and barren trees. One thing he liked about this room: it had a window. He hated the dark, tomblike rooms in the interior of this godforsaken building.

Behind him, MacGregor said, "Wow. Castro must have shit a brick when they told him the bad news."

He looked at MacGregor. "Yeah. Probably got that stupid-ass expression on his face. Like he's constipated."

Danforth smiled. "Wait till he sees what's in store for him. But we gotta get going on it."

Witherspoon coughed from all the smoke. "He's really just a piss-ant dictator on a shitty little island. He must love being the center of strategic interest again like he was when the Russians were kissing his ass. I'll bet he's built up enough hatred to be really dangerous this time."

"Been noisy lately," MacGregor said. "He and his buddy Olusegun Obasanjo in Nigeria and the rest of the Group of Seventy-Seven. All beating the drums again. Complaining about the big bad capitalist rats starving them out."

Witherspoon eyed MacGregor, who seemed to be getting pumped up. "Same old crap," he said. "He's always on the warpath about something. The usual trick to maintain a united Cuba."

"You're right, Don," said MacGregor. "Castro doesn't *want* improved relations with us. It benefits him to play the martyr. Otherwise, his little kingdom would crumble."

When someone knocked on the door, Witherspoon stepped over and opened it. A professional-looking woman peeked in and said that Grant Love had arrived a few minutes early. Witherspoon told her to make him comfortable and ask him to wait for Blackwell.

"Should be arriving any moment," he told her, consulting his watch. "When he shows up, please escort them both to the guest room."

She nodded and left. Witherspoon shut the door and flopped back into his chair. As Danforth and MacGregor spoke about their guest of honor, he reflected on the work they had each done recently. They had been gathering mounds of information on terrorists and rogue states worldwide, an incredible number of foreign countries and splinter groups that were out to get the United States. It was a painfully slow process. At times, he felt it was endless, a lot of grunt work.

Witherspoon tuned out his colleagues as he thought about recent developments. Two CIA agents he knew well had been killed in a wild car chase a couple of weeks before in Hong Kong. That made this more personal. The two surviving agents had found the evidence in the wrecked Rolls in a single file box, all of it detailing China's plan to back Cuba militarily. This was an unexpected windfall. It gave them a quantum leap of intelligence that had thrown the CIA into high gear.

"Operation Smoke-Out" had gotten the green light after a quick round of meetings with select CIA personnel in the tombrooms, with Witherspoon and John MacGregor tapped to spearhead the operation. Although he'd put in years with the agency, this was something special. Few people knew about it, for one thing. It was covert to the max, a major black op. He and John answered only to Cecil Danforth, the head of the internal elite. He was part of a small and special CIA task force that was unaccountable, uncensored, and officially nonexistent. Buried under layers of bureaucracy, it was called the AMD, the Anti-Mass Destruction unit. Its sole purpose was to thwart the advance of weapons of mass destruction. The theme was popular enough in these times and easily justified in the present global climate. The operatives called themselves MDs, an attempt to stress their focus on the preservation of human life amid the looming threats against the U.S. Had

AMD not been secret, he thought, no doubt it would have been generally agreeable to the public anyway, post-September eleventh. But, he reminded himself, it was still outside the law.

He knew that Smoke-Out might be the most covert operation of its kind in forty years. If they failed, the result would surely be a huge international incident, not to mention personal career suicide. Witherspoon shook his head and smiled. He didn't know if he was excited or scared. Probably both.

Clifford Blackwell stifled a yawn as he rode in a taxicab through the crush of Washington's early morning traffic. He caught a glimpse of himself in the cabbie's rearview mirror; his neatly combed dark hair looked fresh, but his face was lined with fatigue. The day before had been long and tiring, what with his sudden departure from Monaco, the transatlantic flight, and a restless night at the Hyatt near Capitol Hill, just minutes from where they had touched down at Reagan International. He hadn't eaten dinner until almost three in the morning. He had reviewed the instructions that Grant Love had left for him while he ate and tried not to think too often of Victoria, away in another world.

Now he was rolling through the gray morning, as directed, heading across the Potomac River to Langley, Virginia, and CIA headquarters. The ride seemed too long, but eventually the cab pulled up in front of the familiar site, and Cliff paid and got out. He took a deep breath of the chill air. His stomach seemed to be full of broken glass. He entered the looming building and strode across the great seal of the Central Intelligence Agency toward an information desk. A uniformed guard intercepted him.

"I'm here to see a Mr. Donald Witherspoon," he said to the guard.

"Mr. Blackwell?"

"Yes."

"Follow me." He led the way toward a corridor on their left.

They exchanged no words as they marched past nondescript offices down the long hallway. Finally they turned to the left and walked through a pair of tall wooden doors. Cliff was relieved to see Grant Love. The older man stood to greet him.

"Am I ever glad to see you," Cliff said, shaking Grant's hand. He was also glad to see his escort depart without a word.

"Good to see you, Cliff. But what a place to meet." He leaned close and said, "Can't imagine what these people want. At the moment it feels stacked in their favor."

"This place is kinda creepy."

Before Grant could reply, a slender young woman in uniform entered the small room. She asked them to follow her and turned and walked away without waiting for a response. She directed them into an empty private office and asked them to be seated.

Grant thanked her, and she left. He touched Cliff's arm and said, "Don't say anything in here that you don't want overheard."

Cliff nodded.

They sat quietly for what seemed like a long time while Cliff studied everything in the room. The place had no pictures or other decorations. Before them stood only a large, circular conference table, along with eight armless chairs and a water cooler. Telephones were conspicuously absent.

"Looks like this room's used for just these occasions," said Cliff, smiling. He tried to take a deep breath and couldn't catch it.

Just then the door opened, and three men filed in and locked it behind them. After an awkward moment they introduced themselves as Donald Witherspoon, John MacGregor, and Cecil Danforth.

Witherspoon was a tall man with short, sandy hair and mustache, friendly eyes, and a relaxed manner. He held a gray fedora. Cliff felt better somehow now that he'd seen this guy. MacGregor was a compact, clean-shaven, dark-complected man, neatly turned out. He seemed like a coiled spring. Danforth was older and appeared to be the real leader, as if he always had the last word and knew it—a man who had been there and done it all twice. Unlike his colleague Witherspoon, Cliff thought, this guy had an edge to him that kept people off balance, which was probably where he wanted them.

The three men stood together, filling the space with their combined energy. Eventually MacGregor looked directly at Cliff and said, "Thank you, gentlemen, for coming here."

Cliff nodded, hoping he looked agreeable.

Witherspoon said, "I'm sure you're both wondering why you're here." He seemed articulate and polite.

"Of course we are," Grant said.

Cliff was happy to have Grant open the dialogue on their behalf.

MacGregor produced a handkerchief and coughed into it. He turned to Cliff, his eyes watery. "We have important business to discuss with you, Mr. Blackwell. But before we ask Mr. Love to excuse us, we want to assure you both that this meeting is unrelated to any of your past dealings with the federal government."

"You can take our word for that," said Witherspoon. "And the reason you're here is top secret. To get to the point, Mr. Blackwell, we need to ask for your help."

"But before we continue," MacGregor said, "we must ask Mr. Love to wait outside. This conversation will be quite sensitive."

Cliff peered at Grant.

When Grant raised a bushy eyebrow, Cliff shrugged. "Oh, all right," Grant said. He rose and walked toward the door as Witherspoon pulled it open.

"I'll make this as quick as possible, Grant," Cliff said, hoping he'd have the control he needed to do so.

Grant nodded to him and withdrew. Witherspoon locked the door again. The three men gathered around Cliff. "Now then, Mr. Blackwell," Witherspoon said quietly.

"I'm listening."

MacGregor said, "You're in a unique position to help us, sir,

partly thanks to your close relationship with the Chicago outfit."

Cliff's mouth went dry. "Actually," he said, "I have no current involvement with them."

"We're aware of your long association with them," MacGregor continued as if he hadn't heard, "specifically with Mr. Russo, the *consigliere* of the Chicago outfit, also known as The Brain, and with that *capo*, Mr. Zanotto." MacGregor's hard stare bored into him.

"Yes," said Cliff, feeling his hackles rise, "but Zanotto's been replaced by Badalamente. I barely know him, and I don't like him."

Witherspoon delicately cleared his throat. "The fact remains, Mr. Blackwell, that you've known Mr. Russo for twenty years, and we know you're well respected at the top of their, uh, organization. This particular family, Mr. Blackwell, has been no less than the single most powerful criminal organization in America for most of the last century."

"Okay," said Cliff, "but why is my *relationship*"—he paused to give the word an ironic twist—"of interest to the CIA?"

"Well," MacGregor said evenly, "we need you to assist us with something. A project we've labeled 'Operation Smoke-Out.' "

Cliff chuckled. "Operation Smoke-Out? What the hell is that?"

"Listen, Mr. Blackwell," Witherspoon said. "We're dead serious. This matter concerns national security, and it will have critical international consequences."

There were those words again—*national security*.

"I've heard that one before," Cliff said, looking directly at this guy Cecil Danforth, who obviously was in charge.

"We understand," said Witherspoon, maintaining his polite approach. "We don't blame you if you have reservations, sir." He took a small step toward Cliff. "But please hear us out."

"Okay, shoot," said Cliff, leaning back in his chair. "I'm all ears."

Danforth approached Cliff and folded his arms. "Before we

proceed, Mr. Blackwell, we must warn you not to discuss this conversation with anyone. Not even with your friend Grant Love. We will tell you about an important covert operation that will affect the international arms race and, we hope, will avert another highly probable attack on the United States."

Cliff felt pinned to his chair by this guy's steady glare, as if he were a lab specimen.

"Furthermore," Danforth said, "this could happen at any time. We have to trust you to keep it a secret no matter what. Our experience with you has been good so far. Let's keep it that way."

Cliff returned Danforth's stare. "I have no reason to say anything. To anyone."

MacGregor said, "Your life could be in danger otherwise, Mr. Blackwell."

Cliff stiffened. "Is that a threat?"

"No," said Witherspoon quietly. "Just a fact."

"All right," Cliff said. "I can't imagine how I can help, but I'm listening."

As if on cue, all three men relaxed and found a chair.

Once they were seated, Witherspoon said, "Recently, we caught the Chinese, red-handed, you might say, in the act of supporting Cuba militarily." His voice was flat, as if he read from a script.

Cliff worked on his dry mouth. The heaviness in his chest telegraphed what these men were up to.

"They may already be backing them financially," said MacGregor. "We don't know."

Witherspoon said, "We've done a lot of work since this came up last month. The situation with Taiwan appears to be the key. It's pushed the Chinese over the edge."

That piqued Cliff's interest. "I read about the Taiwan-China problems recently," he said. "Do you mean the kind of backing Castro got from the Russians in the early 1960s?"

"Precisely," said Danforth.

"Long story," said MacGregor. "But the short of it is that those individuals who organized this plan and the shipments to Cuba of weapons, military personnel, and technical support were all killed at once last month. Car accident."

Oh, yes, the car accident. The skin on the back of Cliff's neck prickled. A lot more had to be going on. He searched their faces for clues, but found nothing.

MacGregor said, "The fact that they were together in the car is curious enough. But they carried with them incredible secrets we wouldn't have learned for a long time, if ever." He rubbed his forehead. "Or in any case, too late."

"Blackwell," said Danforth. He stood and walked absently to a picture on the wall, peering at the small oil of battleships at sea, as if in thought. "This discovery was made very recently. We still don't know if that first shipment went to Cuba." He turned and faced Cliff. "Imagine if we had discovered, in advance, the plans of the terrorists to fly commercial airliners into the World Trade Center and the Pentagon. This is bigger. Much bigger."

Cliff swallowed hard. "You don't know if the first shipment was sent?"

Danforth's eyes looked darkly serious. "I'm afraid not. We do know that more shipments were planned. Of course we can only move so fast ourselves, and it has taken us a few days to analyze the material, verify what we can, and formulate the right plan of action. Needless to say, we cannot allow this to turn into a public debate. As it is, we're still a month and a half away from pulling this off. We can only hope to God that nothing happens between now and then."

Cliff nodded. "But what can you possibly want from me?"

MacGregor took a breath and let it out slowly. "Like we said, we know you're well connected with the Chicago outfit."

Cliff stiffened. "Wait a minute. This sounds like déja vu to me. You want the Mob to knock off Castro?"

All three men gave him a deadpan look.

"You're serious!" Cliff said. He turned to the boss. "Won't it be obvious to the whole world?"

"Don't get us wrong, Cliff," MacGregor said, switching to his first name. "We'd rather remove him ourselves. Certainly we have the trained operatives. But the agency's been under attack since the Bay of Pigs. Everybody blames us for not stopping the 9/11 mess, even accuses us of knowing about it and doing nothing!" He shook his head, looking wounded. "Listen," he said. "We've had everyone crawling up our ass. It's nearly put us out of business."

Cliff eyed him carefully.

Danforth said, "The accusations piled up until we had a meltdown." His tone was confidential, as if Cliff was now his trusted ally. "The press loves to jump on any hint of charges against us, true or not. And the media and the public only cared about themselves, until recently. Now everyone's gotten patriotic."

Witherspoon said, "That's why we'd rather engage Chicago for this job." He stood and approached Cliff. "We know they're effective assassins. If they decide to do it, we know they'll do it right." He shrugged. "And that'd leave us out of it, you know, directly."

Cliff wrestled with amazement and anger. "Yeah," he said, "but that's what you thought last time, I'm sure, and look what happened."

"But it's better this way, Cliff," Witherspoon said, placing a hand briefly on Cliff's shoulder. "Besides, they have a long-standing vendetta against Castro. Maybe they perceive him now as weakening. He was sick as hell for a while there, not that it stopped him. Anyway, maybe they'd like to take back what they felt was theirs before someone else does. Maybe they feel they can open up gaming with Castro out of the way. Who knows?" He shrugged. "Better them than us, even if we *are* suspect. In the end, everyone that matters wins."

Cliff thought about that for a while, hunting for the traps, the pitfalls that could affect him. He almost wanted to laugh. "High stakes," he said finally.

"Indeed, Mr. Blackwell," Danforth said, rising from his big chair. "What happens if China gets their weapons into Cuba? They'll be close enough to spit at us." He shoved his hands into his pockets. "Maybe all they want is to neutralize relations, but I doubt it. There's nothing to stop China, or Castro, for that matter, from waging biological warfare against us. What does Castro have to lose? He's an old man now, with a sense of history. Give him that. He can go for broke."

"Coercive diplomacy," MacGregor said sourly.

"You know, Cliff," Witherspoon said, "China likely has other plans. Probably even Castro doesn't know. In fact, I bet once they're firmly rooted in Cuba, *they'll* get rid of Castro. How can they trust him? Why do they even need him?" He sliced the air with his hand. "China's there for China, not Fidel. Then China will be our next-door neighbor. If we haven't banished Castro in forty years, how the hell will we get rid of the Chinese?"

Cliff studied him. Spots of color had appeared in Witherspoon's fair complexion.

"Personally, I'd rather whack the bastard myself, right now," Witherspoon said. "I have three kids I love."

The three men stared at Cliff. "What if they don't want to do it?" he asked.

"Let's put it this way," MacGregor said. "I don't think they have a choice."

"Is that right? You know I've been squeezed between you people and the Mob before. You guys aren't saints."

"Neither are you, Cliff," Witherspoon said. "Remember, we can be persuasive."

Cliff glared at him. "I've fucking had it with your tactics and your innuendoes. You made my life, and my fiancée's life, a living hell once. You're not doing it again."

"Calm down, Mr. Blackwell," MacGregor said. "We need you to be a willing participant."

"I don't care if you do, MacGregor. I'm lucky I'm not dead. Sorry, gentlemen. I can't help you." He rose and started for the door.

"Actually, Mr. Blackwell," Danforth said, "you don't have a choice. Neither does Chicago. We need you. Get my drift?"

Cliff stopped. "Oh, yeah, I hear you, but I won't play." He was suddenly filled with a sense of dread. "And neither will Vic."

Witherspoon extended a hand. "Look, we don't want to make threats, Mr. Blackwell. We're on an important mission, and we need your cooperation."

"A mission?" Cliff said. "Like the Blues Brothers. Terrific."

MacGregor said, "Look, Blackwell. If you won't do this for us, then think about the thousands of innocent Americans who were killed on September eleventh by the terrorists. Your decision here could save thousands more. Maybe hundreds of thousands."

Cliff let his breath out slowly, shaking his head. "You guys are too much. Anyway . . . Victoria has to be involved in this decision. I need to go back to Monte Carlo and discuss this with her first."

"Jesus Christ, Cliff!" Witherspoon said. "We don't have time for that. What if she says no? We'd be screwed. They could be closer to dropping nukes on us now than you would care to imagine."

Danforth said, "That's true, Mr. Blackwell. I'm afraid we don't have time."

Everyone fixed him with a grim look. Cliff returned to his chair. He raked his fingers through his hair and stared at the floor. Finally he said, "All right. I'll help." He looked at Danforth and said, "But I can't guarantee the Mob's participation. In fact, I make no guarantees of any kind."

The three men stared at him in the humming silence.

Later that day, at six P.M. Washington time but about midnight in the Adriatic Sea, a stout, swarthy sea captain stood at the wheel of his sleek, thirty-eight-foot Fountain speedboat, lulled by the sound of his engines but alert to his darkened surroundings. So far the trip had gone smoothly. Usually the night crossing through the inky seas between Vlore in Albania and Otranto on the heel of the boot of Italy was no problem. Smuggling guns and drugs paid off well when everything went right, but he knew that the trip could be a disaster if the wrong people came along. Especially lately, he thought, with the recent addition of his new cargo—refugees.

But he had to admit he liked this new booty. It was lucrative and easy enough to conceal. And, if he got popped, the charges were less than for smuggling drugs and harder to prosecute.

His crew of three Albanian "tour guides" stood with him near the helm, all keeping watch. His job was to speed the craft to its destination, and theirs was to alert him to any trouble and to make the human cargo stuffed into his hold as compliant as possible.

The tall one called Enrico lowered his binoculars from the dark horizon and turned to him. "So far, all clear, Captain," he said.

"Good," the captain said. He turned to the beefy blond guy on his right. "Hey, Vitaly, how many warm bodies do you have below tonight?"

"Thirty-two. Crammed in like Portuguese sardines."

The captain grunted. *Thank God we don't have to take them to friggin' Spain.*

He thought about this new business. His only job was to deliver them. But he knew something about the story, and it read like a catalogue of despair. Albanians, Kurds, Bangladeshis, Iraqis, Iranians, Turks, Bengalis, Kosovars, and Pakistanis—all fleeing abuse and poverty and all seeking a new life. Anything was better than what they had left behind.

He knew without looking that most of the souls crowded below deck would be women and teenaged boys and girls who had, through involuntary exploitation, succeeded in making it this far. Those poor devils. They'd been duped into this "opportunity," but what other choice did they have? Once on land his passengers would be within the EU borders and, in theory anyway, able to travel with relative ease through former border checkpoints. Any disputes by Italian authorities, known for lax law enforcement, would likely be deflected by falsified travel documents provided by their "travel agents."

An errant wave slapped against the hull, then the speedboat settled.

Gradually, the illegal immigrants would venture north like the others to their ultimate destinations in Switzerland, Austria, and Germany and possibly beyond to Antwerp, Amsterdam, and London. There they'd hook up with family, get jobs in the homes of the rich serving afternoon tea, or use their recently learned trade and work as prostitutes. Later, they would try to obtain legal papers as political exiles.

The captain lifted his broad shoulders in a dismissive shrug and squinted through the spray as his fast boat bucked over the murky waves. What did he care? He just had to deliver his freight.

Squatting in the darkness of the cramped hold, a fifteen-year-old Kosovo girl fought the rising panic of being sandwiched among a dirty gang of strangers. All she knew at the moment was the whine of the powerful engines and the jarring thud of the boat. But her hopes were high. She tried to hypnotize herself to still her fears. She struggled to remain strong and optimistic amid the press and stench of all the others. She squeezed her eyes shut and mouthed a silent prayer.

She tried to remember how glad she was to be out of the nightclubs in Macedonia. *Yes, the boat is cramped and stifling,* she told herself, *but also it is freedom. I am away from that disgusting Blagoja, who used me like a public toilet. My parents would die if they knew I hadn't already made it to the job in Italy, making good money as a dancer. They don't know about my secret journey from home in Odessa to that horrible place called Macedonia. They never will. If they did, their dreams of my becoming a famous ballerina someday would surely be smashed. I am a little fool to have answered that ad. And I had worked so hard!*

She took a deep breath of fetid air through her mouth and listened to the drone of the motors and of the people around her. *I mustn't dwell on this moment. Before, they held me captive, and I could not escape. If I tried, I was beaten and sometimes raped, or both. I just had to lie down. That's all. Lie down for money. For them, for the pigs.*

When she took another breath, her head swirled from the stink of the people and the petrol. A body crushed against her. *Now I am free from the swine. I will send Mother and Father money someday, and then they will know I made it.*

Topside, the captain decided to repeat his instructions to Vitaly and Giuseppe, who kept track of a large gun but little else, and to Enrico, who stood slightly apart, scanning the dark water with powerful infrared binoculars.

"We will be in Otranto soon," he said. "Remember, we must get them all off quickly. Then we go straight back tonight."

The two closest men nodded, but suddenly Enrico lowered his high-tech goggles and whirled, shouting, "Another boat, coming out too fast!"

Giuseppe snatched the glasses away, his assault rifle swinging from one shoulder, and had a look for himself. He nudged the captain. "We are too far from port."

The stocky captain spat a curse and shoved the levers forward, kicking both of the 572-cubic-inch, supercharged engines into full throttle, using every bit of the thousand horsepower at his disposal. The engines roared, and the boat leaped ahead, accelerating quickly.

Enrico steadied himself and grabbed the binoculars for another look. "They are gaining on us, boss."

The captain cursed again. "Okay, okay," he said, trying to remain calm. He looked at Vitaly. "Do we have time to dump them?"

"Maybe."

"Do it!" he shouted, jerking the throttle controls back. "Open the hatch, get them out."

The captain knew the drill. Vitaly would unlock the hatch cover and explain that they had reached their destination, that everyone would have to swim to shore—a possibility they had all known in advance. Thrilled to reach Italy and freedom, they would all babble excitedly, and like good boys and girls they would leap into the sea, with no idea that they didn't stand a chance out here.

Mother of God! How he hated this work sometimes. This wasn't the first time he'd had to scuttle his human cargo. It was bad for business, but to escape the law he had no choice. The floating bodies would be a great diversion for the humanitarians in pursuit, and without his heavy load he could squeeze a top speed of a hundred and five out of her, maybe more. No other boat could outrun him. Later, they would circle back to Otranto to deliver the rest of the shipment, a small stash of drugs.

"*Shit!*" the captain said, his curse lost to the thunder of engines. He could avoid getting busted, but he also had his reputation to think about. What would his blockhead boss say? This screwup might be one too many, he thought, remembering the headlines in the Italian press the last time this had happened.

When the hatch above her opened, the Kosovo girl's heart jumped. Her mouth sucked in the blessed salt fresh air. The big, friendly blond guy who had helped them on board appeared, his face squinting down and barely visible against the black sky. The engines spooled down, and the boat lurched and rolled with the sudden deceleration.

"Okay, folks," Vitaly said into the darkness. "Good news. We are here! But I am afraid you will have to swim a few meters to the shore." He smiled and nodded. "Do not worry. Small boats are around to help you and make sure you are safe. Now climb up here quickly and jump off the side, into the drink."

As the small crowd surged toward the exit, the girl's hopes soared. The blond man spoke encouragements as the people hurriedly squeezed their way topside, one by one. When it was her turn she clasped his strong hand, and he hauled her into the overwhelming freshness of the dark night.

The deck tilted beneath her trembling legs as passengers leaped into the water all around her. She clutched a plastic bag that contained everything she owned in the world. The blond fellow helped her to the side and then stopped and looked into her eyes. He liked her, she could tell. Just then, in her happiness, she could have hugged him.

Then he snapped his head away. "Just go," he said. "Jump and do not look back. You will be fine."

She turned away from him, clasping her bag to her stomach, and took a deep breath. She leapt into the black sea, went under, and flailed back to the surface, stunned by the cold water. She thrashed around with one arm, searching for the others, panic clutching her throat. Suddenly she felt lost and helpless as those around her splashed and cried out, clawing toward nothing.

2

Rogue's Gallery

At noon on the following day Cliff left his Gulfstream V at Palwaukee Airport in a northwest suburb of Chicago and hurried through the November chill toward the usual waiting black limousine. His thoughts were ugly, embracing the events that had shattered his quiet existence since the phone call on his yacht. Only two days before, Victoria and the good life, now a life beyond reach.

Cliff greeted the driver and ducked into the back of the limo. Russo's personal chauffeur secured his luggage, started the car, and headed south. Cliff settled in for the ride and thought about meeting his old acquaintance, Sydney "the Brain" Russo, the top boss of the Chicago outfit.

They had made plenty of money together and had had some memorable experiences, too. Then came the memory of his dear friend Max Thornton, who had been murdered in the sky lounge on his yacht. Cliff's hands bunched into fists. He knew that Carlo was tied to that death. When he thought about Max's risky funeral at sea, the grief was just as sharp as ever.

Cliff opened an air-conditioning vent and let the cool air hit his face. There had been the big Mob meeting in Tahoe, next door to his house on the lake in Incline Village. That day he had met Johnnie Badalamente for the first time. The small hairs on the back of his neck stiffened just thinking about that guy. The man had the eyes of a cold-blooded killing machine, and he clearly didn't like Cliff. The feeling was mutual.

When the limo reached Willow Road and turned left instead of right, another bad feeling chilled him.

"Where are we headed?" he asked the driver casually.

"Mr. Russo wants to meet at his home."

Cliff swallowed around the sudden tightness in his throat. Previous meetings with Russo had always taken place at The Dollar Club in Mt. Prospect. He always felt better seeing the big boss in a public place like that, and he also got to see his old friend Patrick Antonopolis, the owner, also known as the One-Armed Bandit. Cliff leaned back and closed his eyes against the bleak landscape scrolling by, willing himself to relax as the limo headed eastward toward the North Shore. He thought about Grant Love, who had helped him so much in the past. *Poor Grant. Flying all the way from California just to be kept in the dark.* The CIA had used him just to lure Cliff into their grasp. *Screw them. I'll tell him everything anyway, just as soon as it's safe.*

He had mulled over the conversation with Danforth, Witherspoon, and MacGregor during the flight to Chicago. *Damn them!* Just when he was feeling free of the government's grip, now he had to dance to their tune again. But the situation was also perversely amusing. An important arm of the almighty U.S. government needed him, just one man. And for what? To ask the Mob to do a job for them. Unbelievable.

Cliff had encouraged Grant to return home right after the meeting, and Grant seemed to understand. Then he called Sydney Russo, who was surprised to hear from him but agreed to meet today. During the long, quiet evening in his Washington hotel suite he planned how to approach Sydney. He figured the old dago would turn him down flat. The outfit had been burned many times by the feds, including once before over Castro. They had been scorched by Castro himself. *Why should Sydney even listen to such a crazy idea?*

Of course, the CIA had probably contacted the FBI, and maybe they had something on the Chicago boys that the government could use as leverage. The FBI would gladly turn up the heat on them for the CIA. Also, his CIA friends had implied that they could arrange other unpleasant consequences, as if they had learned a few tricks from the Mob itself. He had to smile.

Maybe such incentives would work. Maybe Russo and Badalamente would take the agents seriously. But with Cliff as the conduit, they might not take the proposal seriously enough. Not for Cliff, anyway. Unfortunately, they had him just where they wanted him. The whole thing clamped like a vise. He was just a money man, a civilian, not a killer like everybody else in this game. But he still had to make them see that trying to kill Castro for the CIA again was a good idea. Jesus. Badalamente's cold eyes probed across his memory.

But one persistent thought had given him an idea for a plan that would satisfy everyone. If only he could sell them on it. Otherwise . . . He didn't want to consider the otherwise. He had already experienced some of the Mob's muscle once. Victoria mustn't know what he was up against . . . she had to be safe, out of it.

He had gotten Grant to call her for him to reassure her, to explain that he couldn't contact her until later. The cold from the vent was soothing. He adjusted the flow. Just as well her father hadn't been in the room to hear about this scheme.

The limo swayed into a turn. Tall evergreens floated by, dark shapes against the gray sky. He closed his eyes for a moment, gathering his wits. *Showtime* . . .

Cliff's plan was a crapshoot. Too many things could screw it up. But it was bold, it had promise. If it worked, the Mob would make a fortune, the government would lose Castro, and everyone could continue living the American Dream. No more tragic terrorist or nuclear nightmares, no more threats from dark forces that wanted to destroy us. He smiled at the burlesque proportions of this business, enjoying a certain ironic elation. *If I make it through today, and if all else goes well, I'll be okay. Maybe I'll even score big. Imagine having a piece of the next Las Vegas.* He had always been a sucker for the long shot.

He shifted in his seat, looked around, and turned on the stereo. A familiar tune filled the compartment, one by Frank Sinatra from the Rat Pack days.

The limo turned right on Green Bay Road, and a few minutes later it made a left at Winnetka Avenue. Soon it cruised past New Trier, a stately old brick high school founded by a German immigrant in the late 1800s, where, Cliff knew, Ann-Margaret, Rock Hudson, Charlton Heston, and even Donald Rumsfeld had graduated. The street dead-ended at Sheridan Road, which ran along the lakefront. There the car turned north to Sinatra's refrain and tooled past several mansions. Then it swung into the long, sweeping driveway of a large lakeside estate on the Winnetka shoreline. Cliff gazed out the window. Wide, sweeping lawns and carefully tended landscaping surrounded a white, two-story Mediterranean mansion with barrel-tile roof, black wrought ironwork, and red trim, with the darkness of Lake Michigan brooding beyond. A collection of expensive cars crowded the curved driveway. *What's the occasion?* He knew it wasn't a funeral or Russo's birthday. And his visit wouldn't smoke this many people out of the woodwork.

A butler stood in the doorway, apparently waiting for him. The driver opened the door for Cliff, and the butler escorted him into the reception area. They paraded in silence down a short, carpeted hallway lined with dark, gilt-framed paintings and into an empty library. The butler motioned him to an overstuffed, leather, high-backed chair. Then he left without a word, leaving Cliff abruptly alone in the hushed room. He had seen no one else on his way in. Something felt strange about the place.

He took in the rich surroundings. The dark room was mahogany-paneled and crowded with heavy, expensive furniture, fine art, and shelves filled with old books. The place resonated with the power of the man who used the prominent burlwood desk that stood before him. A massive, marble-manteled fireplace filled one corner, where a small fire snapped against the winter chill, offering a gentle warmth to the vaulted space. Cliff gazed through the high windows at the gray lake. It was a fair enough day for November in Chicago, he thought, as stray shafts of pale sunlight broke through the overcast.

"Hello, Clifford."

Cliff flinched and looked over his shoulder. A wiry old man stood in the doorway. As usual, he was immaculately turned out in a dark, shiny suit.

Sydney Russo crossed the room, moving as if the winter chill had settled into his joints. "Good to see you, young man."

Cliff stood and managed a smile. "Been a while, Sydney," he said, carefully taking the old man's dry, fragile hand. "Haven't seen you since that day in Tahoe at Tony's place."

Russo nodded and smiled thinly. "That day I wondered if we'd see each other again." His watery eyes had a faraway look as he studied the gray lake as if for the first time. After a moment he shivered and turned his attention to Cliff. "How's that fine girl of yours?"

"Victoria's doing well. She's been with me since those days. Staying on my yacht in Monte Carlo."

"I love Monte Carlo." Sydney shuffled to his grand desk and seated himself carefully, a fragile contrast to its heavy wood presence. "Marry her, Clifford." He placed a crooked hand on the desktop, then waved it at him to sit down. "A woman like that you don't find every day. Marry her and start a family." Watery eyes found the windows again. "Nothing is more important than family."

"You're right, Sydney. Believe me, my caution is not because of her." He smiled. "Vic's about perfect. In fact, she's probably smart enough to turn me down."

Russo peered at Cliff. "You're afraid to care too much and lose everything again, I think. You suffered deeply when Catherine and your son were killed. But if you don't expose yourself to tragedy, you also miss out on real happiness."

Cliff bowed his head. "I know." *What must she be thinking? How will she feel when I finally speak to her again?* The pain of it sliced at him.

The old man grunted. "How things been since winding down your old company?"

"Peaceful."

"Some little gold mine you had going for yourself."

"True."

Russo's chair creaked in the quiet room. "So what brings you to Chicago?"

"Actually . . ." Cliff forced himself to meet the old, familiar eyes.

"Yes?"

Cliff wiped at his jaw. "You won't even believe what I'm about to tell you."

"Hell, Cliff, I've worked for Capone." Russo chuckled, his eyes suddenly bright. "I think I've seen it all."

"I just came from Washington."

"Yeah?"

Cliff told him the whole story, beginning with the phone call from Grant Love. He stopped short of the punchline.

Russo sat back, embraced in his big leather chair. "So why you telling *me* all this?"

A log in the fireplace gave way with a thud. Sparks flew, dancing up the chimney.

"They want you guys to kill Castro."

Russo did not move. The eyes skewered Cliff and he felt the power. When his response came it was deceptively mild. "Are they fucking nuts?"

Cliff put his head in his hands.

"Clifford?" Russo asked quietly. "What's wrong?"

Cliff willed himself back together. "I'm just thinking about the well-made box those bastards stuffed me into."

The thin smile came again. "That's the way they always play it. Cliff, look at me."

Cliff looked up.

"Your secret is safe with me. Try not to worry. And don't worry about Victoria." Russo got up with an effort and went to the bar. Glassware tinkled as he fixed drinks. He returned to the desk and handed Cliff a half-filled tumbler. "Let's talk," he said, taking the chair next to Cliff.

"Thank you for the kind words, Sydney," he said, aware of the slight tremor in his voice. The old man's presence reassured him. "And thanks for the drink."

"I'm not telling you anything new here," Russo said. "I was involved with the CIA in the late fifties and early sixties. Another Castro deal." He sipped his drink. "We helped them. Getting Castro's not so easy, though. Before that, we tried to do business with him. That didn't work either." He smoothed a hand across his balding head. "Double-crossing bastards. No honor, no loyalty, my friend. Took our money with one hand and tried to screw us with the other." The *consigliere*'s gaze was cold. "That was their mistake."

The vision of his murdered friend filled Cliff's mind again.

"What's a matter?"

"Nothing."

"What do you mean 'nothing'?"

Cliff's nerves went, frayed under the calm of this old mobster schooled in manipulation and bargaining. He got to his feet and clunked his glass down on the desk. "Just what I said!"

"Sit down, and don't spill alcohol on this fine desk." The eyes brooded. "Maxwell Thornton. Am I right?"

"Where was honor and loyalty then, Sydney?"

Russo leaned toward Cliff. "We had to protect ourselves. Besides, killing Thornton was a mistake. That goon was supposed to whack your brother-in-law, the shithead from the NSA. You know that."

Cliff nodded. "Yeah, but you didn't trust me, Sydney. You murdered him, too."

The fragile hand moved delicately, a dismissal.

"That was another mistake, Cliff. We were paranoid, to a fault. I apologize." Russo stood up, air passing from his concave chest. He touched Cliff's arm. "We learned again that you're a man of honor."

"How do I know it won't happen again?" Cliff shook his head. "I must have rocks in my head to be standing here."

"Our friendship is better than that. Come on. You have my word."

Cliff took in the warm concern in the old man's eyes. His jangling nerves settled. "All right, Sydney," he said finally. "But—"

"I said you have my word. Now sit down again and let's talk like friends."

"Double-dealing bastards," Cliff said, taking his seat and reaching for his drink.

"Exactly. The last time, fortunately, I stayed behind the scenes. Probably why I'm still here. I had front men like Johnny Roselli and Sam Giancana. They did the dirty work. I had other business to tend to—Hollywood, Vegas, Chicago. You know." Russo eased into his chair, looking reflective. "I handled finance and strategy. Had to keep the other families happy, too." He winked at Cliff and the mood lightened. "Me and Lansky had some good times."

The fire popped and cracked. Cliff studied the old man's lined face.

"I know that look, Clifford. Tell me."

Cliff took another drink for courage. "How does the idea of a new Vegas strike you?"

"Havana?"

"If Castro's dead, why not?" He eyed Russo closely.

"We tried that once before, with Castro alive. Even had his cooperation for a while." Russo thumped a thin knee. "Then he turned on us."

"Now's different," Cliff said. "We'd have an edge. Better yet, a monopoly."

"A monopoly? How do you figure that?"

Outside, the sunlight had faded, leaving the room in semi-darkness. "Listen to this," Cliff said, and laid out the CIA's plan and its advantages to the Mob.

Russo listened. He sat immobile, staring at him expression-lessly. Finally he said, "You do think big, Cliff. But we got a lot of ifs there."

"Sounds that way, but bear with me. The alternatives don't look good. The feds want our voluntary cooperation, they say, or else."

"Ah, shit," the old man said, massaging his temple. "I'm sick of those assholes making threats. Who the fuck do they think they are?"

"They do have balls," admitted Cliff. "They came on real strong."

Russo took a long pull at his drink and gazed at the darkening windows. He seemed lost in a different place and time.

Cliff let the old *consigliere* chew on everything for a while. "Listen," he said finally. "I understand if you've heard enough."

Russo focused on Cliff again. "No. Go on. I gotta hear this."

Cliff went into detail, explaining the circumstances presented to him by the CIA, including their stubborn intentions to include both Cliff and the Mob. "They're afraid," said Cliff, "that if they take the time for a new president to rubber-stamp this operation, it'll be too late. These guys think they're doing what's right for the country, even though it'd be a disaster if they fail. A media frenzy and a political nightmare with international repercussions."

"Anything else?"

"No, Sydney. That's it." Cliff grinned. His nerves had settled.

"Except you make a great martini."

Russo chuckled. "And you make a good argument." He took another sip of his drink and savored it for a moment. "We tried to help the CIA with Castro for money. But also for patriotic reasons. We're Americans, too, ya know. I like what you said, Cliff. You're a smart cookie."

Cliff shrugged.

Russo crossed his legs and relaxed. "Poor Meyer. Dumped all his retirement money into the Hotel Riviera. Fanciest joint on the Vedado waterfront in its time. Fortunately, he made even more money later." Russo gazed at the paneled ceiling, replaying the memory. "Then that fuck Castro confiscated the Riviera and threw Meyer out. I could kill Castro just for that."

"Then let's do it."

"Maybe we should buy back the Riviera," Russo said with a wicked smile. "For old time's sake."

"Good idea, Sydney. Bet there's tons of good buys down there."

Russo tapped the arm of his chair decisively. "We need to see Tony Carlo, Cliff. He could pull this off. You know he revived Vegas, made it what it is today."

"Yes."

"Imagine what we could do in Cuba." Light burned in the old man's eyes.

"Havana could be the new Las Vegas, Sydney. But even bigger, better, more beautiful."

"More profitable, too. People will get bored with Vegas. We've pulled them from all over the world. But when they hear about Havana . . ."

"I agree." Cliff enjoyed the vision. "Could be bigger than Vegas."

"Hell, we'll build the grandest casino resort you could imagine. That'll grab their asses. Matter of fact, Tony has plans for a place like that. We cashed outta the Mecca before he had a chance

to build it. But this one's a beautiful Italian palace, fancier than anything in Vegas today."

Cliff nodded and smiled, his mood expanding with a sense of
the future as the fire snapped, bright in the darkening room. He
had leaped the first hurdle. He had Sydney Russo's support. And
he would need that to stay alive.

Half an hour later, after more talk about the future of Havana, Russo guided Cliff through the dimly lit hallways to a room
filled with the rumble of voices. Russo paused outside the door
and motioned for Cliff to join him.

Cliff stepped forward and looked into the roomy salon at the
gathering of men. All conversation ceased at the sight of them.
Cliff stared, stunned. Maybe a dozen guys stood in small groups
or lounged in big club chairs. Their combined energy was as palpable as the expensive cigar smoke that hung in the air. He had
met a couple of them. A few others he knew only by reputation.

Russo said, "I'll speak with you gents later. First I have some
business to discuss with Cliff here." The men nodded, a couple
waved their cigars.

Russo led Cliff to the kitchen, where he issued some orders
to the help, then escorted him to the dining room. They sat at one
end of a long table already set with crystal and sterling silver, all of
it gleaming under the subdued light of a twinkling chandelier.
White-coated waitstaff appeared and bustled about.

Cliff was feeling a lot better about things now. "Sydney," he
said, "an area called Varadero is close to Havana. I hear it could be
the next Waikiki. Might be the perfect spot for your Italian palace."

"Yeah, I know the area. It'd be perfect." His hand orchestrated the vision. "A whole strip of casinos and gambling resorts."

Cliff nodded. "Las Vegas, international style. With a fabulous
beach. It'll knock out everyone."

"You can help make it happen, Cliff, like you did with me and

Tony and the Mecca."

A fire caught in Cliff's belly.

"Without you to show us the offshore angle, I couldn't have pulled it off. Allowed us to remain anonymous. That was critical."

Russo's face glowed. Cliff thought he looked ten years younger.

"Your offshore financing methods," said Russo, "your investment strategies. All brilliant." He gave a wheezy laugh. "Hell, we know how to run casinos. But if the government knew the whole story we'd a been kicked outta town before we said hello."

Cliff laughed. "You may be right." He was genuinely flattered to hear what Russo really thought. "But Hugh Knight was instrumental, too, remember, with those junk bonds. Great while they lasted."

Russo grinned. "You know, we got the perfect vehicle for this project. Remember the *SS Vegas Heiress?*"

"Sure," said Cliff. "Ben Siegel's old idea. The world's largest floating casino resort. I saw the model at Tony Carlo's house last year in Tahoe. How's that going?"

"Great. Spun it off the Mecca a while back, and it's trading on NASDAQ now. Operating it outta Miami. People love it and it's profitable. But we gotta expand the ports of call."

"Havana?"

"Yeah, yeah. Perfect tie-in. Bring in captive business. We also got plans to build other ships. Have 'em cruise the Caribbean." His face took on more color as his crooked fingers toyed with a fork. "The thing is, when we quit the Mecca the buyers wanted all the premier properties. We spun off the subsidiary cruise ship deal and took it public, too, and dumped the other Vegas properties."

"Sounds good."

The fork made dents in the tablecloth. "Yeah, it has been. We turned around and sold those dogs outright. Between that and the cash for our interest in the Mecca, we got over a billion dollars after taxes, all sitting in the corporate kitty. Plus we still have the *Vegas Heiress.*"

"Not bad. A perfect position to make acquisitions with credit, securities, and cash, if necessary. And with Tony's reputation you'll attract all the investors and lenders you need. Plus viable projects to acquire." Cliff smiled. The Chicago outfit was in even better shape than he had hoped.

"Actually, that's why these fellas are here today," Russo said, gesturing toward the hallway. "*Consiglieres* from other families around the country. We're going over a few joint investment schemes." He looked directly at Cliff. "I need to spend a billion before the public shareholders get restless." He smiled. "That's tricky. I don't want to make any wrong moves."

Cliff touched Russo's forearm. "I think you just found the perfect project. But you have to wait to share it with them until Castro's dead. Besides, I don't want you giving away my position."

Russo patted Cliff's hand. "We won't tell them until we're ready. Meanwhile, we need to talk about your part in this venture, Clifford. Let's fly out to Vegas tomorrow in that jet of yours and lay this on Tony. He's gonna die."

Cliff tensed. "You think that's safe?"

"We'll swear him to secrecy. He knows what that means."

"All right, Sydney. But talking too much is like playing Russian roulette."

"I know the game, Cliff."

"What if Tony doesn't want to play?"

"Believe me, Tony'll love it. He's been a little lost lately." Russo picked up a spotless knife and polished it with a linen napkin. "Look at this, the help need to wipe these off. Actually, Tony needs this project. And remember, I call the shots. Tony made a fortune with the Mecca, but even then most of his interest was ours. Except for us, he'd still be a nobody. This, my friend, he knows." He motioned to a waiter. "Tony's a swinger, Cliff. Forget about it. We'll see him tomorrow. You'll see."

Cliff smiled at Russo, thinking how fortunate he was to have a man like this for a friend.

* * *

Cliff and Russo enjoyed a leisurely lunch while they caught up on the past and speculated about the future. Afterward, the butler arrived with a selection of Cuban cigars. Cliff indulged himself. This was a time for celebration.

"When we're finished here, Cliff," said Russo, "I'll introduce you to the real board of directors of Vegas Heiress Enterprises, Inc." He smiled wryly. "The ones not listed on the annual report."

Cliff nodded and smiled, too. He took a draw on his cigar. He blew the fragrant smoke into the air, reflecting on the corporate name. "You know, maybe after Castro's gone and we announce our plans for Cuba, we can change the name of the corporation to something better. Like Vegas-Havana Casino Resorts Corporation." Cliff liked playing this what-if game. "We can play on the credibility of Vegas and expose the public to our other plans. Who knows, maybe you'll want to get into Vegas again someday and buy back the Mecca."

Russo chuckled, squinting at him through the smoke. "Already crossed my mind, Cliff. Problem is, I'd wanna steal it back. What a cash cow. Hated to give that up, but at least the timing was good." He puffed on the cigar. "Market was strong and the offer . . . well, irresistible. We'll do it again, you wait and see."

Cliff felt good watching Russo's special brand of enthusiasm. He was just as sharp as ever. No wonder he was the brains of the outfit for so many years. Johnnie Badalamente, the new *capo*, Cliff realized, was clearly just a figurehead. Probably only muscle.

Russo stood up, brushing at his shiny suit. "Bring your stogie." Cliff followed him to the living room, where they joined the group. They spent the long afternoon discussing business, politics, and the economy.

Later, after the others had left, their limousines pulling out of the driveway, Cliff accepted Russo's offer to stay over as his guest.

* * *

Ivan Penkovsky felt weary after the flight from Budapest. As his cab negotiated the hilly road and approached his old villa overlooking the Black Sea, he hoped he could rest for a while before tackling the next bit of business.

He watched his rambling private retreat come into view, knowing there he could escape the demands of Moscow and the daily responsibilities of bossing his vast organization—this thing that many now called the Russian Mafia. He wondered how many of his special "clients" were in temporary residence now, preparing here in Hungary for their new life in the West, in western Europe, perhaps, or somewhere in the United States.

When his driver opened the door of the Mercedes, he took his time unfolding his long, lean frame from the back seat and adjusting his clothes. The chill evening air smelled clean and salty. "Ah! Thank you, Stefan. This is much better. See to my bags, please."

He marched to the heavy wood front door with its framework of ivy, feeling glad to be back. These trips were becoming tiresome. But he was shrewd enough not to trust everything to his lieutenants in Moscow and Budapest and the other cities around the world. Go see things firsthand, stop in unannounced sometimes, look the little bosses—the *smotryoshohiy*—in the eye, and ask the hard questions. That was the best way to maintain control, was it not?

He stepped into the warm vestibule and smiled at the lovely creature who stood waiting for him, a young woman who introduced herself as Tatiana. He admired her cool Slavic beauty, the high cheekbones and icy blue eyes.

He handed her his overcoat and asked her to find Viktor. When she hurried away he strode to a favorite sofa and collapsed, still taking inventory of his surroundings. Several young women and boys—more than before—went about their business. A few others lounged here and there. He smiled at the familiar scene.

Viktor bustled into the room, out of breath, with Tatiana on his heels. "Greetings, Ivan," he said, a smile on his pink face. "What a surprise!"

"Hello, Viktor." He always enjoyed watching the little man puff and bluster in his presence. "Yes, it has been a while."

Viktor nodded vigorously, rubbing his hands as he glanced at Tatiana. "Something to drink, Ivan?"

"Vodka, please." The young woman nodded once and disappeared.

"Sit down, Viktor," said Penkovsky. "Relax a little. How are you doing these days?"

Viktor sat on the edge of a big upholstered chair, wearing a now uncertain smile. He unbuttoned his jacket and then buttoned it again. "Good, good, Ivan."

Penkovsky fired questions at the man until Tatiana returned with the drinks and placed them on the glass coffee table. He eyed her until she had left the room.

"Keeping her for yourself, are you, Viktor?"

"Actually, yes, Ivan. She makes things run so much smoother. You know, with the young girls and such."

Penkovsky smiled. "I can imagine."

Viktor looked away.

"But let us get back to business, Viktor. You were saying?"

Business in the Ukraine, in Odessa, was going well, Viktor said. They had an unlimited supply of clients there now, and, well, the demand was high.

Penkovsky was pleased with all of Viktor's reports—and with all his business operations. Their various international smuggling schemes were all doing especially well. They were moving drugs, strategic metals, chemical weapons, military hardware, and even people. Trafficking in humans, he knew, had great potential, limited only by imagination. Women, especially young ones, and even boys could all be exploited successfully and with relatively little risk, because they were lured into "better" jobs "voluntarily." All of them felt good about their new opportunity after a few days or weeks at this charming villa.

He considered how delicious this trade could be. Once the human commodities left here, they worked nightclubs in various cities, dancing and serving drinks for long hours with little pay, and doubling as prostitutes. All payments went to the establishment, of course. The young ones were kept as virtual prisoners in substandard living conditions, all of them believing they were headed to a major European city for a good-paying job. Instead, they were shuttled from nightclub to nightclub and city to city along a slow course to their desired destination. No guarantees, of course. He smiled at how easy it all was.

They now had many well-established routes from India and the Middle East to Istanbul. His organization controlled the transshipping points in Odessa and Macedonia and worked closely with the Turkish Mafia in Istanbul and the Vlore Mafia in Albania. The runaways could be ferried across the Black Sea to Odessa, where they might make it to his villa here or to another secure holding point in the port city. Then they could be routed through the Ukraine and Poland to Austria, Germany, or Switzerland or maybe to Istanbul and Macedonia through the West Balkans and on to Slovania. Other routes existed, too, and Penkovsky had creative ideas about establishing even more.

He smiled and stretched with satisfaction. What a growth industry! They were now shipping thousands of people across multistate boundaries.

Penkovsky felt pleased and stimulated. "Well, Viktor, I believe you are doing a good job."

Viktor's flushed face lit up. "Thank you, Ivan."

"Keep up the good work and play straight with me and I will let you in on a little opportunity."

Viktor chafed his hands. "I would like that, Ivan."

Penkovsky threw back the rest of the vodka. "We are working on new routes. We have the Sicilian Mafia in our pocket now, so we can move things from Tunisia to Sicily. That could be an important route. Then Africa. We can use more ways to move diamonds, and lately we have good business with the terrorists."

Viktor's eyes watered as he listened, nodding. "This sounds very good, Ivan."

"But," said Penkovsky, "Poland joined the EU. They have a huge border, more than a thousand kilometers, mostly dense forest. On the other side is Lithuania, Belarus, and the Ukraine."

Viktor looked excited now. He produced a pack of Papirosi, pulled one out, and lit it, his eyes hungry. He took a deep drag and said through the smoke, "This could be wonderful, Ivan."

"Good, Viktor. I would like for you to supervise the whole operation. This could be our biggest venture yet."

"What do you need, Ivan? Name it."

Penkovsky waved a hand at him. "Do not worry, Viktor. I am happy. Just keep doing what you are doing." He nodded and smiled his practiced smile, glancing around the room, looking for Tatiana.

She stood in a corner, just out of earshot, watching them. He crooked a finger at her. "Darling, come here." He patted his knee. "Sit."

She approached them gracefully. "I suppose, Viktor, that you are entitled to such perquisites."

She stopped in front of them and looked down at Viktor, her face expressionless.

"You are incorrect in your assumptions, Ivan. Tatiana is yours." When Viktor looked at her to see if she understood, she nodded once and reached down to take Penkovsky's hand. He stood and let her lead him away. Behind him Viktor said, "One last thing, Ivan."

Penkovsky squeezed Tatiana's hand and turned around. "What?"

"Dr. Gerleman has a big request."

"Yes?"

"He needs twenty young organ donors in Geneva as fast as he can get them."

Penkovsky sighed. "Well, where do we stand?"

Viktor shrugged. "We have them. They can leave immediately."

Penkovsky slipped an arm around Tatiana's slender waist. "Tell him double. Ten thousand dollars each, and we give him special delivery service." He pulled Tatiana closer and kissed her cheek. "I think the good doctor must be doing very well in his practice."

"Very well, Ivan," said Viktor. "I will make the arrangements." His fingers fiddled with his jacket buttons. "See you in the morning."

Penkovsky took Tatiana's arm. She stood patiently, but her ice-blue eyes told him nothing. He held out one hand. "After you, my darling," he said, and she turned and led him down the long hallway toward his private quarters.

At dawn the following morning Cliff and Sydney Russo settled into their seats on Cliff's Gulfstream V as the engines spooled up. Cliff toyed with a growing optimism as the big jet taxied across the tarmac. He grinned at Russo, whose dark brown eyes twinkled with new signs of life. The *consigliere* seemed younger away from the projected power of the mansion.

"So, Clifford," Russo said, "how will you participate in our new project?"

"I figure ten-percent ownership in the public company for bringing them to you is fair. You guys'll make billions." He studied Russo's face.

Russo cleared his throat. "Remember, Cliff, we do all the work and put up all the money. First we knock off Castro, and who knows who else. And there's no guarantee the feds won't investigate us. Charge us with murder or worse, assassinating a foreign leader, toppling a government, all kinds of stuff. The CIA can't make any promises since they're acting illegally themselves."

"You're right, Sydney, but by killing Castro your chances of getting into Cuba are good. Legal or not, you're acting at the request of the U.S. government." Cliff listened to the thump of the jet's tires as it taxied towards the runway.

"True. We never let the prospects of an investigation discourage us before." He chuckled. "Anyway, the government finds out the CIA's involved, they'll hit the cover-up button. Protect their own asses." He wagged a gaunt finger in the air. "And they'd better, or we might talk."

"You can count on that."

Russo gazed out the window as the aircraft made its takeoff roll. Finally he turned and bounced his fist on the armrest as they lifted off. "Okay, Cliff," he said. "Ten percent."

"Something else, Sydney."

"Yeah?"

"I can be an even bigger asset to this project."

Russo's eyes narrowed. "Like how?"

"Couple of ways," said Cliff. "But first I want the CIA to explain what happens after Castro. What we can expect." His stomach sank pleasantly as they left the earth. "If it's similar to what I outlined yesterday, then I'll tell them you'll cooperate, but only because you want to develop gaming and tourism in the country. That you'll invest billions over the next few years. But you'll need certain assurances and assistance before you proceed."

"That's good," said Russo, a brief suspicion fading from his eyes. "Their response will be interesting."

"We better present this up front so they know what to expect."

"Good, Cliff."

"How can they not agree? They need us."

"Right. Good idea. Turn the tables on them."

"Exactly. If everything goes right, they'll find themselves in our well-made box instead."

Russo laughed. "I like your attitude, Cliff."

Cliff's longtime steward, Bill, arrived with orange juice and coffee.

"Something stronger, Sydney?" asked Cliff.

Russo declined.

Cliff stirred his coffee. "I'll let them know we want a meeting with the transitional government to discuss business, and we want them to influence the new people for us. After all, we're giving the CIA what they want—a dead Castro."

Cliff sipped his custom-blend coffee, feeling better all the time. The more he thought about things, the more he could see how to pull off his part in the whole affair. If only everyone else held up their end. If the plan backfired, he knew the feds would crawl up his ass as well as those of the CIA and the Mob, and it could get real ugly and expensive. But he knew he could deal with that if he had to. In his mid-forties he was a world-class corporate executive, and still felt like a tiger ready for a fight.

Russo drank some orange juice. "A classy ride." He smiled and gazed out the window.

"Glad you like it," Cliff said. "This brings me to where I began." He waited until Russo turned back to him. "I'll convince them that it's in their best interest to help us, too."

"A nagging question, Cliff. What'll stop them from backing out after we whack Fidel?"

Cliff smiled. "We have a little secret of theirs that they'll want to keep quiet, maybe?"

Russo's thin, dry lips worked against each other. He sipped his juice.

"Getting rid of Castro's only part of their problem, Sydney. They'll need someone friendly in there, and some way to maintain order, and an election. I hope that's already been planned."

Sydney picked orange pulp from his mouth. "The CIA can do all that shit by the numbers. This won't be the first big shot they've taken out."

"That's true, Sydney, but it is our first."

Russo arched a craggy brow.

"Okay, Sydney," Cliff said. "My first. Anyway, if I can get them to agree, I think the new government will cooperate. If so, I'll push to meet the temporary president. We'll make a deal before any election."

"A deal?"

"Monopoly."

"You keep saying that, Cliff. How do you figure to get a monopoly?"

Cliff peered out the window, feeling as free as his aircraft and as open as the blue distances that seemed to reach forever. "You'll pay me a fat retainer, and I'll paint a rosy picture of Cuba's future for the president. All of it thanks to good old American capitalism." He tapped Russo on the arm in rhythm with his words. "When he hears about billions of dollars in investments, how can he say no? Hell, the man'll be a hero. The savior of his poor, beleaguered country. They'll build statues of him."

Russo nodded and looked pleased. "Okay, but what's with this fat retainer of yours?"

"I'm going to earn it. What's a monopoly worth to you?"

Russo massaged his temple. "You can really do that?"

"Why not? I'll curl up in a corner and wait to strike." He shrugged and said, "Hey, you need me. I'm the right guy for the job."

"I can feel the poison working already."

"The temporary president'll welcome us with open arms," Cliff said, warming to the subject. "We promise to invest a certain sum in gaming over a given period, attract the right business to their shores, and give them a piece of the action. In exchange, we get a ten-year monopoly in Cuba. Simple as that."

"Holy Mother!" Russo said, his features flushed, eyes like an eagle's. "That's all we need. By then we'll be way ahead of any competition. With a strong foothold and all politically connected-up. Like the early days in Vegas, only better—outta the reach of the goddamn U.S. government."

"Exactly." Cliff smiled. "So what's that worth to you, Sydney?"

Russo remained quiet for a while, his coffee cup poised unsteadily in his hand. "A lot."

"Then how about sweetening the deal?" Cliff let it out. "Ten percent of the gross. The whole Cuba operation."

"Christ! Paralysis is setting in."

Cliff shrugged. "Okay, five percent. Take it or leave it."

"All right, all right. You got it. That's a sweet little compensation package for you, Clifford. But if you can do it, you'll have earned it."

Cliff leaned back in his seat, feeling both exhausted and elated. "Good. We can work out the mechanics later."

They rode in silence for a while on the whistling drone of the jet engines. Then Russo extended his hand. "Let's make it official," he said. "Incredible project, Cliff. Very exciting."

Cliff took the bony old hand. "Thank you."

"Want me to put you on the payroll?"

Cliff knew this was just a polite gesture. "I don't need a paycheck, Sydney, or a title. Only your word 'til we get everything down on paper."

"Forget about it, Cliff." The light still glowed in Sydney's old eyes. "This is a deal never to be broken." He studied Cliff, a *consigliere* checking, confirming. "You really think you can do it?"

Cliff grinned. The old man's words produced a warm surge of adrenaline that felt almost erotic. But then came a feeling of dread and danger, which he fought to push aside. He looked at his old friend. "I feel very good about this, Sydney. If I have to be involved in another government cover-up, at least we can make a lot of money out of it."

"Good, Clifford. That's good."

"One thing I'll insist on when the temporary president signs the agreement with us. It has to be grandfathered in. That way, the successors can't change the contract."

Russo agreed and fell silent, savoring the details of the future. Before long, the old man nodded into a nap. Cliff glanced at him from time to time, noting the porcelain fragility to his sunlit profile, and feeling a vast contentment even as he struggled to keep his nagging fears at bay.

As the Gulfstream rode the thin air toward Las Vegas, Cliff's mood buoyed him to the top of his own private world. For the remainder of the flight, he willed his thoughts to paint exotic pictures with a broad brush of a glittering Caribbean Waikiki supercharged with Las Vegas-style pizzazz.

A line from a pop song came to him. *The future's so bright I have to wear shades.* That seemed to be true now. All they had to do was achieve the impossible. Cliff sat quietly, sipping his coffee. He thought of Victoria, the phone call, the first fear. He had turned it around, by God. At least for the moment.

3

Risky Business

CLIFF STRODE THROUGH THE FLASHING LIGHTS, sounds and babble of the crowd at the Mecca casino on his way from the front desk with a small entourage escorting him to his suite. The consciously cultivated ambiance of chance and money made him feel both stimulated and edgy. He and Sydney Russo had left his private jet at McCarran International Airport in Las Vegas just thirty minutes before. He had already learned that the Chicago outfit still had plenty of clout in Vegas. Russo had made one phone call to Tony Carlo, and the new owners of the Mecca fell all over themselves to accommodate their guests, the former owners of the joint.

Cliff listened politely to one of his escorts, a striking young brunette who managed to be both seductive and coolly professional. She catalogued all the wonders of the house as they walked.

He was glad to end the guided tour at the penthouse suite, which looked like a sultan's summer house and was just as luxurious. A butler and maid came with the place and would remain at his personal disposal. The casino had gladly comped Cliff and Russo this and an identical suite, both of which were normally reserved for international high rollers, known in the trade as the "whales."

Cliff tipped the bellman and thanked the striking brunette and the two smooth men from management who had escorted him. They repaid him with wide smiles, bid him a memorable stay, and departed. He scolded himself for taking a moment to admire the rear view of the brunette. Victoria etched into his thoughts.

When the door finally clicked shut, Cliff allowed the persistent tug of a looming dread to surface. He was in Vegas with the Mob, on the orders of the CIA. He was far from Victoria and his floating home. And he could feel the danger, a lethal presence.

He shoved these thoughts from his mind and explored his new digs. He padded soundlessly across the plush white carpet to the window wall and took in the tawdry glamour of Las Vegas—the car-choked Strip and the ragged patchwork of civilization that ended abruptly at the empty desert, with the sunburned mountains brooding in the hazy distance. The patterned ceilings of the suite seemed to vault to the sky, and the split-level floor plan flowed from a sunken living room to a spacious dining area and gourmet kitchen. Beyond that was a large, private room with an oversized bed, a vast bathroom with two of everything, a full spa, and a compact gym. Great design, he had to admit. Garish comfort and entertainment. Nothing had changed since his last visit.

The Hispanic maid had finished unpacking his clothes and was brushing one of his custom-made suits from Sam's Tailor in Hong Kong when someone rapped sharply on the door. It startled him, and he watched the butler quick-step from the kitchen to answer it.

Two men in gray suits filled the doorway, craning their necks as the butler retreated. He recognized Witherspoon and MacGregor immediately, but he was surprised to see them so soon, and here, in a world so completely removed from the dreary officialdom of CIA headquarters. He took the butler aside and said under his breath, "I thought this was a secure floor."

"Yes, sir, it is," the baldheaded man whispered. "Shall I call security?"

Cliff steeled himself. "No, that won't be necessary."

"Mr. Blackwell?" Witherspoon called from the door. "Would you kindly join us in the hall?"

Goosebumps crawled down his arms. "You fellas sure showed back up fast," he replied, trying to sound casual. "What's new?"

"We need an update," Witherspoon said. He glanced at the butler and the maid, who just stared, slackjawed. "Could you just step out here for a moment?"

Cliff looked around the room, then shrugged and walked into the corridor. His door closed behind him automatically with a sturdy click.

Cliff waited for his eyesight to adjust to the subdued light. Before he could speak, the next door down snicked open, and Sydney Russo appeared. Everyone's attention shifted to the old man.

Russo seemed to take everything in quickly and took a step toward them. "Is everything all right, Cliff?" His voice resonated in the hallway, the calm of it authoritative and sinister, a tone Cliff had never heard before.

Cliff shifted the momentum. "Yes, of course, Sydney." He held his gaze for an extra second on Russo's watchful eyes. "These gentlemen just dropped by for a little chat. You go ahead. I'll catch up with you later."

"All right, Cliff. But if I can be of help, let me know." Russo gave the strangers a meaningful look, turned slowly, and reentered his suite.

The agents huddled up with Cliff. MacGregor said, "Could we just go outside and talk for a while, Mr. Blackwell?"

His gut did a little dance. "Why not?" He led the way toward the bank of elevators. The odd thought accompanied him: he was more at ease with the Mob than the U.S. government.

Standing alone in his suite, Sydney Russo tapped his carefully manicured fingernails on the telephone. He had picked up Cliff's signal, so he knew the visit by these two suits was a surprise. Something wasn't kosher. He should call Tony Carlo, the former owner of the joint. Yeah, he should be in the house now. He picked up the phone, always a conduit of his sometimes lethal power.

Tony answered his private line on the first ring and heard him out. Once he got the picture, he said, "Go after 'em, Syd, but watch yourself—you're too valuable. You ain't on the street for Capone no more. I'll getcha some backup soon as I can."

"My guess is they're government goons," Russo said. "I want you should know, we don't come right back, we got trouble. Don't let me down." He carefully replaced the receiver and made his way down the hall to the elevators. His legs felt old. Capone and his youth were long gone.

Downstairs he scanned the sprawling casino floor. Hundreds of people milled about amid the clatter and conversation of gaming. Russo headed off in one direction, then chose another. His chest cramped painfully, not used to the sudden exertion. There would be a car. Cops and mobsters had similar methods. He pushed his way through the crowd toward the valet area. He emerged into the bustle of expensive cars and jogging attendants, and there were the suits, climbing into the backseat of a black Ford SUV, Cliff between them.

"Mother of God!" His voice was a wheezy croak. Where the hell were they taking him? He clutched his chest and flailed an arm at a waiting cab.

The cab pulled forward smartly, and he was inside before the doorman could grab it for two other guests. "Follow that black piece of shit! Don't lose 'em. Pay you triple." He broke into a fit of coughing.

The Pakistani behind the wheel threw up his hands helplessly and wagged his head, playing dumb.

Russo wiped at his mouth as he stuck his sweet little Bulldog revolver under the guy's long nose. "Do it, or you'll be kissin' the ass of Allah."

The driver slammed the car into gear, laid rubber, and wedged them into the flow of traffic, ignoring a blare of horns. He kept up a steady chatter of Arabic, smacking his forehead repeatedly.

Russo steadied his breathing. "Shut the fuck up and drive," he said. He stowed his piece and squinted through the dirty windshield. The government car was not far ahead. "There he is. Stay on the fucker." One hand still clamped to his chest, he fell back onto the greasy seat and tried to ease the tightness around his heart. Christ, he wasn't up for this. Too much sitting at his fancy desk and riding limos.

He kept an eye on the black vehicle. It cruised through the intersection onto the Strip, and as they scooted to catch up, the stoplights blinked from yellow to red.

"Go, goddammit!" Russo coughed again.

The cabbie stomped on the gas pedal, causing cars to brake violently. The SUV threaded through the traffic efficiently and gained some distance. When the next light turned yellow, the cabbie sent the taxi veering into the bicycle lane, then he swerved violently back into the slow lane of the Strip, cutting off a Volkswagen that had to slew to a sideways stop.

The SUV gained more ground. Russo squinted, trying to keep it in sight. The SUV made a series of quick, evasive moves. The cabbie uttered a string of Pakistani curses. The car shot across two lanes of traffic on the left, taking a big gamble, but got caught by a red light at a major intersection.

"Get him!" Russo shouted.

Dark brown hands wrenched the wheel and they careened around two lines of traffic as the SUV bolted into the intersection. Cars on every side slammed to a stop. They were gaining when the cross-traffic closed ranks again. The cabbie screeched to a halt. Russo groaned as the SUV sped away, overtaking the slower traffic crawling toward the freeway on-ramp.

Russo compressed his hand over his chest, trying to ease the ache there.

The Pakistani looked at him, gesturing wildly. "I tried! Please don't shoot me!"

"Ah, shut the fuck up." What would happen to Cliff?

Cliff's heart tripped more quickly every time he thought of the implications of being taken for a ride into the Nevada desert. He wondered about the wild race through Vegas to the freeway. Someone must have been chasing them. But who? He never got a good look at the action behind them. Was the chase car still on their tail? Probably not. They had roared onto the freeway and sped northwest for several miles through the tiled-roof landscape of the suburbs. Now the CIA guys who had him sandwiched in the backseat were silent and relaxed, and the driver had backed off to the speed limit.

Where the hell were they taking him, and why was no one talking? He felt foolish now that he had come willingly, just climbed right into their damn car like a jerk even though he had been surprised when they suggested taking a ride. Now he wondered if that quick decision was a deadly mistake.

He kept his mouth shut and concentrated on the passing landscape, memorizing details of their route, just in case. When the suburban sprawl thinned, the freeway narrowed to three lanes each way, then to two as they sped into an ochre-and-khaki expanse of open desert framed in the distance by contrasting levels of mountain ranges. The looming heights looked unreal, but he took comfort in their beauty.

The silent treatment was getting old real fast. He cleared his throat and said, "So what's the rush?"

Nobody made a sound. Shit, now he was invisible, too.

The car accelerated along the empty stretch of county road, climbing as the mountains seemed to converge before them. They headed through a narrow pass, and as they rounded a bend, the desert panorama opened wide. He had never witnessed such vast openness, except at sea. They drove for a few more miles before the car finally slowed.

Cliff peered through the dusty windshield. They had come to a sketchy intersection, no more than a dirt road that approached from both directions through the distant wastes and simply crossed the highway. The driver braked and turned left onto the unpaved track. Soon they were kicking up plumes of dust as the SUV rocked and bounced along this trail, which seemed to lead to nowhere, carrying him farther and farther away from anything at all. He fought to hold his silence and to keep a grip on his fears.

Suddenly the guy to his left, Witherspoon, shifted in his seat and coughed. Cliff jumped as if a corpse had moved.

"We know for certain," he said, "that out here, no one will hear our conversation."

Then the guy on his right, MacGregor, said, "Blackwell, you haven't had much time, but we need to know your intent."

The driver remained focused on the road.

"Listen, gents," Cliff said, his heart banging in spite of himself, "I haven't stopped working on this since I left your office. I'm a willing participant, remember? What else do you want from me?"

"Does it look feasible to you?" Witherspoon asked.

"Yes." Cliff tried to keep his voice even. "Yesterday I met with Russo in Chicago, and as you can see"—he gestured toward the empty wasteland—"we came to Vegas today. Precisely because of this. In fact," he said, punching the air, "we've put a helluva lot of time and energy into this thing already." He felt like a coiled spring.

"Get to the point, Blackwell," MacGregor said.

"Hey!" Cliff shouted. "Listen. We'll get along better if you'll show some courtesy. You guys come three thousand miles, bang on my door unannounced, and screw up my plans. You drive me, without even small talk, to the middle of fucking nowhere and demand that I get to the point?"

When MacGregor started to speak, Cliff made a sign with his

hands. "Okay, time out." He took a breath to calm himself. "One more thing. How about calling me Mr. Blackwell, like you did before?"

Both Witherspoon and MacGregor waited to make sure he was finished. Finally Witherspoon said, "Our sincere apologies, Mr. Blackwell," as MacGregor stared pointedly out the window. "We're just a little, ah, anxious."

"I can see that," said Cliff. He gathered his thoughts and decided to regroup, take control, and try to lighten up. "Anyway, you're in luck." He smiled. "Mr. Russo's interested. Evidently you've dealt with him in the past."

Witherspoon seemed glad for the change in tone and the good news. "Never worked directly with Russo," he said quickly, "but some of our people worked closely with his associates, Mr. Roselli and Mr. Giancana. Ancient history now. Actually, we'd like to forget it." He smiled grimly. "New era now."

Cliff ignored his sudden stream of chatter. "It took some convincing, guys, but Mr. Russo generally has no reservations about working with you. But . . ."

"But what, Mr. Blackwell?" MacGregor asked.

"Russo wants Castro to get what he deserves. As a patriotic American, of course. But he's also a shrewd businessman. I had to paint it like a golden opportunity." Both agents hung on his words.

He looked directly at Witherspoon. "Once he saw the opportunity," Cliff said, "he was on board. He'll get the job done, and more."

"More?" asked Witherspoon. "Like what?"

"I told him with Castro gone he could open up gaming in Cuba."

MacGregor opened his mouth and shut it again.

Cliff plunged ahead. "I trust you gentlemen have already devised a post-Castro plan?"

"Of course," MacGregor said. "Why get rid of Castro if his brother should just take over afterward? That's why we, well . . ."

"Go on."

"We need to kill them both. At once."

"What about maintaining civil order?" Cliff asked. "The military'll try to take over. Hell, they will take over."

Witherspoon nodded. "We're planning for the worst." He grabbed the seat in front as the car lurched over a hole in the road. "I can't explain how, but believe me, once Castro's dead, we'll secure the island."

"Good," Cliff said. That was a relief. But should he feel glad about a double assassination? A cloud of dust boiled around the SUV as it bumped slowly through the desert.

Witherspoon said, "A temporary president will be installed right away. We have a man already."

"Very friendly to the U.S., I assume."

"Of course. The perfect guy to pave the way for a democratic election. We'll keep a hand in the process."

"I'm sure," said Cliff, watching the changing terrain outside. The rig had slowed, making the ride more comfortable. He looked at Witherspoon. "I have a group of investors prepared to pump several billion dollars into Cuba. For gaming, tourism, and related services." He picked at a fingernail while a few seconds ticked by. "The risk is high. They want an advantage."

"We can appreciate that," Witherspoon said. "What exactly are you thinking?"

"Monopoly." Cliff smiled to himself. Control. It was all about control.

"Monopoly?" MacGregor asked. He placed a fist on the front seat and twisted to look at Cliff. "Wait a damn minute. Look, we want a democracy. No more dictators and communists hanging around just off our shores. How do you think you'll get a monopoly out of a democracy?" He shook his head. "Christ. You push too much."

Cliff shrugged. "Monopolies exist in the United States, which at last check was still a democracy."

"Yeah," Witherspoon said, "but they were broken up, or they need to be, or they will be." He looked flustered.

"Sure," said Cliff. "But remember, you're talking about the United States. I'm talking about Cuba. Democratic or not, it'll be ages before they'll need to bust up monopolies."

Witherspoon nodded. "Good point."

MacGregor said, "How do you propose to get it, Mr. Blackwell?"

"I figure you fellas will have a great incentive to encourage it. You know, put in the good word?"

"I see." The muscles in MacGregor's jaw tensed as he looked out the window.

Cliff said, "I want to meet with the new temporary president once he's in office. You'll arrange it. Everyone will appreciate someone pouring money into that poor economy. Right?" Cliff looked at one and then the other. Both men stared through the windshield. "How can you say no?"

Witherspoon said, "Well, maybe not no, but more like we don't know. Your idea sounds logical. Their economy can certainly stand the help. It's been screwed up for so many decades, they barely have an economy. But with Castro gone, tourism's gotta increase anyway."

"Sure," Cliff said, "but think about the existing accommodations. Those places have gone to hell, too. Changing that picture could be tricky. But any investment capital would be a shot in the arm."

Witherspoon pulled at his earlobe. "Personally? We don't give a flying fuck if the Mob's involved in Cuba or not. We just want a democratic Cuba. But a strong economy would help Cuba's independence." He looked at MacGregor. "Maybe we'd be stupid not to support Mr. Russo's interest in Cuba."

"So you'll make the new president receptive to the idea?"

"Mr. Blackwell," Witherspoon said, "you people are helping us. We'll do our best to help you."

"Good." Cliff stopped picking at his fingernail. "Russo and company can handle Cuba's makeover as brilliantly as they can take out Castro. And . . . I also have enough personal incentive to help them."

The men glanced at each other. "We're convinced you'll be a significant factor, sir," MacGregor said, finally sounding respectful.

"Good. But Mr. Russo's probably getting all the wrong ideas by now. He was the man in the hallway, remember? So can we go back now?"

"Oh," Witherspoon said. "Sure. Sorry." He shook himself and glanced out the window, looking as if he didn't know where they were. Then he tapped the driver on the shoulder. "Let's kick this off-road wonder in the ass and get back, pronto," he said.

The ride back to the paved road was faster and rougher. Bracing against the bumps, Cliff said, "Mr. Russo and I have some business to finish here, then I'm going back to Europe. I'll give you the number of my satellite phone. You want to talk again, call first. No more goddamn surprise visits, okay?"

Both men nodded.

"I'll be in Miami in a week or so. I have to pick up a new yacht and do some business in the Bahamas."

MacGregor said, "Agreed. Meanwhile, don't waste any time. We're counting on you people."

The rig bumped hard one last time as it reached the highway. Cliff relaxed for the trip back to the Mecca.

"Actually, Mr. Blackwell," Witherspoon said, "the Bahamas would be a great place to meet again."

"All right. I'm leaving here tomorrow, and I'll plan on seeing you there."

Witherspoon let go of the front seat and leaned back. "That'd also be a good time for us to see Mr. Russo. And anyone else we should meet before we tackle Cuba."

"I'll suggest that," Cliff said, feeling like himself again. "By the way, when does Operation Smoke-Out happen?"

"January first," MacGregor said. "And we have a lot to do between now and then."

Witherspoon said, "We'll go over the details with you when we see you in Nassau."

The late afternoon sun was low behind them, and before long the first of the evening's twinkling lights of Las Vegas appeared in the distance. Cliff hoped that what lay ahead of them would not be like that glittering vision: odds stacked against them, all dance and dreams of success, ultimately leading to failure.

Shortly after their return to the Mecca, Cliff knocked on the door of Russo's room. He felt drained after his desert adventure, and new concerns had eroded his good mood. A sharp pain throbbed in his temple.

"Clifford!" Russo exclaimed, looking relieved. "Where the hell you been? Come in, come in!"

Cliff stepped inside and said, "Assholes took me for a drive in the desert."

"I figured. Just didn't know if you were coming back. Who was it? Looked less clean-cut than the FBI."

"CIA. You saw two of them in the hall, the ones I met in D.C."

"Christ on a crutch! Sit down, sit down. I'll get you a drink." Russo went to work at the wet bar. "I knew I smelled something wrong." He told Cliff about chasing him in a cab.

"Thanks, Sydney. I appreciate your effort. They really had me, like something from a movie." Cliff gratefully downed the brandy. He told Russo about the drive out of town and down the long dirt road to nowhere. "I thought they were going to kill me, but I didn't know why."

"Yeah," Russo said. "I'd of felt the same way. So what did they want?"

"A progress report."

"For Chrissake! Din' you just see 'em a couple days ago?"

"Yep. Think they're a little anxious, or what? Insecure, too."
The brandy warmed his belly, relaxing him.

"The CIA insecure?" Russo barked a laugh. "That's a good
one."

"Made me realize how much they need us."

"Good."

"I laid it out for them," Cliff said. "Told 'em you were shrewd.
Not that interested in whacking Castro, even if you are a patriotic
American. You wanted something meaningful. Like a monopoly
on gaming in Cuba." He waggled his empty snifter. "Got another
one of these?"

Russo chuckled and refilled the glass with brandy. "They
musta choked on that."

"More or less." Cliff stood and walked over to the windows.
Purple streaked the desert twilight. He turned back to Russo. "I
asked about post-Castro Cuba. It's just like we figured, so I
explained our expectations, and they actually conceded . . . to
everything."

Russo spread his arms, a peculiarly Italian gesture. Cliff smiled.
" 'Course, they can't guarantee the monopoly, but they agreed to
twist the new president's arm. And arrange a meeting with him for
me."

"Just like that?"

"Just like that. We have a deal, Sydney. I let them know that
it's a go for us, under our terms."

"Excellent, Cliff." Russo sat down and rubbed his chin, a
smile playing on his thin, old lips. "You know, you just might pull
this off. So, what's next?"

"They'll call me in the next week or so. Told them I'd be in
Miami and the Bahamas around then. They think we should all
meet in Nassau."

"Okay. Call me when you hear from them." He joined Cliff
at the windows. The sunset colors had deepened over the western

mountains. "I spoke with Tony. He wants dinner at his favorite restaurant tonight. You freshen up, Cliff, and I'll get the hotel limo to take us over there."

"Is that a safe place to talk?"

"Family-run joint, Cliff," he said with a wink. "Our pal Patrick bought it last year. We financed him. Believe me, it's safe."

"Well, good for Patrick," Cliff said. "All right. Give me forty-five minutes, and I'll be a new man."

"Hey, Cliff. In the old days when we took a guy for a ride, sometimes he crapped his pants."

Cliff grinned. "Don't worry, *Consigliere*. I'm still socially presentable."

Ivan Penkovsky was determined to eliminate the chronic problem with Mr. Potatohead. He sat in the spavined backseat of a creaking cab that nosed through the dark, narrow streets of Velesta. A crumpled newspaper was in his clenched fists.

He was pleased with Viktor's reports and his attitude. And he had enjoyed a night of the sweetest pleasures with the delicious Tatiana. But this problem in Macedonia was a thorn that had to be plucked from his side. He would have enjoyed another day or two at his villa, but such things could not be ignored. He had left the many pleasures of his retreat that morning and boarded a plane to Velesta.

He flattened the newspaper, read the headlines again, and studied the accompanying photograph in the uneven light. Thirty-two lost this time. Such incompetence! He itched to see that fat-headed sonofabitch again. He was sure now that his business and his connections in Istanbul were fine. He just had to fix this little problem with the spudhead, then meet with Sedat, his top contact in the Turkish Mafia—and a man he knew had to be handled carefully.

The cab swung to the curb and lurched to a stop. Penkovsky

paid the driver, climbed out, and nearly choked on the acrid exhaust. The same everywhere, he thought—the stink of automobile fumes and sewage. He marched up the sidewalk past huddled groups of men to the entrance of the Pussycat Club. He pulled open the door, edged past two beefy bouncers, who grunted in greeting, and stepped inside.

The joint was alive with loud rock music, conversation and catcalls. He pushed through the crowd of male patrons toward the runway. A long file of nude young dancers pranced and wiggled down the elevated stage, collecting tips from enthusiastic admirers and doing things that would have shut down a Las Vegas titty bar in a New York minute. Many of the girls squatted among the men and whispered suggestions.

The drunken customers crowded the counter that ran around the perimeter of the runway, or clotted around small tables with standup menus offering all manner of sexual refreshment. Hostesses clad in the briefest of shimmering outfits did their best to serve drinks amid the chaos.

Penkovsky reached between two guys engaged in a loud argument and grabbed a menu for himself. He squinted through the smoke, looking for the man he had come to see. He waded a little farther through the mob. Where is that moron with the fat head?

Penkovsky elbowed his way to the door that led upstairs to the manager's office. Its one-way glass window overlooked the whole scene.

A massive, unfamiliar guy with a sloped forehead and one long eyebrow guarded the door.

"Where is the boss?" asked Penkovsky.

"Stay here." The eyebrow moved against his skull. "I will get him." He disappeared through the door.

Penkovsky stared at the cracked paint on the door, clenching and unclenching his fists.

The muscle returned in two minutes. "He wants to know who you are."

"I am your real boss, you bonehead!" He pushed past and opened the door.

He ran up the stairs with the bouncer behind him. He burst through the door at the top and locked it. The bouncer banged once on the door and shouted something unintelligible.

A young woman with improbable breasts snapped her bleach-blonde head around and gaped at Penkovsky. Her eyes were those of a frightened animal. She leaned over Mr. Potatohead's desk, with the fathead himself, Penkovsky's number-one man in all of Macedonia, pounding her from behind, his pants pooled around his ankles.

"Aha! There you are!" said Penkovsky, striding into the room.

Mr. Potatohead jerked himself free, grabbed his trousers, and yanked them up. "Ivan! My God!"

"Please, don't let me interrupt. I'll just have a seat here and watch."

Penkovsky sat behind the desk, tossed down the menu and the newspaper face-up, and yanked open a drawer. He scooped up a shiny chrome-plated handgun with a silencer attached while Mr. Potatohead scrambled to stop him. He swung the gun toward the ample target of the man's cranium.

The big man froze halfway across the desk. "Boss! Ivan! Please . . ."

Penkovsky made kissing sounds. "Ah, my friend, I hope you have enjoyed your lovemaking tonight. Perhaps you can take that memory with you."

The gun coughed once, and a small, neat hole appeared magically between Mr. Potatohead's thick eyebrows. The girl yelped and cowered as the dead man collapsed heavily onto the desktop and slid to the floor, his pants still undone.

"Polack," Penkovsky said under his breath. The bigger they are, the harder they fall.

The bouncer kicked the door in, took one look at the scene, and fled.

Penkovsky swiveled toward the sobbing girl. "Come here, my precious," he said. He set the gun down and picked up the menu. He thumbed through the pages slowly, casually inspecting the graphic pictures. He glanced back at the girl, who remained hunched in fear. "I said come here!"

She stood up uncertainly, covering her breasts and pubic area like a schoolgirl, and padded to the desk on wobbly legs.

He pointed to a picture and said, "I want one of these."

She dropped to her knees, carefully unzipped his trousers, and went to work. Her mouth was hot, and she knew what she was doing. Penkovsky relaxed and enjoyed every slippery moment. He wondered out loud about the whereabouts of the club's assistant manager. That was one employee, he thought, who would be glad to hear about the corporate restructuring. And that would also be a good time for them to review company policy. He was sure the new manager would have no trouble remembering the rules in the future.

He groaned. The girl was better than good. She was an artist, and she was giving a virtuoso performance. Yes, the Pussycat Club always did seem like a mini vacation.

He gazed dreamily at the bloated face of the late boss and the darkening halo of blood. He looked as if he wanted to ask a question. And his potato head didn't look so big now. Interesting . . .

Another problem crossed off the list. Clean up a couple other administrative details here, and then on to his next stop.

Cyprus.

When she looked up at him, fear in her eyes, he soothed her by stroking her hair. His touch was exquisitely gentle.

Cliff and Sydney Russo stepped into the dim coolness of the restaurant just off the Strip on Sahara Avenue. Cliff felt refreshed, and he was looking forward to seeing Tony Carlo again. The maitre d' recognized Russo immediately and escorted the two of them to a private VIP room in the back of the house.

When they entered the private area, Tony Carlo stood up and opened his arms, a big smile on his face. The table was set for three at one end, and the rest of the space was covered with blueprints, architect's drawings, and bound reports.

Carlo greeted Russo and Cliff with a kiss on the cheek and a bear hug. Cliff knew that this man was an urbane fellow, unlike many of his Italian buddies. He was tall, well proportioned, and fluid in his movements. Gold accessories set off his expensive black suit. Cliff had reserved a nagging distrust for him when they were neighbors in Tahoe, but he had to admit he liked the guy. Carlo projected a natural confidence as he directed them to sit on either side of him at the table.

Cliff glanced at the blueprints and drawings. He knew that Russo had told Carlo he wanted to discuss his "Italian Palace" concept, and that he and Cliff had some exciting new business to talk about. Cliff also knew that Carlo had a lot more free time on his hands since they'd cashed out of the Mecca, even if he was president of Vegas Heiress Enterprises Inc. All the hot properties had been sold. After they had dumped the losers, the only property remaining was the *SS Vegas Heiress* herself, which was operating smoothly and profitably. Unfortunately for Carlo, it didn't have the same glitz of a Strip casino, or the same high-flying clientele he loved so much.

They chatted about business as they ordered drinks and appetizers.

Cliff and Russo had agreed to abbreviate their account of the business in Cuba. Carlo didn't need the whole story now. After all, he was head of a public company and had certain fiduciary responsibility to the shareholders. Russo had sworn Carlo to secrecy until further advised. Carlo had had a lot of experience keeping secrets.

They placed their orders, then he and Russo explained their plans for developing a new Las Vegas in Havana. Carlo listened raptly, his eyes sparkling with life. "Holy shit!"

"A strip of international casino resorts," said Cliff.

"On a beach!" Carlo said. "The Riviera of the Caribbean!" Color flooded Carlo's cheeks. "People will love it. Come to Cuba for Vegas-style gaming in a friggin' paradise."

"You could call it the Palace of Fortune," Cliff said, raising his water glass.

"This'll get international publicity," Russo enthused, stoking Carlo. "Just like Vegas. It'll attract gamblers by the shitload and run up the company stock." He pointed a crooked finger at Carlo. "You'll be on the map again, Tony."

"Brilliant!" Tony breathed, eyes glistening. "How come we didn't think about this sooner?"

"Good question," Russo said. "Been busy with Vegas, for one thing." He regarded Cliff. "For another, Cliff had an opportunity handed to him, and who did he think of?" He spread his hands.

"Okay, but what about Castro?" Carlo asked.

"He don't matter, Tony," Russo said. "Forget about him. Cliff here can get us into Cuba and probably grab us a monopoly, too."

"Forgive my asking," Carlo said, "but how?"

"That, my friend," Russo said, smiling thinly, "is a secret— for the moment." The smile faded, leaving a cruel mouth. "Keep your mouth shut. *Capisce?*"

Carlo nodded. "When will we be in?"

Cliff said, "Early next year."

"Great! Only a couple months away." He looked at Russo. "We gotta sure thing?"

"Tony, this is the best fuckin' thing in years."

Carlo shook his head in wonder. "Shit, we can do it all again, only better. They thought Vegas was finished, what with the lottos, Indian reservations, and riverboat gambling. But we showed 'em, didn't we, Sydney? They had no idea what we had in mind."

Russo smiled. "And they have no fuckin' clue now."

They laughed, smiles all around.

Carlo rapped his knuckles on the table. "You gotta count me in."

"Good, Tony," Russo said. "We need you. You got vision in this business. Gaming's not the same without you."

Carlo raised his drink. "Here's to three big thinkers—and the future of Cuba!"

"Viva, Havana," Russo said, "and our family!"

They all drank, but Cliff's smile faded when he thought of Castro's murder and the screaming international headlines. What if they all ended up in a federal pen, screwed by the CIA big-time?

After steaks and a good merlot, they went over the blueprints and drawings Carlo had brought. Later, when the three of them stood outside in the warm desert evening, Russo assured Carlo that he'd hear from him soon. "So get prepared, Tony. This'll be the biggest gaming deal in history." He took Carlo's hand in both of his.

Cliff admired his old friend's renewed vigor as he stood there in his sharkskin suit and the big black shades he'd put on as they left the restaurant, even though the sun had gone down hours ago. Good business pumped his blood.

Cliff shook Carlo's hand and followed Russo into the waiting limousine. His head swirled with the grand images of a revived Havana. They could make it happen, couldn't they? Bringing Tony Carlo on board was the perfect first step, wasn't it? Sure, sure, he chanted to himself, but a cold chill crept down his neck and he shivered as the big car surged forward into the night.

4

Havana Royale

THE NEXT MORNING, JUST FOUR DAYS AFTER LEAVING the quiet life on his yacht in Monte Carlo, Cliff boarded his Gulfstream again in the rosy Las Vegas dawn to begin the long journey back to the Mediterranean. He felt drained, but his inner demons were as lively as ever. Although he still nursed the guarded high of a clean victory and an enticing future, his mood was shadowed by a sense of impending peril. Christ, this was a dangerous, scary game. His time in the States felt more like weeks than a few days. And Victoria seemed like a benign hallucination now, someone from another life, he thought as he buckled himself into his seat.

Would she meet him as her father had said? How would she feel about all this? He wasn't sure, but he knew that he would find out soon enough.

After more than twelve hours and an uneventful flight, Cliff stepped off his Gulfstream into the shimmering darkness of late-night Monaco. The familiar, unreal sensations of fast travel, with its magical warp of time and place, clung to him, but he was glad to be back.

Victoria detached herself from the crowd, looking happy enough to see him. They fell into a long hug and then walked arm-in-arm to her sleek Bell 407 chopper for the short hop back to the yacht. He knew she was anxious for an update, but she didn't bombard him with questions, apparently out of respect for the sensitivity of the subject. Instead she used her usual sixth sense of him and led him straight to bed and rest without any demand for details. He felt relieved not to be pressured just then.

Before long, Cliff fell into a deep slumber, but he awoke too soon, feeling confused by jet lag. Victoria stirred at his movements, and together they got up and greeted the first light of day on the afterdeck of the yacht, fresh coffee in hand. Standing at the rail with Victoria, Cliff glanced at his watch, trying to get reoriented. Nine-thirty in the morning, Monte Carlo time.

As he shook off the drugged numbness of sleep and sipped his coffee, Cliff recounted the details of his past four days and his travels to Washington, Chicago, and Las Vegas.

Victoria listened quietly and took in everything, her green eyes looking serious and clouded with concern. He knew he was reanimating old nightmares. When he stopped talking she turned on her heel and plunked her empty cup down on a table. Her abrupt movement startled him.

She punched the air and wailed, "Dammit, Cliff!" Her voice was tight with emotion.

"What the hell, Vic?"

She whirled to face him. "You shouldn't have done it."

"Done what?"

"You know!" Color crept up her neck, and her eyes looked dark and cold. "Agreed to anything. Without talking to me first."

"Vic, I already explained that. And you know I normally would have, but—"

She raised a hand. "Oh, sure. I heard the *but*."

"What do you want me to do?" He felt angry and helpless.

"You're a fool!" she cried and stamped back to the rail and stared at the horizon, a fist to her mouth.

"Maybe so, but—"

"You're crazy!" she said over her shoulder. "Just like they are. You expect me to go along with this insanity?"

"Jesus, Vic."

"We were lucky once," she said. "When we got out of the Bahamas alive last year. *Barely.*"

"But, Vic, everything worked out."

"Yeah, right!" Her eyes brimmed with tears. "Don't you remember how scary that was? How we almost died in my airplane? *They sabotaged it!*"

Cliff studied her. He knew she had every right to be upset. Hell, he was angry, too. And now he was also sad to see Victoria so distressed. Her fear was deep and palpable.

"I'm scared, too, Vic."

She spun away from him and yanked a large, blue clip from her hair. "No, I don't think you know what scared is." Her golden tresses swung free, making her look wild, and the hand holding the hair clip trembled.

He edged closer to her. "I'm sorry, Vic."

"That's not good enough, Cliff," she said, her voice rising. "I can't go through this again!" A sob escaped her throat.

Cliff touched her shoulder. "Baby . . ."

"No!" she shouted. She twisted away from him and flung the big hair clip against the nearest bulkhead. "I'm leaving." She fled across the deck, her powder-blue peignoir slipping off one shoulder and her tawny hair flying behind her, and disappeared through a doorway.

"Vic!" he called after her, but she was gone. He slumped into a deck chair and put his head in his hands. He took several deep breaths, fighting back his own sobs. Victoria's outburst had floored him, and he knew he had no right to stop her. A strange sense of loss filled him.

Finally he looked up and gazed at the distant pink sprawl of Monte Carlo dozing in the early morning haze. Even the city seemed sad. Everything felt unreal. He shook his head and stood, feeling weak and dizzy, and dragged himself into the main salon. Nothing moved, as if every living thing had abandoned the ship and even the remote city on the coast and the planet itself.

He shambled on to the master stateroom—not even a ghost there—then continued into the bathroom and took a deep breath. Just a hint of Vic's perfume—Jean Patou 1000—lingered in the air. A bleak pain gripped his heart. He felt lost. Finally he turned on the shower and shed his robe. The hiss of the hot water and the clouds of steam filled his world and comforted him. He stood under the pelting spray for what seemed like hours. But when he stepped out of the shower, the empty feeling crept in again.

A movement in the steamy room caught his eye. Victoria stood there watching him, holding something in her hand.

He summoned a tentative relief. "What do you have there?" he asked evenly.

"Double vodka and tonic."

Thank God her tone was normal again. "Thanks, Vic." He raked his fingers through his wet hair. "You know, I'm really glad to be home."

"No doubt." She placed the tall glass beside the sink and glided toward him in the mist. "Glad I didn't have to make that trip."

He stopped toweling his hair and eyed her. "You okay?"

"I'll be fine. I'm happy you're back." She snaked both arms around his bare waist and looked into his eyes, her lips parted.

"Good." He kissed her gratefully.

She buried her head under his jaw. "I've been crazy with worry."

"I know, sweetheart." He ran a hand through her damp hair.

She leaned back and gazed at him again. "Maybe they really do need you, Cliff."

He shrugged. "I just hope it doesn't destroy what we have."

He didn't like that thought. A warning salvo had already flared across his bow, and he knew that maybe it could. He started to speak, but Victoria put a finger to his lips and took his hand. She smiled and led him from the bathroom.

A little while later, after breakfast, Cliff and Victoria huddled on the afterdeck and watched the sun climb into a translucent blue sky and the day open for business, Monte Carlo-style. With a turn of the head they could scan the skyline of the famous little city, stacked behind its own private harbor filled with boats like their own. Or they could gaze across the open Mediterranean winking peacefully in the morning glare. Only an uneasy truce stilled the tension between them, and Cliff sensed that this might be his last tranquil morning before the inevitable hurl of hazardous events that had already been set in motion.

Upon rising, Cliff had given the crew orders to depart the next morning for Miami, after confirming that his new yacht was ready for delivery. Now he placed a call on his secure satellite phone to Virgil Carter, his right-hand man and most trusted financial advisor in Nassau. In the past when Cliff's offshore investment company, the T.H.E. Corporation, was headquartered in the Bahamas, they had spoken every day, but since liquidating the company Cliff communicated with Virgil less and less. Now they needed to talk only every week or so to keep Cliff abreast of all his financial activities. Cliff knew that his business was in capable hands. Virgil ran a tight ship.

Virgil sounded pleased to hear his voice and asked how things were going.

"Let's put it this way," Cliff said. "I've had an enlightening week in Washington. And Chicago, and Las Vegas." The only response was the muted hiss of the connection.

"Virgil?"

"Yes, I'm here, Cliff. What now?"

"I'd rather tell you in person. We're leaving Monte Carlo tomorrow on the yacht and heading for Miami."

"So it's finally ready?"

"Yep. Just sitting there waiting for us."

"I'm sure it's a beauty, Cliff. Bet you're excited."

In truth he had barely thought about his new yacht during the last few days, and now it was the furthest thing from his mind, but he didn't want that to show. "I'm thrilled. More than last time." Cliff tilted his head and gazed at the bright, cloudless sky. "Anyway, you'll see it soon. After we make the trade, we'll be over to see you. Should be there within two weeks."

"I look forward to that, Cliff."

Cliff rang off and stretched on his big deck chair. This last free morning was degenerating into a struggle to hang on to some hope. Yes, the big new yacht. Just now he'd trade both the damn yachts just to sit in a one-room shack in the deepest woods with Victoria and no worries.

He picked up the *International Herald Tribune* and flipped the pages dully, his mind clattering with random thoughts. Before long a steward brought them lunch. Afterward, Victoria suggested that they retreat to the spa for a while before facing the rest of the day. Cliff thought that sounded like as good an idea as any.

Two hours later, Cliff had just started to drift off to sleep in the master stateroom when his sat phone buzzed him back to reality. He fumbled with the telephone, his heart thudding from a confusing dream that had just begun.

Witherspoon's insistent voice assaulted his ear. Cliff's last shred of peace vanished as he listened to the CIA agent. "Okay, okay," he said, interrupting him. "Let me call you back." He jabbed the button that ended the call much too hard.

Victoria padded into the stateroom from the shower, wrapping a fluffy white towel around herself. "Who was that, Cliff?"

She bent and twisted a smaller towel around her head and flipped it back. Cliff watched her greedily, marveling at how such a simple ritual could derail him from any train of thought.

She adjusted the big towel and said, "Well?"

"The CIA," he said, feeling a pang of stress.

"What now? They know your schedule, right? We're leaving any minute now."

"Change of plans."

"Such as?"

"They wanna meet right away in Nassau. I think they're afraid our cruise will delay things."

"Oh, God. Here we go." Victoria stripped off the big towel and dried one long leg at a time.

"I know. They're pushy bastards," he said, enjoying the show. "Anyway, we'll have to fly, Vic. Take the Gulfstream, be in Miami tonight. Tomorrow the crew'll start taking the *Banc Royale* across and keep an eye on her until we get settled on the new yacht."

Victoria dabbed at the damp hollow between her breasts. "I guess we have no choice. But will the new yacht be ready?"

"It's been ready. But there's plenty to do before we shove off for the Bahamas. We'll see. Maybe they'll have to meet us in Miami, whether they like it or not." He rubbed his forehead, suddenly feeling weary. He had half a mind to tell them all to fuck off.

Victoria placed a hand on his shoulder. "I'll get someone to help us pack." As she shrugged into her dressing gown he tried to tell himself that everything would be all right.

Cliff dozed uneasily in his seat on the cruising Gulfstream, trying to appease his time-zone-raddled brain. The unplanned transatlantic flight this afternoon wasn't helping, but it was uneventful, at least, and he was glad that Victoria was with him this time. With the time changes between Monaco and the States, they would arrive in Miami in time for a late dinner.

As they neared the eastern seaboard, Cliff phoned ahead to the yacht broker. The hour was late for business, but Cliff's studied ear told him that the call was welcomed. And why not? The guy would pocket a fat commission from this deal.

The broker understood the circumstances and that the *Banc Royale*, Cliff's old yacht, would arrive within the next week or so for the trade-in. He offered to pick them up and take them to a hotel or to the new yacht.

"Directly to the ship," Cliff said. "We'll have something to eat on board, if possible, then get a good night's sleep. We'll go over everything first thing in the morning."

With that bit of business completed, Cliff propped his head on Victoria's shoulder and slept again.

As promised, the broker met them on arrival at Miami International and drove them to their new yacht in his black Lexus.

Once aboard, Cliff telephoned the *Banc Royale* and spoke with the captain, who had the yacht well under way and heading for Gibraltar. Cliff told him that they had arrived safely.

"All is well here, too," the captain said. "Don't worry about a thing."

The next morning, Cliff awoke aboard his new yacht as if in a dream. Their arrival the night before had seemed only half real after yet another long flight. He had boarded the vessel and peered at the opulent surroundings vaguely, as if through the eyes of a visitor, skipped dinner, and fallen into bed like an exhausted hotel guest.

Despite their surreal arrival, now he knew that he was literally aboard his new dream yacht. But his emotions were dull. Not even the finest ship in the world could excite him now, he decided. The place was dead quiet, and Victoria was still soundly asleep.

And yet in the hushed twilight of the master stateroom he sensed the fresh, understated luxury that surrounded him. He propped himself on one elbow and tried to let it all sink in, but a strange emptiness filled him instead. He bent and kissed Victoria.

She stirred and moaned. "Wuhtimezit? Oh, Cliff, the ya is sho bi. . . !" she said.

He smiled at her innocent, sleepy words. "I'll say. Actually it's only thirty-two feet longer, but the added length makes it wider, too."

"Wow!" She stretched languorously and scrubbed a hand across her mouth. "I was dreaming we were touring the new yacht."

He hugged her. "Great idea. Let's do it."

Forty minutes later they emerged from the master stateroom bathed, dressed, and ready to explore. Cliff thought the tour should cheer them up. He took Victoria by the hand and led her down a wide passageway toward the main salon. Suddenly he stopped, gathered her into his arms, and kissed the top of her head. Her hair smelled like a field of flowers.

She pulled away and stared at him. "Are you all right? Don't you want to see your new boat?"

He wanted to tell her that he preferred looking at her to everything that surrounded them, preferred the world within the circle of her arms to the expanse of the ship, the sea, and the sky. But again he had to fight off the nagging sense of emptiness and loss.

He forced a smile and said, "Sorry, Vic. Sure I do." They continued down the passageway.

"It'll take some time to get used to all this space," she said. "What were you thinking? Can our crew handle this?"

She sounded so perfectly normal compared to his mood. He nodded, relieved to speak about such mundane things. "Might need to add a couple. They say it typically takes a crew of nine." They walked into the spacious main salon. "But we can do with less."

Cliff glanced around. He was pleased with the dark mahogany paneling that covered everything, even the overhead. The heavy furniture was upholstered in beige, white, and yellow and was grouped for entertaining on a pale, custom-woven carpet.

"It feels like an English country manor," Victoria said.

When she grinned at him he felt his mood start to shift. Smiling, he walked over to a brass telescope that stood on a polished tripod. He spun it toward Victoria and peeked through the eyepiece at her.

She pulled a series of grotesque faces that made him laugh. He leaned across the instrument and said, "Maybe I need to take this thing outside at night, see something besides a clown face."

She stuck out her tongue, and he laughed again. For the moment his worries seemed to have retreated and jumped overboard.

"Look at the lighting," Victoria said, pointing at the tiny overhead spots. "Looks like a constellation of stars."

He rejoined her and took her into his arms. "It's not that much bigger than the *Banc Royale*, but I think it's got a much warmer feel." He squeezed her. "And the extra space is for you."

"So I can't drive you crazy?"

"Exactly."

"But it looks so . . . I don't know. Expensive."

He shrugged.

"Maybe you need to give yourself a raise, Cliff."

"I've already done the math. We're okay."

"I know." She gave him a little kiss. "I wasn't complaining."

"It's our little country retreat. When we need to get away again, we'll haul anchor and leave on that world cruise."

"Okay. If we ever get out of Havana."

The dark shadow had returned to her eyes. He was about to reply when a steward appeared.

"Good morning, sir, madam," he said. "Would you like breakfast? We have a special menu, planned by your broker."

Cliff willed himself to shake off his black thoughts. "Sounds good. Could we possibly eat outside, uh, somewhere on the deck?"

"Sir, it's your ship," said the steward. "You can do whatever you want wherever you wish."

Cliff smiled and winked at Victoria. She still seemed distracted, and he hoped she was all right. Nothing a little sun and some fresh air wouldn't cure, he hoped.

The steward said, "May I suggest the aft deck off the main salon, sir?"

"Perfect. We'll look around some more and be up there in a few minutes."

Cliff sat with Victoria, sipping coffee and enjoying the scenery. The morning was sunny and warm, and they had a panoramic view of the marina. Other fine yachts and boats of every description crowded around them, with brightwork winking in the sunlight and lanyards ringing against aluminum masts in the freshening breeze. In the distance rose the high-rise hotels and condos of Miami Beach. The placid, gray Atlantic stretched away to the horizon. The broker had called just as they were seated for breakfast, and Cliff had asked him to come by within the hour. Meanwhile, two stewards had served their special breakfast and left them to enjoy it alone.

Some color had returned to Victoria's face. Her eyes looked clear and calm when she glanced over her coffee cup at him.

"This boat is very special, Cliff," she said.

"Yes, and I think this is a good change, even from Monte Carlo. Don't worry, everything's gonna be fine."

Without further comment she picked up a knife and fork and started to work on her oysters Benedict.

They spoke little as they dined. When they were finished, the steward returned to clear the table and inform them that the broker, Mr. Barham, was waiting in the main salon.

They strolled inside and greeted the nattily dressed broker, who introduced two other men in business suits, both representatives of the Dutch shipbuilder. Barham explained that the present crew of seven were temporary but sufficient for their needs for the time being.

Because of his change of plans, Cliff had already arranged for an extended sea trial of at least several days, including a run to Nassau and back. After that, the broker told him, they could add any crew members that Cliff required.

The two Dutchmen gave Cliff and Victoria a complete tour of the ship, explaining in detail much of the operating equipment, although some things were too technical to retain from the whirlwind overview the gentlemen provided. Near the captain's sea quarters, one of the men pointed out a comprehensive library and assured them that detailed instructions for all the systems and equipment could be found there. They moved on to the bridge, where Captain Winslow greeted them with a formal salute. Attired in a crisp, spotless white uniform and a captain's hat, he looked the consummate professional.

The captain reviewed the whole layout and its instrumentation, assuming correctly that Cliff already had a working knowledge of luxury yachts and understood his explanations.

"When your crew arrives, Mr. Blackwell," Barham said, "and when you return from the Bahamas, Captain Winslow will familiarize your men with all the instruments and procedures. He'll also demonstrate all the necessary equipment."

Cliff thanked the men. He had enjoyed the tour and the distraction from his cares. He thought he had made the right decision to move into a larger yacht with a uniquely different character in the face of so much uncertainty. A new beginning had to be good, he reasoned, no matter what else might lay ahead.

They had learned about a few modifications to the builder's original plans. One significant addition was a helipad to accommodate Victoria's new Bell 407 helicopter. This had required a redesign of the topside after deck and the relocation of the davits, launches, and lifeboats to the next deck below. When they stood outside in the sunshine again, Cliff admired the empty helipad, picturing the sleek nose and low topline of the chopper fitting in perfectly.

The shipwrights had also added a freight elevator near the bow with a hoist strong enough to stow Cliff's TVR sports car in the forward hold. This had required improvisation by the ship's architect and some clever alterations, but by the looks of things Cliff decided that they had pulled it off well. He was still admiring the handiwork when his sat phone trilled.

Witherspoon identified himself. "I'm in Nassau," he said. "How soon can you be here, Mr. Blackwell?"

"We're leaving tomorrow," Cliff told him. "Sea trial on our new yacht. Should get there by midafternoon or so."

"Call me at the Atlantis as soon as you arrive."

"Got it, chief," Cliff said and punched off.

Cliff and Victoria spent the rest of the day exploring the yacht, making phone calls, and trying to relax. Eventually they decided to check out the hot tub in the master stateroom. Cliff admired his lovely companion as she slipped naked into the warm, churning water. She looked radiant and happy now—and immeasurably sexy. She was sleek, tanned, and toned, a vision of youthful health and beauty. He drew her into his arms, remembering their first physical encounter.

That had occurred after a whirlwind ten days of getting to know and appreciate each other amid the toughest of trials. It had also begun in a spa, that one aboard the *Banc Royale*. Cliff thought about how perfectly they had connected, on all levels, and how emphatically she had ended a long period of often deep loneliness for him—the years of mourning for his lost wife and son. He also recalled how she had stuck by him through some dreadful events. He held her close to his heart, which thumped in gratitude, and stroked her silky skin.

They had grown even closer in the happy days that followed.

Would their happiness survive the events to come? Once, he had craved risk. Now he regarded Victoria and her easy smile wistfully and prayed that he wouldn't lose her.

Cliff and Victoria sat alone on the deck again as shadows lengthened behind the yacht in the waning afternoon. He retrieved his sat phone and punched in Sydney Russo's mobile number. He brought Russo up to date, and Russo asked if he'd heard from their "friends."

"Matter of fact, yes." Cliff squinted through the brassy haze at the famous Miami skyline. "This morning. They're already in Nassau. I think you should go down there."

"I can do that."

"Good. We should get there by late afternoon tomorrow. Let's hook up then, if you can make it." Cliff tried to maintain a businesslike tone of voice while Victoria wiggled her toes between his thighs.

Russo said, "Where should we stay?"

Cliff tickled Victoria's foot, and she clapped a hand over her mouth to muffle her giggles. "Try the Ocean Club. They've got decent bungalows by the pool. Private and peaceful." He stifled a laugh. "Don't stay at the Atlantis. That's where our friends'll be."

"Thanks for the tip."

"We can meet in your suite or my old offices. Either place would be more secure than this boat right now. We've got seven crew members on loan to us."

"Okay, Cliff. Expect to hear from me then," Russo said and abruptly hung up.

Cliff dropped his phone and leapt from his chair. He pounced on Victoria and pinned her to her chaise lounge with a forceful kiss. A pleasant warmth coursed through his blood, and he laughed when he came up for air.

Victoria gazed at him with a lazy, wanton smile, her cheeks

flushed with color. Cliff helped her up and led her to the master stateroom.

Cliff sat on the rumpled bed listening impatiently to syrupy canned music on the telephone, brushing his damp hair. After napping for an hour, he and Victoria had showered together and dressed. Then he had called Andre Martinez, and now he was on hold. Finally the line clicked, and the music stopped.

"Clifford! Where are you?"

"Right here in Miami, Andre. Just took delivery of my new yacht."

"*Fantástico!*" Andre exclaimed with his usual enthusiasm. "Let's get together. I want to see you and your big boat. How long will you be here?"

Cliff explained their schedule.

"What about tonight?" asked Andre. "I'll take you both to dinner."

"Tonight would be good." Cliff felt buoyed by the thought of seeing his old friend so soon. Keep the ghosts at bay for another evening. "But you must be our guest. On the new boat. We'll even christen her while you're here." He gave Andre a time and directions to the marina.

"What will you call this yacht—the *Titanic*?" asked Andre.

Cliff chuckled. "No, the *Havana Royale*."

"Ah, and what a fine name that is." Andre sounded genuinely pleased. "I look forward to seeing you both, my friend."

Next Cliff telephoned his father because he had forgotten to call him before their departure from Monte Carlo. He updated him on their whereabouts and plans and chatted for a few minutes. He was telling his father that he'd call again soon when Victoria walked into the stateroom.

"Gotta go, Pop. Take care," he said and rang off.

"Your father?"

"The one and only."

"How's he doing?"

"Good." Cliff dodged some intrusive thoughts. "I thought I should let him know where we are."

Victoria eyed him. "What's wrong, Cliff? Something's bothering you."

He shook his head. "I made the mistake of mentioning Cuba."

She sat on the edge of the bed. "Why is that a mistake?"

"He's very familiar with the place."

"That's funny," she said with a smile.

"Not really. I don't know. The conversation left me cold."

She raked her hair back with one hand and touched his cheek. "Anything you want to talk about?"

"I guess not. Some things I'd rather forget." He stood, picked up his empty glass, and walked toward the wet bar. "Like some more champagne?"

"Sure."

He filled two clean flutes. "He's a funny old guy," he said with his back to Victoria.

"In what way?"

He returned and handed her the drink. "He doesn't always like to give you the satisfaction."

"What do you mean?"

"Like what you're doing is any good."

"Maybe he's envious, Cliff."

Cliff took a sip of champagne. "Maybe. He always was an independent old bastard."

"Stingy with his feelings? Is that what you mean, Cliff?"

He thought for a moment and nodded. "Something like that."

"Don't let it bother you. He probably just has a hard time opening up. Maybe he wishes he could go to Cuba, too."

He sat next to her. "You're probably right."

"You know me, Cliff, I don't like to probe. But I'm curious about your parents." She took his hand and said, "You don't talk about them much. Especially your mother."

"I know." He sighed. "And I'm not sure if I'm up to it now, either."

"Did they get along?"

"Crazy about each other."

"It's so sad that she died so young. What was she—forty-six? At that age you're only just getting started."

"I'll say," said Cliff. He brought his glass to his lips, then put it aside on the nightstand.

"How old were you when she died?"

"Seventeen."

"And she didn't go to a doctor. I wonder why."

"I told you." He took a deep breath and let it out. "Maybe you forgot because it's so damn illogical." He felt the old grief darkening his mood. "When you have a problem, when you feel crappy, you call the damn doctor, right?"

Victoria touched him gently on the shoulder. "Why didn't she go to the doctor?"

He shook his head slowly, fighting back the images of that time. Finally he shrugged. "She was very spiritual. The doctor thing was not an option for her particular brand of religion."

"I see."

"I'm sorry."

"It's all right, Cliff." She rubbed his back. "That must've been hard on your father."

"Tore him apart."

"And you?"

"Me? A few months later I joined the Marines. The perfect escape, ha ha."

"I bet your dad had plenty of regrets. You know, after someone dies, sometimes their loved ones feel guilty. They wonder if they could've done more, been a better person while the other one was alive, that kind of thing."

Cliff glanced at Victoria. "You're right. Dad had a lot of regrets. I think he still does."

"Such as?"

"Wishes he'd tried harder. You know, less boozing, less time chasing other women. Stayed home some evenings with the family." He waved a dismissive hand to hide his buried anger and sighed. "Ain't life grand?"

"Sure," she said. "Like an eternal senior prom."

Cliff chuckled, feeling relieved.

She cuffed him lightly on the shoulder and bounced to her feet. "Hey," she said. "We'd better get our act together. Andre's probably on his way over here."

Cliff sighed. "Roger that, Captain Vic. Read you loud and clear."

An hour later a steward escorted Andre Martinez into the main salon.

"Andre! Welcome aboard!" Cliff said.

The big man dropped a stack of thin, white boxes onto a couch and gathered Cliff into a bone-popping bear hug. Cliff hugged Andre back, feeling surprised at how good it was to see his old friend again. When they parted, Victoria stood on her toes to kiss Andre's cheek. He hugged her, too, but with less force.

As always, Andre was dressed neatly in freshly pressed clothing that reflected his affluence and his Hispanic heritage. His blue-black hair, slicked back from his high forehead, gleamed beneath the overhead spots, and when he smiled, his Douglas Fairbanks Jr. mustache made a straight line. He looked like an aging, industrial-sized Latin matinee idol.

Andre released Victoria and said, "This boat, it is *magnífico*, Cliff. Congratulations! And you, Victoria, are *bellísima*! Only your beauty surpasses that of this fabulous yacht."

Victoria laughed and said, "Oh, brother! I think you got an early start on the cocktail hour. What in the world do you have in all those boxes?"

Andre gestured toward Cliff. "I bring a dozen shirts to my dear friend Clifford."

"Shirts?" Cliff said. "Andre, you shouldn't have."

"No, no, they are my favorite. Very comfortable. Good for hot weather, and to travel. Cuban-style guayaberas, made by hand." He plucked his own shirt. "I wear them always."

"Wonderful detail," Cliff said, stroking the fabric on Andre's shoulder. "I've seen them on you many times, but I've never seen them in a store."

"You must know where to look, my friend."

"Well, thank you very much. I'll get a lot of use out of them."

"It is nothing, Clifford. Virgil and I passed many good days working together in Nassau while we dismantled your company." He smiled and looked upward, as if reminiscing. "Ah, it was a pleasure—and good money, too. But most of all I enjoyed helping you two. In those days your hands were full."

Victoria took his hand and smiled. "We certainly appreciate your help, Andre. And we appreciate your friendship, too."

He beamed at her and then snapped his fingers. "Ah, I almost forgot." He removed a slender black velvet box from his pocket. "For you, Victoria."

When Victoria opened the box, her eyes widened. A sparkling diamond bracelet rested upon black velvet. "Oh, my God!" she said. "Andre . . ."

"It is nothing." His dark eyes twinkled. "When I saw it, I knew it required an elegant wrist. I have saved these gifts for a long time. I wanted to present them in person. A small token of my esteem."

Cliff said, "You outdid yourself, Andre. That calls for a drink." Just as he had thought, Andre's presence had turned the atmosphere festive. He led his friend to an oversized couch and pressed a button to call a steward.

* * *

Cliff enjoyed the long, leisurely meal that followed, eating more than he needed and chatting happily with two of his favorite people. For the moment his world seemed to be on an even keel.

He updated Andre on recent developments, without going into detail. Andre's eyes widened at several points in the story. When a server was present, they spoke in hushed tones. Cliff assured him that he would provide complete details when it was safe. In the meantime he invited Andre to visit them in Havana.

"I will do that, my friends," Andre said. "Call anytime, and I will come to you. I must hear the rest of this story."

"Excellent!" Cliff said. "Now let's round up the crew for that christening ceremony."

Andre stood, lifted his wine glass, and pronounced, "To the *Havana Royale!*" Cliff and Victoria got up and joined him in the toast.

5

Offshore Reunion

TWO DAYS LATER, ON WEDNESDAY MORNING, CLIFF AWOKE at dawn and slipped away without disturbing Victoria. He climbed topside and inhaled the fresh sea air, happy to see Nassau in the distance, its colors muted by the soft morning light. The cruise had gone well the day before, and he had used the passage to shelve his worries and enjoy the new yacht. He often thought that sea travel appealed to him for precisely that reason—as an escape from the real world.

As he gazed fondly at the familiar skyline, he felt all the more like the voyager returned. This was his first time back to his home base in fifteen months, and he knew that reality—in the shape of Donald Witherspoon—awaited him onshore. He took another deep breath and felt a queasy surge of adrenaline as he thought about the meetings set for later that day.

The *Havana Royale* tested its anchor against the currents, the only large craft in the harbor. Cliff was glad for the momentary sense of tranquil isolation. Before setting sail, the captain had tried to make reservations for a slip or possibly an end-tie to dock the huge yacht on arrival, but his efforts had yielded nothing. Cliff knew that the largest available slips were located at the Atlantis Hotel, close to where their meetings were planned on Paradise Island and across the toll bridge from Cliff's offices. But the marina at the Atlantis was booked solid, and no other facility in Nassau had space to accommodate the *Havana Royale*.

So they had simply dropped anchor in the middle of the channel between Paradise Island and the east end of New Providence Island, where other boats occasionally moored. The first mate had given orders to deploy one of the two seventeen-foot launches so that it would be ready when someone needed to go ashore.

Cliff had contacted Sydney Russo the evening before and found him, as expected, already checked into a bungalow at the Ocean Club. They decided that Cliff should first meet briefly with Witherspoon.

Cliff turned from the rail and headed for the launch, resigned to getting an early start on the day and facing the inevitable.

"This is a good place to do business, Yuri," said Ivan Penkovsky, surveying the streams of humanity that filled the cobbled streets of Cyprus.

Yuri Grovka looked up and replied, "Ya. Nice to get some sun, too." As usual, the small, dark man who sat opposite him at the sidewalk cafe needed a shave, and his dark suit looked slept-in.

"Tomorrow I may do that," Penkovsky said. He felt good just sitting here in the long afternoon shadows and sipping his strong Turkish coffee laced with honey. He always enjoyed visiting this island, where money flowed in many directions.

He leaned back in his wrought-iron chair and grimaced with pleasure as he considered his latest good fortune. He had just received another shipment of cash to fund his global activities. That always made his day.

"Boss," Grovka said, shifting his gaze away, "this time we had a little problem."

Penkovsky stared at his flunky underling. All such men, he thought, were flunky underlings. "What do you mean, Yuri?"

The shabby man chewed a dirty thumbnail. "Airport customs," he said. "They handled the paperwork different this time. They detained us."

"They searched the trunk?"

"No."

"Good. Until they search the trunk, Yuri, no problem."

"Okay, Boss."

Penkovsky scooted his chair next to Grovka. "Listen to me. They aren't looking for money, Yuri. They hope we are loaded with cash. They are *praying* we sneak it all in." He swept a hand through the air. "This fucking place is all about money." He knew that Cyprus was a popular tax haven among Middle-Easterners, conveniently located as it was off the southern coast of Turkey and the western shore of Syria. He made a fist. "But this is no goddamn Switzerland. *Those* assholes screwed themselves. They are cuckoo like their fucking clocks."

Grovka toyed with a spoon and glanced away. Penkovsky sprawled in his chair and said, "Nicosia is a good transportation point. My British banker always pisses his pants when I come to see him."

"You take good care of him, Boss."

Penkovsky sneered. "Even I like the conceit of this rotten place," he said, "and a little feuding between the Turks and Greeks keeps things in balance here."

Grovka peered at him uncertainly. "I suppose," he said.

"Listen," Penkovsky said, jabbing a finger at the little guy's broken nose. "In a couple days, we go. You return to Moscow with the Mercedes, and I go to Dubai to meet a *hawala* banker and that little brown Paki faggot and tell him where he can stick it."

"You mean Mr. Sundaram?"

"Yes, that *govnyuki* shithead. But no matter. India will blow them right off the fucking map soon enough."

Grovka laughed harshly, then quickly added, "Sorry, Boss." He took a quick sip of coffee to cover his offense.

Penkovsky decided to keep going. "You think for one minute I would let that idiot be my financier? Jesus Christ, Yuri, I would need to have a frostbitten brain."

Grovka nodded, his newfound amusement still showing. "I never saw a man so eager."

"Exactly." Penkovsky leaned toward his jumpy little companion. "I have a bigger plan—Edwards. You know, the Gold Man. We have already made a deal. Him, I can work with, my friend. He has two good points. He is filthy rich, and he is totally crazy."

"True," Grovka said, knitting his brows.

"Just imagine—a Russian Cuba. Finally! It makes my head swim."

"You are a big thinker, Boss."

He stabbed a finger at the little man's face again. "You just make damn sure the hardware order is correct. *Then* we transfer funds."

"Do not worry, Boss. I take good care."

Grovka was trying to impress him, he could tell. "All right, my friend," Penkovsky said, thinking that the little shit would probably do as he was told. He was too scared not to.

"Dubai, then Africa?" Grovka asked.

"Congo. The Grand Hotel—a good place to do business. I will flesh out my plan with the Gold Man there. And meet a few new people, when the time is right."

"Then back to Moscow?"

"Yes, my friend," Penkovsky said. "After that—how do you say?—back to the grindstone. Much good progress should be made by then."

The shadows had merged with the evening gloom, and now the streets were alive with the milling after-dark crowd. Penkovsky sprang to his feet, and his little associate jumped as if he had been struck by a bullet. "Now let's find some action. Some Turkish pussy, perhaps?"

"Of course, of course," Grovka said, but Penkovsky was already striding away down the old cobblestone street.

At nine o'clock that morning Cliff bounced through the light chop in the channel, with the fresh wind flapping one of his new guayabera shirts as the launch headed toward shore. He balanced himself carefully and gripped his satellite phone. Preparations for a new day animated the colorful display of Bay Street to his left, and the thick, green vegetation of Paradise Island took on more detail as they approached. He felt ready to tackle the next job in this unlikely drama.

Once ashore he hailed a cab and rode the short distance up the hill to the entrance of the Atlantis. He strolled through the lush portico and entered the cool interior of the hotel. A familiar man who looked uncomfortably warm in a gray suit and matching fedora intercepted him. They exchanged greetings, and Witherspoon suggested a walk.

"Sure. This way," Cliff said. He led the CIA man past the main registration desk, through a bar and waiting area, down a spiral flight of stairs, and through a pair of doors to a walkway that meandered around the grounds.

"Where's your partner?" asked Cliff.

"Reassigned," Witherspoon said. "He's chasing Algerian camel jockeys."

Cliff had to smile at that one.

When they entered the cool gloom of a manmade tunnel banked with aquariums and shark tanks, Witherspoon stopped him and glanced over his shoulder to make sure they were alone. "Have you spoken to Russo yet?"

"Yes," Cliff said. "He and one of his men are here now. They're waiting to hear from us."

"Good. How did your meetings in Chicago and Vegas go?"

"Fine. As I said in Vegas, Russo is prepared to go forward based on what you've said. He's pleased with my involvement." Cliff peered into an aquarium. A trophy-sized grouper stared back, suspended in his green world, working his gaping mouth. "That makes him more comfortable."

"Yes, I agree," Witherspoon said.

"He's prepared to talk." Cliff tapped the heavy glass. "See this big guy here? They rule the reefs in these waters. Good eating, too."

Witherspoon barely glanced at the fish. "You say Russo's ready to talk?"

"Right."

"Good. I am, too."

They left the tunnel and continued their hike around Disney-land lagoons and vast swimming pools to a patio overlooking a brilliant stretch of beach. Sun-worshippers of every description crowded the sand, despite the early hour, their nearly naked bodies glistening with oil. Cliff had always enjoyed the heavy, floral aroma of tourists basting in the sun. Much better than the smell of napalm in the morning, he figured. Just offshore, jet-skis added their whining screams to the canned rock music that thudded in the background.

"Something to eat?" Witherspoon asked, looking jittery. "I haven't had breakfast."

"I think they only have hot dogs out here."

"Shit. I guess I'll pass. Let's find a table in the shade and talk."

Victoria tossed aside the last of the catalogs that the broker had left for them and stretched luxuriously on the padded deck chair. Residual jet-lag and the warm morning sun had conspired to make her sleepy. She would finish making her list of all the custom-designed and personalized china, crystal, silver, linens, towels and such that they needed and telephone the suppliers later.

She had already made friends with the staff and set them all to work. Her mood had improved, but she wished that her inner landscape was as flawless as her physical surroundings. A haunting sense of misfortune nibbling at the edge of their lives kept giving her the shivers. But she didn't want Cliff to know the depths of her fears. She had distracted him from her worries, she hoped, by throwing herself into the tasks at hand. He was troubled, too, she could tell, and she wished she could have given him a hug before he left that morning.

Earlier she had completed a comprehensive list of special foods, wines, spirits, and other consumables that she could not find on the yacht. Soon she would ask the steward to send a couple of hands ashore on the second launch to make the purchases.

For now, though, this delicious Bahamian sun just felt too good. Who could ask for a more picture-perfect day or a more glorious yacht? In a way, she thought—a big way—this was heaven. Wasn't it?

Cliff glanced at his Master Banker watch. Eleven thirty-five. He told Witherspoon that he had to get moving so he could meet Russo at noon.

"Call me after your meeting," Witherspoon said. "I need to see them soon. And you need to be there, introduce me, you know."

Cliff offered him a little mock salute and hurried away. He had to dodge a bikini-clad waitress balancing a tray of hot dogs and drinks. She scowled at him.

Outside the hotel, Cliff hailed a cab and soon felt calmed by the winding drive away from the sprawling grandeur of the Atlantis through the shaded depths of well-tended greenery. When they arrived at the gate of the Ocean Club fifteen minutes later, Cliff gave his name, and the uniformed Bahamian gatekeeper waved them on. The cab crawled through the quiet, manicured grounds and dropped him at the entrance to the lobby. Sydney Russo stood waiting in the doorway.

They shook hands, and Russo gave him his customary hug and a kiss on each cheek.

"You're early, Clifford," he said. "Come. Let's go to my bungalow. I want you to meet someone."

They ambled along a curving sidewalk between low-rise bungalows and lush tropical foliage, then turned at the discreet entrance to Russo's suite. He opened the door and let Cliff in.

A burly guy with a generous paunch turned when they entered the living room. Cliff didn't know this character, but he smiled and looked friendly enough. He shook Cliff's hand respectfully, without applying the macho vise grip. He definitely looked like a made guy, Cliff thought, with his big, tinted glasses, flashy jewelry, and gaudy silk sport shirt.

Russo touched Cliff's shoulder. "This is Joey Corsiglia. Joey, meet Clifford Blackwell. Like I told you, Joey, Cliff here's part of the family."

Cliff shuddered when he heard what were intended to be warm words. *Part of the family?* He wasn't sure he liked that.

"Cliff's the man who got us back in Vegas, Joey." Russo beamed at Cliff. "And as you know, he's our man in Havana."

"You picked a classy joint for us to meet, Mr. Blackwell," Joey said, swinging a meaty hand through the air.

Cliff followed his gesture and glanced out the tall windows at the sweeping lawns, the leafy gardens, and the bright turquoise rectangle of a swimming pool.

Cliff grinned and thanked him.

"Let's get down to business, gentlemen," Russo said. They all found a seat. "How'd your meeting go, Cliff?"

"Quickly. He just wanted to know if you were here and ready to meet."

"Absolutely," Russo said. "Joey and me been over everything. He laid out our resources for the job."

"Good," Cliff said. "Let's pick a place and time, and I'll set it up."

Russo crossed his spindly legs and said, "Tell 'em we'll meet right here. Tonight, seven o'clock."

Cliff plucked a phone from the table next to him, called Witherspoon at the Atlantis, and confirmed the meeting.

When Cliff hung up, Russo stood and offered a box of Cohiba cigars. They all lit up and relaxed for a while, making small talk and comments about the meeting with the CIA man. Russo and Joey Corsiglia did most of the talking.

After twenty minutes, Cliff called his yacht and requested a pickup at the docks. He abandoned his cigar and excused himself. He needed to get back to the comfort zone of the *Havana Royale* and Victoria and take some time to prepare himself for the next meeting. What had seemed like a game to Cliff was beginning to feel all too real.

Cliff stepped out of another cab under the canopy at the entrance of the Ocean Club at 6:50 that evening. A second cab pulled up just behind his. Witherspoon climbed out, still wearing that damn fedora and carrying a fat aluminum briefcase. Cliff greeted him and said, "Follow me."

Formally dressed couples and groups of guests on their way out for the evening eyed them as they passed on the concrete path. A television blared inside Russo's bungalow. Cliff knocked several times before Russo himself swung the door open and smiled at them.

"Cliff. Early again. Come in, come in."

Witherspoon glanced around the room, looking skittish. Joey appeared from another room and killed the television. Cliff made the introductions.

Ocean air from the evening trade winds stirred the open drapes. Witherspoon nodded at the windows and said, "You know, maybe we should close the drapes, Cliff."

"I'll get them," Joey said.

Russo invited everyone to sit down and took their drink orders. Witherspoon requested iced tea. An uncomfortable pause followed as Russo prepared the drinks himself at the wet bar. Witherspoon finally pulled off his hat and busied himself setting up an ominous-looking device on an empty chair. It looked like erector set meets Radio Shack.

"Wait a minute. What's that?" Cliff asked.

Russo squinted at the high-tech gizmo.

Witherspoon said, "Don't worry. It's for our own protection. It's a scanning spectral correlator. For high-level countermeasure sweeps."

"Ah," Cliff said.

Witherspoon said, "Makes sure this place is safe to talk."

"That better be all it is," Russo said.

"No need for paranoia now, I'm sure," Cliff said. "We all know why we're here."

"Mr. Blackwell's right," Witherspoon said. "I'd be stupid to pull anything on you now. You guys know too much already."

Russo nodded slowly and shrugged.

Witherspoon checked his gadget and seemed satisfied with the results. "Okay, if I may begin, am I correct in saying, Mr. Russo, that your organization is prepared to work with us? To eliminate Castro?"

Russo regarded him silently for a moment. "Yes, we are." He filled a martini glass. "We have some reservations, but Clifford here seems well informed. He's very convincing."

"Good," Witherspoon said, sounding in command. "Glad to hear it. This is dangerous business, and the ramifications are astronomical."

"No shit," said Joey.

Russo delivered two drinks, then returned to the bar. When they all had a drink and Russo sat down again, Witherspoon shifted forward in his chair and cleared his throat. "Okay, the mission's called 'Operation Smoke-Out.' Eyes only—top secret, of course.

Until Castro is dead, we're running this strictly on a need-to-know basis. If we have a leak, Cuba and China could be tipped off. That'd blow the whole damn thing."

"Understood," said Russo. He took a sip of his cocktail. "I brought Joey here 'cause he's tapped the right people for this job. They'll take out Castro, no problem—and anyone else you wanna whack."

The Mob boss's casual confidence gave Cliff a cold chill.

Witherspoon nodded and said, "You sure about that?"

Russo gave him a cold smile. "Absolutely. We learned a coupla things from past mistakes."

The implication made Witherspoon squint, but he recovered quickly. "Okay, great. We have detailed plans on how we want to do this. And your part in it. Right now I'm just looking for a meeting of the minds with you."

"We understand the magnitude of this deal, Mr. Witherspoon," Russo said. The agent studied the old man, holding his breath. "As you prob'ly know, I helped the CIA indirectly in the late fifties and sixties through some of my associates, like Johnny Roselli and Sam Giancana. Before the Bay of Pigs. Maybe before you were even born." He eyed Witherspoon wryly. "I was the planner for Chicago."

"I've heard stories," Witherspoon said. "Great. At least you know what we're up against."

"Oh, yes, we do," Russo said. "And we know how you people operate."

This time Witherspoon winced visibly. "Mr. Blackwell here has explained your interest in securing gaming rights in Cuba. We promise to do our best to influence the temporary president. We know him well. We'll explain the idea of granting an exclusive gaming license in return for a significant investment."

"This'll feel good after the screwing we got last time," Russo said.

Cliff jumped in and said, "They're prepared to invest a minimum of three billion dollars in the first five years. And two billion more over the following five years. That's a minimum of five billion dollars in the next ten years. Do I have to draw a picture?"

They all looked at him in silence.

"I'm sure you can imagine the enormous gaming revenue and what it would do for tourism and the whole economy. Peace and prosperity in Cuba forever and ever, blah, blah, blah."

"Yes, Mr. Blackwell," Witherspoon said. "We understand the benefits. Working with your, ah, organization has obvious advantages."

"You keep that in mind, we'll all get along fine," Russo said.

Cliff turned to Witherspoon. "Convey this to the next president. I want a personal meeting with him. All we want is an exclusive for ten years. We made Vegas, and we can make Cuba. It'll even help during the pre-election period. You know, better quality of life post-Castro. The public will see this as bigger and better things for their country. You don't want them electing the wrong man."

"The prospects are good, Mr. Blackwell," said Witherspoon. "That's all I can say now. Of course we can't guarantee anything, but we'll make a strong argument on your behalf, and on behalf of a future democratic Cuba." He caught Cliff's gaze and held it. "As for you, Mr. Blackwell, we're confident that you can drive the point home. The temporary president should be very receptive. He's an intelligent man. Professor of economics at the University of Havana. Well liked by the students and community. Open to change in government."

"Good, good," Russo said, bobbing his head.

Cliff agreed.

"I'll tell you more about him as we go," Witherspoon said, looking at Cliff again. "You'll like him, Mr. Blackwell."

"I have just one question, pal," Joey said. Everyone looked at him. "How do you see us icing Castro?"

Witherspoon eyed Joey, then coughed. "Well, we, ah . . . We have a special device, Mr. Corsiglia." He rubbed his chin in thought, his eyes twinkling in the subdued light. "We're planning to, ah, smoke him out." He chuckled.

Cliff didn't get the joke, and neither did the others. They just stared at the agent, deadpan.

Witherspoon sobered. "We'll get into those details at our next meeting. Lots to discuss."

Joey nodded slowly. "Sounds interesting. When do we make the hit?"

"In less than five weeks," Witherspoon said. "Meanwhile, we have a lotta work to do." He jumped to his feet, as if to regain some sense of authority. "I'd like to meet first thing in the morning. Spend the day going over everything."

"No problem," Russo said.

The agent repacked his equipment, and Russo escorted him to the door. "Call Cliff in the morning, and he'll call me."

They shook hands all around, and Witherspoon scurried away. Cliff stayed behind just long enough to make sure that his Chicago friends were comfortable with everything so far. They seemed to be pleased. He said good night, then marched into the sultry darkness, his head filled with thoughts as far strewn as the stars above him.

6

Thumbs Up

CLIFF WAS RUNNING EARLY FOR THE MEETING AGAIN the next morning when he arrived at the docks of Paradise Island, so he decided to walk the two miles to the Ocean Club and Sydney Russo's bungalow. The heady perfume of exotic blossoms lay heavy on the morning air as he strolled through an area of curving, two-lane streets and small retail shops, past lush tropical growth swaying in the sea-scented breeze, and the lost-city spires of the Atlantis Hotel on his left, heading toward the main thoroughfare that led to the Ocean Club. The late November sun made a pleasantly warm weight on his shoulders. He was glad to be back in Nassau, no matter what. Life seemed to be full of promise this morning. Even with its umbilical bridge to teeming Nassau, Paradise Island felt like a world apart.

Cliff knew that Hog Island, as it was originally called, had known colorful days even before Huntington Hartford, heir to the great Atlantic & Pacific grocery chain, acquired four-fifths of the 625-acre cay in the early sixties and renamed it Paradise Island.

Cliff liked the local history. He recalled the times after Hartford's impulsive purchase when the island became a lurid stage for shady deals and deceit, attracting a cast of questionable characters who were all lured by its fertile promise and the lenient business climate of the Bahamas. A hungry host of financial swingers and jet-setting swindlers beat a path to the international financial haven, where they were received with open arms by the island's bankers and lawyers, who became known as the Bay Street Boys. The incestuous relationships created something of an offshore fraternity that greased the wheels of "creative" business arrangements. Familiar names like those of billionaire Howard Hughes and the notorious Robert Vesco, along with friends of Richard Nixon, all made headlines, while many more remained anonymous behind a scrim of secrecy and subterfuge.

Whatever the history was, Cliff had to admit how much he liked this place. Too bad he couldn't have run with the big dogs in the old days here. That would've been fun. He enjoyed the forty-minute walk and the chance to absorb the feel of the island and to be alone for a while with his thoughts. By the time he entered the grounds of the Ocean Club he felt invigorated. When he arrived at Russo's quarters, he heard several voices inside. He rapped on the door.

Russo appeared moments later and gave him a big smile. "Clifford, you're early again. Good! Everybody's here."

Cliff greeted the old don formally, as usual, and followed him into the shuttered living room. Witherspoon reclined in the same chair, wearing the same gray suit and still keeping company with that absurd fedora. Red lights glowed on the counterspy scanner. Joey Corsiglia made the rounds, refilling coffee cups. He didn't look comfortable playing the role of server, but he was smiling and making an effort. They looked up when he arrived.

Cliff offered his good mornings and took a seat next to Witherspoon, who resumed his conversation with Russo. Corsiglia delivered a cup of coffee to Cliff and pointed out the silver tray of French pastries on the coffee table nearby. Cliff thanked him, then eyed the CIA man. He seemed to be more comfortable with the Chicago men now.

Witherspoon tossed a hand and said, "Isn't this where Resorts International used to be?"

"No, that's where you're staying now, Don—the Atlantis," Russo said.

"And it looks great since the renovations and expansion," Cliff added.

Russo agreed.

Cliff said, "You remember any of the stories about Resorts, Don? Like the one about Nixon's Committee to Re-elect the President? Newspapers said they were receiving questionable funds from down here."

"Yeah," Witherspoon said, "the agency looked into that back then. Ancient history." He crossed his legs and cleared his throat. "The important thing now is the future." He cast hopeful glances at them.

"Exactly," said Cliff. "No point trying to sort out the mysteries of Richard Nixon and his money-laundering schemes now." Cliff decided it was time to cut the small talk. He leaned toward Witherspoon and said, "So what are we using to kill Castro?"

Russo shifted forward on the couch, his old eyes twinkling. "Been waiting for this one," he said. "Pay attention, Joey. This's your department."

Witherspoon crossed his arms and sighed. "Okay, I guess it's time to lay it out."

Cliff used a sip of coffee to swallow the lump in his throat.

Witherspoon opened his briefcase and produced a gleaming rosewood box.

Cliff leaned over to read the hand-carved lettering on the lid and quoted, " 'To our beloved friend, Fidel Castro.' "

Witherspoon lifted the lid slowly. Inside, a single fine cigar rested on plush red velvet. Russo and Corsiglia got up and gazed into the box.

Witherspoon said, "It's a Double Corona from the Hoyo de

Monterrey factory."

Cliff read the inscription on the little brass plate under the cigar. It included the factory code, which was usually found on the bottom of cigar boxes. "It's a ninety-two," he said. "One of the highest-rated cigars ever."

"Oh, yeah?" Russo said.

"That's right, Mr. Russo," Witherspoon said. "It's one of Castro's favorites."

"Hey," Corsiglia said. "Dint you guys try and kill Castro one time with a phony cigar? You know, an exploding one?"

"That's true," Witherspoon said. "But he won't be expecting this one. It'll replace the one they'll probably inspect."

"Ah, the old last-minute switcheroo," Russo said with a wry smile.

"Plus," Witherspoon said, "this'll be presented to him by the president of Cubanos Exports at the International Cigar Summit. That's in Havana in January. Cubanos is the government's world-wide distributor of Cuban cigars."

"That's a ballsy plan," Cliff said.

"Maybe so, but he isn't likely to suspect them," Witherspoon said. "Anyway, people give Castro cigars all the time."

"That's true," Cliff said.

"We also know he usually shrugs off security measures when it comes to his food and cigars," Witherspoon said. "Your concerns are valid, but listen to this. We'll have inside help to make the switch. We have a mole who's high up in the Cubanos organization. Castro won't suspect a thing."

Cliff said, "Maybe he'll decide not to smoke it right away."

"Maybe," Witherspoon said.

"We can do him anyway," Corsiglia said.

Witherspoon ignored that. "This is the actual cigar he'll receive."

Corsiglia said, "So what does this here Double Corona do, anyways?"

Witherspoon's smile carried a hint of pride. "Actually it's a single-shot, thirty-two-caliber gun. Activated and fired by heat. Custom-made to our exact specifications by a Bulgarian craftsman." He touched the cigar lightly with his index finger. "This'll get past even the most sensitive detectors and X-ray equipment, and it looks just like a regular cigar. We've used similar units in the past. And we've perfected our methods over the years."

"Glad to hear that," Russo said, his watery eyes dancing with light.

Witherspoon chuckled politely and said, "When Castro snips off the tip, the safety is released. And when he lights it—*bang*!" He sobered. "Probably blow his teeth through the back of his head."

"What if it doesn't?" asked Cliff.

"If he lights it, Cliff, it'll do serious damage. Anyway, that's where Joey comes in."

Cliff noted his use of a first name.

Corsiglia strained his bulk forward, all ears.

"We'll have backup people," Witherspoon explained. "Agents at the meeting and outside. They can help you. But you need to get somebody inside, close to the target, with firepower."

"I got the right guy," Corsiglia said. "You wan' him to kiss Castro, he can do it." The big man had everyone's attention now. "Johnny Two Fingers. The second that stogie blows, he'll be there to cap him good, point blank."

"Then what?" Witherspoon asked.

"He'll beat it," Corsiglia said. "He knows how to disappear in a crowd." He rubbed his dark jaw thoughtfully. "Maybe get away on a motorcycle to a waiting speedboat."

"What if he gets caught?" Cliff asked.

"Trust me," Corsiglia said. "He won't. And we can put little Sam Del Greco in for insurance."

"Who?" Cliff asked.

"Sammy the Greek, that's what they call him. A former four-time featherweight Golden Gloves champ. He'll dance around alla them like Sugar Ray."

"I hope you're sure about that, Joey," Witherspoon said, looking serious. "They screw up, we're all fucked."

"Now I know the plan, I'll refine it," Corsiglia said. "Just need to get the boys together and coordinate things."

"Of course," Witherspoon said. "Before we head off to Havana, we'll have some meetings in Miami." He gestured at the Chicago men. "But just with you two. We'll have to rehearse this over and over before we go in."

Russo said, "I can meet in Miami, but I won't be goin' to Cuba with you. I'll go back to Chicago. I hand-selected Joey here for this caper. He knows his business, and he has the resources. His guys are all professionals."

"I understand, Mr. Russo," Witherspoon said. "We don't expect you to go. But you need to be in the loop. We want you to endorse your side's participation."

"No problem," Russo said. "You have my okay the same as I was whacking him myself. Don't worry about Joey. He makes good executive decisions. You'll see."

Witherspoon nodded. "We'll review the logistics and refine our plans in Havana. Some of them'll depend on last-minute developments." He closed the rosewood box and returned it to his briefcase. "In Miami I'll explain how we'll communicate and execute our plans once we're in Cuba so we don't get busted." He pulled a roll of paper from a long cardboard tube. "We have a safe house. Double agents, too." He unrolled the sheet of heavy paper on the coffee table.

"What's that?" Russo asked.

"Design plans of our special little 'smoking cigar' unit. All seven and five-eighths inches of it."

They huddled over the drawings.

"It's precision-made," Witherspoon explained. "Our new wizard at the gizmo shop, Dr. Karl Druchenmiller, hired one of his contacts in eastern Europe. The guy makes all kinds of unconventional stuff."

Witherspoon had already told Cliff in confidence about Stanley Rosenstock, the Bulgarian inventor. He was a hunched little man with a droopy mustache who looked more like an old cobbler than the midwife of high-tech weaponry. His wares were discreetly manufactured by hand and hidden from the world in the back room of a small aperitif bar, of all places, located down a narrow, hidden lane in the town of Pazardzhik.

"The guy's a genius," Witherspoon said. "Like a mad scientist. He's developed a lot of innovative things for us. Like a tiny pistol that fires tear gas and thirty-two-caliber ammo, too."

"Very useful," Corsiglia said.

"Another one of his firearms looks like a key fob, but it's actually a double-barreled pistol. You can get both these weapons through airport security. But Interpol's turned up copies of the guns here and there around the world—easy to get on the black market for under twenty bucks." He shook his head.

Cliff glanced at Corsiglia, who seemed to be making mental notes.

"He also invented other stuff," Witherspoon continued, "like the poison-tipped umbrella that killed Octavio, the U.S. diplomat in Chile, and the grenade that looks like a popular cigarette lighter."

"Quite an armory," Corsiglia said. "Whadid you say his name is?"

Witherspoon disregarded the question and bent over the diagrams again. "When Castro waves this baby under his nose, he'll know it's *not* a counterfeit."

Corsiglia chuckled. "You can bet ol' Fidel knows his smokes, too. A lotta phonies floating around these days."

Russo said, "You mentioned a safe house in Havana?"

"That's right. Run by a guy named Toti, a former Cuban MIG pilot. It's fronted by a nice older Cuban couple." He rolled up the drawings. "A few years back, before Toti went to work for us, he was flying missions for an anti-Castro pilot's group known as the

Brothers to the Rescue. He's a real fly-by-the-seat-of-your-pants jet jockey."

"How'd he come to join the CIA?" Russo asked.

"They were rescuing rafters leaving Cuba who were in trouble. A couple of his buddies were shot down in their low-flying Cessna by a patrolling Cuban MIG—both killed. That's when we recruited him. We'd known about him for years. Heard he'd infiltrated Cuban intelligence. He'd also done some freelance work in Miami for anti-Castro exile groups and the FBI."

"Sounds like a good man to have on your team," Cliff said.

Witherspoon nodded. "Toti's a real asset. Castro's got an excellent counterintelligence organization that's managed to infiltrate us *and* the FBI." He made a sour face. "Being down there is dangerous, even suicidal, if you don't have good intel. A lot happens there that the press doesn't get wind of. But we'll be secure at the safe house." He stood and crossed the room and peeked between the drapes.

Russo spoke to Witherspoon's back. "You'll be getting all our expertise on this operation. You can be sure of that."

"I'm counting on that. And I like your ideas, Joey," Witherspoon said, still peering outside. "They sound workable."

Russo nodded. "Good. I think we can work together just fine."

"So when should I go down there?" Cliff asked.

Witherspoon faced them again and said, "No need to be there until Castro's dead."

Cliff felt relieved in spite of himself.

"Too dangerous for you otherwise, especially if you bring that yacht I saw anchored in the harbor." Witherspoon's fingers drummed absently against his thigh. "That's yours, isn't it, the big one? Not exactly low-profile."

"Too bad," Cliff said. "I'm ready to go."

Russo chuckled. "Cliff, remember, we gotta save you for the big play—meeting the new president. Negotiating on our behalf. Can't afford for you to risk your ass down there while the old revolutionary is still kicking."

"I understand that. But my daredevil lady'll be disappointed."

The two Italians smiled. Witherspoon didn't.

Cliff said, "Oh, well, she'll just have to wait. I'll keep her busy in Nassau playing with her new chopper."

Witherspoon frowned at Cliff. "New chopper?"

"That's right."

"I didn't see a helicopter."

"I leased a new Bell 407 for her when we were in the Med. She learned to fly it there. It's on the old yacht. We'll pick it up when we get back to Miami."

"Oh-kay," Witherspoon said.

Cliff stiffened. His own conspicuous consumption made him feel embarrassed sometimes. He pushed the feeling aside and said, "By the way, I was wondering . . ."

"Shoot, Cliff," Witherspoon said.

"What happens right after our friend Fidel is killed?"

Witherspoon crossed his legs and waggled a loafered foot. It was probably Italian—and expensive. "Well . . . we also need to take out his younger brother. Raul. He's his deputy in the Communist Party and head of the armed forces." The agent massaged his temples. "He's Fidel's successor, so he'll take charge if anything happens to his brother."

"Looks like a job for my man Joey," Russo said.

Corsiglia grunted. "Johnny and Sammy can handle him, too."

"Good," Witherspoon said. "He may be more of a psycho than his brother."

"Yes," Cliff said, "but what about when the military finds out that both men are dead?"

"That's where we come in," Witherspoon said. "The military'll probably try to take over. Meanwhile, chaos." He shook his head. "Our agents will have only limited means to secure the area."

Corsiglia sat forward again. "How many agents you got down there?"

"Can't say exactly, but dozens'll be in the immediate vicinity. All undercover."

"Dozens undercover?" asked Cliff. "If Cuban intelligence is so good . . ."

"Yeah, it's as risky as it gets, Cliff," Witherspoon admitted, as if he knew exactly what Cliff was thinking.

Russo slapped his thigh. "Listen, Don, you need a final plan of action that we can all follow. With backup provisions, if necessary."

Cliff nodded. "Absolutely."

Witherspoon plodded to the wet bar. "We're working on that." He opened a cabinet, chose a glass, and turned back to them. "Anyone else?" he asked, and they all declined. He filled the glass with tap water as he said, "I can't give you all the details now, but I know we can pull this off if you just do your part." He returned to the group with his drink. "Special ops groups will be in position near the cigar summit, and military personnel will control the Cuban troops and secure the country from threats." He drank all the water and set the glass aside.

"Is President Caldwell aware of this?" Cliff asked, knowing he was pushing the envelope.

Witherspoon said, "No, not yet, Cliff."

"Gentlemen," Russo said, "I think we all know what we're up against. Don, we trust that you and your people know what you're doing. It's your show. We'll follow your lead."

Witherspoon looked relieved. "Thanks, Mr. Russo. This is the most delicate assignment we've ever worked. It'll make the history books."

"That's an understatement," Russo said with a rueful smile. Then he clapped his thin hands and said, "Well, how about some lunch now?"

"I could eat," Joey Corsiglia said. "I could use a smoke, too."

"Let's go, then," Cliff said, getting to his feet. "The Ocean Club beats the hot dogs at the beach."

* * *

They returned to the bungalow an hour later to review a map of Cuba and some intelligence reports that Witherspoon wanted to read. Cliff sensed that they had established a bond of camaraderie and mutual respect, perhaps because their common goal was something they had all secretly desired. Fear and suspicion always loomed large in their separate orbits, so any experience to the contrary was probably oddly fulfilling for each of them, he thought.

When the meeting began to wind down naturally, Witherspoon opened the drapes and the windows. Brassy late-afternoon light and fresh tropical air filled the room. Cliff felt a welcome shift in the atmosphere.

He stood up, stretched, and announced, "I'm returning to Miami on Friday, right after Thanksgiving. Need to pick up my regular crew. They should be there soon on the trade-in yacht."

Corsiglia laughed. "Must be tough, kissing the little boat goodbye." His sarcasm was almost benign.

Cliff tipped him a grin. "Hey, I'm sentimental about that boat. Anyway, after that I'll come back here until we get the word to head for Havana."

Russo touched Witherspoon's arm briefly and said, "When are you going there?"

"I'm out of here tonight and back to Langley. Then I've got visitation with my kids over the holiday. We'll all meet next week in Miami. I'll slip into Cuba after that."

"Well, looks like history will give you guys a second chance," Cliff said. "If at first you don't succeed . . ."

Everyone smiled and nodded, then shook hands and wished one another a happy holiday. Cliff went through the motions, but he didn't sense much real mirth in their good humor. As he marched away he wondered if Fidel Castro celebrated Thanksgiving.

7

Christmas in Havana

DONALD WITHERSPOON SAT IN THE OFFICE OF HIS BOSS, Cecil Danforth, in Langley, Virginia, two days before Christmas. Since the meeting in Nassau, he'd had his kids over for Thanksgiving, then had deployed to Cuba to meet with Joey Corsiglia and the others to work out more details for Operation Smoke-Out. Now, with just a little over a week left before the event, he'd slipped out of Cuba to update Danforth in person. He didn't tell anyone, but he was flying high on his own private roller-coaster, and he was having the time of his life.

"Sounds like we're on track, barring any last-minute surprises," Danforth said, looking pleased and optimistic.

That made Witherspoon feel even better. "I think so," he replied. "I'm happy with Corsiglia and his crew. They arrived less than a week ago. They take his direction well and seem acclimated to their assignment."

"Good, good . . . But listen to this." Danforth had his game face on now.

Witherspoon braced himself for a curve ball.

"Last we talked, Don, we hadn't made any progress on the

Chinese problem and those suspected arms shipments to Cuba."

"I know."

"Remember that box of documents and disks our guys snatched in Hong Kong?"

Witherspoon nodded.

"It also contained a schedule for the shipments. But we couldn't tell if they'd still happen after the death of those five big shots. We thought the Chinese might back off after they learned their plan had been compromised."

Uh-oh, here it comes, Witherspoon thought.

"We knew the shipments were scheduled every two weeks and that Chow Hwa's organization, the Happy Fortune Shipping Company, was handling them. But we didn't know which ships they'd use. Figured they'd be registered in various tax havens, though." He opened the top desk drawer and produced a set of eight-by-ten, black-and-white photographs. "Here's some interesting evidence."

Witherspoon leaned across the massive desk for a closer look. "Spy satellite photos. Yeah?"

Danforth pointed to a freighter entering a port. "See that ship?" Then he slid another print under Witherspoon's nose. "See that?" It was a close-up shot of the transom of the same vessel, dated November seventh.

Witherspoon read the words *Four Seasons, Liberia.*

Danforth separated five more photos from the collection one at a time. He stabbed a polished fingernail at each one and recited the name, registry, and date when it had made port. The dates were about two weeks apart in November and December.

The old CIA spook leaned back in his black leather chair. "Of course the arms were probably only a small part of the manifest, hidden among the rest of the cargo. But even so, those ships could deliver quite an arsenal."

Witherspoon nodded and said, "But how do we know if these ships are connected to Happy Fortune? The registration disguises the ownership."

Danforth shrugged. "We don't know. At least not about all of them. But the registrations in tax havens made me suspicious." He swept the photos together and squinted at the top one. "We've been working on this for weeks. Tracked down the offshore companies that own these freighters. Got the names of the directors and had agents call on all of them. The corporations are all fronts." He shuffled the photos into a neat stack. "All run by lawyers. All bound to their country's secrecy laws. Nominees posing as corporate directors for the real owners."

"And?"

"We tried bribing them. All but two told us to fuck off." Danforth removed his glasses and rubbed his eyes. "That cost us a hundred grand, but we got the info on two of the companies and their principals. Both shareholders are the Happy Fortune Shipping Company." He sighed. "Same with the others, probably, considering their arrival times." He replaced his glasses and allowed himself a tired little smile.

"Damn!" Witherspoon said. "They must be close to having a launch facility. If this stuff's coming in, they'd be all over getting the site built."

Danforth chose another photo and tossed it across the desk. "This one was taken yesterday."

"Looks like just trees and bushes."

"Look harder." Danforth pointed to a dark green area between two ridges. "See right there?"

Witherspoon shook his head.

"Get your eyes checked." Danforth pulled out yet another photo and pointed. "Right there."

"Oh, yeah. Camouflage nets. Jesus!"

"Now check this one," Danforth said. "From our files, taken six months ago."

The same two ridges showed plainly—but with bare land between them. "Jesus, Cecil. So the shipments arrived."

"Apparently so."

"Then we're too late."

"Maybe not. But keep up all that praying to Jesus that we don't fuck up."

"Who knows about this?"

"Only the director. Had meetings with him all day yesterday, after we got this photo. And this morning."

Ah, yes, Witherspoon thought. *Our fearless leader, General Alexander Dietrich. Old Iron-Ass.* He said, "I'm sure he's not thrilled about this."

"Nope. He'll be meeting with the president later today."

"So before I leave I'll know if it's still a go."

"Correct." Danforth leaned forward and lowered his voice. "Personally, I don't know how he could say no, even if he is tactically challenged."

Witherspoon knew how his boss felt about President Caldwell, but this was the first time he had voiced a criticism. He decided not to go there. "Did you tell Dietrich about our involvement with Chicago?"

"Only that we uncovered a plot to kill Castro. That we were gathering information and would report to him shortly."

"Did he ask who?"

"Told him we think it's the Mafia."

Witherspoon's mouth had gone dry. "Did you mention us?"

"Naturally."

"You didn't."

"Shit, no!" Danforth said, smiling like the Cheshire cat.

"Christ!" Witherspoon didn't care if he was talking to his boss. "You lied to him?"

"You expected me to tell him the truth?"

"I guess not."

"You guess correctly." Danforth sat back and clasped his hands behind his head. "He doesn't know about the anti-mass destruction unit. He knows that our duties are part of the CIA's responsibility, but he has no idea that we have a special task force.

You know that, Don."

Witherspoon nodded.

"And don't forget. Our unit is buried under layers of bureaucracy in this agency. Invisible. Answers to no one."

"In theory."

"And in theory, telling Dietrich would be prudent. But that could complicate things. Our number-one job now is to make Smoke-Out happen. We could kill Castro ourselves, but we can't provide the backup necessary to stabilize Cuba afterward. We could create a monster."

Witherspoon agreed.

"This way, Dietrich'll tell President Caldwell, and the president will have no choice but to support the CIA and send in our troops, I hope—if he doesn't try to stop the assassination."

"Some big ifs there."

Danforth stood and strolled to a window in silence. He squinted at the bleak winter sky, his hands clasped behind his back. Finally he said, "Look at it this way. We're probably the only ones who could stop the assassination. This is our show, so that's not likely. Which leaves the question of the follow-up." He turned back to Witherspoon. "Do you think he'll wait till it's too late to involve the U.S.? On January first the Cuban military'll know that Castro's been murdered. Who knows if those damn missiles are operational yet? If they are, they could hit us before we can act."

"Maybe this thing's gotten out of hand."

Danforth returned to his desk and perched on a corner. "Maybe, but if we hadn't gotten that box of stuff from Hong Kong, we'd find out the hard way what the Chinese had done. Probably too late. At least now we have a chance to stop them."

"I guess you're right. I hope the president doesn't smell a rat."

"We'll know soon, Don. Maybe tomorrow."

"Only nine days left. Is that enough time?"

"Barely."

Witherspoon slumped in his chair and exhaled as if he were

blowing out smoke. He wondered how much luck they'd need to pull all this off. Too bad MacGregor wasn't here to help. He could use him. He asked Danforth how his partner was doing.

"John's fine," his boss said. "With a little luck he'll stop those terrorists with the dirty bomb."

The luck factor again. He didn't like depending on that. The roller-coaster ride was fun and exciting, but he preferred knowing exactly where it was going and how it would end.

General Alexander Dietrich admired the postcard panorama of the White House scene from the back seat of his limo. He had always loved this Christmas thing. What could be more purely American? Festive lights and ornaments beamed and winked everywhere on the snowy grounds, and a tall, gaily lit evergreen glittered through the thick, bulletproof glass of a front window. He felt a little twinge about interrupting the president's evening, but what the hell. History didn't take holidays.

Three staff members greeted him cordially at the West Wing entrance, obviously informed of his visit, and one of them escorted him directly to the Oval Office. President Caldwell welcomed him just as warmly when he arrived there and offered him coffee.

He declined politely. Caffeine, he thought, was a mind-altering substance that should be avoided like an illegal drug, and so was nicotine. Filthy habits, both of them. Crutches for the mentally unfit.

They settled onto two striped, satin-covered couches opposite each other. He remembered to extend holiday greetings to the president and his family before he began.

"My apologies, Mr. President, but we must discuss an urgent matter."

The president put his elbows on his knees, clasped his hands, and nodded—his usual get-down-to-business position. "Shoot, General."

"A week ago we uncovered an assassination plot against Castro."

"Again?"

"Yes, sir. They plan to kill him on January first, during the International Cigar Summit in Havana."

The president grimaced. "Great timing. Van Buren will be taking office soon."

Dietrich agreed, trying to ignore another one of the president's BFOs. The man was noted for his blinding flashes of the obvious.

"Hell, Alex," the president said, "there've been lots of attempts on the old bastard's life over the years. Why are you worried about this one?"

"We think the Cuban military's behind it." *That little detail should kick his pansy ass*, he thought.

"A military coup? In Cuba?"

"We think that's a strong possibility."

The president ridged his brow in thought—or what passed for cognitive skills, in Dietrich's opinion. The general knew that Caldwell had had to sit for his bar exam three times, and he was familiar with his lackluster record as governor of Massachusetts. The president, he believed, couldn't even spell the word *coup*.

The Commander-in-Chief gave him the look of a constipated chimpanzee and said, "Are you suggesting we intercede?"

"I haven't suggested anything, Mr. President."

"Okay. Then what *would* you suggest?"

"We could step in, but I don't know if that'd be in our best interest. On the other hand . . ." He took a moment to choose his next words carefully and decided it was time for a little political science 101. "As you know, sir, over the past forty years we've made several attempts to eliminate Castro ourselves. Every one of them unsuccessful."

Now there's a BFO that should help this man, he thought.

"You see, sir," he continued, "with Castro out of the picture, we'd no longer live with the, uh, threat that always exists in our hemisphere."

He was trying not to sound patronizing as he approached a conclusion that should be perfectly clear, as old Dick Nixon used to say. "Actually, sir, this could be an, uh, *opportunity* for us, you see. Stabilize the situation, open up the country for democracy, goose the economy, improve the quality of life." *What bullshit*, he thought.

The president rewarded him with a simian smile. "I understand. Go on."

"In October two of our agents in Hong Kong made an important discovery."

The president looked uncomfortable.

Dietrich thought he was probably worried that another one of his past transgressions had surfaced and that it would ruin his holidays. "We've learned that the Chinese have been working with Castro on a plan to make Cuba a Chinese satellite—in exchange for substantial funding and arms."

"Jesus, Alex! What're you saying?"

For God's sake, did he have to paint him a picture? "Since we found concrete evidence of their plans, we've been checking it out."

"And?"

Dietrich dragged his battered briefcase onto his lap, removed a stack of photographs, and handed them to the president. "We've spent the last two months collecting evidence, including these U2 and sat photos."

The president sat blinking at the top picture.

Dietrich gave him a detailed description of each photograph, in order of importance, and summarized the other evidence purchased from the foreign attorneys.

"Unbelievable," the president murmured, chewing his lower lip. "Damn! I've already had enough bad press over the friggin' Chinese."

"I know, sir."

The president set the photographs aside and held his head in his hands. He massaged his temples with his thumbs for a while.

Dietrich figured he was getting one of his famous migraines, probably caused by trying to think too hard.

Finally Caldwell looked up and said, "Can they do it?"

"Yes, I think they can."

The president sighed and seemed to shrink inside his perfectly tailored blue suit. "What if . . ."

Dietrich said, "They're close to launch capability of short- and medium-range missiles. If they're not already there. Question is, would they use them?"

Caldwell shook his head. "This coincides with the 374 million-dollar so-called trade credit Cuba just received from China."

"Not a coincidence, I'd say."

The president looked exhausted now and about ten years older. Probably glad he could bail out of the White House soon, Dietrich thought. Even he must know that he wasn't up to playing Kennedy in another Cuban missile crisis.

"Guess we'd better make worst-case preparations," Caldwell said wearily. "Castro has been bad enough, but the idea of the Cuban military running the show, in bed with China, is even worse." He shook his head. "We're in deep shit. With or without Castro."

Caldwell would never be a candidate for the Mensa Society, Dietrich thought, but at least he saw the big picture now.

The president rubbed his temples again. "Oh, hell, let's just let 'em kill him. Then we can go in and stop the Cuban military from taking over."

"That's what I would suggest, sir."

"With this evidence we're justified, aren't we? National security and all that crap?"

"Absolutely."

Caldwell shook his head again and managed a snide smile. "We didn't expect a new arms race to begin tomorrow. Van Buren's gonna be up to his ass in alligators. Thank God it's happening to a Democrat."

"Shit happens, as they say, if you'll pardon me, Mr. President. Like nine-eleven."

The president nodded as wisely as he could manage and got to his feet. "So is there anything we can do to guarantee, you know, Castro's death? I mean, short of stepping on our own dicks?"

Dietrich withheld a smile. "We're already working on that. And we can have special-ops personnel in Cuba, ready to move as soon as he and his brother are taken out. They'd secure the immediate area until we can send in the troops."

"Castro's brother, too?"

"That's what we hear."

He let out another big sigh. "I guess I'll be busy over the holidays."

"Sorry, sir."

"Don't be. You're doing a fine job, and I needed to know this." The president crossed to his desk and punched his intercom button. "Get me Admiral Dallenbach right away," he said. "Tell him it's urgent."

Dietrich was pleased to see the chief running with the ball.

Caldwell returned to the couch and said, "We need to call an emergency meeting of the Joint Chiefs. The National Security Council, too. I want you to be there."

"Of course, Mr. President."

The general smiled, thinking that this was going to be a merry old Christmas, indeed.

"So is the chief going to play ball with us, or what?" Cecil Danforth said.

He was in General Dietrich's private office at CIA headquarters on a quiet Sunday morning—Christmas Eve. The facility was officially closed, but security personnel manned their posts, as usual, while maintenance crews cleaned up after Friday's office parties.

"You should've been there, Cecil," Dietrich told his right-hand man. "Handling President Einstein was a piece of cake."

Danforth smiled at the casual insult.

Dietrich told him that the president would commit the military and that the Joint Chiefs of Staff would meet that day. "They should call me any minute now. Don't worry. The troops will be in Cuba on New Year's."

"Outstanding! How'd he take the news?"

"Pretty surprised, as you can imagine. He should read all of his daily briefs. He'll bring Van Buren up to speed before he takes office on January twentieth."

Danforth chuckled. "Caldwell's last days in office will be memorable."

"That's an understatement. If all goes well, he'll come out smelling like a rose, the slick bastard." Dietrich grinned. "I'll be spending some time with Van Buren, too."

"Maybe you can ask him to give us a raise after this is over."

They both laughed.

"I'll keep you posted, Cecil. Meanwhile, you'd better ready your troops."

"Roger that, sir."

Ten minutes later, Danforth met with Donald Witherspoon in his own private office and told him the news.

"Thank God!" Witherspoon replied. "Man, I've about shit a brick worrying how this thing could bite us in the ass. After all the years we've had to deal with goddamn Castro, I kept thinking, What if we can't stop him again? Shit."

Witherspoon sat back and stretched his long legs, looking relieved but worn. "My kids came to mind. And the holidays. Christmas's a bad time to have these thoughts."

Danforth said quietly, "Sometimes you think too much, Don. Don't worry. I think we have the right people this time. Just stay on top of Corsiglia. You've done a good job so far. Keep it up. You know that Castro has got to be history. He's gone too far."

Witherspoon nodded thoughtfully. "Our guys'll like this news. But they're worried about military support. Without that . . ."

"They'll be there in force. Don't worry. But we have to move fast. Time is short." Danforth stood to end the meeting. He had a million things to do today.

Witherspoon dragged himself to his feet. "Yeah, merry Christmas. I have to catch a flight soon. I'm stopping in Nassau on the way to Havana. I'll see Blackwell, tell him in person that it's show-time."

"Forget the airlines. Take our Boeing business jet. You'll be gone as soon as you can pack a bag. I'll arrange it."

"Thanks, Cecil."

Danforth shook his favorite agent's hand and said, "Thank you. And good luck. You better be at my victory dinner when this is over."

Ivan Penkovsky manned his desk in his Budapest headquarters, talking to the world and taking no breaks. He grabbed the phone when it buzzed again. It was Yuri Grovka, calling from Moscow.

"Tell me something good, Yuri."

"Our plan worked. The order is ready."

The little man's voice sounded quite assured, for him.

"Good work, Yuri."

"Thank you, Boss. What now?"

"Wait for my call, comrade."

"I will do that. You can count on me."

"A good supply is still available? Same stuff?"

"Yes. Also, a new gold mine. Radiothermal generators."

Penkovsky rubbed his nose while he considered that idea. "That could be of interest." But now he had other things on his mind. "One other thing, Yuri. I have a new friend. He had some business in Dubai and the Congo. We had a few drinks at the

Grand Hotel bar."

"Anyone I know?"

"His name is Boyd. A big arms trader." He smiled as he re-called their evening together. "Maybe we will make more business with him."

With that Penkovsky ended the call, his thoughts already racing ahead to the next conversation.

Witherspoon left the unmarked jet late that evening at Nassau International Airport and commandeered the last cab available. When they rolled away from the terminal he lowered his window to enjoy the warm, tropical air. The Bahamian driver cruised through the darkness around the north end of New Providence Island, heading for Nassau. Witherspoon felt weary, and he was annoyed and tense, as usual, by traveling down the wrong side of the road. Why couldn't the whole world get its shit together and use the right side? But he was feeling amped by the latest news and couldn't wait to talk with Cliff Blackwell.

He punched the number for Cliff's yacht into his mobile phone.

When Cliff came on the line, Witherspoon told him where he was.

"Tell the driver to head to Hurricane Hole on Paradise Island," Cliff said. "I'll have a launch waiting for you there."

Working with a rich guy like Cliff sure had its advantages sometimes, he thought.

When a small boat growled around the end of a row of fancy yachts at Hurricane Hole, Witherspoon recognized Cliff at the helm, waving at him as it approached. He was alone.

"Ahoy, mate!" Cliff shouted.

Witherspoon met the launch. "Running your own errands

tonight, huh?"

"I wanted to talk with you before we get back to the yacht. You know."

Victoria, Witherspoon thought. "Good idea, Cliff."

He had to speak over the sound of the burbling engine to bring Cliff up to date. He left out the part about the Chinese and the missiles.

"I'm glad you got the go-ahead, Don. I guess."

Witherspoon felt genuinely glad to see Cliff again. He liked this guy and his quicksilver mind, his guts, and his easy optimism. "I'll keep you updated the best I can. But at this stage of the game you may hear things sooner by watching CNN."

Cliff laughed.

Smiling at his own wit, Witherspoon said, "You mind if I stay on board tonight?"

" 'Course not. You're more than welcome."

"I'm catching a commercial flight to Havana around eleven tomorrow morning."

"This ain't such a bad place to lay over," Cliff said, pointing.

Witherspoon took his first look at Cliff's new yacht. It was lit up like a national monument—and damn near as big as one, he thought. He was stunned by its grandeur. He read the gold-lettered name on the beamy transom and said, "*Havana Royale*?" The irony of pulling this yacht into Havana Harbor made him burst into laughter.

At first Cliff just gave him a blank look. Then he caught on and laughed, too.

Donald Witherspoon arrived at Jose Marti International Airport in Havana early on Christmas morning and caught another cab, this one a dusty black 1949 Chevy piloted by a scrawny old guy the color of Cuban *café*, minus the *leche*. Not much of a ride, but at least the Cubans knew which side of the road to use. He had the driver drop him half a mile from the safe house and hoofed it the rest of the way, heading southwest into the outskirts of Havana. Oddly enough, he felt glad to be back in a Communist country run by a cranky, anachronistic dictator, even if it was too damn hot.

He was more than ready for a cold beer by the time his goal was in sight, but he went through the drill anyway. He detoured down a hard-packed dirt path that ran along a field of sugarcane, forcing himself into a casual, ambling pace, then waded through knee-high grass to the foot of the hill where the house was perched. The old wooden, tin-roofed structure hunkered its two modest stories beneath the crimson glory of a venerable royal poinciana tree, nearly hidden by stands of banana plants, tumbling bougainvillea, and tropical shrubbery.

He squatted in a clump of broom sedge and eyeballed the house. Everything looked quiet. Too quiet, maybe? Then Mr. Nunez emerged from his canted tool shed, fiddling with something that looked like a small electric motor. He placed it on a table in the yard and returned to the shed.

Business as usual, Witherspoon decided. He trudged up the rough incline toward the front porch.

Everyone looked surprised when he walked in. He'd been away for days, and he hadn't announced his return. Joey Corsiglia seemed especially happy to see him, although he had a big question in his eyes. Witherspoon took him aside to talk.

While they spoke he glanced at Mrs. Nunez. He felt comforted somehow just by watching her puttering around in the kitchen, fixing a holiday dinner. He knew that Castro had outlawed Christmas in Cuba many years before, but she had told him slyly that she intended to make her guests feel at home anyway. What was one more secret in this house? she said with a wise twinkle in her eye.

When he and Corsiglia parted, he stuck his head into the kitchen and learned that Mrs. Nunez was preparing *Pierna de Puerco Asada,* a local favorite. The whole house was redolent with the rich aroma of the main dish. Witherspoon inhaled the heavenly scent and thought that this meal alone would probably keep him from feeling too homesick.

While the food cooked, Mrs. Nunez busied herself with polishing a tarnished set of serving plates and utensils—prized possessions, no doubt—taking sips from a little glass of straight Havana Club the whole time.

Witherspoon also noted that her husband, Francisco, avoided the guest-filled house as much as possible. He tinkered with an ancient lawn mower for more than an hour, then cut the browning grass in the small, scraggly lawn.

He returned to the living room, thinking that this old couple and this house were the perfect facade for a black op. They also had a large-screen TV and a small satellite dish, courtesy of American taxpayers, which pulled in channels from around the world. He joined Corsiglia on the spavined couch, where they sat glued to a soccer game from Argentina like children waiting for Mother's call to the table.

Then Toti walked in, almost as if on cue. He looked the part of a dashing jet-jockey—tall and athletic, Hollywood handsome, in his mid-thirties. His gleaming black hair swept back from his tanned face, and he sported a Howard Hughes mustache and a steady twinkle of humor in his watchful brown eyes.

He plopped next to Witherspoon and asked how the planning was coming along. They had already spent several weeks together taking long walks, getting a feel for the geography, meeting other CIA agents, and holding secure powwows to discuss the logistics of the big event. They had all had too much to do and think about in too short a time. The safe house had become a welcome retreat for everyone involved at one time or another.

Witherspoon felt a lot more relaxed now, speaking with Toti and surrounded with the mouthwatering smells from the kitchen and the soft laughter and conversation from other rooms. He liked this little house. Mr. and Mrs. Nunez had lived here for all their married years, and they were well liked by their longtime neighbors, only one of whom was within shouting distance. Sometimes they climbed the narrow staircase and sat in rocking chairs on a shallow balcony, which was the only place in the house with a view of the ocean. Until they received the television, that had been their only glimpse of the larger world. Now, he thought, the world was coming to them.

Witherspoon wondered about this childless couple who had opened their house and their hearts to the CIA and their people. They had decided to stay in Cuba many years before, he knew, even though they didn't like Castro or what he was doing to their country. Like many other Cubans, they believed that another revolution was long overdue. They knew that Castro wouldn't live forever, but they thought it was high time for him to leave the scene, one way or another. What could they lose? They were old now, too.

The sounds in the kitchen and the dimmed lights told Witherspoon that dinner was ready. Corsiglia had dozed off on the couch. He killed the TV and followed his nose. Several bottles of wine and champagne stood on the long wooden dining table. Mrs. Nunez lighted the cluster of slender red candles in the homemade centerpiece of local blossoms.

Toti strolled into the kitchen with a guitar, expertly fingerpicking a sweet Spanish Christmas carol. Before long his smooth, plaintive tenor had gathered everyone to the humble Yule feast.

The atmosphere filled Witherspoon with a special glow. He was far from old friends and family, but he felt part of something warm and special here, something hushed and forbidden, and therefore acutely precious. This would be a merry Christmas, after all, he thought, even if the whole world seemed to be going mad.

8

The Big Smoke-Out

THE LEADER OF THE TWO-MAN U.S. NAVY SEALS TEAM
stood frozen on the beach of Cuba's northern coast in his scuba
gear and scanned the surroundings—the long, empty stretch of
sand dreaming away in the soft light of the half moon, the jungle
sighing in the mild breeze. He choked his MP5 submachine gun,
every nerve ending humming as his senses collected data. This
was the real thing. Later tonight, his briefing officer had told him,
another special team would take out the big guy in Havana, not far
away. But that was then, and this was now. They had to move fast
to their objective—a small military installation.

Satisfied that their drop had gone undetected, he unlocked
his tall, angular frame and turned toward his partner, Cobb, who
squatted about three meters away. "Let's move out," he said under
his breath.

Cobb glided almost soundlessly to join him, his CAL-15 an-
gled skyward, and whispered, "You want I should take point, Mac?"

He'd never known a guy who could move so silently with so
much gear strapped to his ass. Cobb was a good man to have by
his side tonight. He replied with a hand signal and let the stocky

figure of his teammate take the lead toward a break in the trees.

Eighteen minutes later they were still snaking through the heavy growth like a single creature when he spotted their target. He touched Cobb lightly on the shoulder. They both crouched and stared. He squinted in the dim light and ran the CIA description of the place through his mind. Just three prefab buildings, each with a tin roof, and a modest radar tower. Radio shack, barracks, and an equipment shed, all enclosed by chain link and barbed wire. A couple of Soviet-era trucks and a jeep. No guardhouse at the open gate. Yep, this was the place.

He surveyed the facility for three more silent minutes and mused about what was already happening in Havana. The military strategists must have had fun planning how to move personnel into the area of the cigar summit disguised as Cuban soldiers using Soviet-made army vehicles. They could park on the fringes of the shindig and move all around on foot without arousing suspicion. And then . . .

Nobody moved among the buildings or across the hard-packed dirt yard. The compound looked deserted, but he knew that wasn't true.

He caught Cobb's eye and motioned again, and they crept through the gate and double-timed silently toward a lighted window in the barracks. They huddled against the building and caught their breath. Someone fired a staccato burst of Spanish inside. Another man laughed.

Mac popped up just long enough to take a quick peek through the open window. What he saw allowed him a second, longer glimpse. Two Cuban soldiers sat at a small wooden table under a single naked light bulb, playing dominoes. A portable TV flickered nearby. No other men in sight. Mac signaled to his partner, and they backed away into the shadows behind the shed. This looked like a piece of cake.

He told Cobb about the two domino players. "If there's others, they're sleeping."

"They don't have a clue," said Cobb with a frosty smile.

Mac unpocketed a watertight, secure military satellite field phone, plugged in the earpiece, and punched in the number to contact the Navy vessel that lay well offshore. He relayed his findings to his C.O.

Mac secured the phone and said, "Let's go back and keep an eye on those guys. Make sure nothin' disturbs their little game."

Cobb glanced at his watch and frowned.

"What's wrong?"

Cobb rolled his eyes at him. "When will they get here?"

Mac shrugged. "Relax."

They ghosted back to the barracks to stand their watch and wait for contact by the invasion force. Every inch of Mac's being thrummed with energy. This was a biggy, but it was hard to remain this still and this alert. How long would they have to hold fire like this?

Fifty minutes passed like that. And then, finally, several shadows materialized from the dark treeline. SEAL Team Six had arrived. Sixteen men, and the first of ten teams just like them. They'd be followed shortly by the scouts for the First Marine Expeditionary Force, and then the whole division would roll ashore.

Mac glanced through the window again. The game continued, *click, click, click*, the two soldiers looking pretty damn oblivious, not a care in the world. Mac knew that they could have been detected when they breached the old British radar system. But the CIA had said that the equipment was shoddy. Well, they were right.

He also knew that this was just another night for the Cuban military. Only a handful of soldiers were normally on round-the-clock duty. The last thing they'd expect tonight, or any other one, was another Bay of Pigs. The most excitement they ever had was maybe just the occasional drug runner.

"Like taking candy," Cobb said, obviously reading his mind, as usual, and shaking his shaved head.

Mac had to smile, even though they'd be in the shit soon.

What a great life this was. Last week a secret mission in Somalia, and now this—an invasion of Cuba. Hot damn! Just like in the movies. He just hoped that Castro's military muscle had atrophied as much as everyone wanted to believe. They'd find out soon enough. No turning back now.

He motioned to Cobb, and they scuttled across the compound and through the gate to meet the Six team leader. After that, things played out quickly, by the numbers, just as they had rehearsed it. The SEALS surrounded the outpost within minutes, surprised the two domino players, and had them frozen at gunpoint along with three of their sleepy-eyed comrades. Same thing at the radio shack, where they found another young soldier nodding in front of a radar screen. Nobody had fired a shot.

Colonel Everhardt, the bulldog C.O. of Alpha Force, ordered one sixteen-man team to hold the facility and remain in contact with the rest of the troops, who would roll into Havana in a couple of hours.

Mac knew that the plan was simple—but dicey. Get into Cuban military gear and proceed to the event site in the vehicles they had captured here and others that were coming ashore soon from the LST. Once everyone was in place, they were ordered not to act, unless they were attacked, until the Castro brothers were confirmed kills. Then they had to surprise the Cuban military, take control quickly, and secure the site. Mac couldn't wait to get going.

Two hours later, as the Marines established a beachhead, they finally saddled up and filed onto the narrow, blacktop road to Havana, a little convoy of vehicles with no lights. As they rattled along, Mac tried to maintain his famous cool head. This was going to be some party.

Joey Corsiglia sat at a table set dead center in the spacious convention hall that was the scene of this year's revival of the International Cigar Summit in Havana. As animated groups of formally dressed guests filled the space, he eyed the podium sitting on the stage thirty feet in front of him and found it hard to picture Castro himself standing right there, soon to address this bunch. Harder still to imagine was the little surprise they had arranged for this party and that he, Joey Corsiglia, would witness a real historical kinda thing, plus the end of Castro. He shivered.

Would the plan work? Who could say? Now that he was here, he could barely believe any of it. He knew that security would be tight here. At least a thousand people from all over the world would pack the joint. This was the country's biggest annual party. And even though Cuba was poor, it was doing well in one way. Nowadays, everyone thought it was cool to smoke cigars.

This time was special, though, more than ever. Because this time Castro would be here. Probably he had decided that he should get behind the cigar industry, the one thing that made his country okay. Being a more public kinda guy probably made sense to him now. Ever since that little boy, Elian what's-his-name, got saved in the ocean, Castro seemed almost like a celebrity again, showing up at charity to-dos and talking to the reporters. Stuff like that. Seemed like old Fidel was having more fun than ever.

Corsiglia tried to settle down by admiring the classy room. The big party was coming off this year in a hall called the El Laguito Protocol Salon, where they usually held official state events. The place was already crawling with representatives from distributors and cigar factories, along with people who just loved cigars. He couldn't get over it. He liked cigars, sure, but a bash like this, just for cigars?

He had arrived early and nursed a Coca-Cola while he watched the chattering people arrive and the party shape up. He couldn't help but notice several stunning young broads with their raven hair and flashing dark eyes, all shrink-wrapped into those little black dresses. Cuba could turn out more than fine cigars, he decided. Too bad they were all leashed to fat, bald Cuban guys, and too bad they'd be just as fat someday.

By now the joint was noisy and almost full up. He hoped he'd kept a low profile while he had hung out there, waiting impatiently. Finally some middle-aged guy in a shiny black suit showed up at the podium and banged a hammer, and everyone got real quiet. Good. Now maybe they'd get this show on the road.

He took a deep breath and tried to relax as the guy up front introduced another guy coulda been his twin and said he was the president of the International Cigar Association. Corsiglia wasn't here for the speeches, but he was glad to hear spoken English, the official language of the summit this year. Those who didn't speak English had a translator.

This president guy gave a speech in broken English. And then the real fun began. While the guy struggled on, the wait staff brought out all kinds of great food and some wine, too. Then more guys talked to the crowd, and sometimes everyone applauded. Corsiglia didn't pay much attention. Instead, he eyeballed the frisky little dame at the next table, who sported a miniskirt and honey-colored legs that went all the way up to her neck. Um-*umm*! Couldn't be more'n nineteen. He fidgeted through almost an hour of yadda-yadda by an import agent from Costa Rica, the chairman of the exclusive Cuba cigar agency in Canada, the publisher of a trade magazine, a consultant who blabbed about counterfeit cigars —a big problem for the industry—and at least six other cigar honchos. The best part, he thought, was about the counterfeit cigars.

The butterflies in his stomach didn't help his appetite, but he tried to enjoy the dinner anyway, because he thought the food was spectacular. First they served fancy appetizers, then all these different cheeses, then not just a salad but all kinds of salad, and then some prime rib or seafood for the entrée. That choice was easy. He picked the beef. And he couldn't pass up the wine, either. They brought French wine and Spanish wine and even champagne. Champagne, for shit's sake, and they weren't even toasting anything! After a meal like that, all the sinful desserts looked like extra pounds of fat, and that made him remember his growing paunch, so he passed.

Some cigar big shots got awards next, and then they served liqueurs, fine cognac, and some great cigars from the different Cuban factories.

As the servers passed out the cigars, Corsiglia remembered why he was here. His overstuffed gut sizzled with a hot current of adrenaline when he realized that the big moment was getting close. He knocked back the rest of his cognac and tried to hold his pricey cigar steady in an uncooperative hand while he surveyed the crowd. Without being too obvious he kept an eye on Johnny Two Fingers and Sammy the Greek, who sat ahead of him, next to each other and near the podium. They looked happy enough as they each toked on a fat stogie. He knew that the two hit men had gladly indulged in all the food, but they had gone light on the booze. They kept sharp eyes on things, too, including the uniformed guards stationed nearby. They also knew that undercover intelligence agents floated around, dressed like regular guests.

Corsiglia left his seat and strolled nonchalantly between tables, a sappy smile pasted on his puss, avoiding eye contact all the way to the patio outside. He tried to look unconcerned as he lit a cigarette that he didn't want and inspected the floodlighted grounds to see if everything was okay.

Two old motorcycles waited patiently in the driveway near the front door, obscured by shrubbery, ready to take his guys the hell out of there. Uniformed Cuban military troops patrolled everywhere. *Too many uniforms!* A big, black Mercedes Benz 600 Pullman limo—the president's ride—stood nearby, crowded by several black Soviet-made sedans. A chauffeur and at least a dozen military jokers hung around the official cars. Farther down the driveway several cabbies huddled near a row of colorful old taxis, talking and smoking while they waited for all the hoopla to end.

Despite all the uniforms out here, Corsiglia felt satisfied. He knew that CIA guys should be in place all around the grounds, hidden in the shadows—maybe even some disguised as cabbies—

and that some of those uniforms concealed U.S. special forces guys. That would make things interesting in a little while. But now he had to get back to his table and in position before the main event. He flipped his cigarette into the bushes and returned to the hall.

The rush of noise stopped him. Someone had turned up the juice on the party machine. The crowd was really pumped now, and the atmosphere was smogged with excitement. You could cut it with a knife.

He wandered casually through the crowd and took his seat. Johnny and Sammy were still part of the scenery, both of them looking like they were having a swell time, like they'd been coming to these affairs for years. Each of them wore a name tag that matched their fake identity, just like he did. The hit men were supposed to be cigar distributors from the Dominican Republic, and he was a rep from an obscure tobacco grower in Honduras. With their swarthy Italian looks Corsiglia knew that they all blended right in.

He also knew exactly what to do when the time came, and so did his two button men. They had run through everything over and over again in the weeks before Christmas and many more times on location in Havana during the last week. They were ready.

Somewhere in the crowd, Corsiglia knew, lurked more undercover CIA agents, but he didn't know where they were. They were supposed to stop anyone from interfering, help to disperse the crowd, and secure the area. The special forces teams would help, too.

Knowing all these things helped, he guessed, but he was surprised at how jittery he felt, now that the time had come. His big meal had started to think about coming back up. Corsiglia tried to swallow, but a stone had found its way into his throat, and his mouth was full of sand.

* * *

Johnny Two Fingers sat near the podium, fidgeting on a seat that had grown sharp springs, fighting a belly full of snakes. All of a sudden he didn't feel too good. Why had he eaten so damn much? A hot pulse drummed behind his burning eyes, and the hair on the back of his neck bristled. Too many things he didn't like now, things he hadn't liked from the beginning. Like the way the conference was set up and the layout of the surrounding grounds. Plus too many unknown factors. He knew that Castro was a bright guy, and he was, as always, very well guarded. No doubt they had the best strategies for protecting him during such a public gathering. The CIA had calculated all this stuff, but sitting here now, he thought the Cubans could be holding the better hand.

This wasn't just any hit. This one had called for some careful planning with the big wheels from Chicago and some kinda special CIA agents. They were all depending on him, because he was the insurance man. He had to make damn sure that Castro was snuffed for good, right then and there, and whack his brother, too. No way could the pricks get off only wounded. Johnny Two Fingers had to finger them both for sure. What a job! A real career-maker—and a fast ticket to a fat retirement. Then maybe he could feel happy living in his skin for a change. But right now he wanted to jump right out of it.

Maybe the big boys like that old fuck Russo and that fat-ass Corsiglia thought he was a dummy, but Johnny also knew he was just a little cog in the big wheel. This job wasn't like pulling the Italian rope trick on one of your old pals, dumping the body into the trunk of your Cadillac, and planting him in an orange grove. Nope. This was major league. Earthshaking. Historical. In the scramble of the aftermath, the world would ask, would *demand* to know, who did it. The Cubans, the CIA, the Mob, some rag-head terrorist, a rogue state, a world power—who? Somebody had to take the fall, and he figured that it might be him—probably was him. *At least I'd go down in the history books,* he thought. *Me, Johnny Two Fingers. The man who iced Castro. Historical.*

But that thought didn't comfort him. Instead he tried to breathe normally and pretend to listen to the speakers.

He pictured Castro standing up there, taking the cigar box, listening to the usual bullshit, everybody smiling. Then he takes the cigar in his left hand, snips off the tip with the tool in his right hand. Sticks the cigar in his mouth, lights up. Then *boom!* The place would come apart like a cheap suit. Maybe his legs would feel like overcooked pasta when he ran up there to finish the job, feeling all those eyes on him. *Shit, the whole world will be watching!*

He muttered a little prayer. It was something about hope—hoping to make the hit clean and get the fuck out before they jumped him, and hoping to have the old steam, after the adrenaline kicked in, to escape on foot, dodging armed guards and gunmen, and get to the motorcycle, get the damn thing started, and speed away to the waiting boat. A lot to hope for. He needed a prayer.

Sammy better keep up with me, he thought. *'Cause sure as shit I won't be waiting around for him.*

Johnny knuckled perspiration from his eyes and glanced at his partner. Sammy sat there calmly spooning up his dessert, actually paying attention to the latest speaker. That made Johnny feel a little better. At least Sammy looked cool and in control.

Joey Corsiglia didn't like the way Johnny Two Fingers looked now, sweat running down his forehead like that. The friggin' guy was getting real twitchy, he could tell. Not a good sign. Sammy seemed to be fine, thank God, but Johnny was the A-man. *Shit!* If Johnny choked, and if Sammy couldn't get to old beard-o . . .

Corsiglia was there to help, if possible. But he knew that was a big if. The plan said he could maybe cause more confusion, be a distraction, act like a big dummy and get in the way, maybe yell something to throw the security guys off. Then his boys could get away. But if Johnny blew it . . .

He kept scanning the joint casually, trying to make the CIA

agents, Cuban intelligence, U.S. and Cuban military, and plain-clothes guards. He picked up some clues, but you'd need a pro-gram, for Chrissake, to have a fighting chance. The plan was solid, but, baby, they'd need a lotta luck to get this thing done.

His gaze kept landing back on that one Latina babe. Her mini-skirt had scooched even farther north. *Mama mia!* A little more and he could see forever. Why was she hangin' with that old fart? Prob-ably owned a monster tobacco plantation or something. Man, if he didn't have a coupla other little things to do tonight, he thought. But, hey, maybe Witherspoon could get him a pass for the next cigar summit, too, so he could have some time to, like, help im-prove international relations.

Corsiglia rode that happy train of thought until the last guy finished his thank-you speech. Then the air seemed to get thicker as the crowd noise settled down to a watchful buzz. Corsiglia stiff-ened. The audience knew that the big moment had come, and so did he. Like him, most of them had grown up, and some had grown old, with images of Castro, but also like him, he guessed, few of them had ever actually seen the guy. Castro was kind of a legend—or a legend in his own mind, as his pal Vinny C. liked to say—and now the big man himself would be standing right up there in a minute. The gathering grew still and hushed. His heart started mak-ing like a pile-driver on speed.

The president of Cubanos Exports, S.A., returned to the podium and gazed around the room with a big, shit-eating grin, milking it. Then he got into his introduction, blabbing away like some friggin' politician. He made it sound like he and old Fidel were asshole buddies from way back. When he finally shut up for a few beats, those seconds seemed like they were charged with electricity. Finally he made like a ring announcer and almost shouted, "Ladies and gentlemen, Mr. Fidel Castro, the *presidente* of *Coo*-bah!"

Corsiglia jumped up as one with the crowd and found himself applauding and cheering just as enthusiastically as everyone else.

Fidel Castro appeared like a hallucination and marched to front and center stage. He acknowledged the thunderous greeting with a self-indulgent smile and a flourish. *El presidente* was dressed impeccably in a double-breasted navy blue blazer that sported a single white rosebud in the lapel.

Corsiglia stole glances at his two hit men. They clapped and smiled, playing their part, but he knew they were also copping all the little details, including which nonuniformed men who materialized onstage were probably there to protect their boss. Castro himself looked especially calm, Corsiglia thought, like he was enjoying the limelight.

When Castro retired to the podium, five equally stunning Latina women joined him to form a deliciously human backdrop. What a picture! It reminded Corsiglia of an old Robert Palmer music video. Before long Castro flapped his right hand, with a hint of impatience, and the crowd quieted and sat down.

The man of the hour captured the podium in a firm grip and thrust his wild, salt-and-pepper beard toward the microphone. Corsiglia thought his lined face looked more tired than calm now. "I am so very pleased to be here tonight," Castro said in accented English, his voice surprisingly resonant and as assured as ever.

Corsiglia goggled at the great man as he spoke at length, feeling just as entranced as everyone else in the audience seemed to be. Castro's English was pretty good, he thought. The *presidente* thanked all the key people, praised the award-winners, and addressed the issues of counterfeiting and the future of the cigar trade. Corsiglia thought he spoke like some kind of visionary captain of industry. He also cracked a few lame jokes, smiling each time so nobody missed the cue to laugh politely. Near the end he sounded more like a football coach as he made the usual promises about the future of his anticapitalist revolution.

When the speech and the applause had ended, the bigwig from Cubanos Exports approached the podium, smiling proudly. He carried a wooden cigar box. Corsiglia suddenly had a problem with his windpipe.

The businessman leaned into the microphone. "Mr. President," he began, offering the gleaming box to Castro as if it were a religious relic, "a gift from us to you. It is a 1992 Double Corona from the Hoyo de Monterrey factory." He adjusted his half-glasses, focused on the lid of the box, and read, " 'To our beloved friend, Fidel Castro.' "

The *presidente* manufactured a pleased smile, but he looked aged and weathered as he accepted his present, nodding graciously. He caressed the cigar box with the hands of an old man. Then, slowly, he lifted the lid. Corsiglia flinched, as if he had expected an explosion.

Castro smiled again, then leaned forward and said, "This is a fine moment, my friends." He tossed one hand. "I am so happy to attend this event on the forty-second anniversary of having the honor to serve as *presidente* of Cuba and the leader of the people's revolution."

Two of the lovely young women stepped forward to hold the box for him, beaming as he paused to admire the cigar resting on its velvet bed. Then, as if in slow motion, he picked it up reverently and, with the tremble of age, raised it to his eyes, then to his nose. He made a show of inhaling its special fragrance. The collective voice of the audience moaned, "Ahhh!"

Corsiglia didn't make a sound. His windpipe still wasn't producing enough air.

Castro placed the Double Corona in his mouth and rolled it ceremonially, then drew it out with his left hand and regarded it with narrowed eyes.

Corsiglia came down with a case of rigor mortis. *What's he looking at? What the fuck is he looking at?*

In a graceful flurry Castro produced a cigar clipper, snipped the end, and exchanged the clipper for a gold lighter. He positioned the cigar dead center in his mouth, applied fire, and sucked the Corona to smoky life. Moments later, when he tilted his head back and exhaled, the two vivid chicks standing with him dissolved into a blur behind the smokescreen. He rewarded the rapt audience with a smug, satisfied smile.

Corsiglia tried to focus on Castro. *Fuck me! First I can't breathe, and now I can't see too good.* Everything around the old revolutionary had receded into a bleary cloud that pulsed with a surreal light. Castro stood like a stone sculpture wrapped in fog in the middle of it all, like the centerpiece in an old religious picture.

Dreamlike, Castro sucked on the cigar again as if he drew in the very breath of life.

Half blind, Corsiglia gave in and choked for air.

A sharp explosion cracked the suspended silence. Castro froze as if time had stopped, the fingers of his right hand still caressing the Corona, his gaze fixed on nothing in this world. A woman in the audience tittered, undoubtedly thinking this was some kind of gag. A couple of heartbeats later the beauty standing on Castro's left shrieked like steel plate ripping, stuck her pretty knuckles into her mouth, and staggered back, staring in horror at the twin who stood just behind Castro. An abstract pattern of dark stains spackled the girl's bewildered face and white lace bodice.

That did it. Everyone in the room jumped up and let fly with a roof-raising chorus of screams, shouts, and curses. Tables and chairs banged onto the floor, linen napkins kited aloft, china crashed, and cutlery clattered away in every direction. The audience morphed into a panicked herd of animals seething toward the exits.

Corsiglia sprang to his feet but stood his ground amid a scene that looked like something from *Titanic*. He squinted at the stage and tried to pick out his guys. Castro remained rooted in place, looking eerily the same, as if nothing was wrong. Wreathed in smoke, his frozen face still beamed an unearthly glow. But he stood alone now. For the moment, at least, the stage was empty. A second later his whole body shuddered briefly just before he collapsed onto himself in a boneless heap, like the Wicked Witch of the West. Then a blur of movement blocked Corsiglia's view.

* * *

The way things look to him, Sammy the Greek figures that Castro is dead meat already. But now Johnny's up there on the stage to make sure. Three men race from the wings toward Castro's body. The one in the army fatigues has to be Raul, Fidel's brother, that faggot. Weird that none of them has a gun. But Johnny does. He whips out his compact 9 mm Glock with the homemade silencer and goes to work. *Heeere's Johnny!* Raul first. Two rounds into his face and one more to the heart—*thup, thup, thup*—real fast, just like that. Then he spins and takes out the other two dudes—*thup! thup!* One killshot to the head for each. That Johnny's efficient, man! No wasted ammo. A pleasure to watch him do his thing. Before he gets off the stage two more guys wrench themselves free of the surging mob and go for him, guns leveled. Only one guy manages to snap off a shot that goes wild before Johnny plugs them both good. They go down hard and disappear under the pounding hooves. *Fuckin' sardine city in here, man!*

Sammy fights his way through the packed humanity, all knees and elbows and knuckles, until he can latch on to Johnny's free arm. Time for him to go to work now. All the noise and the muscling crowd help. He slams against Johnny, makes eye contact, and gives him a big smile. Johnny smiles back. Sammy hugs him, still smiling, and pistons his fist. Five quick thrusts of the blade— in, up, and out—avoiding bone. Johnny goes limp, a look of puzzled surprise in his peepers before he crumples.

Sammy glances back a few seconds later, swallowed by the stampede again. Two suits the size of NFL linemen shove people aside and dive onto Johnny like he was a fumbled ball. *Too bad, Johnny don't have no bounce left in him now.*

"*Mierda! Esta muerto!*" one of them shouts as he holds the lean, rag-doll body of Johnny Two Fingers. He curses again and drops Johnny like a sack of week-old garbage.

Yeah, he's dead. Thanks for the news flash, shithead. Sammy squirms and salsas through the crush, finds a broken window, slips out, and scurries toward the parked motorcycles. A river of yammering guests sluices through the broken doors and down the steps, streams down the circular driveway, and straggles across the lawn, leaving a scatter of high-heeled shoes behind. Gunshots ring out, inciting more screams. Sirens yowl in the distance.

He vaults onto a bike like a rodeo cowboy, kicks the starter, and peels off. The bike tears up the turf as he roars across the front lawn, heading for the service lane beside the hall. He's memorized the street maps and walked the route, knows that the alley leads to a dark back street that will take him to the docks and the boat. Running almost flat-out with no headlight, he squints into the darkness and focuses on the road, thinking, *Just a few miles and a few more minutes. Just a few minutes and I'm home free.*

Nine minutes later, Sammy wheezed with relief when he spotted the boat and the familiar Chicago foot soldier standing at the helm, waving him on. When he let the bike stall and dropped it, he was glad to hear the big marine engines grumbling at idle, ready to rock. He jogged down the short dock on spaghetti legs and leaped aboard.

"Where's Johnny?" asked the pilot.

"Didn't make it. Let's boogie."

They blew past the mouth of the harbor, heading toward open water, almost before Sammy knew it. He had crashed after the adrenaline high and felt sorta blue and a little disoriented now. This goddamn boat bouncing his ass around didn't help much, either. He sucked in a big gulp of sea air and fought the nausea uncoiling in his guts, trying to hold on until they met the other boat that waited not far offshore. Maybe he should sit down for a while. Shit, maybe he should lie down somewhere.

Standing next to him at the wheel, the captain said, "Great getaway boat, huh?" He showed Sammy a set of long, horsey teeth that gleamed dully in the moonlight. "Confiscated by the DEA and on loan to the CIA. An i-go speedboat. For special assignments."

"No kidding?" said Sammy. "Say, you gotta beer on board?"

"In the fridge." He pointed. "Below, in the galley. Grab me one too, will ya?"

Sammy ducked into the cramped cabin, found the beer, and banged his head painfully as he struggled topside again. He handed over one of the bottles, not feeling too happy about it. *Dipshit smiling at me. Thinks it's funny I'm hurtin'.*

The helmsman stopped grinning long enough to throw his head back and take a long pull from the bottle.

How convenient, Sammy thought. *A perfect target.* He got the knife into his fist and used just one quick motion to saw it through the guy's main cables almost to the neck bones. The beer bottle thudded onto the deck just before the grinning idiot did. Sammy yanked the throttle back to neutral and waited for the boat to settle into the water. He sucked down a couple of swallows of the cold beer, taking his time, enjoying the feel of it going down the pipe. That should help his stomach.

The jerk was tall and rangy and too damn heavy, but Sammy managed to work him up and over the side. His body made a nice sound like *blunk!* when he hit the black water. Maybe he sank, and maybe he floated. Who cared?

Sammy returned to the wheel, took another mouthful of beer, and shoved the throttle lever forward. The twin engines roared, and the boat leaped ahead, plowing a creamy furrow through the dark water.

A few minutes later a bright light flashed behind him. A spotlight, probing the night for him. Shit, it looked like another speedboat hot on his ass. *What the fuck?*

The chase boat had almost caught up with him before he could think of an answer. Oh, Christ, he didn't know shit from boats! He cranked the wheel and made a couple of awkward evasive moves, nearly losing control, but it was no use. The speed-boat stuck to his tail, bucking in his frothy wake.

Controlled bursts of gunfire stuttered behind him. The wind-shield shattered, and bullets tore off chunks of fiberglass all around him. Sammy flinched and ducked uselessly, noting the heavy voice of the gun. Fifty caliber, probably. It was tearing him to pieces. *Shit! Who were these guys?* He swerved erratically to the right, then to the left.

The gun fell silent. Then came an emphatic *thump*, like when they launch fireworks. The black water geysered just off his port side. He jerked the wheel and cranked the long bow away from the shower of seawater. Then another *thump* and nothing else for a while but the labored whine of inboard engines and the hollow bump of plastic hulls hammering the chop. Then Sammy's eyes went blind in a flash as bright as all creation, and he marveled at the sudden odd sensation of stepping off a speeding train without getting hurt, maybe somewhere way out west of Chicago, in the country, someplace where he could stretch out in the cool shade of a big ol' tree, kick back with a good cigar, and take a nap.

9

Deadly Games

CLIFF SNAPPED AWAKE IN THE PREDAWN DARKNESS of his stateroom on January second, glazed with perspiration, his mind tumbling with dream images of the Big Smoke-Out. Victoria purred in deep sleep beside him in the warm bed. He got up carefully, pulled on a robe, and tiptoed into the still darkness of the main salon, wondering how events had played out the night before and how the world would react.

He padded to a window and squinted into the gloom. The bracelet of steady lights on the distant Bahamian horizon seemed curiously normal, as if nothing of any real consequence could have happened anywhere in the world. But Cliff knew otherwise. He settled onto the edge of the couch, punched on the TV, thumbed the volume down, and tuned in CNN. Bile rose sharply into his throat in anticipation.

A routine business report filled the screen. Cliff was glad to hear that the DOW Index was still holding up. Then another announcer's voice cut in. Cliff's pulse quickened. The picture changed to display the words *Chaos in Cuba* and the familiar image of Fidel Castro's face.

Looking appropriately grim, the equally familiar CNN staffer proclaimed Castro's death by assassination just hours before in tones of smug solemnity. He went on to report the shooting death of Raul Castro.

Adrenaline tickled Cliff's sour stomach.

"Havana appears to be under martial law," the newsman continued. "Details are still sketchy, but authorities believe the assassinations were part of an attempted military coup."

Cliff sensed movement behind him. He snapped his head around and jumped at the wraithlike vision of Victoria hovering in the doorway, dressed only in a filmy peignoir. "Jesus, Vic!" He gulped air and pointed to the TV. "You catch that?"

She ghosted across the salon and put a trembling hand on his shoulder. "My God, Cliff! They did it!" Her frightened eyes glistened in the ambient light. "What have we done?"

He held her gaze for a few moments, struggling with a riot of emotions, and then turned back to the screen. "I don't know."

The scene switched to a live satellite feed from the grounds near the scene of the murders and to another familiar talking head. Sirens wailed, and lights swept the background as the newswoman spoke excitedly.

Cliff wondered how CNN had gotten there so quickly.

"CNN has learned that the Central Intelligence Agency uncovered an assassination plot here recently, but even more disturbing is another discovery, which is why the United States has intervened in this rapidly developing situation."

"What the hell does that mean?" Victoria asked.

The announcer went on to relate the news about China's recent delivery of short- and medium-range nuclear missiles to Cuba. "The assassinations and the missile threat appear to be related. Apparently the Cuban military decided to take advantage of the shift in Cuba's power. But it's still too early to confirm this, or much else."

The camera panned as she strolled in front of a large building festooned with colorful streamers and bunting. "We do know that U.S. forces were deployed to Cuba yesterday, and they're moving rapidly to control the situation. Gunfire filled the streets of Havana until just minutes ago. We're told that the U.S. will quarantine the island until the threat can be accurately assessed and, hopefully, eliminated."

The telephone rang, startling them. Cliff snatched up the receiver.

"Cliff, did you catch the news?" It was Sydney.

"Yeah, I'm watching it now."

"They *did* it!" Sydney sounded excited and more than a little pleased.

"Looks that way." Cliff felt too shell-shocked to share Sydney's emotions. He glanced out a picture window. The first rays of the sun gilded the edge of the world. "Say, any word from you-know-who?"

"Not yet."

"Nothing? What about the other two?"

"*Nada.*"

"Hmmm. That doesn't sound good, Sydney."

"Not to worry." The old man sounded unusually relaxed. "Maybe something changed their plans. I hear from them, I'll let you know."

"You do that, Sydney. Thanks." Cliff hung up abruptly, his head whirling with whys and what-ifs.

Victoria looked up at him from her seat on the carpeted floor with a question on her lips.

"That was Sydney."

She squeezed his thigh. "And?"

Cliff sighed and told her what the old don had said.

"Shouldn't they be out of there by now?"

Cliff nodded and looked at the TV screen. "Look. The president."

Caldwell, dressed casually in a sweater, stood at the podium in the crowded White House press room, looking tired but confident. He confirmed that U.S. troops were in Cuba in force and that the assassinations had signaled the start of a military coup. "The situation in Havana is far from stabilized," he said, "but so far I'm pleased with our progress."

The president glanced at his notes and furrowed his noble brow. "Evidently, Fidel Castro had worked out a financial aid-for-arms agreement with China, disguised as a trade deal. China's leaders have not yet responded to our demands for an explanation. Fortunately, the Secretary of Defense reports that the immediate threat, the nuclear missile site, has been captured and secured."

Cliff and Victoria exchanged glances.

"Therefore," the president said, "we have successfully averted the possibility of an attack on the American people. Until we can assess the situation, we will continue our military buildup in Cuba, and all of our armed forces will remain on highest alert. I have also requested an emergency assembly of the United Nations in order to form a coalition peacekeeping force in Cuba."

President Caldwell thanked everyone and strode from the room, waving off a storm of questions from the clamoring White House press corps.

After a brief and redundant summary of the president's remarks by the CNN anchor, the scene shifted back to the site of the cigar summit in Havana and more repetitious monologue.

"Did we cause all this, Cliff?" Victoria asked.

"No, Vic. We were just their puppets."

"Really?"

"Look, Vic, if the Mob and the CIA hadn't gotten together, maybe Castro could have carried out his plan. Who knows what could've happened then?" He stroked her tousled mane, trying to believe his own words. "At least the Cuban military is contained now, and the whole thing's out in the open."

She nodded slowly. "I guess you're right."

"I wouldn't want to be the Chinese now. I just hope they stop here."

"Yeah, egg foo yung on the face beats World War Three."

He smiled at her, glad for that sign of her plucky humor. "How about an early breakfast?"

She jumped up. "Give me ten minutes."

The Gold Man stood in a small clearing near the center of his self-proclaimed "Gold Reserve," his well-stocked natural but privately owned game preserve on the Masoala Peninsula in Madagascar, and surveyed his domain. The preserve existed in one of the poorest nations on Earth, yet some of Africa's most notable wildlife called it home. Many of these creatures were on someone's endangered species list.

It was already late afternoon and darkening quickly in the rain forest. The Gold Man inhaled the heavy but cooling air lustily, feeling happy and in his element again. Nearby, Mr. Tambolo, his Man Friday, busied himself setting up a makeshift campsite. As brown as an African river, the wiry little man of mixed French descent was a native of the region.

We must do this more often, the Gold Man thought with a private smile. *Yes, much more often.* As the host of his own annual big game hunt, he thrilled with excitement to be engaged in one of his favorite activities.

"I think this is a good place to spend the night," he said to his man.

Tambolo nodded. *"Oui, par la,"* he said. "I could not have found a better one."

The Gold Man nodded once, feeling pleased at the rare compliment. He took another deep breath of the fragrant air and thought about the goddamn government and their three-thousand-acre park next to his reserve. They had developed it thanks to a handful of bleeding-heart international organizations, supposedly to protect the country's natural resources and biodiversity. Bullshit, he thought. More tourist dollars is what they want. They had tried to annex his two thousand acres to expand the park, but he had stopped them cold. He would never give up his big game hunt. Not for anything or anybody.

This year, as always, he had chosen an interesting fellow to be his guest on the hunt. And, as always, the fool thought he was one of ten lucky guests who were invited on the safari, one of the chosen few to share a once-in-a-lifetime tournament. What his current visitor didn't know was that he was the only guest—and the only hunter. And yet not a hunter at all, but the prey.

"Delicious," the Gold Man said with a dry chuckle. He sucked in another draft of the fecund air and grinned.

By now Tambolo had erected the compact tent and started a campfire. All the creatures of the night stirred to life, making faint, furtive sounds just beyond the reach of the flickering yellow fire-light.

The Gold Man lowered himself into a folding chair and watched Tambolo as he gathered the ingredients for a coarse meal. He pulled a flask from his safari jacket and took a long pull of the tequila inside. The fiery liquid coursed down his throat, boosting his floating feeling of well-being. He thought about his current guest, his human prey, an American this time, now at the end of his fourth day of the hunt, or, more accurately, his torment.

What great sport! the Gold Man thought. Nothing else like it. And it doesn't cost me a dime. An amusing diversion before I have to go back to work and deal with Penkovsky again. He frowned at that image. That sonofabitch better not fuck up, or I'll make him my next guest.

That thought made him laugh out loud. Tambolo turned and gazed at him evenly, his face as inscrutable as ever. The Gold Man tipped his man a theatrical wink and barked another laugh.

He took another drink as he savored the details of the hunt. It was a microcosm of his other favorite sport, his global business game. The private safari gimmick always worked. No self-styled man of the world would turn down such a tempting proposition, would even kick in fifty grand of his own for the experience and a shot at a cool million before returning home with fat pockets and the bragging rights to the overblown title of "The World's Greatest Hunter." That sounded pretty lame, but any jerk with a healthy male ego was lured by the exclusive competition, the easy money, and the chance to show off the gaudy bronze and walnut plaque to everyone.

The hunters were scored on a point rating system based on the type of animal killed, with more points awarded for the fastest, largest, and most exotic or rare animals. The Gold Man's Madagascar reserve was full of such game.

He smiled, picturing some of the odd wildlife and wondering how many of them lurked nearby. He thought about the forsa, related to the mongoose, which looked like half dog and half cat. And the serpent eagle, the red owl, the red-ruffed lemur, and the cuckoolike birds known as the sickle-billed vanga. And what about the giant jumping rat and the ground roller? The list of critters here read like the damned manifest of Noah's ark— Noah's ark on acid. He loved them all.

That was part one of the story. Part two featured the end of the hunt on the west side of the island, on the broad and fertile plains, a large section of which he owned and had stocked with zebra, giraffes, hippos, rhinos, elephants, cheetahs, and other game typically found in Kenya. This was an unfair lure, of course, an irresistible temptation for any corrupt hunter, who would incorrectly assume that he would enjoy the second half of the hunt fulfilling a dream that would make Marlin Perkins roll over in his grave.

That image made the Gold Man giggle until Tambolo looked at him again. He could hardly wait for the next day.

The American hunter dragged himself through the unfamiliar forest in the darkness. When his boot hooked a vine he stumbled, dropped his gun and suitcase, and toppled painfully onto his knees. "Shit!" he cried weakly, then collapsed onto his side, panting. He felt like a wounded animal, stalked by some alien beast in the teeming darkness and finally run to ground. The festering cuts and sores on his face, arms, and hands made his whole body throb hotly, and his parched throat threatened to glue itself shut. He told himself to get up and struggle on. He had to run for his life. He knew that now. But to where?

That sadistic madman! The gun and the Pelican case had become deadly liabilities. A million dollars? Lucky you, cowboy! Fucking stuff gets heavy real quick. Can't live with it, can't live without it. He knew that the crazy bastard figured he wouldn't leave the island minus the cash, that his greed wouldn't let him drop the goddamn case to lighten his load.

He took stock of his situation dully. He had a gun, sure, but he couldn't see his pursuer to shoot him. And all the while that maniac taking potshots at him now and then, without warning, and obviously missing him deliberately. The crazy fuck! He wants to drive me nuts before he kills me.

Groaning, he dragged himself to his feet and picked up the case of money and the rifle. Before he had stumbled three steps his spinning head forced him to drop both burdens again and sit on the case to rest.

How the hell does he keep finding me?

He dug through a pocket until he realized he'd already eaten the last granola bar. He sucked the last swallow of warm water from his military-style canteen and dropped it at his feet.

Grimly he willed himself to find some shred of hope. It's okay. I can still make it. In the morning I'll find a stream and fill the damn canteen again. Sure. He wheezed a laugh and shook his head. Here I am, sitting on a million bucks. Literally. And I'm in the worst shape of my life. Christ!

He dropped onto his knees. He couldn't help himself. He dragged the case closer, popped the locks, and flipped up the lid.

He pulled out his tiny penlight and shone it on the cash. What a picture!

He closed his eyes and shook his head, unable to fight back a choking sob. He lowered his sweaty forehead onto the banded packets of bills and retched miserably. I'm stuck in the fucking Twilight Zone! I'm going to die for this goddamn money!

He wept quietly for a few minutes, then sat back on his haunches, feeling drained and depressed, and scrubbed his gritty face with a bleeding hand. Jesus, how does he always know where I am?

The new idea struck him like a fist. Slowly he looked down at the yawning Pelican case, the neat bundles of hundreds. It's in the goddamn case!

He clawed furiously at the packets of cash, raking them onto the ground until his raw fingers found a small, hard object. He snatched it up, clicked on his penlight, and gaped at the little gadget in horror, his heart pounding. Holy shit! A homing device! The slick bastard is tracking me! He slumped in defeat, the last of his pride evaporating. How stupid could he be? Even now the Gold Man could be out there in the darkness, close by. He imagined the lunatic's eyes burning into him.

But wait a minute. He glanced at his Rolex Submariner. Just after ten. The Gold Man hadn't fired at him since midafternoon. Maybe he was far away, taking it easy and feeling overconfident. He could be asleep by now. But I could find him standing over me when I wake up, if I'm pathetic enough to fall asleep. Christ, I wish I'd stuck to hunting bighorns in Idaho.

Wearily he returned the money to the case and latched it shut. He shook his head again as he stared at the Pelican case, feeling cursed. It held everyone's fondest hopes, and yet it weighed him down hopelessly. He wanted to laugh, but he couldn't summon the energy.

What a perfect setup this dream hunt was. The Gold Man had given him his choice of weapons, but the options were limited. He had picked the best of the lot, a Glaser Heeren System rifle. A respectable weapon made in Germany, sure, but a single shot, manual feed? A pretty crappy choice, really.

He picked up the rifle and considered it, then gazed at the suitcase. He stuck a hand in a pocket and fingered the bullets, counting them. Ten. Only ten.

He used the penlight to probe the dark jungle around him with its narrow beam. Nothing but trees and leaves, most of the trees no thicker than his arm, crowding as far as the light penetrated, going on forever, it seemed to him.

Just then another idea popped into his mind. What if . . . ? He quickly panned the light around until he found a likely spot. Then he dragged the case behind a big, tortured-looking tree that dangled nets of aerial roots, and camouflaged it with leaves and branches.

He retrieved the rifle, feeling hope for the first time in four days. His cracked lips curled into a grim smile. Okay, you crazy bastard. Let's have some fun.

Then he stumbled into the black night to look for a good vantage point. There he would wait, patiently, for a new day.

During their light breakfast on the afterdeck, Cliff and Victoria made small talk, avoiding the obvious topic. Cliff was just beginning to relax when the hotline rang again. This time it was Donald Witherspoon.

"I'm on my way there, Cliff," he said. "We need to talk privately. Can you pick me up at the airport?"

"When?"

"One hour."

Cliff checked his Master Bankers' watch and found the East Coast time zone. "Nine-thirty?"

"Exactly."

"You got it, chief."

"I'll meet you out front."

Cliff hung up. Things had shifted into high gear again, and the world tilted off center.

"Who was that?" Victoria asked.

He told her about meeting Witherspoon.

"Oh, boy," she said. "Here we go again."

"I just had the same thought."

He sat drumming his fingers, thoughts banging around in his head. Finally he called Virgil Carter and felt buoyed by the sound of the familiar voice when he answered.

Cliff told him he had to pick up a VIP at the airport. "Can you meet me at the dock? Soon as you can get there."

"No problem," Virgil said. "You know, I've been watching the news, and—"

"You know as much as I do, Virgil. See you in a few minutes."

He sprang from his chair and hurried forward to the launch that the crew lowered every morning, just in case.

"Stay out of trouble," Victoria called after him.

He turned and waved at her. She stood rigid, her hands clasped. He threw her a kiss. "Don't worry. See you soon."

Virgil Carter idled onto the dock in his new silver Mercedes 500 sedan just as Cliff stepped out of the launch. Just the sight of him made Cliff feel better. Cliff climbed into the car beside his key man and told him they would return to his office and drop him off.

"You can have the car as long as you want," Virgil said. "You know, I've been watching CNN. . . ."

Cliff thought he looked nervous, but that was nothing unusual for Virgil. "I know, I know. I saw it, too."

Virgil kept his eyes on the road. Traffic was light.

Cliff wanted to tell him everything, but he couldn't. "So far I only know what everyone else who watches CNN knows. I can't wait to see what's next."

Virgil nodded solemnly and rolled his eyes at Cliff. "Same here," he said.

Thirty-five minutes later, Cliff pulled up to the curb at the Nassau International Airport where Witherspoon stood waiting, one hand holding his fedora in place against a brisk Bahamian breeze. Cliff smiled at the picture. *Now I'll get the real news.*

"Nice ride, Cliff," Witherspoon said, following his briefcase into the car. "You keep this onboard, too?"

Cliff smiled, sensing the agent's good mood, and glanced at his watch. "You made good time."

Witherspoon chuckled. "Bermuda Triangle tailwind."

Cliff nosed the Mercedes into a crawling line of cars and headed for the winding access road, not feeling as lighthearted as his CIA pal seemed to be. "What'd you fly on?"

Witherspoon pointed at an odd-looking jet plane that was taxiing toward a parking area. "On that."

Cliff was surprised to see the stunning aircraft. "Looks like a corporate job."

"Yeah, an AASI Jetcruzer 500, converted to a reconnaissance plane."

"They just loaned it to you?"

Witherspoon nodded. "It was doing recon work over Cuba. When I had to leave, an Air Force general snagged it for me." He beamed, an unlit cigarette dangling from his lips. "A stealth fighter escorted us out of Cuban airspace. And here I am."

They neared the airport exit and crossroads. "So where are we headed?"

"Just drive around, Cliff. I only stopped by on my way to Washington to give you a quick update. Thought it'd be best to meet in person."

"Have you spoken to Russo?"

"No."

Cliff glanced at Witherspoon and said, "I just talked with him. He hasn't heard from his men yet. Seems strange."

Witherspoon toyed with his cigarette. "He won't be hearing from Johnny, uh, what's his name? Two Fingers? Or from Sammy the Greek."

Cliff's pulse jumped. "What the hell happened?"

"The cigar went off just as planned," Witherspoon said. "Did Castro in right away."

He recounted the basic events, making it sound upbeat, as they cruised along John F. Kennedy Drive. Cliff tried to digest the news about Johnny and Sammy. He didn't like that, and he wasn't thrilled about what he was hearing now. That little alarm bell was ringing in his head again. He yanked the steering wheel and braked the car to a shuddering stop just off the road.

He looked Witherspoon in the eye and said, "Let me get this straight. The SEALs caught up with Sammy. And Sammy ends up with various parts missing, floating around in the drink. Okay." Cliff killed the engine, his gaze still locked on to the agent, who suddenly rediscovered the cigarette in his hand. Witherspoon pocketed it awkwardly and looked out the window.

"I don't get it, Don," Cliff said. "How'd the SEALs know that the boat docked down there for Sammy would transport Castro's assassins out of the country? And if they knew who Sammy was, why would they kill him?" He had the dreadful sense of knowing the answer.

Witherspoon turned back to Cliff and said, "Listen, man. This is a sensitive situation. We can't have some little hit man for the Mob walking around, shooting his big mouth off about stuff like this."

"Oh, of course not," Cliff said. "Silly me." Suddenly he had a queasy feeling about his own safety.

"No guarantee he'd stay quiet," Witherspoon said. "Not discreet like you, Cliff." He searched Cliff's eyes for understanding. "Come on. Let's keep driving while we talk. This brings up something important."

Cliff got the car going again, and the winding road took them along the postcard shoreline and through tunnels of tropical vegetation and eucalyptus trees. Witherspoon remained silent for a long time, taking in all the sights like a tourist.

Finally he said, "Listen, Cliff. Some things you know even the president of the United States doesn't know."

"Let me guess. The phony military coup?"

"We had to get the president's support, Cliff." He placed a hand lightly on Cliff's shoulder. "You understand, right?"

Cliff shook his head. "You're too much." He took a deep breath. "Don't worry. I won't talk about any of this. Or do you plan to kill me, too?"

"Jesus, Cliff, get real. We know you're tight-lipped. How could you even think—"

"Okay, okay. Tell me more."

"The U.S. military was well prepared."

"No doubt."

"Special ops groups from the Navy, Army, and Marines were air- and sea-dropped so that military backup was right there at the cigar summit."

"Must've surprised the Cubans."

"You bet," Witherspoon said. "But the main thing is they captured the 'Doomsday'—the Chinese-Cuban nuclear missile site. That unplugged our biggest worry."

"Thank God."

"And our special forces. Our flyboys are on hand now, too."

"Covering the whole island?"

"All six hundred miles," Witherspoon said. "Flying their whole arsenal. F-22 Raptors, F-15 Strike Eagles, F-16 CID Fighting Falcons, F-111 Aardvarks, A-10A Thunderbolt II Warthogs, and a few F-117 Nighthawks."

"Some list. What about the Navy?"

"One carrier group from the Sixth Fleet arrived last night. More ships are on the way."

"So we're in control?"

Witherspoon shrugged. "Basically. But shit could still happen."

Cliff glanced at the agent, who was still gawking like a tourist. "Okay. Now what?"

"We have to contain the Cuban military, keep civil order. And keep any ambitious foreign states or terrorists the hell out of there."

"Peace in the western hemisphere," Cliff said, still trying to shake the surreal feeling of what he had helped to create.

"As quickly and inexpensively as possible," Witherspoon said. "We don't want a protracted situation."

Cliff thought about that, knowing how little stomach the U.S. had historically for nation-building.

Witherspoon turned away from the window. "We have to get back to D.C."

"We?"

Witherspoon ignored the question. "Would you contact Russo after you drop me and tell him that his three men did a great job, but, unfortunately, they won't be back?"

This guy never ceased to amaze Cliff. "Yeah, yeah, I'll tell him if I have to. You ready to go back now?"

"Sure," said Witherspoon. "Thanks."

They traveled in silence while Cliff envisioned his call to Russo. Great job. But they won't be back. How would the old man react? Cold fingers brushed the back of his neck.

"What about Joey Corsiglia?" Cliff said.

Witherspoon gave him a sheepish smile. "He's fine. He's, uh, relaxing right now. On the Jetcruzer. Probably having a cocktail."

"He's with you? Why didn't you say so?"

"No need for you to know."

Cliff felt relieved until another thought struck him. "Don, didn't you just ask me to tell Sydney that his three men didn't make it?"

The agent stared straight ahead and remained silent. Something in his face chilled Cliff to the bone. Murder. Cold-blooded murder.

Finally Witherspoon said, "I, uh, have one stop to make on our way to D.C. You understand, don't you, Cliff?"

Cliff suddenly realized how fast they were traveling—way over the speed limit. He tightened his grip on the wheel and let the car coast. "All right, I'll tell Russo exactly what you said."

The agent looked relieved. "By the way, I had a good meeting with Professor Perez, the man who'll replace Castro until the election." He tapped Cliff on the shoulder. "He's very open to meeting with you. Wants to discuss your investment ideas."

"I'm glad there's some good news to tell Sydney."

"I put in a real good word for you. I think you'll have a deal."

"At least Sydney'll be glad to hear that."

"Sorry about the other business, Cliff. I hate giving bad news to people I really like." He gave Cliff's shoulder a buddy-buddy squeeze. "The agency appreciates all the help you gave them."

"It's not over yet."

Witherspoon nodded. "Actually, Cliff, you should feel good about this, and about yourself. It's a thankless job, we know, but thanks to you, Americans can keep living the American way of life."

Oh, brother! Cliff thought. Next he'll start singing "America the Beautiful." "Yeah, maybe we saved western civilization."

"Right!" Witherspoon said eagerly. "Who knows how many lives we've spared? You made the right call, Cliff, when we asked for your help."

Cliff thought the guy might break into song yet. He actually sounded sincere.

They were nearing the airport again. Cliff banked the Mercedes around another curve and stopped at an intersection. Then he turned left and swung onto the circling roadway that ran past the old DC-3 displayed in front of the airport entrance. When they reached the terminal building he wheeled up to the curb smoothly, feeling relieved about shedding his passenger—and about his reprieve from the post-assassination hit list.

Witherspoon made a quick exit, pausing only to collect his briefcase and hat. "Thanks, Cliff," he shouted over the airport noise. "Call me if you need me."

Then he strode briskly away and swept through the swinging doors, gone almost as soon as he'd appeared, thought Cliff, almost as if he'd never really come.

"The new president's invited Dietrich over to the White House for an evening conference," Cecil Danforth announced, cradling his telephone. He cracked a wry smile. "I guess he needs all the ammunition he can get for the next few days."

An after-hours meeting in the Oval Office that included the director of the CIA was hot news, but Donald Witherspoon was too weary to do anything but nod at his boss. Despite his fatigue, he had arranged this urgent meeting at Langley to update his immediate superior. That was done now, and Danforth had relayed the information to Dietrich.

Witherspoon slumped in his leather chair, trying to find enough energy to go home. It had been a long and eventful day. All he could think about now was a hot meal, an even hotter bath, and a soft bed.

A sudden rustling sound made the American hunter jerk awake. His chest contracted around his thudding heart, making it hard to breathe. He knuckled his burning eyes and scanned the jungle, looking for signs of movement. Early morning sunlight beamed through the greenery, and a freshening breeze stirred all the leaves of the rain forest into a steady murmur.

Nothing. He sucked in as much air as he could and exhaled through his open mouth. Thirst had become a madness. He would skin his mother alive for one mouthful of water.

He tried to focus on the tree with all the aerial roots. Then he saw him.

The slender black assistant of his murderous host stood at the edge of the clearing, peering around. Then he shrugged off his heavy pack and eased it to the ground. He crouched and surveyed the small clearing again. Finally he stood and took a step toward the tree and the hidden case, as if he had made a decision.

The American held his breath.

When he reached the tree Tambolo pawed through the brush carefully. Then he stood erect and called over his shoulder, "It's here, boss!"

The Gold Man materialized moments later, his khakis already dark with sweat. "Good man, Tambolo! Open it."

Tambolo dragged the case into the open and flipped up the lid.

"Well?"

"*Comme ci, comme ça*," the black man said with a helpless gesture.

"So it's all there."

"*Oui.*"

"Good," the Gold Man said. "Then he's almost done. But he'll be back for it." He squinted as he scanned the forest around them. "Leave it. We'll get it later. No point letting the sucker slow us down." He removed his hat and raked his fingers through his long, sweaty hair. "Anyway, he comes back, we'll know."

The American had him in his sights, but he was trembling with hunger and exhaustion, afraid he'd miss. Then he'd be screwed. He fought the urge to squeeze the trigger, then relaxed. No, he would play the fox's game instead.

Tambolo nodded. "*Mais oui*, boss. *Déjà se fatigue* if he left all the money behind."

The Gold Man looked around again. "Only problem, which way did he go?"

"Paff!" Tambolo said with a dismissive wave. "Not so far."

The black man retrieved his pack and struck out into the

trees, heading eastward, and the Gold Man soon followed. The American counted slowly to one hundred before he returned to the clearing and opened the case. He dug out the homing device, glanced around, and scraped a hole in the loamy soil. Then he buried the little gadget, grabbed the case, and toiled off in the opposite direction.

The Gold Man spat a curse and slung his floppy hat onto the ground. He glared at Tambolo, as if he was to blame, and said, "I think we've been fucking tricked."

Tambolo shrugged. "I think no, *monsieur*." He tapped a monitor the size of a watch on his wrist. "The case, she has not moved."

The Gold Man wasn't convinced. It was high noon already, and they hadn't found a single hint of the American. No other guest had been this difficult. Now here he was, stuck on a cold trail, suffocating in the heat and sweating like a pig. This was no fucking fun at all! When they found that pretty American playboy he would just wound him first and then kill him slowly. Stinging ants and a jolly little barbecue came to mind. But his boiling anger couldn't kill a seed of doubt. Maybe this guy was different. Maybe he had enough left to be a problem.

He shoved Tambolo rudely and shouted, "Move your ass! We're going back."

The little man cowered. "Very well. As you say, *monsieur*."

They hurried through the rain forest at a frantic pace. Tambolo eventually fell behind, drooping under the weight of his heavy pack. The Gold Man stopped and whirled on him. "Come on, goddammit, you black bastard! We're almost there."

When they had regained the clearing, the Gold Man stomped to the tree and tore through the vegetation. "Bloody hell! Where is it?"

"What, *monsieur*?" Tambolo asked, panting.

"The fucking case! It's gone!"

"I think no, *monsieur*." He pointed at the tracking monitor.

"Stop pointing at that fucking thing. The case, you bloody fool!"

Tambolo dropped to his knees and examined the spot. No Pelican case, but the soil had been disturbed here. He dug frantically with both hands while the Gold Man stomped and cursed. The black man stopped and whispered "*Merde!*" when he found it. With one hand he held up the small tracking device. "*C'est ici la chose, monsieur.* But the money?"

"Fuck me! He tricked us, you idiot!" The Gold Man slapped the gadget from Tambolo's hand and booted him to the ground. "We . . . will . . . kill this sonofabitch. Do you hear me?"

Tambolo scuttled away from the Gold Man on his butt. "*Oui, monsieur.* We will kill him good."

The Gold Man loosed another string of curses when he checked the sun again. It was low in the sky now. They had worked their way west all afternoon, all the way to the grassy plains, but still nothing. That miserable son of an American whore! I'll drink his blood and eat his beating heart! Crouched in the tall grass, he fussed with his rifle while he waited for Tambolo, who was off somewhere nearby, checking a game trail. Damn his black soul! What good was he, anyway? Maybe he would kill him, too, for being so worthless. He wished only to find that American shit and to watch him die piece by piece.

And then, as if wishing had made it so, some movement caught his eye. A hazy figure appeared near a thin tree line, no more than eighty yards away, backlit by the low-angled light, slowly dragging that bloody case of money. For one painful moment the Gold Man thought he was hallucinating. But, no. The American was right there, moving in painful slow-motion. An easy target. Yes!

He flinched at a whisper of footsteps behind him. It was

Tambolo. The Gold Man made a faint sound like "Zit!" that stopped him in midstep. He motioned for him to get down, then jabbed a finger toward the trudging figure. His aide stared with bulging white eyes.

The Gold Man slipped the sniper's rifle from his shoulder and crept to a fallen tree trunk nearby. He motioned for Tambolo to join him. The little man moved quickly and soundlessly and stretched out next to him. The Gold Man could literally taste the blood in his mouth. He peeked over the trunk and found his prey again. The American limped as he dragged the heavy case through the diffused orange light. He could get a clear shot if he hurried.

He laid his rifle across the tree trunk and peered through the scope. The forlorn figure jumped into view, surprisingly big in the powerful lens. He centered the crosshairs on the man's back, precisely over the heart. He took a deep breath and held it. Steady, steady . . . Time contracted and stopped just as someone hit the Mute button. He had entered the zone.

Steady . . . Now! He squeezed the trigger.

The recoil drove his meaty shoulder back ten inches, and birds exploded from the trees like shrapnel, all in suspended silence. The American turned to stone, quivered, and toppled onto his face. The Goldman waited a few beats, still not breathing, looking for signs of life. But his prey stayed down, motionless, the Pelican case abandoned at his feet. Dust swirled in the golden light.

The Gold Man released air in a rush, inhaled, and turned to Tambolo, curled stiffly beside him. "Okay, let's have a look."

The Gold Man felt better when they found the body in the scrubby grass. It hadn't moved a bit. The American looked smaller now. Like a used rubber, he thought. He motioned to Tambolo, and the little man grimaced, then reached down tentatively and rolled the body onto its back. Blood was everywhere, black in the dying light. The American's blue eyes stared sightlessly into the darkening sky. They made him look stupid, the Gold Man thought, even more stupid than he was in life. The .50-caliber bullet had gone straight through easily. The Gold Man smiled. It was a perfect killshot. Clean and neat. Right through the heart.

He didn't feel angry now. The little game was over, and it had been amusing—more fun than the others. The hell with eating the guy's exploded heart. What he wanted now was a thick, juicy beefsteak. A bottle of Dom, too. And maybe one of those little Madagascar maidens for dessert.

He tossed his rifle to Tambolo and hefted the money case. "Let's go," he said. "I'm starving."

10

Monopoly Money

THE NEXT MORNING, JANUARY THIRD, CLIFF AND VICTORIA huddled in the high-tech media room of the *Havana Royale* watching CNN on the giant plasma TV screen. Every news channel carried the same story. Talk about the stunning events in Havana had been on everyone's lips for the past twenty-four hours. Now the president of the United States was about to speak. Cliff thought that the whole world must be tuned in.

"Nothing like having a front-row seat to history," Cliff said.

Victoria managed a wan smile, but Cliff knew how tense she was.

Looking tired and grim, President Caldwell spoke in somber tones, but as he explained the developments in Cuba he also projected a cautious optimism.

Afterward, as Cliff only half listened to the broadcasters' postmortem, he thought that the best part of the thirty-minute speech had dealt with the future of Cuba and how the United States proposed to deal with its new redheaded stepchild. Cliff could hardly wait to see how everything played out. The U.S. clearly had appointed itself as midwife to the birth of the new

Cuba. Washington had developed a strategy or, more likely, had trotted out an existing plan to address a situation like this. Whatever the case, the president's actions appeared to be endorsed by the United Kingdom, most of western Europe, Japan, and other U.S. allies. The jury was still out for other countries of the United Nations. But Cliff felt reassured by the president's remarks and thought he had a workable plan that the U.N. would endorse eventually. After all, who could really question the United States on this issue? Ultimately, Cuba was America's problem.

Cliff was also glad to hear about the proposed democratic elections, which would allow the people of Cuba to determine the future of the island nation. And he thought the U.S. had made a good choice by appointing a Cuban from academia as interim president. That man was Dr. Diego Perez, a professor of economics from the University of Havana. According to the president, Dr. Perez shared the same democratic ideals and believed that change was paramount. He would lead the country through the transition period and help to insure fair elections—an exciting milestone in Cuban history.

Victoria took Cliff's hand and sighed. "Maybe everything really is under control. That makes me feel better."

Cliff squeezed her hand, pleased to hear her singing an upbeat tune. "Things should work out just fine. You heard the president. No more trade embargo. Financial aid. Unrestricted travel for Americans to Cuba. And help with attracting investment capital. That's just what Cuba needs, for starters. And the U.S. will continue to provide economic support as long as the new leaders play by the rules."

Rosie entered the room with a coffee service for two. They both took a cup.

"I suppose you're right, Cliff," Victoria said, "but what about this huge military buildup? Sounds like the U.S. is turning Cuba into one big armed camp."

"I'd say we don't have any other choice. Things will be unstable for some time, I'm sure. There's bound to be some hostility in the Cuban population, especially in the military. And then there's China and who knows what other external threats. This guy Perez may be a puppet, but we need someone like him now, and we need to hold elections as soon as possible. The whole thing could fall apart without strong military support."

Victoria nodded thoughtfully. "I guess that's true. And we also need the new elected president to sign that treaty banning all weapons of mass destruction."

"Which couldn't be modified by any future Cuban leader. That would be a real landmark."

"I'll say." She smiled more brightly this time and nudged him. "So how does it feel? You had a hand in all this, Cliff. You've made a real contribution."

What could he say to that? He shrugged and turned back to the TV screen. "Well, who knows? But this is an important moment. And the president sure took advantage of it with that speech."

"Oh, yeah," Victoria said. "The American public'll eat it up."

That afternoon, Cliff paced the varnished teak of the sun-deck, gazing at the vast, whitecapped Atlantic, his mind filled with visions of a future Cuba, until his satellite phone rang. It was Witherspoon. Now that President Perez had been appointed, the agent said, the door was wide open. Cliff could come to Cuba.

"How's that sound to you, Mr. Blackwell?" Witherspoon asked cheerily.

"I'm there," Cliff replied.

Cliff hurried below decks and forward to the bridge, fueled with new energy. He had grown weary of the long wait, and he knew that Victoria was anxious to see Havana. He told the captain to make ready for departure immediately. Then he sought out Victoria to give her the news.

* * *

Near noon three days later, Cliff and Victoria joined the captain on the bridge of the *Havana Royale*. Cliff's spirits soared at the sight of the skyline of Old Havana drawing closer as they cruised into the Bahia de la Habana. The captain maneuvered the big yacht toward a commercial wharf where he had booked a spot for them to dock indefinitely.

Cliff had learned as much about the situation in Cuba as he could during the run from Nassau. He had shared much of this information with Sydney Russo and Tony Carlo, who were practically foaming at the mouth to get there. He knew they had arrived earlier that same day, because Sydney had called him from his suite at the Hotel Riviera. He told Cliff that he was enjoying some vivid memories of the place his good friend Meyer Lansky had built, and he was charmed that the present owners had retained the Fifties ambiance along with the modern Cuban splendor.

Shortly after docking in Havana, Cliff also received a call from his Miami attorney, Andre Martinez. After listening to President Caldwell's speech, Andre was even more curious about Cliff's recently expressed interest in Cuba. Cliff admitted that he was representing some major players who were interested in long-term investments in Havana and that he was headed there on a reconnaissance mission on their behalf.

Andre said that he, too, planned to visit Cuba soon, because Diego Perez, the new temporary president, was a former colleague of his. What better time for a reunion with his old friend? Andre also offered to introduce Cliff to Perez.

"Funny you should suggest that, Andre," Cliff said into his sat phone as he scanned the city from the main deck. "I've got tentative plans to meet with him. In fact, he's expecting me."

"He is?" Andre said, sounding surprised. "Excellent, Cliff! I know you will like him. He's a good man. It is a good thing for you to meet."

"Maybe you could let him know I'm here," said Cliff, admiring Victoria's sleek helicopter as it sat on its new perch. "Perhaps the three of us could get together."

"Done, Cliff," Andre said. He sounded excited by the idea. "My pleasure."

· *Thank the gods for Andre,* Cliff thought. *He's going to make this easy for me.*

Less than forty-eight hours later, Cliff and Andre hunched together over a little table at a sidewalk café near the Hotel Sevilla, where Andre was staying.

"I saw enough firepower at the presidential palace to take Fort Knox," Cliff said. "Are you sure we don't need an appointment?"

Andre Martinez winked at him over the rim of his coffee cup. "Do not worry, my friend. Diego knows we come sometime this morning." He smiled. "Cuban time."

Cliff returned the smile, thinking that Andre had used New York time to get here so quickly. He took another swallow of his tarry Cuban coffee and tried to calm down. He eyed the colorful streams of people that eddied around them. Cubans of all ages hurried about, chattering away and gesturing broadly, paying little attention to the teams of U.S. Army Rangers who patrolled everywhere. An occasional transport or Humvee whined slowly down the street, parting the crowds like a shark in a school of fish.

The bustling scene did little to calm Cliff's nerves. But the gregarious and charming Andre seemed to be in his element. He was all smiles this morning. He grinned and nodded every time Cliff offered him another crumb about his reasons for being in Havana. Cliff chose his words carefully so that his involvement in recent events would not be misunderstood.

Cliff could count the people he really trusted on the fingers of one hand. Andre was one of them. But he couldn't be too careful now. Andre wasn't your average backstreet lawyer. Raised in

Mexico, the son of an important governor, a firsthand witness to the crapshoot of politics. But not the best scholar in the world. The black sheep of the family. Born in California, so he was also a U.S. citizen. That and a few pulled strings had gained him entry to a prestigious law school and the rich life of high-end lawyering, not to mention quite a few fat business deals. Above all Andre was a shrewd businessman who could run with some of the bigger dogs anywhere in the world if he wanted to. He was multicultural, multilingual, and sophisticated. And he was one of the few legal beagles that Cliff had called upon repeatedly over the years whose talents he truly respected.

"You worry too much, Cliff," Andre said, stirring his coffee. "I will introduce you to Diego. You two will be *muy simpáticos*. This I know." His brown eyes twinkled.

Cliff braved a tight smile. "I hope so, Andre. I sure hope so."

They rode to the presidential palace in a cab that Cliff guessed to be a '54 Buick. At the main gate Cliff kept his mouth shut and let Andre charm the U.S. Marine Corps guard, who finally made a call on his cell phone. Moments later, the combat-uniformed guard saluted them smartly and waved them robotically into the compound.

Cliff took in all the ornate Spanish colonial architecture as if in one breath, and then he felt breathless. The glories of the past seemed to blend uneasily with the realities of the present. Armed sentries and security cameras intruded everywhere in the postcard scene of the capitol of Cuba. As they marched to the main entrance, Andre explained that the new president occupied Castro's old office for now, assuming that it was the safest place in Havana.

Inside, after they passed muster at the makeshift command post, a dark-suited staffer wearing a discreet earphone showed them to the presidential suite. When the Marine guards let them in, Diego Perez rose from his oversized, deflated leather chair and greeted them. He was tall and slender, with movie star good looks. His black hair fell in a comma over his swarthy forehead, and his mustache was razored into a perfect line. Cliff noted his pricey tailored suit and his fancy cowboy boots.

Andre and the president shook hands, embraced, and exchanged cheek kisses. Perez beamed at his old friend, his eyes dancing with good humor and affection.

Andre made the introductions. Cliff shook hands with Perez.

"Your fame precedes you," the president said, obviously assessing Cliff. "And you bring impeccable credentials." He tipped his head toward Andre. "Most important, you come with a high personal endorsement."

"Even I am impressed," Andre said.

Perez chuckled and invited them to sit down. When he had settled behind his desk, he eyed each of them in turn and smiled. "Destiny unites us here, gentlemen."

Andre nodded. "This is more than we could have hoped for, Diego."

"Yes, I know this in my heart, Andre." He looked down at his carefully manicured hands and frowned in thought. "Never we could guess it would pass in this way. Always we thought Castro would die—how do you say?—a 'natural' death, which maybe is never."

Andre chuckled. "The spotlight shines on Cuba now, no?"

"*Sí, es verdad.* It shines very bright." He glanced out the window and seemed to get lost in the rhythm of wind-blown palm fronds. "Now begins the real work. The path is long, but we must begin at some place."

"*Dios mío!*" Andre said. "I am so content to see you again, my friend." Andre gazed at the high, ornate ceiling and then swung his arms to include the whole room. "Who could imagine it would be within these walls? Who could have guessed that you, my dear friend, would sit in just that chair, so well worn by someone so important, now gone forever?"

Perez lifted his hands, palms forward, and shook his head.

"Yes, yes, Diego. You deserve this honor. You have labored long for your people here when you could have had so much more in the States."

Perez nodded. "Yes, a long time. More than fifteen years since I closed the practice in Miami. But I have no regrets."

"I practice in three countries and six U.S. states," Andre said, "and I have made embarrassing amounts of money. So one could say that I have no regrets as well." He looked at Perez with a straight face, and then both men burst into laughter.

Andre threw his hands into the air and said, "But look. Now I have something rare—a true chance to make something important during a critical moment in Cuba's history." He smiled rakishly and added, "As my late mother would say, God bless her, 'Better late than never,' eh?"

They laughed again.

Cliff took the opening. "Andre's right, Mr. President. It's an honor to be in your position. A calling. You'll touch many people with your positive leadership, even if it is only temporary."

"Perhaps I run for office myself," Perez said, smiling. "Or join a ticket with another."

"Why not?" Cliff said.

"Yes, my friend," Andre said. "You can create prosperity and many new opportunities for your people. No one will forget." Andre clamped a big, warm hand onto Cliff's forearm. "This man who comes to see you today can help to make these things happen."

"Yes, so I understand," the president said. "You are well connected, Mr. Blackwell, so I don't doubt it. May I call you Cliff?" He made the word sound like Cleef.

"Yes, by all means."

"And you may call me Diego." He rose from his chair and gestured toward the door. "I wish to show you the gardens."

Cliff and Andre followed the president through the double doors and onto the gravel path of the courtyard. Lush and green with tropical plantings, here was a private retreat right in the middle of the capitol compound, where the president could enjoy the outdoors and the security to hold casual, private meetings.

Perez strolled slowly, his hands clasped behind his back, glancing occasionally at the cloudless blue sky. They matched his pace. Finally he said, "Recently I had a meeting of great interest. A Mr. Witherspoon came to see me." He looked at Cliff. "He told me that you are instrumental to the U.S. government in some very top-secret business."

Andre glanced at Cliff, his eyes alight with surprise and respect.

Cliff winked. "I hope you won't hold that against me, Diego."

Perez stopped and smiled at Cliff. "You make the joke, my friend, but I know that you are a serious and honorable man. And a powerful one."

Andre puckered his lips and shook his head.

"You both must know that I would not stand on this spot today except for the U.S. government. They appointed me." Perez turned and led them down a path bordered by explosions of floral beauty. "They did that, I must conclude, only after careful consideration of my personal history, my political views, my vision for the future of Cuba, and my cooperation." He approached a life-sized equestrian statue of some obscure, dead statesman, leaned against it, and addressed Andre. "Their first point of business concerned your Mr. Blackwell here and his group of investors. They have proposed certain financial arrangements that would benefit everyone. Great sums of money are involved." He looked at Cliff. "Is that not correct, Cliff?"

"That's right, Diego."

"Come. Let us sit for a while." Perez turned and headed for two ornate stone benches that were all but hidden in an arbor that was ablaze with scarlet bougainvillea.

"This I wish to hear," Andre said.

"Be patient, my friend, and you will hear everything. That must be part of the bargain. Perhaps Cliff will be kind enough to enlighten both of us further, yes? I am—how do you say?—all ears. Because what I have heard so far pleases me very much."

Cliff pocketed his sat phone, returned to the table, and apologized for the interruption with a crooked smile.

"Let me guess," Victoria said. "Sydney Russo?"

"Bingo. He couldn't wait to hear about my meeting with the president. He's thrilled. And he's excited about a deal he and Tony made today. Tentative, but it's to buy the Hotel Riviera. They also found some large tracts of land on Varadero."

"That was fast."

"Sydney doesn't waste time. They're nosing around some other important properties, too. Could be a good time to invest."

Victoria arched an elegant eyebrow. "Uh-huh. I know what you're thinking."

Cliff grinned, trying to look casual. "Yeah, well I told him I might want to go in with them on a couple of things."

"Really. I thought you were done with the gaming industry."

"Well . . ."

"Never mind. Tell me more about your meeting and your impressions of the new president."

Cliff gave her the blow-by-blow as they relaxed at their open-air table, sitting just out of the mid-afternoon sun. They had stopped for a drink here after a long walk around Old Havana, where they took in all the crumbling colonial architecture, with its graceful wrought ironwork, weathered stone, and bright primary colors applied like brave gestures of faith and hope across a canvas of neglect and despair.

"Bottom line, it looks like we'll lock in a monopoly deal," Cliff said, squinting across the sunny plaza. Tides of humanity filtered in and out of the many small bars and cafés. Brassy jazz music floated on the air. Nearby, four old gentlemen in black berets hunched over a small, crippled table, slapping down dominoes as if the percussion was as important as the dots on the tiles.

Victoria produced a mischievous smile. "A monopoly deal, huh? So what are they using for money?"

"What do you think?"

They both laughed.

Then he took her hand, lowered his head, and said, "One thing bothers me, I have to admit."

"What's that?"

"Bringing that super yacht down here." He shook his head. "Poverty's everywhere. Makes me feel a little embarrassed."

"I know. It's about as subtle as the *Queen Mary*. People must wonder what it's doing here."

"Yeah, and of course I had to name the damn thing *Havana Royale*. Like I'm here for the kill."

"Well, aren't you, Cliff?"

He sighed. "I guess you're right." He fingered the diamond-studded ring on her right hand, the one he had bought for her in Monte Carlo. "I've been thinking about a lot of things, Vic. Sometimes I don't think I deserve all this, including you. Then I remind myself how hard it was clawing my way to the top, blah, blah, blah. Chatter like that."

Victoria put a hand on his forearm and said, "Fortunately there's some kind of balance in the universe. You're part of it all, and you're right where you're supposed to be."

He looked into her soft eyes, considering her words, but still felt lousy.

"You're not a bad guy, Cliff. Overly ambitious, maybe, but not a bad guy."

"I know I can be a self-absorbed jerk sometimes."

"Shhh, Cliff." She squeezed his arm with both hands. "You may be a little obsessive-compulsive sometimes, but you aren't greedy. I don't care what you say."

"But I—"

She placed her fingers on his lips. "That's enough, Cliff."

"But—"

"No!" Her eyes sparked emerald fire. After a moment she smiled at him fondly and withdrew her hands. "You're too good a man to punish yourself like this. Promise me that you'll put these thoughts away for good."

Something in Victoria's voice and in her eyes broke the spell of gloom. Cliff shook his head and sighed deeply. "Okay, Vic. I promise."

"Good. Thank you very much. Now let me give you something else to think about."

Cliff smiled and nodded, feeling grateful for this woman. "Shoot."

"I have some ideas about that international children's education fund you talked about. Remember?"

"Of course, but I'm surprised that you do."

She stuck out her tongue at him. "I happen to recall every detail of our early days in Nassau, Mr. Smart-Ass."

"Oh, yeah? And?"

"I want to do it," she said. "It's a . . . a noble project."

Cliff leaned back in his chair and stretched, recalling what she had said about balance. Did she think the children's fund would even the scale against the dirty business he had been involved in lately—and the dirtier money he'd make from it eventually? Maybe. Should he bring that up now? Probably not. Why ruin the mood?

The busy plaza looked even brighter and more colorful now somehow. Raucous Latin dance music had replaced the jazz. "I'm glad you feel that way, Vic. And you're the perfect person to head it up. Who else could get a ton of money out of a jerk like me?"

She pursed her lips and whipped a napkin at his face, and then they both laughed. The afternoon sun had crawled across the cracked sidewalk and set fire to her platinum mane, morphing her into an icon of vibrant youth and beauty. Maybe he didn't deserve her or the *Havana Royale* or the money. But he hoped to God that this moment wouldn't end up as just a frozen memory, like a photograph hiding in a drawer.

11

Caviar and Vodka

CLIFF NOSED HIS BRITISH-MADE TVR SPORTS CAR through the narrow streets of Old Havana with care, enjoying the bright morning sunshine of a mid-February day. He was headed to the Hotel Riviera in the Vedado sector to meet with Sydney Russo, who had become something of a permanent resident of the place. Cliff had awakened that morning buoyed by a sense of being in full swing with his colleagues, of building something special in this new and democratic country. The time was ripe to connect with Russo again. A couple of critical meetings with important hotel operators were on the agenda today. Cliff thought his participation could add some fuel to the fire. And anyway, he loved this stuff.

Now that a lot of the dust had settled, he thought the future looked promising, to say the least. Law and order reigned, more or less, and the streets felt relatively safe now. Victoria had also begun to throw herself into life again, which made him feel good. She had held up bravely during the rough going, and now she was back in the game, immersing herself in the Cuban culture and making plans. How good it felt, he thought, to have a partner who could grasp the unique possibilities of these volatile circumstances. On the downside, a niggling sense of dread still dogged his thoughts. So much could still go so terribly wrong. But for now he fought to hold that feeling at bay, keep it to himself.

That was easier to do on a sun-drenched day like this. The Vedado neighborhood hummed with the health of a normal, business-as-usual morning in the streets. You had to give the Cuban people credit. They certainly could roll with the punches.

Cliff checked his map of Havana again, turned right at the next corner, and soon spotted his destination. The Riviera was a modern, glass and concrete high-rise that towered over a wide, tree-lined boulevard in front and a wide stretch of beach behind. He turned his car over to the valet and strolled inside.

The place looked like Miami in the '50s, with touches of South Beach art deco, and it still wore the proud luster of better times. A kid with Valentino good looks called Russo's room from the front desk and then directed Cliff to a bank of elevators.

"Penthouse, sir. Twenty-first floor," he said in thickly accented English.

A bell captain accompanied Cliff to the elevator and used a master key to access the special floor. The guy's immaculate uniform made him look more like the captain of a cruise ship. He accompanied Cliff to the top, discreetly palmed his tip, and bid him a cheerful good day.

The door to the suite was just off the elevator lobby, and it was open, with Russo leaning against the jamb. He looked older than usual, and painfully thin.

"The penthouse, huh, Sydney?"

The old man embraced him and kissed him on both cheeks. "Come in and get a loada this view. The ocean forever, and off that way, Old Havana. It keeps me from forgetting where I am."

Cliff admired the spacious interior and its expensive but venerable furnishings. Not bad in a country where the accommodations had long been in decline. Russo was right about the view. "So how's business, Sydney?"

"Lotsa meetings, Cliff." He checked his watch. "Got another one in an hour."

"Good. I'd like to tag along, if you don't mind." He grinned. "Gets me off the boat."

"Anytime you want," Russo said, returning the smile. "Have a seat."

Cliff chose an upholstered armchair and said, "I think the sooner the properties are tied up, the better."

"Absolutely," Sydney agreed. "Good news is the sellers seem flexible. Say, you want I should call room service?"

Cliff declined.

The old man eased himself onto the couch and said, "I've been looking at some real beauties. This place, for example." He swept a hand through the air. "And the Hotel Nacional, the Capri, and . . ."

For a moment Russo had seemed to regain his youthful facade, but now he wore a lost expression. He brought his floating hand to his forehead and rubbed it. "Of course," he said finally. "How could I forget? The Copacabana."

Cliff wondered if Sydney's mental faculties were holding up in all this excitement. That concerned him. "Good properties," he said, watching his old friend closely. "What about the Hotel Sevilla?"

"Still trying to get an appointment with the big wheels."

"These four- and five-star places can be turned into money machines fast."

Sydney got up stiffly, tottered to the floor-to-ceiling windows, and stood there looking out. "I know. Instant cash flow."

Cliff joined Russo and gazed at the distant sprawl of Old Havana. The antique Spanish architecture blazed in the yellow morning sunlight—a perfect picture from this distance that revealed none of the extensive decay that overwhelmed anyone who stood in those narrow streets. Russo seemed to be mesmerized by the scene.

Cliff said, "Don't forget that vacant land on Varadero."

"Our meetings have gone well," Russo said, as if he hadn't heard. "The fellas we're meeting today have a lot of clout."

"I'm glad to be in on it."

"They're being cautious."

Cliff studied Russo's face, wondering what was happening behind those old eyes. "Sydney, you stole that parcel we looked at there together." He touched his arm. "For the Palace of Fortune? A perfect spot."

Russo looked at Cliff and shrugged. "Sure, we can hardly lose. We got too much time in the business." He nodded toward the cityscape. "And in Cuba. And now you got us this ten-year monopoly."

Cliff felt relieved to see that the old fellow was indeed plugged in. "The president was very cooperative," he said.

"This'll kick Wall Street in the ass."

That was the old Sydney. "And with Tony at the wheel," Cliff said, "this is just the beginning."

"Vegas will be green with envy. Now we just need a little luck."

"Conserve the cash," Cliff said, stabbing the air with a finger.

Russo gave him a long and appraising look. "Thank you, Clifford."

"For what?"

"Everything. Including your little offshore bank. Came in handy for a few sensitive transactions."

Cliff smiled.

"Maybe we should discuss you handling all our offshore stuff again."

Cliff bit his lip, images of the past flashing in his mind. "Maybe, Sydney. We can talk about it sometime."

Russo nodded and gazed out the window again. "Okay, Cliff. Good. Things haven't been the same since the days of T.H.E."

"I'm flattered," Cliff said, then glanced at his watch. "We should get going. Reminisce any more and we'll miss that meeting."

* * *

Ivan Penkovsky squinted into the glare of the window beside his first-class seat as the big Aeroflot jet made its approach to Miami International Airport. Below him a seemingly endless clutter of beachfront high-rises reflected the late-afternoon sun. The long flights from Moscow and London had been tiresome, but he was revived by the sight of this sun-kissed city. The land of opportunity. He smiled when he thought how easy it was to move around the world anonymously and unquestioned, even here. Stupid Americans. They thought their borders were more secure these days. And yet here he was, a fox with a phony EU passport, entering the henhouse. The underpaid Customs and security drones would never recognize him as the *pakhan*, or Russian godfather, as Interpol and the CIA had labeled him, of the fastest-growing, most dangerous crime organization in the world. Nothing would stop him from setting his newest plan in motion.

When he had cleared Customs and retrieved his bags, Penkovsky proceeded to the hotel located within the terminal complex and checked in. A few minutes later he dumped his baggage in the privacy of his own room and looked around with distaste. *What a country*, he thought. Airplane to terminal to hotel room without even stepping outside or feeling one ray of Miami's generous sunshine. And the room had no windows, so travelers could "visit" Miami, stay overnight, and depart without even seeing it.

No matter. He had other concerns. He quickly showered and changed into a Hugo Boss suit, rode the elevator back to the lobby level, and strode into the bustle of traffic outside. Dying sunlight filled the smoky concrete canyon between the main terminal and the parking garages. He bulldozed through a family of Japanese tourists and grabbed the next cab in line.

"Where to?" the Cuban cabbie said.

"Pinky's."

The driver nodded and got going. They merged into the flow

of traffic and headed toward North Federal Highway, an area littered with bars and nightclubs. Penkovsky ignored the sights of this gritty side of Miami, with its anemic palm trees and strip malls, and thought about the man he was going to meet—Boris Forostenko, the local kingpin of the *grooperovka*, better known in the States as the Russian Mafia.

Boris "Pinky" Forostenko had built a crime organization of nearly a thousand street criminals, mostly of Russian descent— the largest such mob in the U.S. Their activities included brokering weapons, laundering money, smuggling narcotics from Latin America, dealing drugs on the streets, extortion, protection, gambling, and prostitution. They also traded in plutonium, enriched uranium, and chemicals for bombs and weapons.

Even better, Forostenko had established new channels for brokering some heavy stuff, from RPGs and artillery to anti-aircraft missiles, helicopters, and attack jets—and even an occasional submarine or warship. With the dismantling of the USSR and the economic chaos of the 1990s, supply was readily accessible. Available, that is, with lots of *kapusta*, or "cabbage" in American slang, paid to the appropriate syndicate in Russia and the military personnel guarding it.

Penkovsky was pleased with the progress they had made here. He was even more pleased with Forostenko's prized possession—a Soviet-era-built, Foxtrot-class attack submarine, which he had acquired for the heavily discounted price of six million greenbacks wired into an offshore bank account. The "Pink Sub" had been refitted as an oceanographic-research vessel, a deceptive disguise for Forostenko's drug operation, which transported forty tons of cocaine at a time from Central America to offshore transshipment points destined for Florida, the Gulf coast, and Southern California.

Penkovsky knew that Forostenko's organization was also muscling into Seminole Indian casinos, horse racing, theme parks, hotels, on-line gaming, Internet pornography, banking, finance, and the securities brokerage business. Besides all that, Redfellas were infiltrating other cities throughout the U.S.

The taxi swerved suddenly and slammed to a stop near the covered entrance of a one-story, concrete-block building. Pink neon strobed the interior of the cab and the crushed-shell parking lot. Penkovsky paid the fare, skipped the tip, and climbed out. The air had grown much cooler, but it was still heavy on vehicle emissions.

When he entered the club he had to stop and adjust himself to the gloom and the abrupt change of atmosphere. The club was nearly deserted, but it thrummed with a hidden life that seemed ready to burst. He backed into an alcove and scanned the main room. Mirrored walls, black lights, and a scatter of cheap tables and chairs. A bar at the far end and a horseshoe-shaped stage in the middle. Finally he spotted Forostenko sitting at a private table in a glassed-in booth. As usual, the big man had planted himself unobtrusively where he could talk privately and yet keep a sharp eye on all the action in his strip joint. A chesty brunette with big hair crowded him on the left, while his right-hand man, Sergei "The Count" Yezhov, maintained a more discreet distance where he belonged, on Forostenko's right.

Penkovsky wasn't surprised to see the Count, who was a small man. Damn near a midget, really, less than three feet tall. He'd become a trusted soldier of Forostenko's years before in Moscow, before Penkovsky moved with his own team to Budapest, the fast-growing haven for Russian mob leaders. The Hungarian capital was also becoming the new crossroads between Russia and Eastern Europe. That was why Penkovsky lived there now as an absentee crime don.

Penkovsky regarded Sergei Yezhov with distaste. The little man, also known facetiously as "the count that doesn't count," looked like a circus freak, he thought, but he had his uses. He had come from a long line of true Russian counts during the pre-Soviet era. He would have inherited that honor if his father hadn't been stripped of the title—the price of embarrassing the wrong politicos during a shift of power.

Despite his appearance, the Count had one special talent that Penkovsky appreciated. He could garrote a man's head from his body like snipping the stem of a rose. He was known to be a stealthy and effective assassin, and his version of the Italian rope trick was widely admired. Penkovsky smiled just thinking about that. Yes, the little prick could be useful indeed. He had plans for him.

Penkovsky lumbered across the room through the flashing lights and the heavy thud of rock music. A few more customers had arrived, and two leggy dancers dressed only in G-strings worked the pole onstage listlessly. As if he had radar, Forostenko looked up and noted his approach.

Penkovsky entered the private booth and smiled.

"Outta here, you two," Forostenko said, snapping at his comrades without greeting Penkovsky.

The Count jumped to his feet, gave his boss a sharp nod, and scuttled away, looking rejected. Miss Boob Job stood reluctantly, her scarlet lower lip thrust at Forostenko. The big man rocked his head sympathetically and said, "Is hokay. You go now." He slipped his hairy mitt up the back of her tight miniskirt. "If you good, honey doll, you get big raise." He handed her a key. "Here, go to cooler and get a couple big jars of caviar for me and my friend here."

"No caviar for me, Boris," Penkovsky said. He had always made it a point not to call this man Pinky. Too chummy. You had to keep some distance with underlings.

Forostenko acknowledged that order with a nod, then looked at the girl. "Also get me spoon. And bring couple vodka on rocks." She heaved a sigh and trotted off on six-inch spikes.

Forostenko hoisted his bulk upright and clasped Penkovsky in a bear hug. "Ivan!" he said. "It has been too long."

"Boris," Penkovsky said, pushing his host away. "You look good."

"Thank you, Ivan. You know, I'm watching my waistline." He

patted his considerable paunch, grinning. "New girlfriend."

"I see that. Can I sit the fuck down now?"

Forostenko apologized, then started to babble. Nervously, Penkovsky thought. The babe returned with a tray and served the food and drinks. "Anything else, fellas?"

Penkovsky thought longingly of the food he liked best in the world. "Quail eggs?"

"Swimming in sake," Forostenko said proudly.

Penkovsky beamed at Forostenko and lifted his glass. "Comrade!"

Forostenko puffed up with pleasure and told the girl, "Get for my friend, honey doll. Chop-chop." She made a face and took off.

Penkovsky raised his glass again and declared, "To our good health. Everything else we can buy."

Before long Penkovsky had his quail eggs and another glass of vodka. Forostenko shoveled Beluga caviar into his mouth right from the jar. Some of it stayed behind on his mustache and beard. When he was finished eating, Penkovsky fired up a Papirosi, sucked in the smoke from the Russian and Turkish tobacco, and sighed, letting the smoke drift out slowly. The refreshments had lightened his mood.

"Boris," he said, "I have a job for you."

Forostenko squinted at him and grunted. The crowd had grown, and so had the noise. Four dancers worked the stage now amid bright strobe lights.

Penkovsky leaned close to his man. "Moscow wants to take out the new Cuban president. Right after the election."

"Why?" Forostenko said. "To fuck the Americans?"

Penkovsky nodded. "Leverage. To get those *ublyudoki* bastards in Washington by the balls. The temporary Cuban president just took office, and so did the new U.S. president, Van Buren. Things are not so stable. We can catch them all asleep."

"Sounds risky."

"Everything we do, Boris, is risky." He shot a look over both shoulders and said, "Listen, the Russian economy is a wreck. Moscow doesn't have the money they need. You know that. They need a quick fix. So we rub out the new spic president. That will help, and we will make many new friends."

"The Chinese probably plan to do this, too."

"Those *otmorozheni!*" Penkovsky banged his fist on the table. "We will beat them to it."

Forostenko shrugged and looked down. "Hokay, hokay, I hear you say this, but—"

"Boris. Don't be a *duraki*. This is no time to be stupid. We need more clout in Moscow."

"I understand, comrade."

Penkovsky raised his hands. "Look at the big picture, Boris. Everybody is fighting for position now. A new international arms race has begun. We don't want to be losers, do we?"

"No, Ivan."

"Since the beginning of January we have been sending arms and troops to Cuba. Right under their noses." He sneered. "Hidden in shiploads of rice. We trade rice for drugs, tax free, to replace the supplies they lost in the last hurricane."

Forostenko's left eye twitched the way it always did when he was excited. "Very clever, comrade."

Penkovsky splayed his hands on the table. "We are spreading it out. The shipments arrive weeks apart. See, they think they stopped the real threat—China. Now they are all loose and easy and don't expect another surprise."

"So what is your plan, Ivan?"

He leaned toward Forostenko, into his fishy caviar breath. "We will use your submarine. Separate from the military operation. Drop off our man in the night. Bang, and then we pick him up later." He smiled. "No problem."

"I suppose you have someone in mind to do this thing?"

Penkovsky nodded and smiled again. "The perfect man. A

master of disguise and an expert with explosives."

Forostenko's eye twitched. "A simple plan. But very risky."

The brunette reappeared at their table. "How are you fellas doing?"

"Just bring the bottle, honey doll," Forostenko said and shooed her away. He turned to Penkovsky. "How do we take control after the president is whacked?"

"The military will be there and ready to move. At the same time, the big nuclear submarine comes, and after that a whole fleet of Russian ships." He jabbed his finger into Forostenko's meaty arm. "We will force the Americans' hand."

"You seem very sure about this."

Penkovsky nodded. "We will also organize some ugly demonstrations. That will make our point clear. It will send shock waves around the world. Believe me, Boris, they will give in."

Forostenko shook his head, looking uncertain.

"Do not worry, Boris. If we do our job, Moscow will win this little war."

"How? Mother Russia can't even fight a war. How can we win one?"

Penkovsky opened his mouth, then closed it again, letting Forostenko continue.

"Russia's military arsenal is old, Ivan, and much of it cannot be repaired. No money! We could not defeat the Afghans or the Chechens. How can we face the Americans?"

Miss Boobs returned with a new bottle of vodka in a bucket of ice and clean glasses. Penkovsky scowled and motioned for her to get lost.

"Boris, you are right. It is not like the old days. But we still have plenty of muscle. And we still have the bomb. We take over Cuba, the Americans will back off. Van Buren has no balls. He knows if they don't, we will blast them off the fucking planet. As for financing—" He swallowed half of his glass of vodka. "Do not worry. We have a backer."

Forostenko squinted at him. "A backer?"

"Someone who will pay for the whole goddamn thing."

"Who has such money?"

"The Gold Man."

Forostenko nodded slowly. "I have heard of this man, but I thought it may be just a story."

"He is very real, I assure you. He is a Belgian, educated in Europe, lives in South Africa. His family has been in the commodities business for generations. And he controls most of the gold market."

"A very powerful man, I do not doubt. But can he be trusted?"

Penkovsky shrugged. "He is a crazy bastard." He told Forostenko about the Gold Man's game hunts. Then he wondered if he had said too much. Maybe it was the vodka. "But it is no matter if he is a little fucked in the head. We can manipulate him. He also hates the United States with a great passion. He has been dreaming about destroying this big ugly beast for years."

Forostenko knocked back his whole glass of vodka, banged the glass onto the table, and swiped an arm across his mouth. "The plan is too ambitious, Ivan."

"The World Trade Center was too ambitious."

Forostenko bobbed his shaggy head thoughtfully. "I see that you have already made up your mind. Hokay. Maybe I can help. But in the end we could all be dead."

"That is why we will not fail, Boris." Penkovsky polished off the rest of his drink and handed over a slip of paper. "My number at the hotel. Call me tomorrow. We will go over the details. And I want some ideas from you."

Penkovsky didn't wait for a response. He muttered a curt good-bye, slipped out of the booth, and pushed through the front door into the swarming Miami night.

12

Election Day

"THIS PLACE IS MAGNIFICENT, CLIFF," VICTORIA SAID, gazing around. "Reminds me of Spain."

"It's a fine example of a real turn-of-the-century luxury hotel. A mixture of Spanish and Moorish architecture."

"Very exotic," she said, smiling. "And the view from up here is really something."

Cliff knew that Victoria would appreciate the Hotel Sevilla and having lunch in the Roof Garden Restaurant. Sharing it all with her made him feel even better than he had expected on this special day—election day in Cuba, the first of April. The streets below them were clogged with people, blaring bands, vendors, and raucous, ragged parades. The carnival atmosphere made him wonder why he had been so edgy for the past six weeks. Those damn premonitions. Would he always be plagued with the fear that his carefully constructed world would collapse like a house of cards at any time? Not today, certainly. The tide of history had changed in Cuba. Nothing could stop it now.

He returned his gaze to Victoria. She was a vision in white today, like a photo in *Vogue*, only better. She had breasts.

"I hope Andre can join us," she said, derailing that train of thought.

"He said he'd try. But I know he has meetings all day."

"Maybe he can tell us more about the election returns."

"Probably. But I think our man Ernesto Vivo and his New Line Democratic party will take it by a landslide. The Socialist Party candidate looked like a beaten man already on TV this morning."

A young male waiter dressed in starched black and white approached their table, moving with the practiced aplomb of a bullfighter. He greeted them formally and presented their menus with a flourish. They ordered drinks, then made small talk while they studied the luncheon selections.

Cliff put his menu aside and leaned across the table. "I didn't say anything before, but last evening I had an interesting conversation with Witherspoon."

Victoria's eyes lit up. "Really? Why didn't you tell me?"

He dodged the question with a shrug and said, "Congress has dropped the investigation into Operation Smoke-Out."

"Oh, thank God, Cliff. What a relief."

"That's for sure."

"Why the sudden change?" She took a baguette and broke it over her bread plate.

"They started by focusing on the three Italian-Americans from Chicago," he said, accepting a piece of bread from her. "But then they received some convincing counterintelligence from Cuba. They decided that the Italians had been hired by the Cuban military, in—and get this—'a cheap attempt to cloak their own activities.'"

"Wow. How's that for ironic?"

"Convenient, too, since none of the three Mob guys made it back."

"A cover-up?"

"Of course. Nobody wants a Cubagate."

Victoria put down her bread. "That's too much."

"Ah, the machinations of politics," he said, chuckling. Then he remembered Joey Corsiglia, waiting there on that damn corporate jet and enjoying a highball, thinking he was home free.

Two beaming young women arrived with their lunch—plates generously heaped with hearty Cuban fare, elegantly presented. They both dug in.

"I'm really glad we came out today, Vic."

"Same here," she said. "I really enjoyed walking around, seeing all those happy people. Made me feel, you know, part of history in the making. And I love being with you, Cliff."

"Not always," he said.

Her expression turned serious. "You aren't the only one to blame, Cliff. I know I can be difficult sometimes, and I'm sorry for that." She offered him a tentative smile.

He touched her cheek. "Everything considered, I think you've done quite well. Don't worry about it."

Cliff steered the conversation into calmer waters as they returned to their meal. A few minutes later, Andre Martinez bustled to their table, bringing an air of tension and concern with him.

He apologized for interrupting their lunch and spread his arms in a helpless gesture. "But here I am, at last."

Cliff waved off the apology with a smile, shook Andre's hand, and offered him a seat.

"No, no, thank you so much," Andre said. "I had a long meeting, and it turned into lunch."

"Have a drink, at least," Cliff said. "We're almost finished."

Andre smiled broadly and sat next to Cliff. When he had caught his breath, he said, "It looks like Vivo will be the new president."

"Gosh, that's great news," Victoria said.

Cliff was pleased to hear this. "Is it a sure thing?"

Andre heaved a sigh. "Not yet, but I think it is close. He has fifty-nine percent already."

Cliff thumped his friend's meaty shoulder. "Excellent! That means Diego is the new vice president. He must be feeling great."

"Of course," Andre said. "This is good news for him, for Cuba, and for the world."

The balletic waiter returned and took Andre's order for mineral water. When he was gone Andre said, "So how is business going for you, Cliff?"

"Can't complain."

"I see that the corporation's stock is healthy."

Cliff nodded. "We just made our first public offering. The price went through the roof." He pushed his plate away and patted his lips with a linen napkin. "I think the investors trusted the polls about the New Line Party winning the election. And they wanted to get into Cuba before the world knew that Vivo was in."

Victoria said, "The stock went from twenty-four dollars a share to forty-three fifty. All in one day."

Andre whistled quietly. "Impressive."

"Of course," Cliff said, "it went back down, but it's been holding steady at around thirty-three to thirty-six."

"You should be proud of yourself, Cliff," Andre said.

"We're pleased."

The waiter brought Andre's drink.

"The stock announcement had a lot of sizzle, thanks to Vic's father," Cliff said.

"And Tony," Victoria added. "He's a real ham."

"Ham?" Andre asked. "What does it mean?"

"Tony's a real showman," she said. "Loves the spotlight."

"Ah, yes."

"Wall Street liked what they saw," Cliff said. "A strong market helps, too."

Andre took a long drink of the bubbly water. "What about the hotels?"

"Tony and Sydney have already acquired some of the choicest four- and five-star hotels here. And they're working on this one."

Andre pursed his lips and nodded with obvious respect. "This one, eh?"

"Yes, and the Riv, the Nacional, and Sydney's favorite, the Copacabana."

"Incredible."

"They've already starting converting some to gaming properties," Cliff said.

Victoria refolded her napkin and said, "And they bought a great piece of vacant land on Varadero to build the Palace of Fortune. When it's done it'll be the biggest gaming resort in the world."

Andre gave Cliff a wry smile. "You have been very busy, my friend."

Cliff winked at him. "We also grabbed some other choice places on Veradero. It'll be a strip to rival Vegas one of these days."

"Perhaps I could offer you my services."

"Why not? I'll get you some Reg 'S' stock you can put offshore. Maybe some free-trading, too."

"Wonderful, Cliff. Thank you."

Victoria said, "How about joining us for the groundbreaking ceremony for the Palace on April fifth?"

"How time is flying," Andre said. "Of course. I would be honored."

"Sydney's doing a great job," Cliff said. "Sometimes he amazes me. With all the investor interest and the shares holding strong like they are, he's enticed nearly every seller to accept a bundle of stock and nearly nothing in the way of cash."

"How is their credit?"

"Luckily, that just doubled. Wall Street analysts have praised the company, and credit institutions gave it their highest ratings."

Andre took another pull at his mineral water. "Looks like your people are all set to make a killing."

"We hope so. It's been a challenge getting this far. But thank God for the peace and relative stability around here. That's helped immensely."

Victoria touched Andre's hand. "So what have you been up to lately?"

Andre flashed his bright Latino smile and filled their ears for ten minutes with tales of his exploits in Havana.

When Victoria excused herself to powder her nose, Andre leaned close to Cliff. "Listen," he said, glancing around. "I didn't want Victoria to hear this."

"Hear what, Andre?" A warning signal sounded in Cliff's head.

"The president of this hotel turned up dead this morning."

Cliff swallowed hard. "Are you suggesting what I think you are?"

"I am not saying anything. But it was clearly murder. And so far the news is, well, mostly secret."

"And they want it to stay that way, right?"

Andre nodded.

Cliff massaged his chin and thought about that for a while. Then he thanked Andre for the tip.

"I thought you should know, Cliff. This won't reflect well on what you are trying to accomplish here."

"You think somebody didn't like the guy's plans, his dealing with us?" Another possibility had occurred to him, but he didn't want to mention it.

Andre examined him with his dark, liquid eyes, but didn't reply.

Victoria returned wearing a bright smile, then stopped short. Her smile faded. "Everything all right, fellas?"

Andre got to his feet and said, "Just fine, Victoria. But now you must excuse me. I have another appointment." He gave them a courtly bow and hurried away.

Victoria sat next to Cliff. "Is he all right?" she asked, her face darkened with concern.

Cliff pulled her close so she wouldn't see his face. He gazed out the window, his thoughts as dark and churning as the distant sea. "He's fine, Vic," he said. "Let's head back to the boat."

* * *

Later that afternoon, Roberts, the senior steward, glided into the main salon and told Cliff that he had a visitor—a Mr. Witherspoon. Cliff thumbed off the TV and asked Roberts to show him in.

The agent stepped into the whispery, cool dimness of the room moments later. "Get a load of this place!" he exclaimed as he glanced around with obvious appreciation. "Onassis would feel at home."

Cliff chuckled. "Thanks. I guess."

Roberts took their requests for iced tea.

"How about that election?" Cliff said. "Looks like Vivo's in."

"Oh, right," Witherspoon said. "Swell."

What kind of an answer was that? "Is something wrong, Don?"

Witherspoon's expression grew serious. "You won't believe it."

"Don't tell me. The Chinese are at it again."

Witherspoon shook his head and leaned forward on the couch. "No, Cliff. The Russians are coming."

"What?"

"We just heard about it today ourselves." The agent scrubbed his hands together and looked at the carpet. "A nuke sub is heading here."

Cliff gripped the arms of his chair. "Are you serious?"

"It could show up soon."

Shit, he was serious. "Does the president know? The U.S. president, I mean."

Witherspoon nodded wearily and ran one hand over his face. "He's probably in the war room right now with the Joint Chiefs of Staff."

Holy shit! How will I break this to Vic?

"You can bet they're planning some sort of military action. We're in DefCon One now, and so is Great Britain."

"Why are they involved?"

The steward returned, poured their drinks, and glided out.

Witherspoon took a quick sip of his drink. "Some MI6 agent stumbled across their activities. The prime minister took it so seriously that he called Chick himself."

"Called who?"

"Chick," Witherspoon said. "The president's nickname."

"Great," Cliff said. "I can't wait to tell Victoria the good news."

"What good news?" Victoria said as she entered the salon behind them.

Cliff glanced at Witherspoon, who gave him a bilious smile, then stood to greet Victoria.

She took the chair next to Cliff. "Well," she said, looking from one to the other, "what's up?"

Witherspoon cleared his throat and said, "I've got some classified info. It has to stay here in this room. You understand?"

She nodded, fixing him with a worried look.

He said, "The Russians are coming."

She gaped at both of them. "Are you trying to make a joke?"

Witherspoon shook his head and told her about the nuclear sub, speaking in a hushed voice.

Victoria turned her stricken face to Cliff.

"It's all right, Vic. They're not here yet."

"True," Witherspoon said. "But they could be here by tomorrow."

"Let's get out of here," Victoria said.

Witherspoon smiled indulgently and said, "That wouldn't be a smart move."

"Why not?"

"In a few hours we'll know the president's position on this, and . . ." He gestured helplessly. "Well, they'll seal off the island. Then send in the military."

Victoria jumped to her feet. "I don't give a damn about the president's position!"

Cliff thought she looked more upset than he'd ever seen her before.

She whirled on him. "Cliff? Are you just going to sit there?"

He gazed steadily into the dark pools of her eyes, his heart clenching at the sight of the panic there. "Probably best we wait to hear what the president says. We don't want to complicate the problem."

Now she looked hurt as well as angry. "You're doing it to me again."

"We don't have much time, Victoria," Witherspoon said quietly. "Let's just see what the president plans to do. We need more information. It'd be foolish to try to leave."

He stood up, eyed Cliff oddly, and started to leave. Then he turned back with a softer look in his eyes. "We should know more soon. Meanwhile, not a word to anyone, either of you."

Cliff stood. "All right, Don. But I'm counting on you. Keep us on top of this."

"I'll come by later," Witherspoon said, "as soon as I know more." He marched to the door, then looked back at Victoria. "It'll be all right."

She tossed her head, turned away, and folded her arms.

When the agent was gone, Cliff took her by the shoulders and tried to turn her into his arms, but she had become an ice carving.

"I feel sick," she said with disgust. "I think I'll take the chopper and leave."

"Don't do that, Vic. Please. I need you." Her body trembled under his hands.

She wrenched herself from his grip and fled the salon.

Wonderful, Cliff thought. *As if the Russians weren't bad enough.* Now he'd be sitting through a lonely dinner and an even lonelier night.

After an early dinner alone, as he had expected, Cliff called Sydney Russo at his hotel.

"Yeah? Who is it?" a gruff voice answered on the first ring.

"Cliff Blackwell. Who's this?"

"Hey, Blackwell, it's Johnnie Badalamente."

Cliff tensed. More bad news. "I need to speak to Sydney."

Badalamente grunted. "He's busy."

Anger flared in Cliff. "Don't give me that shit. Put him on the goddamned line."

"You better watch yourself," Badalamente mumbled.

Cliff listened to muffled sounds for what seemed like a long time before Russo picked up.

"Cliff, glad you called," he said. "I've got some business to discuss with you."

Friendly chatter, but something didn't feel right. "Sure thing, Sydney," he said, covering his simmering anger. "Glad you guys are busy."

"Hell, Cliff," Russo said, "it's going like gangbusters. Makes me wish I was forty years younger."

"Gangbusters" seemed like an odd choice of words for the old don. "I like your enthusiasm," Cliff told him.

"Say, Cliff," Russo said, his tone dropping like the temperature in a Chicago winter. "You don't sound so good. What's eatin' you?"

"I can't tell you over the phone."

"Oh, yeah? Are things as bad as you sound?"

The old man's still pretty sharp. "Could be," Cliff said. "Something that could put a stick in our spokes."

Russo sighed. "All right. I'm coming over. Right now okay?"

Cliff checked his watch. Nearly half past six. "How about eight-thirty?"

"Eight-thirty? You keeping me in suspense that long?"

"Vic doesn't feel well, Sydney. Anyway, by the time you get here, I should have either better or worse news."

Russo agreed, but he didn't sound happy about it.

"Oh, and Sydney?" Cliff said. "Be sure to come alone."

* * *

Cliff told the staff about his expected guest, then retreated to the quiet solitude of his study. He sat in a pool of soft light at his large cherrywood desk and treated himself to his first smoke of the day—a Cohiba. He meditated in the swirling smoke, letting his gaze come to rest on a model of the *Moonshine*, his authentic 1930s woody motorboat that he had once kept at his Lake Tahoe estate. It made him think about the great leaps he'd made over the years in personal achievement and financial success—and about the spectacular disasters he'd also suffered and yet somehow managed to weather.

Was disaster about to strike again? The darkness that grew in the pit of his being gave him an answer he didn't like. Everything had gone so well recently, in so many ways. But now, alone in the silence of his sanctuary, the darkness seemed to be closing in, and something sinister came along with it—something more than just a little bad luck, like a hiccup in the stock market. This time it felt more like death in the air.

Maybe the end would come as swiftly as his meteoric rise in the world. He tried to find some pleasure in accomplishing what had seemed impossible. It had cost him long, hard years of work and had required a lot of patience and guts, maybe more guts than he really had. But eventually the hard work and a relentless desire to endure in spite of extreme adversities had paid off. Handsomely. But now he was filled with conflicting emotions, and he felt strangely powerless, unable to fight or flee. He could only sit tight and hope for the best.

He had been here before. This sense of doom, of something threatening to take it all away, everything he'd sacrificed so much for, leaving him like a hollow man stuck in drying cement, left to see if he could escape somehow, live to do it all again.

Cliff shook his head. He got up and paced across the plush blue carpet to the mahogany-paneled wall, where he paused to admire the giant oil painting of a splendid sailing ship cutting through a tossing sea, a biblical nimbus of golden light filling the sky behind it. He turned away, wandered to the wet bar, and built himself a stiff one—Stoli on the rocks, splash of vermouth. The ice popped and cracked in his heavy crystal glass, sounding too loud in the whispering stillness.

He prowled around some more, examining everything as if for the first time. Shelves packed with old books. He'd read them all. A heavy oval frame with a portrait of his great-grandfather, a turn-of-the-century fortune builder, pioneer, visionary, and leader of men. An ornately framed picture of the Blackwell family's coat-of-arms with the family motto engraved in Old English script on a brass plate—"*Fortes fortuna juvat.*" He whispered the translation: "Fortune favors the brave." Words to live by, he thought. He raised his glass in salute and took a swallow. The family seed had been planted long ago. I'm like a perennial cousin of this tree. I come back after the snows every year, each time like the time before.

A picture of his father sat on a corner table under a pseudo-nautical lamp. Charlie Blackwell. The one-eyed tiger himself. The photo had been taken many years before in Newport Harbor. His father stood tall and lock-kneed on the foredeck of his old wooden yacht. He wore a blue sailor's cap tilted rakishly on his head, a black eye patch that covered his past, and a smile that made you think he possessed an important secret of living. He looked strong, viral, stubborn, and without a care in the world. Yep, that's my old man. Cliff smiled with mixed feelings of pride and chagrin. Charlie always had something interesting to say. The bard in him was always just below the surface, ready to tell an enchanting story that left little Clifford spellbound. And he had a million stories—tales of great and powerful people he had known or read about, along with his own colorful exploits. Several of those old yarns unreeled in Cliff's mind as he picked up the framed picture and studied every detail. Suddenly something in the photo seemed to change. He moved it under the lamp and looked again. He swore he'd seen the old man move.

"Buckshot," Charlie Blackwell said.

Cliff smiled, knowing that his old man wanted his full attention.

"Don't forget. When the going gets tough, the tough get going."

Those corny old words struck a chord. Hot tears welled in Cliff's eyes.

"Thanks, Pops," he whispered. Of course I'm standing here with a problem that's bigger than Dallas. But not too much bigger. Just the possibility of World War Three. He replaced the picture, wiped his face, and tossed back the rest of his drink.

Voices nearby startled him from his reverie. He listened more closely. Sydney . . . and Victoria. Oh, boy. Time to face the music. He peered once more at his father's photo, pooled in lamplight, a slice of time flash-frozen. The voluble Charlie Blackwell had nothing more to say. Cliff gave him a jaunty salute and said, "Gotta go now, Pops. Wish me luck."

"Hello, Sydney," Cliff said as he entered the main salon. He glanced at Victoria as he shook hands with the old don. Her polite smile had vanished.

"Vic, Sydney and I are going to talk in my study. Why don't you just relax for a while, maybe watch a movie."

She shot him a dangerously deadpan look, whirled, and stalked from the salon.

Russo turned to him with one eyebrow hiked.

Cliff took Russo's elbow and piloted him toward the aft passageway.

"Cliff, is this a bad time?"

"No, no. She's just a little upset. You'll know why in a minute."

"I can hardly wait."

They sat down in facing chairs behind the closed door of Cliff's dimly lit study. "Witherspoon came here this afternoon. Something's come up."

"Top secret?"

Cliff nodded. "But you and Tony need to know, so I'll give you what I've got so far. You want a drink first?"

"Single-malt Scotch?"

"How's twenty-five-year-old Macallan suit you?"

"Perfect. On ice, if you got some."

Cliff made the drinks quickly and returned to his seat. Russo tasted his Scotch, his gaze fixed on Cliff. Cliff considered various ways to launch their talk, but ended up using Witherspoon's hack phrase.

The old man's wary eyes widened. "The Russians are coming? What the—" He gaped at Cliff, and then he burst into hoarse laughter.

"Sydney, I—"

"Cliff, that's priceless." Russo clapped his bony knee and laughed again.

"Listen, man, this is no joke." Cliff told him about the nuclear sub and the impending military blowup. "Thousands of lives, maybe, and billions of dollars are all on the line. That's not so funny."

Russo waved him off while he gasped for breath. He put his drink aside, still chuckling, and wiped his eyes. "Jesus, Cliff, that was worth the trip over here."

"I wish I found it so amusing."

"Lemme tell you something, Clifford. Fuck the Russians. They're not spoiling this old man's fun."

Cliff had to smile. The guy really was some piece of work.

"We both know this game, Cliff. Somebody's always ready to shit on your Wheaties." He retrieved his drink and took a swallow. "So what else is new?"

"I know that, Sydney, but . . ."

"Don't get all stewed up, Cliff. This is life. Why not join the party? Man, I can't wait to see how Washington'll handle this hot potato. Bet the White House looks like a fuckin' Chinese fire drill."

Cliff shook his head, amazed by the old man's rejuvenated spirit.

"Say, the big inaugural party at the Presidential Palace is just four days from now, right? You and Victoria goin'?"

"Wouldn't miss it."

"Good. Rub lotsa elbows for me." The old man still looked amused. "No way Tony and me'd be caught dead there."

That reminded Cliff about Andre's bad news. "Speaking of the dead—"

"Oughta be interesting," Russo said. "Tables have really turned in forty years. We got it made in Cuba now with Martinez, Perez, and now Vivo, Russians or no Russians."

"Yes, and you want to keep it that way."

Russo turned sober. "You started to say something about the dead."

"Badalamente's in town, huh?"

"Arrived this week. Had some business to take care of."

"So I heard."

"News travels fast."

"Bad news travels faster."

Russo eyed him warily. "What're you tryna say?"

"Get rid of him. He's trouble."

Russo banged a fist on his knee. "We need him, goddammit!"

"For Chrissake, Sydney!"

"The guy was a problem. Made the mistake of threatening Badalamente to his face." The old man's eyes had turned black and cold.

"Probably just didn't want to be run out of business, Sydney."

Russo looked away and shrugged. "Like the kids say, shit happens."

Cliff got up and jabbed a finger at Russo's face. "That's bull-shit, Sydney, and you know it! Get that fucking Badalamente out of here. I mean it. I don't like him."

Russo jumped to his feet like a young man and swatted Cliff's hand away. "Don't tell me what the fuck to do. I run this operation."

"You have blood all over your hands."

"And so do you."

Cliff could hardly breathe. "Look, I risked my ass to get you in here, goddammit!"

"Big fuckin' deal."

Something broke loose in Cliff's mind, and a bloodshot fog blinded his eyes. After that he was vaguely aware of movement, but he was too busy trying to get enough air to think about it. His arms and hands burned with effort. When his vision finally cleared he froze in horror at what he saw.

Russo sprawled in his chair, his head wrenched back awkwardly, making wet, gagging sounds and clawing the air. His eyes bulged with terror. Cliff had his hands clamped around the old man's throat.

That sight pulled the plug. Cliff released his grip, and Russo catapulted forward, coughing raggedly and gasping for air.

Cliff stumbled backward on spaghetti legs and dropped onto his desk. He shook his head until the pink mist dissolved. "Oh, God! Sydney! I—"

The old man clawed a white silk handkerchief from an inside pocket and hacked into it for a while. In time he raised a trembling hand and flapped it at Cliff feebly. "Water," he said in a froggy voice.

Cliff brought him a brimming tumbler and a bar towel. His trembling hands caused some of the water to slosh onto the blue carpet. Panting, the old man took the glass and got some of the water down. Then he sat back and used the towel to wipe his face.

"Sydney . . ." Cliff began again. "Christ . . . I don't know what to say."

Russo waved the towel, rested his head on the back of his chair, and considered Cliff with an icy stare. "Guess I made a small . . . miscalculation," he said. His voice was a low rasp.

"Sydney, I'm so sorry. I can't believe what just happened."

"People do shit like that usually turn up dead."

"I said I was sorry. Please don't threaten me."

"I don't need to make threats."

"Of course not. You have animals like Badalamente to do all your dirty work."

"That's enough, Clifford. You made your point."

Cliff took a breath and clamped his shaky hands onto the edge of the desk. "I'm not finished yet. You got everything handed to you on a silver platter here. Killing that hotel owner was just plain stupid. This isn't Chicago in the 1920s. You let Neanderthals like Badalamente run loose, you're shitting on your own Wheaties. You better lose him fast."

Russo stared at him with narrowed eyes for a long time. Cliff thought he could read something new in their watery depths. A shrewd respect, maybe.

Finally Russo took another drink of water and cleared his throat. "Okay, Cliff. Maybe you're right. I'll take care of it."

"Thank you, Sydney. That's playing it smart."

"One more thing."

Cliff raised an eyebrow.

"Never put your hands on me like that again."

After a trip to the bathroom, Russo accepted a fresh drink from Cliff and returned to his seat. He tasted it, smacked his lips and said, "Maybe we should talk about them Russians some more."

Cliff finished telling Russo everything that he had learned from Witherspoon. The old man listened carefully, not laughing now. "If that sub is only hours away, the U.S. will have to act damned fast to intervene. I don't know if they can manage to do that."

"That's not much to go on."

"No, but Witherspoon said he'd come by tonight and update me. I hope he does."

Russo drew himself up. "Those fuckin' Russians! Pullin' this shit only months after the Chinese got pinched. They're nuts."

Cliff rubbed his chin. "That's a good point. Could be this is a rogue operation by some wacko splinter group. Thinking this is a good time to make their move. A long shot, but they could pull it off if they're lucky."

Russo polished off his Scotch and shook his head. "Bad timing for us. Un-fuckin'-believable."

Cliff said, "You want a refill?"

"Is the Pope Catholic? Man needs a few drinks after a near-death experience."

Before Cliff could reply, the intercom on his desk beeped. He pushed the Talk button and said, "Yes?"

A steward's voice said, "Mr. Witherspoon's here, sir."

"Good. Bring him to my study, please."

The CIA man joined them only moments later. His face didn't change when he saw Russo. He greeted the old man politely enough but with little enthusiasm.

"Maybe I should be going," Russo said, leaning forward.

"No, Sydney," Cliff said. "Relax. I want you to hear this, too." He looked at Witherspoon. "Sydney can stay, right? We're all in this together anyway."

Witherspoon considered Russo with a blank expression.

Cliff thought about Joey Corsiglia again.

Finally the agent said, "Sure, why not?"

"Good. I've already briefed him."

Witherspoon's face changed just enough to reveal a hint of displeasure, but he didn't respond to that. He said, "What I'm giving you will be front-page news tomorrow, anyway. But till then, keep a lid on it."

Cliff and Russo agreed. Russo said, "What the hell is going on with the Russians?"

"Same bullshit, different day," Witherspoon said. "We're ready and waiting for 'em now."

"We?" Cliff asked.

"Our boys," Witherspoon said. "Two carrier groups are haulin' ass here now. One's off South Florida, and the other isn't far behind."

"Got your hands full," Russo said. "I know how that goes." He rubbed his neck and looked at Cliff.

Witherspoon ignored the comment. "One group should arrive early tomorrow. A couple of subs are coming, too."

"Wow," Cliff said. "They aren't wasting any time."

Witherspoon eyed the wet bar. "Say, you mind if I . . . ?"

"Sorry, Don," Cliff said. "Help yourself."

While he fumbled with bottles and ice, the agent said, "Besides the carrier groups, Marines and Army airborne units are mobilizing as we speak. Good thing we brought in all those troops after Castro was assassinated."

"Yeah, we noticed," Russo said.

Witherspoon poured three fingers of bourbon. "All the armed forces are ready to rock, and the flyboys are providing complete air cover. With AWACS, Nighthawks, tankers, you name it."

Cliff said, "I just hope they know their targets when the shooting starts. Lots of tourists and business people are around right now, not to mention all the Cubans."

Witherspoon shrugged. "Collateral damage will be kept to a minimum, I'm sure."

Cliff didn't think that sounded very reassuring.

Russo said, "So where is this damn Russian sub now?"

Witherspoon returned with his drink and took Cliff's executive chair. "Not sure exactly, but we know it left Russian waters over a week ago. It could arrive any time."

"Before our ships get here?" Cliff said.

"Possibly."

"Does President Vivo know about this?"

"Yes, we're keeping him posted."

Cliff said, "I hope you remember that the inaugural party's in a few days."

"Of course. Unless it's canceled. If it happens, the grounds'll be heavily guarded by the Marines and a lot of special ops people."

"I'd hate to see it canceled," Cliff said. "So much preparation's gone into it."

Witherspoon nodded. "It'll come off on schedule unless things are really bad. We're all under a lot of pressure to make it happen. Show the world everything's under control in Cuba."

Cliff said, "That makes sense. Just be sure to let me know if they call it off at the last minute. Vic and I have been invited. Hate to look stupid, all dressed up and nowhere to go."

The other two men smiled.

"Will you be there, Mr. Witherspoon?" Russo asked.

"Yep. Should be interesting."

Russo flashed an ironic smile. "Well, isn't that just dandy? Like a family reunion. Only ones missing are Joey, Johnny, and Sammy."

Nobody moved a muscle until Witherspoon shifted uncomfortably in his chair and took a drink.

Still wearing a wry grin, Russo got to his feet and said, "Well, gentlemen, this old man's gotta go and get some rest. Looks like tomorrow will be a busy day. I may have to unpack my Tommy gun."

Cliff chuckled and said, "I'll show you out."

"Don't bother, Cliff. I know the way."

For some reason the darkened room felt more claustrophobic when Russo was gone. "Unless you have to take off, too," he said to Witherspoon, "let's go to the billiard room."

"Sure," the agent said. "But I'll warn you. The guys at Quantico used to call me 'Fast Donny.' "

Cliff laughed as he turned and led the way.

Donald Witherspoon didn't need much time to show Cliff that he still had the touch. He cleared every ball except one from the antique Brunswick table on the first round and left Cliff with an impossible shot.

Cliff made a low whistle. "I think I'll concede that one to

you, Don. Let's start again. My break."

Witherspoon smiled as he gathered balls and racked them. "Everything okay, Cliff?"

"Not with my pool game."

The agent snickered and said, "I mean here in Havana. I hope your friends don't get you into trouble."

"They're the least of my worries at the moment."

"Then what is it? You're chewing on something, I can tell."

Cliff chalked his stick while he made up his mind about trusting Witherspoon. "Listen, Don. I have an idea, but there's not much time."

"Let's hear it."

"I can't tell you right now." Cliff tossed his stick onto the table. "But I need your help."

"Sure, sure, Cliff. But calm down."

"Sorry, ol' buddy. No time."

"What is it?"

"I gotta get to Nassau tonight."

"Nassau? You can't do that now."

"I have to. Something important's come up."

"But, Cliff," Witherspoon said. "The Russians."

"I don't care. Vic and I have to take off as soon as she can warm up her chopper."

"Jesus, Cliff!"

"I'm sorry, Don, I can't explain everything now. We won't be gone long." He headed for the door. "I'll tell you when we get back, okay?"

Witherspoon shook his head. "This better be good. You're hanging your ass way out."

Cliff whirled to face him. "I'm hanging it out standing here talking to you. You'll have to excuse me now. I've gotta tell Vic. You know the way out."

"Wait a minute, Cliff. Aren't you forgetting something?"

"What?"

"You need special clearance to fly out of here."

"Well, get it, goddammit!" Cliff spun and hurried through the door and down the passageway.

"Give me thirty minutes," Witherspoon called after him. "I'll get an escort for you."

Cliff stopped and took a few paces back. "One more thing. Somehow you gotta get Johnnie Badalamente out of this country tomorrow. Talk to Sydney. It's critical."

He trotted off without waiting for Witherspoon's reply.

Victoria was sitting up in bed with a hardback book in her lap when Cliff burst into the master stateroom. "Oh, good, you're still dressed," he said, short of breath.

She gave him a dubious look and returned to her reading.

"Vic, I know you're pissed off at me, but I need your help."

She ignored him.

"Vic? Please?"

"What now?" she finally muttered, speaking to her book. "The North Koreans launch all their missiles at us?"

"No, Vic. I have an idea. We gotta get out of here now."

She closed her book with a resounding thump and looked at him with cold fire in her eyes. "What are you babbling about? Are you drunk?"

"No way. Please, just listen to me for a minute."

She huffed a big sigh and hugged her knees. "All right, all right. Let's hear it." She still wouldn't look at him.

Christ, he didn't have time for these games. They had to get moving right away or else forget the whole thing. But at least he had broken the ice with her. "Honey, I know you're scared and upset about what's happening," he began, trying to sound calm and reasonable. "I am, too. And I hate just sitting and waiting. I think we can do something, but we have to hurry."

She turned her head and rested it on her knees. Tears trembled on the edge of release. "Go on," she said quietly.

"All right. That's my girl." He gathered his racing thoughts. "Okay. First, something I haven't told you before. A few years ago, shortly after my wife and son were killed, I went out with a British secret agent. Met her in a London nightclub."

"You dated a spy?"

"Counterespionage agent." He sat down tentatively on the edge of the bed. "She was with MI6. You know, the British counterpart of the CIA."

"Yeah. Like Bond. James Bond."

"Very funny. Anyway, I was an emotional wreck in those days. Just looking for escape. I must've done every damn nightclub in western Europe."

"You told me that part."

He nodded. "I call that my 'Dumb and Dumber Phase.' When I finally cleaned up my act, I buried myself in work. Then I started the T.H.E. Corporation."

"I know. But what about Mata Hari?"

"Nice girl. Too much into her work, though."

"Not like you."

"Don't interrupt, please. Let's just say I could see it'd be difficult to maintain a long-term relationship with her."

"What made you think of her now?"

"Don said it was a British agent who got onto the Russians. Then he and I are down in the poolroom. Sasha—that's the agent —she and I used to play a lot of pool together. She was damn good."

"I bet."

She wasn't making this easy. "Hang in there with me, Vic. There's more."

"No doubt."

He sighed and shook his head. "I heard from her again, in Nassau. Before I met you. She's still with MI6."

"She's not the only British agent, you know."

"That's true, but she told me some things. Makes me think

she might be the one. Anyway, I want to see what I can find out."

She just stared at him.

He threw his hands into the air. "Well, do we want to just sit here and do nothing and trust these CIA spooks? I'd feel better doing something."

No response.

"Don't you see, Vic? We need to know what's really going on. A level playing field. We need someone we can trust, to cover our butts."

"Not the best choice of words."

"C'mon, Vic, you know what I mean."

"She may not be interested, with me in the picture."

"Give me a break, Vic."

"Do you know how to find her?"

"Yes. Witherspoon's not happy about it, but we're getting outta here tonight. I see a tiny window of opportunity."

"Does he know what you're planning?"

"Hell, no."

"So what are you thinking?"

He pointed a finger upward. "Your chopper."

"Damn. I knew you were being nice for some reason."

He grinned and checked his watch. "We'll slip over to Nassau, then take the Gulfstream to London. Tonight. Find Sasha at the Blue Max."

"She'll be there?"

"That's my best guess."

"What about clearances?"

"Don's taking care of that."

She closed her eyes while precious seconds ticked off in Cliff's head. When she opened her eyes again she didn't look at him. "All right," she said finally. "I wanted to get the hell out of here anyway. I'll pack a small bag and warm up the bird."

Cliff jumped up. "Attagirl!" He headed for the door. "I'll tell the staff and then call Virgil and tell him we're coming."

Cliff hustled forward, carried on a current of adrenaline. Join the party, Russo had said. What the hell. Why not? At least Vic was talking to him again. He hoped that his efforts would patch things up. And he hoped that they would have enough luck to locate Sasha soon.

13

Byzantine Ways

"WE'RE ALMOST THERE," VICTORIA SAID IN HIS HEADPHONES two hours later. The big Bell 407 helicopter that carried him, Victoria, and Bill, one of the ship's stewards, had just cleared Andros Island as it roared toward New Providence Island and Nassau at top speed.

Cliff checked his Master Banker watch for the twelfth time, then peered into the darkness. "Must be those lights."

Victoria nodded.

"Excellent," Cliff said. "With luck we'll get there just in time to jump on board the Gulfstream before they close the airport for the night."

Victoria said, "I'm looking forward to some rest on that flight. This trip's been nerve-wracking. Thank God we had an official escort."

"We can thank Don for that," he said, feeling amazed himself at how the agent had come through for them.

* * *

Bahamian customs in Nassau knew they were coming, so Cliff's party wasted little time getting through the terminal and onto his waiting Gulfstream V. Thirty minutes after takeoff they had climbed to the cruising altitude of forty-one thousand feet, and Bill had served them refreshments.

Victoria slumped in her seat and exclaimed, "Phew! We made it."

"Thanks to you, Vic," Cliff said. "You're an ace pilot."

She picked up her glass of champagne and smiled with a hint of pride. "I hope we can get a square meal on this bird."

"Of course. And a movie, too."

Victoria gave him a guarded smile. "Before we get to the featured attraction, I want to know more about this lady friend of yours."

"From the top?"

"The whole enchilada, baby."

Cliff glanced at his watch. "Well, I guess we've got plenty of time."

"More than enough, I'm sure. How long to Heathrow?"

"Twelve and a half hours."

"Just in time for our second dinner."

"And if we can get some sleep, we should feel pretty good when we get there."

She jabbed his arm. "The story, Cliff."

"Not much to it, really," he said. He adjusted his seat back a few inches. "We met at a nightclub in London called The Backstage."

"I've heard of it. Isn't that where the 'three A.M. girls' hang out trying to meet guys like Tom Cruise and George Clooney and dig up dirt on them?"

"That's the place," Cliff said. "I'd been hopping all over Europe, but when I met Sasha I stuck around for a while."

"I wonder why." That wary smile appeared again.

Cliff managed a crooked grin and decided to hit it head on. "She was stunning, world-class. Later, when things got hot and heavy, she confided in me, said she was a British agent."

"A little added attraction. How nice for you," Victoria said, her green eyes flashing.

"Come on, Vic."

"C'mon yourself. I remember when we first met. Don't you?"

"How could I forget?" He squeezed her knee. "Let's not get into the jealousy thing, Vic, please. You're here. She's not."

"She will be soon."

"Man, you go straight for the jugular, don't you?"

"If I have to."

"Don't worry, babe. You won't have to." He patted her leg. "In fact, I think the two of you could hit it off nicely."

She gave him a dubious look. "So what happened with this fairy-tale romance?"

"She didn't think I was ready."

"And she was?"

Cliff shrugged.

"Was she married before?"

"I don't think so."

"So she wanted you, but you weren't rising to the bait fast enough for her?"

He sighed. She wasn't going to let this go easily. "I guess so."

"If she's still on the loose, she could try again." Victoria leaned away from him as far as she could and put down her glass. "I hope you know what you want, Cliff, 'cause we could be skating on some thin ice here."

He was struck by the admonishing tone of her voice. Maybe he had said too much. "Give me some slack, Vic. I know what I want, and she's sitting right here."

"Good answer, Cliff. But suddenly we're in an awful hurry to find her." She looked away.

"Listen, Vic. Maybe she can help us. When you're in a desperate situation, you think of anything that might help you survive. Petty emotions don't even count."

She looked at him sharply. "Thanks a lot."

"No, I mean, she's the one person that I feel might be able to shed some important light on this mess."

"That's a longshot." She hugged her breasts and looked away. "The only sure thing is she'll hit on you. Big-time."

Cliff sat back and clamped his hands on the armrest. He was just about at the end of his rope with all this nonsense. "All right already. Maybe she will, and maybe she won't. But I guess it's up to me if she succeeds. So what's the big deal, Vic?"

"You'd be defenseless against such an attack."

"Oh, really? I—" He almost choked on the words. "You sure give me a lot of credit."

Victoria stared straight ahead, her long legs crossed, bouncing one foot.

He unglued a hand from the armrest and placed it tentatively on her knee. "Vic, all that's ancient history. I can handle it."

"Maybe. Maybe not," she said. "If it's over, then you shouldn't mind talking to me about her."

"I don't. What else do you want to know?"

"Give me the math on this bitch."

Cliff had to laugh. "No problem, honey. Numbers I can do." He leaned back and let his gaze drift to the overhead of the dimly lit cabin as he pictured Sasha. "She's tall, about five-eight, mid-thirties by now, flaming red hair, big blue eyes, great skin tone—"

"Wait a minute," said Victoria. "What do you mean by 'great skin tone'?"

"A nice, firm body," he said bravely, knowing he was pushing his luck. "Athletic, you know? And freckles all over."

She glared at him. "I must be crazy to be sitting here."

Cliff picked up his martini on the rocks and took a swallow. "Trust me. It never would've worked out." He rattled the ice. "I'll be honest. The physical attraction was powerful, incredible, but—"

"Stop it, Cliff!" She dropped her fisted hands into her lap and accused him with tear-shot eyes.

"No, *you* stop it, Victoria!" he almost shouted. Out of the corner of his eye he caught sight of Bill coming down the aisle carrying a tray. The well-trained steward stopped, did an about-face, and retreated to the galley.

Victoria glanced at the steward and said, "Stop what?" in a hoarse whisper. All the color had drained from her face. "I suppose you love me for my mind."

"Actually, that's true," he said softly. "You're much more intellectual, thank God, and more compassionate about people and the world. I love that about you—and, dammit, I love you!"

He gathered her hands into his own and opened them. They felt hot and sweaty. "I'm not even going to mention that you're beautiful, because you'd probably just miss the goddamn point." He held her tearful gaze. "We're a perfect match. And I feel all warm and alive just thinking about you, Vic. I mean it."

She dropped her head onto his shoulder and sobbed.

He pulled her closer, kissed her hair, and whispered, "Someday I hope you'll see how much I'm in love with you."

They remained that way for a while, until her sobs resolved into an occasional hiccup.

When Bill reappeared at the head of the aisle, Cliff motioned him forward and told him they were ready for dinner and a movie.

The steward nodded gravely and turned away.

"And, Bill," Cliff called, "I know just the flick. Make it *Casablanca.*"

Fifteen minutes later, Victoria returned from the bathroom looking better, with some color in her cheeks and fresh mascara. "Now tell me the rest, Cliff," she said, obviously making an effort to remain composed.

"Are you sure?"

She nodded. "Just promise me that you won't let this woman come between us."

Cliff sighed and picked up his drink. "Don't worry, Vic."

"I'll try," she said. "Go on."

Cliff began by telling Victoria that Sasha Volga was a British subject from a Russian family, trying to keep it casually objective. She had been a prime candidate for MI6, with her high IQ and a foreign background. Her grandmother had been a spy, too, and a woman who had stolen the heart of an English aristocrat. The Russian spy and the British journalist were a dashing couple who pursued a high-profile life among the insulated upper crust of British society. Nobody knew about her secret identity and scandalous background until the Soviet Union disintegrated in 1990, when she was a widow in her eighties, living in genteel poverty in Mayfair. That's when Sasha appeared on the MI6 radar screen.

They liked what they saw. The young woman had been educated in private schools and at Oxford, she was fluent in Russian, French, and German, and she had the perfect pedigree for handling sensitive work in the former Soviet Union. They also learned that she had been steeped in her grandmother's stories and that she was an adrenaline junkie, always looking for a new adventure. Just the kind of person they needed.

"What happened when the news broke about Sasha's grandmother?" Victoria said.

"Fleet Street jumped on it, of course, but MI6 persuaded the prime minister to intervene, and he got the publishers to call off their dogs. A matter of national security and all that."

A few months later, Cliff told her, Sasha had effectively disappeared, because the secret service was keeping her under wraps. They trained her for two years, provided her with all the right paperwork, and sent her on her first assignment in Chechnya. Her handlers gave her fifty-fifty odds of returning alive. They were happy when she did, and they were pleased to see that she had nerves of steel and the capacity to kill, if necessary.

Victoria shook her head and said, "Incredible. And you believe all this?"

"Absolutely. And so will you when you meet her." Cliff was ready to drop the subject, and he was hungry. He signaled to Bill and asked for dinner. He checked his watch. "We still have enough time to watch Bogey and Bergman before we need to catch a few hours of shut-eye."

Victoria settled into her seat as the cabin lights dimmed further. She looked calm now, but Cliff sensed the distance between them. When Bill served their food she just picked at her salad and vegetables in silence and pretended to watch the movie. She declined coffee and dessert and drifted off to sleep long before the final scene at the foggy airfield.

Cliff smiled at the smooth innocence of Victoria's relaxed face. *So beautiful,* he thought. *And so special, too.* But like many smart and attractive women, she also possessed a sweet vulnerability that endeared her to him that much more. If Sasha had a similar flaw, he had never seen it. She was all woman, but she was a tough cookie. Would Sasha see that chink in Victoria's armor? And would that encourage her to make a play for him? The incomparable Sasha Volga's charms would be hard to resist, but he wanted her to remain a thing of the past. And he hoped that she wasn't as beautiful as he remembered.

Bill roused them at six-thirty that evening. The Gulfstream made the usual noises in preparation for landing. "Next stop Heathrow," he said. The steward worked his way around the cabin, raising the window shades.

"Oh, my God!" Victoria cried. "I have to get ready." She gathered her things and rushed away.

Cliff yawned. Sleep had eluded him for most of the flight. "Yeah," he told himself, "I better get my act together, too."

"The limo's down there waiting for you, Mr. Blackwell," Bill said. "And so's the Savoy."

"Good. I hope customs won't tie us up long."

* * *

Victoria replaced her demitasse cup and said, "That meal was delicious, Cliff. It's been years since I was here with Daddy."

They had just finished dinner at the restaurant in the Savoy, even though it was after 11 P.M. Cliff felt sluggish after the big meal, but he was anxious to get going on the next phase of their mission.

"Been a long time for me, too," he said as he retrieved his credit card from the gold tray. "You ready?"

Victoria pulled her wrap around her shoulders. "I hope this goes well, Cliff."

"All we need is a little luck."

"So where are we headed?"

"You'll see. Not far from here."

"A nightclub?"

Cliff shook his head and grinned. "More like a ritzy pool hall."

Victoria smiled, too. "Sounds like an oxymoron. Are we dressed for the occasion?"

"We'll get by."

Fifteen minutes later their black cab rolled to the curb in the Knightsbridge district of London. A red flame flickered on the lamppost outside an Olde London-styled brick rowhouse establishment. Below it a modest brass plate stated "The Blue Max." A uniformed doorman ushered them inside.

Cliff took a few seconds to adjust to the low light. The spacious reception room looked the same as he remembered it—royal blue carpet, potted palms, several heavy, upholstered chairs, and gold detailing. The walls had been painted black.

He strode to an old-fashioned elevator cage and inserted a key into a circular slot in a metal panel. The elevator door rattled open instantly, as if by magic.

"*Voila*," Cliff said.

"Still have the key, huh?"

"Lifetime member."

"Of course."

They rode the lift to the next floor. When they stepped out, a raven-haired hostess greeted them. She glittered in a sequined black dress that accentuated the lush curves of waist and hips.

"Wow!" Victoria whispered. "This is swank."

Cliff piloted Victoria through a gathering of well-heeled folk all dressed expensively in varying degrees of what he considered to be good taste, including a few tuxedos and evening gowns. Several hostesses wearing full-length black dresses glided among the patrons, serving drinks and cigars. He took it all in, savoring the remembered scene—the sophisticated players, the subdued buzz of polite conversation, the sharp crack of billiard balls, and the smell of expensive smoke, money, and danger. A Mozart sonata drifted from hidden speakers. The joint was low-profile but classy.

"What do you think?" he asked Victoria.

"I'm wondering who comes here," she said in a hushed voice.

"You'll see," he said, smiling, and led her past a lounge and into a quiet corner. "Our friend, for one. She's gotta be around here somewhere."

"What makes you so sure?"

"Well, she usually is. Or was. And if she isn't, someone here will know where she is. Which is good, because I didn't keep up with her moves."

"We could've just telephoned."

He gave her an indulgent smile. "I can be more persuasive in person."

She glowered at him.

Cliff cleared his throat. "I mean, she spent a lot of time here. Champion player, you know."

"Ah, a pro," said Victoria.

Cliff decided to slide right by that. "One of the best pool players in the world." He looked at her with a straight face. "She taught me a few things."

"I'm sure."

He peered over her shoulder into a nearby room where several red felt tables were in play. "She beat the black widow more than once," he said. "Unofficially, of course."

"Didn't want the publicity?" Victoria asked.

"Something like that." He glanced around. "Hey, I see someone here who can help us." He put a hand on Victoria's arm and said, "Wait here."

Cliff zigzagged through the crowd until he reached a busy bar in a far corner.

"Hey, Corky!" Cliff said over the drone of conversation.

The bartender turned to him and exclaimed, "Saints preserve me, if it ain't Mr. Clifford Blackwell!" He threw back his head and laughed. "Where the hell you been?"

"Around."

"Good to see you, my boy."

Corky McLaughlin, the longtime mixologist and resident philosopher of The Blue Max, looked the same, too, with his big, florid face, mischievous blue eyes, and wild shock of reddish gray hair.

The barman moved closer and dropped his smile. "Say, I'll bet you're looking for our lady friend."

Cliff leaned forward and said, "As a matter of fact, I am, Cork. Got some important business I need to discuss."

Corky put his forearms on the gleaming wooden bartop and moved close enough for Cliff to catch a hint of Irish whiskey on his breath. "Been gone almost a week. But she'll be here tomorrow. That you can count on, me lad."

"Big match?"

"The biggest."

Cliff lowered his voice. "Where is she now?"

"Nowhere nearby."

Cliff's heart sank. "What do you mean?"

"Don't look so forlorn, Clifford, darlin'," said Corky. "Can't say as I blame you, though. As I said, she'll be back tomorrow."

Cliff grabbed his forearms. "Too late, Corky. Where the hell is she, right now?"

Corky backed off and scowled. "I've already told you, nowhere around here. I hear she's got something going in Turkey. In Istanbul."

"Damn! Where in Istanbul?"

"You'll have to ask her yerself. Tomorrow she'll be sitting right there, pretty as you please," Corky said, jabbing a finger at a nearby barstool.

"Look, Corky. I can't wait."

"No? So then what? Go to Istanbul?"

"I guess I have to."

"Come on, laddie. Tonight?"

"Tonight."

"You always were in a hurry, Mr. Blackwell."

"Not as much as I am now." Cliff pulled a crisp, new five-hundred Euro bill from his pocket and palmed it across the bartop. "Sorry. Ran out of pounds. How do I find her?"

Corky glanced around furtively, then pocketed the money. Finally he sighed. "All right. She'd likely pay me to find you, too." He snatched one of the house business cards, scribbled something on the back, and handed it over. Cliff read the unfamiliar words—Cemberlitas Hamann.

"Go there," Corky said. "Any cabbie'll take you. If she's not there, they'll know how to reach her." The bartender wiped his hands on a signature bar towel and winked at him. "Be sure to tell her I said hello."

Cliff smiled at him with gratitude and relief. "Will do. Thanks, Corky."

Cliff found Victoria in a far corner, watching the play at an uncrowded table from a discreet distance. "You won't believe this," he said.

"Let me guess. She's in Havana, looking for you."

"Ha, ha, Vic. No, it's weirder than that."

Victoria raised an elegant eyebrow.

"She's in Istanbul."

"What?"

"You heard me. Come on, we gotta go." He took her arm.

"Holy cow, Cliff. I don't believe this," she said, standing her ground. "I want to go back."

"Back? To Cuba?"

Victoria frowned and looked away.

"Come on, Vic. Why go back to Cuba? Think about it."

She looked at him and smiled weakly. "I guess it is like a catch-22."

He squeezed her arm. "Wait till you see Istanbul. You'll love it." She allowed him to trot her back to the elevator. "I need to go back to the room and make some calls. Then back on the magic carpet."

"Magic carpet? What—" Victoria stumbled as she tried to keep up with him. "What're you talking about?"

He winked at her. "You know—the Gulfstream."

A little more than two hours later, their private magic carpet streaked over the European continent, locked on to a heading for Istanbul. Cliff peered out the window at the black night, squinting to see the scattered sprays of light below.

He chuckled and said, "Gateway to the cradle of civilization."

Victoria stifled a yawn. "Thank God we took a little nap at the hotel before dinner. I'll be dead tomorrow anyway."

"Let's hope not," Cliff said, not thrilled with her choice of words.

"What did you find on the Internet?"

"A five-star joint called the Merit Antique Hotel."

"Sounds quaint."

"Presidential suite. Six hundred bucks a night."

"You make a reservation?"

"Yep. Thirty percent prepayment required."

She nodded. "This should be interesting."

"The suite has a French bed."

"What's a French bed? Like we'll have time to use it."

Cliff glanced at his watch. "Maybe I'll get lucky."

"What do they speak in Istanbul?"

"Turkish, Kurdish, and Arabic."

"No English?"

"Maybe as a fourth language," he said. "But a first-class place like that hotel should have people who speak English. And a couple decent restaurants."

"I hope it's not a holy day. With fasting or something like that."

"Don't worry, Vic." He patted her thigh. "We'll find something to eat."

"Or maybe a holy war."

Cliff smiled. "You never know." He caught Bill's attention and requested cold drinks.

Victoria combed her hair back with her fingers and said, "I really hope all this running around is worth it." The lack of sleep made her sound cranky.

"So do I."

"Let me see that card again."

He handed it to her.

" 'Cemberlitas Hamann.' What is it?"

"Don't know, exactly. Corky just said that they'd know where to find her."

Victoria frowned and shook her head.

Cliff looked at his watch again. "We've been in the air two and a half hours. Istanbul is fifteen hundred miles from London.

At our cruising speed, we should be there soon."

"Like another half hour or so?"

"More or less."

Bill brought the drinks, and before long Victoria closed her eyes while Cliff tried to concentrate on a copy of *The Economist*, hoping once again that they weren't on a wild goose chase.

When the Gulfstream banked and turned to make its approach to Ataturk International Airport, Cliff looked out the window just as the sprawling, whitewashed city materialized from the early morning haze. The pilot made a perfect landing, as usual, and less than thirty minutes later Cliff and his gang emerged from the gauntlet of Turkish customs with their passports dutifully stamped.

"Stand by, fellas," Cliff told his crew. "We may not be here long. Grab a nap if you can."

Cliff found a hotel telephone and called for a ride, then he and Victoria strolled outside to wait. Cliff noted how the air smelled and felt different in every foreign city. The scented breeze of Istanbul seemed exotic somehow and not unpleasant at all. A few minutes later the driver from their hotel pulled up in a black, late-model Mercedes. He flashed a toothy smile and greeted them warmly as he got out of the car.

"The Blackwells?" he asked. "May I take your bag, Miss?"

"Oh, thank God. English," Victoria said, hugging herself.

Cliff chuckled. "What's your name?"

"Yualchen," the driver said cheerfully.

Cliff extended a hand. "Well, it's good to meet you, Yualchen. I'm Cliff, and this is Victoria. We appreciate your English."

Yualchen bowed and showed his long, white teeth again despite his bristling mustache. "The hotel, I think, keeps me around just for that reason."

The driver loaded their bags, escorted them into the car, and settled himself behind the wheel. "It is not far," he told them brightly. "We will be there in just a few minutes."

"Great," Cliff said. "Say, can we drop our luggage at the hotel and then hire you for the morning?"

Yualchen smiled and nodded, the lines around his eyes deepening.

Victoria leaned forward and showed him Corky's card. "Do you know where this is?"

Yualchen squinted at the words for a moment. "Ah, yes, I know this place." He glanced at them over his shoulder. "It is for ladies only. You know what I mean? But I can recommend a similar place for you, sir."

"I'm not sure what you mean," Cliff said. "What kind of place is it?"

"A bathhouse," Yualchen said, grinning. "Turkish-style, of course."

Victoria looked at Cliff with wide eyes.

Cliff shrugged.

"Oh, well," she said. "I could use a rubdown about now."

Cliff kept his amusement to himself. "All right, Yualchen. After we check in at the hotel, we'd like to go straight there. I'll wait outside if I have to."

Yualchen bobbed his head and donned a pair of aviator's shades. "Whatever you say." He nosed the car into the traffic and headed toward a cluster of minarets in the hazy distance. The sun was fully up now, and the traffic was pressing and noisy.

A few minutes later they stopped in front of hulking gray 1920s-style building fronted by high windows arching up from street level and rising four tall stories toward a scalloped roofline. The place seemed to cover several blocks. Two liveried bellmen took charge of their bags and escorted them up a few steps into a bright, expansive lobby. Burgundy period furniture stood perfectly arranged around marble coffee tables on rich Turkish carpets, and a dozen chandeliers glittered overhead, even though it was morning. They were led to the reception area on the right.

The two male clerks spoke fluent but heavily accented English. As Cliff signed in, Victoria said, "This hotel is beautiful, Cliff." She looked around with awe.

"Yes, very nice," he agreed.

A bellmen led them to their spacious suite, which was heavy on draperies and dark. They lingered there just long enough to freshen up and admire the Istanbul skyline basking in the morning sun from their tall window. They hurried to meet Yualchen in the lobby, as planned.

Yualchen drove them along wide boulevards and then through ever narrowing back streets toward the cinnamon-colored hills that surrounded the city. Finally they entered a quiet, cobbled road dominated by a plain, sand-colored building topped by a single large dome. He turned into a narrow side street and stopped.

Yualchen opened their door and said, "You will remember, sir, that this place is for ladies only, yes?"

"Right," Cliff said. "I'll play dumb, see how far I can get."

Yualchen smiled and shrugged. "As you wish. I will wait for you here, if you get kicked out or—how do you say?— indisposed."

"I appreciate that."

As soon as they entered the cramped, austere, white-marbled lobby, a middle-aged woman greeted them, speaking quietly and deliberately to them in Turkish, no doubt, Cliff thought, about their ladies-only policy.

Victoria smiled and took over. "We have just come to see one of your guests," she said.

"No English," the lady said in perfect English.

The two women worked things out in sign language as Cliff looked on, wearing what he hoped was an innocent smile. Finally Victoria arranged her own admission as a day guest, which seemed to be the best compromise.

"I can't believe you've gotten me into this," she told Cliff, looking indignant and more than a little skittish. "But I'll try not to enjoy the services too much and forget my mission to find your beautiful ex-girlfriend."

Cliff gave her a hug. "That's right, don't forget why we're here. And good luck. I'll step outside and have a smoke."

The hostess eyed him sternly and pointed to the door. He nodded and headed out. What else could he do? Victoria had to run with the ball now.

The receptionist made a fuss of getting Victoria signed in, still speaking in Turkish or Arabic or whatever it was. Victoria decided that it was time to stop playing games.

"I'm looking for someone," she said.

The woman's attitude had changed once Cliff had disappeared. But now she looked at Victoria blankly, apparently without a hint of understanding, and gave her an ingratiating smile. Then she took Victoria's elbow and led her into the labyrinth of the interior.

They entered another room, smaller than the first and made completely of pearly marble. Another dark-haired woman, this one younger and wearing only a black bikini, stepped forward and took charge of Victoria. The receptionist bowed and disappeared.

Again Victoria withstood the barrage of a strange, foreign language. She smiled bravely and said, "I only speak English. Oh, and some French and Spanish."

Her new hostess shook her head and made motions that told Victoria to remove her clothing. The young woman opened a closet door, removed a pair of hangers, and repeated the undressing pantomime.

Victoria froze with uncertainty. The hostess cocked her head and propped one hand on her hip as if to say, "Well . . . ?" Finally Victoria decided that she'd better go with the flow if she wanted a chance to find this hot dish of Cliff's, but she wasn't happy about it. Just the thought of this Sasha bitch made her emotions swing between morbid curiosity and homicide.

She took a deep breath, stripped off her clothes quickly, and handed them to her hostess. The slim, dark-skinned woman gave her a pair of black bikini bottoms just like hers, and Victoria pulled them on. She waited for the matching top, but that was evidently not part of the wardrobe.

Next the hostess took her hand and led her to a large, round room with a dome-shaped ceiling and stained glass skylights above. The atmosphere was hushed and discreet. Several other women lounged on heavy massage tables, some naked, some with just the bikini bottom or draped with a towel, a massage therapist working slowly on each of them.

All the women seemed to be Middle Eastern. No stunning redheads in here. Victoria smiled to herself. Okay. Cliff can wait. What else could she do? She allowed the hostess to lead her to an empty table and stretched out.

Yet another dark-eyed beauty appeared and began to work on her silently. Victoria relaxed and closed her eyes, surrendering herself to the strong hands and the fragrant oils, feeling perversely amused that Cliff was anxiously cooling his heels outside.

Soon she was practically purring with pleasure, but she couldn't rid her mind of thoughts about finding this mystery woman from Cliff's past—and a spy at that—and getting out of Turkey as soon as possible. What if she's just not here on this particular morning? Then what? These unanswered questions repeated themselves until they faded away into a black, echoing well.

Victoria awoke to gentle fingers tapping on her shoulder. The massage was over. Her troubling thoughts returned again as she sat up. My God, what if Sasha was nowhere to be found? That could be worse than finding her. How long can we keep up this crazy chase? We have to find her. We need help. And maybe she can help. Victoria did not want to go back to Cliff with empty hands.

When she sat up, the massage therapist pointed in the direction she was supposed to go. The showers, no doubt.

Wrapped in a fluffy white towel, Victoria padded across the cool marble floor into the misty changing room. A new guide approached her and pointed out the locker where her clothes were waiting. She evidently had some options now, Victoria thought, but a shower seemed logical. After that she could explore the baths.

She dropped the towel, peeled off the brief bikini bottoms, and stepped into the round marble room of the community showers. One other woman stood under the hard, steamy spray, facing away from her. Victoria stopped cold, her heart quickening in her chest.

The young woman turned and arched her neck, letting the water soak her full mane of dark red hair. She had a tall, perfectly sculpted body that looked hard and toned, like an Olympic athlete's. And she had freckles everywhere. Victoria swallowed. My God, this has to be Sasha!

Victoria inched closer to her and turned on a shower. She jumped back with a squeak when the needles of cold water hit her warm, oiled breasts and sluiced down her front. The other woman eyed her suspiciously. Shit! Victoria apologized to her for the intrusion with a feeble smile, feeling like a jerk. She adjusted the temperature of her shower, trying to get a grip on her emotions and think of something to say.

Finally Victoria just said, "Forgive me. Do you speak English?"

"Yes," the woman replied with a hint of surprise.

"Uh . . . well, good." Victoria tried not to stutter. "I mean, do you know how late this place stays open?"

The woman cocked her head, looking guarded. "Until ten o'clock."

Yes! The accent was perfect Oxford. She had to be Sasha. So just go for it. She took a breath and said, "Are—Are you Sasha Volga?"

The woman's face turned to stone. "I don't know what you're

talking about, miss."

"You must be Ms. Volga," Victoria said carefully. Now that she had her, she couldn't let her off the hook.

"Leave me alone." The woman shut off her shower and headed from the room.

"Wait! I'm a friend of Clifford Blackwell."

The woman halted and turned slowly. "What did you say?"

Victoria knew she had found her mark. She breathed a sigh of relief and said, "Clifford. Blackwell."

The stunning redhead regarded her icily, but her eyes held a flicker of recognition.

"You know him, don't you?" Victoria asked gently.

"What if I do?"

"Then you must be Sasha Volga."

The woman's glistening breasts rose and fell when she heaved a sigh. "All right," she said. "I'm Sasha Volga." Then she smirked, struck a pose, and raised her hands, palms up. "In the flesh."

Victoria had to smile. Sasha certainly was some package, she had to admit, and she had a sense of humor, too. What normal man could resist her? She squared her shoulders and said, "I'm Victoria Love. And I must say I'm reluctantly pleased to meet you."

"I could say the same thing," Sasha said, adopting an ironic smile.

Victoria stepped forward and thrust out a hand. "What a place to meet."

Sasha broke her pose and shook Victoria's hand awkwardly. "Indeed. So where is the famous Mr. Blackwell these days? He sent you to do his dirty work?"

"I'm sure he would've preferred to do this dirty work himself. But they booted him out."

"Good Lord! He's here?"

Victoria bristled at Sasha's reaction—the sapphire sparkle in her eyes and the color that flushed her cheeks—but held herself in check. "He's waiting outside," she said.

Sasha managed to look disconcerted and pleased at the same time. "I don't believe it. But then I do believe it. That devil." She couldn't hide her delight.

Victoria struggled to maintain her cool. "I see you actually do know him."

Sasha's attitude became guarded again. "Yes, I do. But what exactly is going on, if I might ask?"

"Don't worry. Cliff can explain. Let's get out of here before I turn into a prune." Victoria led the way to the changing room, where another Turkish woman handed them thick towels. She told Sasha about their wild rush to find her.

"I see," Sasha said. "This should be interesting."

Cliff paced the cracked and buckled sidewalk and fiddled with an unlit cigar. When the heavy front door of the bathhouse swung open and the two women appeared, his tension burst like a party balloon. He hurried to meet them, arms extended, his gaze radar-locked on to Sasha.

"The two Graces," he said. "Thank God!"

Both women accepted his embrace. The smiling Sasha raised her mouth to his ear and whispered huskily, "Hi, handsome."

He covered his reaction by giving Victoria a quick kiss on the top of her damp head. Then he held both women at arm's length. "Sasha," he said, putting on his serious face, "we need to talk." Breathing became a chore while she surveyed his face, her gaze narrowed but rapt. "Something very big is about to happen, and you may be the only one who can stop it."

14

A Pink Day

"DINNER WAS GREAT LAST NIGHT, CLIFF," VICTORIA SAID. "The company, too."

Sasha eyed Victoria and said, "Indeed. And so was breakfast."

Cliff was in no mood for small talk or feminine games. Some fresh air was more like it. He opened the French doors and stepped onto the balcony. Everything looked peaceful on this brassy third morning of April in Istanbul, but the atmosphere in the parlor of their suite at the Merit Antique Hotel had an edge to it—something like an "uneasy truce," as the newspapers always said. The two women kept eyeing each other like a cobra and a mongoose. But he didn't know which one was the cobra.

He thanked his lucky stars for finding Sasha. At the same time he hoped he hadn't made a mistake by bringing her into the mix. The combination of the two women could be volatile, he knew. Risky business. Today was sure to be the first of a series of interesting days. Maybe too interesting.

Cliff turned back to the sunny room, where his two lovely companions stood gazing at him now, neither one offering any hint about what was in her mind. "Istanbul is certainly exotic," he said to no one in particular, taking a deep breath of the heavy air.

Sasha joined him on the balcony and said, "I'm glad you tracked me down, Cliff. Thanks."

Her Slavic beauty ranked with Victoria's all-American good looks, but she played it down. No makeup. Comfortable black slacks, T-shirt, and leather jacket. Sensible shoes. Very low-profile. Necessary for her trade, no doubt. He smiled at her and said, "Can't think of anyone better for the job. I'm not entirely comfortable with getting all my information from only one contact—and a CIA contact, too."

Sasha nodded. "That's playing it smart." She glanced around. "Can I use the phone?"

Victoria had joined them, her bland expression unreadable. She pointed and said, "Be our guest."

Sasha found the phone on an ornate side table by the couch. She rummaged through her big leather bag, retrieved a palm-sized electronic device, and clamped it onto the mouthpiece. Cliff assumed that it was some kind of a scrambler.

She glanced at them and said, "I'll call my boss, see what I can learn."

Cliff and Victoria turned away to give Sasha some privacy and sat on the stone balustrade. Victoria took Cliff's arm and said, "Having fun?"

The question was bait for an argument, but he decided to admit his true feelings anyway. "Yeah, Vic," he said firmly. "You could say that. Mainly because I think Sasha can help us." The look on Victoria's face said they might need some privacy of their own. He got up and pulled the French doors closed.

While Sasha waited for the connection to MI6 headquarters in London, her heartbeat increased with the sheer excitement she felt every time she was on to something. But this one was special for a number of reasons. She couldn't wait to speak to Sir Walter and get the latest intel on this intriguing situation.

When he finally picked up, she was glad to hear his cultured, old-school voice, and he sounded happy to hear from her, too. She assured him that her end of the line was secure and brought him up to date, then prodded him about what she'd learned from Cliff. He withheld the information for a while, teasing her as he always did, but finally gave her the names.

"The Godfather of the Russian Mob and the Gold Man?" she said.

"Yes. They're the ones behind this so-called Russian invasion."

"Good Lord! I didn't even know they knew each other. Why are they working together?"

Sir Walter chuckled at her surprise. "The Gold Man is financing the Russian Mob in Cuba. I needn't tell you why, now, do I, my dear?"

"No, sir, indeed you needn't. But you must explain why I'm not on this assignment." She breathed heavily through a long pause.

"In point of fact," he said finally, "I was just about to send someone out to Cuba. I dare say it might as well be you, don't you think?"

"That's brilliant! Thank you so much, sir." Her heart rate increased even more. "Tell me," she said, lowering her voice, "how are they managing it?"

"Russian-made sub. Might have nuclear weapons on board."

"No! When did you hear this?"

"Just two days ago. Ought to be big news soon."

"You wouldn't happen to know where those two men are, then, would you?"

"Actually, I've just learned that they plan to meet soon—on the island of Malta."

"When?"

"Twelve noon, Malta time."

She whistled lightly. "I'd give anything to be there."

"You could be if you used that jolly little toy you're packing around."

"The STU! Of course! That's brilliant, sir!" Sasha knew that the Shadow Trek Universal, on loan to MI6, was an experimental technology developed by a small research firm funded by a CIA venture capital company in the Silicon Valley. It just might work. She hoped she could control her excitement and not let it show too much over the telephone.

She took a deep breath and said, "I just need the coordinates."

"Righto. I'll transmit them to your STU," Sir Walter said. "Get on it straightaway, young lady."

"I owe you one, sir."

He gave her an indulgent chuckle. "You owe me many more than that, my dear."

"Agreed. Wish me luck. Cheerio!"

When the French doors burst open behind them, Cliff turned to see a Sasha who was beaming and flushed with excitement.

"Great news!" she exclaimed. "I've been assigned to Cuba!"

"That's perfect, Sasha," Cliff said.

Victoria shot him a sharp look.

Sasha moved closer as she pushed up the sleeve of her jacket. "Look at this." A black device that looked like a larger version of a cheap digital watch was strapped to her wrist. When she pushed a button, a small LED screen glowed.

"What's that?" Victoria asked.

"First let me tell you what my boss just said." Sasha gave them the juicy news without wasting a word. Cliff liked seeing that old fire in her eyes again, but he could hardly believe his ears.

"They're meeting today," Sasha concluded.

"Where?" Victoria asked.

"Malta."

"Incredible!" Cliff said. "But we were planning to leave soon to get back to Havana in time for the inaugural party. Day after tomorrow."

"Oh, we can do that," Sasha said. "But first we may just get a bird's-eye view of the meeting."

"What do you mean?" Cliff asked.

Sasha pointed to the device on her wrist. "We can be *at* the meeting without actually going to Malta."

Cliff wondered if Sasha was more of a magician than he'd imagined as he stared at the device on her wrist.

She followed his gaze. "You're getting the idea, Cliff. This pregnant wristwatch can 'beam me in,' if all goes well."

"What?" asked Victoria, looking confused.

"I can't tell you much about this thing," said Sasha, wagging a slender finger. "Classified, you know."

"But, Sasha," Cliff said, "I—"

"Just wait, Cliff. You'll see how it works soon enough."

"When?"

"One P.M. here."

"Today?" asked Cliff. He glanced at his watch. "Damn! We'll run out of time."

"I don't think so," Sasha said. "The meeting will likely be quite brief."

Feeling slightly high, Cliff checked his watch again. "All right. It's almost eleven A.M. now in Istanbul. The meeting's in about two hours. If it lasts for three hours, that would take us to four o'clock here."

"Then another couple of hours to get to the airport and get clearance," said Victoria.

Cliff studied her serious face and wondered what she was really thinking. "Right, Vic. Putting us at six P.M. here, nine A.M. Nassau time."

"How long was your flight from Nassau?" Sasha asked.

"Twelve and a half hours to London," said Cliff. "Another three hours getting here. But a direct shot'll be quicker."

"Need we stop in London?" asked Sasha.

"We?" Victoria said.

Sasha grinned. "Yes. I'll need to go with you." Then she sobered. "If you'll have me, that is."

"Of course," Cliff said.

"Brilliant!" Sasha gave both of them a luminous smile. "That'll cut through a lot of red tape."

"We don't need to stop in London," Cliff said, "but you'll miss your big tournament tonight."

Sasha shrugged and grinned. "This kind of sport is much more interesting."

"Okay," Cliff said. "Then we'll play it safe and refuel in Spain, fly to Nassau, then take the helicopter back to the yacht."

"Excellent!" Sasha said.

"From Nassau, it's another three-hour ride," he said. "And we still have to clear Bahamian customs."

"So when do we get back?" Victoria said. She didn't sound very enthusiastic.

Cliff couldn't read anything in her expression. He looked at his watch yet again. "Hmmm. If the meeting doesn't end until four . . . We could make Nassau in fifteen hours."

"Don't forget we're nine hours ahead of Nassau and Havana," Victoria said.

Cliff nodded. "So nine A.M. here, minus nine hours for the time difference... That's midnight at the oasis—Nassau, that is."

"And then four hours to Havana," Victoria said. "Allowing an hour for changing aircraft, clearing customs, and getting a departure clearance, we'd get in sometime around four A.M."

Cliff tapped the crystal on his watch. "Shit. We still need a clearance into Havana."

"How can we do this, Cliff?" Victoria asked.

He touched her arm. "How can we not do this, Vic? At least

we'll have the next day to catch up some before we go to the party."

"We need to get moving," Sasha said.

Cliff agreed. "Excuse me while I make a few calls." He scooped his sat phone from the table on the balcony and turned away. Victoria groaned and hurried inside, muttering under her breath.

Sasha approached Cliff and put her hand over his. Her palm felt warm and damp. "Let me know if you get good reception, Cliff. If you do, I should be able to pick up the meeting in Malta from out here, too."

Cliff gave her a nod and a thumbs-up. Anticipation had rewired his nervous system, making the telephone tremble in his hand. Could Sasha really tune in to that meeting and learn something valuable? Could they get back to Havana in time to do some good? And could he keep these two dynamic women from declaring their own personal war and scuttling the whole show?

Rivulets of sweat coursed down Boris "Pinky" Forostenko's face as he cruised through the darkness of the muggy Miami night, thinking, What a fuckin' place. Three-thirty A.M. and the car feels like a fuckin' sauna. But maybe it wasn't just the humidity. Maybe it was all those shots of vodka. Or maybe he was getting too old for shit like this. The Count sat small and erect beside him, craning his excuse for a neck to scan the old warehouses that crowded the derelict neighborhood south of Miami.

Soon they came to the end of the littered street. Forostenko nosed the black Mercedes onto the buckled concrete quay at the all-but-abandoned docks. He wanted to play it cool and casual on this mission. He tried a smile on for size, but his high blood pressure and the vodka waging war in his generous gut turned it into a grimace. Although he and the Count had rehearsed their moves endlessly during the last few days, now he felt as if he just might burst.

The Count's tiny head bobbled as he looked around, making Forostenko think of those stupid dolls Americans liked to put in the rear windows of their cars. Obviously he was jumpy, too. "Do not worry, Sergei," he said. "The plan should work good."

The little man replied with a pained smile and bobbed his head again. "Yes, boss." Then he coughed a dry laugh. "They'll never suspect a Trojan horse."

"My people got the palace bugged," Forostenko said. "Lucky thing we heard about their little surprise."

"What surprise?" the Count practically squeaked with his high-pitched voice.

"Calm down, you bonehead. You know. The new presidential limo. The gift. The Cadillac they will deliver to the inaugural party."

"Oh, that surprise. I will feel better when the car is inside the gates."

Forostenko tried to manufacture a reassuring smile. "You will do fine. Just get a clamp on yourself, as the Americans say. If we screw up, we better just keep going."

They pulled up to the last dock, and Forostenko cut the engine.

"You can count on the Count, Boris," the little man said, repeating his tired joke. He pushed his door open with some effort and jogged lightly toward the darkened pier.

Forostenko thought he looked like some kind of crazy wind-up toy. He shook his head and grinned despite his grumbling stomach.

Sasha, Cliff, and Victoria huddled on the balcony just before one o'clock, preparing for the meeting of Ivan Penkovsky and the Gold Man in Malta. Sasha checked her watch again and said, "Forgive me if I ignore you. I'll need to concentrate on the STU."

Her companions muttered their agreement and backed away. God, how she hoped this thing would work. She had gotten lucky.

This time she was in the right place at the right time. She desperately wanted to score big on this one, not only for Queen and Country but also, she had to admit, for her brilliant former lover, Clifford Blackwell.

Sasha knew that the STU was a prototype offered to MI6 through a cooperative technology exchange program with the CIA, who wanted to test it in the field. She had been thrilled when Sir Walter Conway gave her the nod to try it first, saying he thought she might find some use for it in Turkey and Iraq during her investigation of new terrorist cells.

A series of words and numbers appeared clearly on the tiny monitor of the STU. She stored the secured data, as she had been instructed, and cleared the screen. Then she pushed several buttons on the side of the gadget to bypass the firewall of a collateral retrieval system that was used by authorized personnel of allied foreign agencies. This gave her direct access to the impervious Interlink, the vast intelligence network of the U.S. Department of Defense. She pressed more buttons on the face of the device and received a special, frequently reissued, double-X security clearance code. Once the STU had verified her right thumbprint and voice —bingo, she was in.

Sasha exhaled with relief. Now she was free to choose from a host of options. She let her fingers do the walking straight to Project 3S. Once there, thanks to the National Imagery and Mapping Agency, she could view any place in the world via one of the "eye-in-the-sky" satellites of the new Shadow Spy System. Sasha's Shadow Trek Universal unit had been developed as an integral part of Project 3S and the Shadow Spy System as a tool that could be used easily by operatives in the field.

This beta-test model of the STU, she knew, had multiple viewing options that were similar to looking through the lens of a 35 mm SLR camera. She could zoom in with its telephoto capability and also take high-resolution digital pictures. With the push of a button her subject could be locked into the crosshairs of the coordinates, and then, by using special contact lenses, the viewer could see a projected image of up to twenty-four inches square suspended in midair about eighteen inches from the STU. Digital enhancement made the picture detailed enough to read lips. Fortunately, with this newer model, that shouldn't be necessary. If the STU worked as advertised, she could just push a button and receive real-time sound.

Sasha also knew that the STU could be equipped with even more useful features. Her particular unit, model number 2002-B, could link to any computer and provide the precise time anywhere in the world, with the time corrected once a day to the millisecond by the Atomic Clock in Colorado. It could also access the Global Positioning System, provide the weather anywhere in the world, and, since many of its users had a physically stressful occupation, monitor the wearer's vital signs, too. What would they think of next?

Now it was time for her STU's maiden voyage. Sasha whispered a prayer as she punched in the coordinates for the meeting on the small Mediterranean island of Malta. If their intel was valid, the STU would soon display a live feed of Ivan Penkovsky, the brutal *Pakhan* of the Russian Mob, and Dr. Jonathan Edwards III, the infamous Gold Man, meeting somewhere in the old, stone-walled city.

Recalling details from previous assignments, Sasha assumed that the Gold Man had flown there from his headquarters, Consolidated Global Exploration, Ltd., in South Africa, and Penkovsky had come from Moscow or maybe Budapest, the two cities where he lived and conducted business and banking.

The monitor on her STU flickered, and then an image appeared, but Sasha couldn't make out any details. She glanced at Cliff and Victoria, who stood behind her in rapt silence. "Bloody hell!" she said. "I nearly forgot."

She removed two small cases from pockets in her slacks and opened them carefully. Small lenses that resembled contacts rested in little cups filled with liquid. "Here, put these on your eyes. Use your fingertip and just pop 'em in."

Mimicking her, Cliff and Victoria fumbled with the lenses but soon had them in place.

"Good show!" said Sasha. "Most people have trouble with that."

Cliff smiled. "You kidding? I'd poke my eye out before I'd miss this."

She winked at him. "Now watch this." She thumbed a button, and a two-dimensional image suddenly jumped into the air between the STU and her face and hung there like magic. The black-and-white picture was large and detailed. When she pressed another button, the image enlarged and refocused, plainly showing two men in close-up.

Sasha felt almost intoxicated as she prepared to test the last button. As soon as she pushed it, an audible hiss issued from the STU, and with a few more clicks the volume increased. She felt as if she were hovering just above her subjects, eavesdropping on their conversation. Her excitement was almost too wild to suppress, but she remembered to click off and save a few still shots.

"Amazing!" Cliff said under his breath.

"Listen!" Sasha said. "Voices."

"—to see you again, my dear Dr. Edwards," Penkovsky said in his thick Russian accent around a fat cigar.

"Likewise, Mr. Penkovsky," his companion said in a Belgian accent. "You certainly picked an out-of-the-way place to meet."

"As you requested, Dr. Edwards."

"Indeed, Ivan, this place looks like it will do just fine."

Cliff and Victoria goggled at the projected display, open-mouthed. The three of them exchanged broad smiles.

The two men stood on a bridge that spanned a dry channel, like a moat, and led to the gate of the medieval city. Sasha knew the spot. It was on the verge of an old, shaded park that bordered Mdina, also known as the Silent City. A good place for them to discuss their plans—quiet, with few tourists.

"Let us walk," Penkovsky said, taking his companion's arm. They strolled toward the gate of the walled city.

Sasha noted the contrast between the two men. Penkovsky was tall and lean, and he looked small beside the heavily built, square-headed Gold Man. Dressed in his frumpy black overcoat and Homburg, the Russian looked like a Stalin-era *komissar*. That didn't jibe with Sasha's previous image of the man. Maybe he was playing a role, presenting himself as a rude Soviet *politchik* as a way to disarm the Gold Man, who looked quite GQ in his tawny top-coat of what was probably expensive camel hair.

The two men ambled along the cobblestone streets, halting their small talk for the occasional passerby. "See how they designed this city?" Penkovsky said. "The streets, they are all curved. And every building is like a fortress. This way, when the enemy is in pursuit, his arrows cannot follow you."

Dr. Edwards cackled. "Quite clever. It's a strange place. So silent, like an abandoned citadel."

Sasha smiled as they drifted along with them. Thanks to her high-tech gadget, they could round corners that ancient arrows could not, even from faraway Istanbul. If Sir Walter were here, she would kiss the old boy full on the mouth.

The men turned left and continued their stroll down a narrow side street. "I think you will enjoy Mdina," Penkovsky said. "You know, it is many hundreds of years old, and behind the walls, in grand homes, live descendants of former residents from the old times." He smiled. "And as you see, automobiles are forbidden. So is all noise except church bells. The people who live here must park their cars outside the gates, in the town across the bridge."

"Extraordinary," Dr. Edwards said, gawking like any tourist.

Penkovsky finally stopped and announced, "Here we are." A weathered sign hanging on a stone wall read "The Dungeon."

The Gold Man scowled. "What is this place?"

"A restaurant and bar. You want a drink?"

The scowl faded. "Why not, comrade?"

Sasha held her breath as Penkovsky pulled open a heavy, wooden door. Would they lose the image when their targets went indoors? The image projected by the STU jittered and dissolved.

"Oh, no!" Cliff said.

"Hold on," said Sasha. "Thick walls. But the signal should come back." She wiped her brow. "I hope."

As the two men stepped into the chill gloom of the stone-walled foyer, Penkovsky felt pleased to be back in one of his favorite watering holes. Built into an appendage of the city's ancient outer wall itself, The Dungeon was appropriately named. It reminded him of the dank, secret chambers that lay deep beneath the streets of Moscow, where the stone walls weeped tears from the Moscow River. He loved the place.

They stepped into the deserted main room. Penkovsky pointed and said, "Notice all the interesting things hanging on the walls. Many clever devices of torture."

Smiling with appreciation, Dr. Edwards moved away to get a closer look. "Authentic?"

"Of course. From right here in Mdina. Below the city are real dungeons." The Gold Man looked mesmerized as he studied each artifact. Finally Penkovsky took his companion's arm and broke the spell. "Now let us see if we can find a real bartender."

They wandered through the darkened dining room to the long bar in the back. A tall, swarthy bartender looked up as they approached, smiled politely, and offered them refreshments.

Dr. Edwards turned to Penkovsky. "You think this torture chamber has any cactus juice?"

Penkovsky looked at the bartender. "Tequila?"

"Certainly," the man said. "On the rocks?"

Dr. Edwards nodded, and Penkovsky ordered a double Russian vodka on the rocks.

"Make mine a double, too," Dr. Edwards said, "and hold the ice. This joint is cold enough already."

When the bartender had walked away, Penkovsky said, "So, my friend, how is the gold business?"

"As you must know, it's taken off, pushing seven hundred dollars an ounce. Beats the stock market." He scowled and looked away, eyeing the bartender without interest. "Not to mention, it beats the South African rand."

Penkovsky removed his hat and placed it on the bartop. He pantomimed sympathy with a shrug and a shake of his head. The bartender returned with their drinks.

Penkovsky raised his glass. "I know what you mean. That worthless paper." He spat theatrically. "Diamonds are better business."

Dr. Edwards took a drink and grimaced with pleasure. "Probably those goddamned currency speculators," he said, wiping his mouth. "Why do you mention diamonds?"

"We have many holdings in the Congo."

"Then we must make another deal sometime, swap gold for diamonds." He gazed at the dark, heavily timbered ceiling, rubbing his chin. "I must make some international payments outside the banking system. I need an asset that's easy to transport."

"No problem, comrade," Penkovsky said. "With your gold production you can make a killing. You will shake up the market."

"Thank you," Dr. Edwards said. "And you, Ivan. I assume you're doing well with that diamond smuggling operation of yours." He twirled his glass on the shiny bartop. "Maybe even our gold shares will finally take off."

"We will drink to that, comrade," Penkovsky said, raising his glass.

The Gold Man gave him an emphatic nod, and they both took a swallow. "Meanwhile, subsidizing this Cuban caper is expensive. But if it gets the fucking Americans, I would gladly pay double." Just then a small, bright red light began to blink on his heavy gold watch. He looked at it and pushed a button. The light kept blinking. He whispered a curse. "You must excuse me for a moment, Ivan."

Penkovsky nodded, and when his companion hurried away he wondered what the hell that was all about.

The Gold Man retreated to an adjoining room, deeper into the bowels of the dungeon. He didn't want to upset the Russian by telling him that his ICU—the Identity Countermeasure Unit strapped to his wrist—had detected an electronic spy. By pushing a button he should be able to scramble much, if not all, of his conversation and, he hoped, his image, too. At the same time, the device should also indicate the precise location of the intruder.

He jabbed the button. Nothing. He pushed it again. Still nothing. He cursed violently under his breath.

Penkovsky swallowed the last of his drink as the Gold Man lumbered back to the bar. "What is wrong?" he asked, looking pointedly at the man's watch.

"Nothing," Dr. Edwards said. "My watch is not behaving like a good Swiss machine."

Penkovsky shrugged, raked up his change, and left a small tip. He had an idea. He grabbed his hat and motioned to the Gold Man, then headed for an old stone stairway.

They climbed the timeworn steps to a large, bright room and approached another heavy, wooden door. "I will show you something now," he said. "An ancient garden. Once an important place, too. Here you stand on top of the great wall. You see miles around, everywhere." He dragged the door open and led the way.

* * *

Sasha flinched when the STU bleeped again. The device had finally reacquired its signal. "About bloody time," she said. Once again they were all glued to the projected scene.

The two men were outside again. Their images flickered on the brightening picture.

"Look at that," Cliff said.

No one had spoken during the long break in the signal, and Sasha was too spellbound to speak now.

Penkovsky and the Gold Man roamed across a grassy expanse, backed by a bright, clear sky filled with the sunlight of a breezy spring day. Sasha knew that the wind would have a bite to it. The men strode past a large sculpted horse's head and continued to the outside wall, where they pocketed their hands and gazed across the rooftops of the old buildings below. Beyond the island the Mediterranean shimmered all the way to the horizon.

"A remarkable sight," Dr. Edwards said clearly, his long, dark hair whipping in the wind.

Penkovsky adjusted his hat and said, "Malta is a place I love. Most times I stay at the Corinthian Palace Hotel. Very nice. This is also a good entry point for Libya."

"Ah, I see," Dr. Edwards said, nodding. He stepped back and inspected his watch.

Sasha fiddled with the STU until the picture zoomed in for a closeup. A small, bright spot of light winked on the face of the Gold Man's fat watch.

Dr. Edwards pushed a button on his timepiece, peered at it closely, then broke into a wide smile.

"What the hell do you do with that clock of yours?" Penkovsky asked.

Sasha zoomed out.

"Just checking the time at home, comrade. Let's go and sit down." He led the way around a hedge to a wooden table and chairs.

A thin, young male waiter appeared as if from nowhere and asked if they needed anything. Both men declined.

Damn! Sasha had hoped that they would continue to drink. Loose lips sink ships and all that.

Then, as if to please his invisible viewers, the Gold Man reached into his coat and retrieved a silvery flask. He twisted off the top and took a long pull. "Mmmm," he said, then turned to Penkovsky, said something unintelligible, and laughed.

Sasha shook her wrist. The Gold Man offered the flask to Penkovsky, who shook his head and moved his lips without making any sound. "Bloody hell!" she said, smacking the STU with two fingers. "Stupid techno-rubbish!"

"New president—" Penkovsky said as he gazed at the distant sea.

Dr. Edwards nodded and said, "—time . . . action."

"You . . . acquisition hardware . . . budget," Penkovsky said.

"When . . . in Cuba?" Dr. Edwards asked.

"—ussian sub . . . now . . . warheads—" Penkovsky's voice crackled in and out. ". . . rest . . . armament . . . soon."

"Good," Dr. Edwards said.

"Fucking CIA!" Sasha cried as she banged the STU with the heel of her hand.

Cliff and Victoria huddled closer.

"Our . . . in Miami will . . . Cuba . . . the Count in two days. They—" Penkovsky's voice cut out again.

Then, "Fine job, Comrade Penkovsky," Dr. Edwards said with perfect clarity.

"Za, Leningrad," Penkovsky replied, grinning as he patted Dr. Edwards on the shoulder and shook his hand.

Dr. Edwards slapped the Russian's back and declared, "To Ophir!"

"Those American ublyudoki bastards! When do you plan to go?"

"Tomorrow. I wish to see this myself."

"Do you know the old KGB retreat?"

Dr. Edwards took another swig from his flask. "I was there

once, a few years ago."

"Good," Penkovsky said. "I will catch up with you there before they come."

"Excellent, comrade! We will reunite in the new communist Cuba." He held his flask aloft. "Viva Russia!" He took a long drink, then once again offered it to Penkovsky.

This time the Russian accepted it and held it high. "Viva new order!"

Suddenly the picture shivered, broke up, and disappeared.

"That's it?" Victoria asked.

"I guess so," Sasha said. "I better call London straight away with this. Then I suppose we better get on our bike."

"Good," Cliff said. "That didn't take too long. My God, that was incredible, huh, Vic?"

Sasha looked from him to Victoria, who gaped like a silly cow.

"I'll call the bell captain and then the driver," Victoria said breathlessly, flouncing away.

Sasha couldn't dismantle the sneer before Cliff saw it. His brave smile looked apologetic. "Right," he said. "We better get going."

15

Havana Heat

"WELCOME BACK!" CRIED ROSIE, GREETING CLIFF with a sunny smile when he breezed into the spacious domain of her galley on the *Havana Royale*. "Want breakfast?"

"Sure. Would you bring it to the afterdeck, please? I think I'll watch some TV there."

Cliff felt unsteady on his pins as he strolled aft, and his head was clouded with jet-lag, but he was glad to be back in Havana aboard his yacht, where he could decompress before the inaugural party the next evening. He was also feeling agitated by his own uncharacteristic grumpiness, no doubt caused by the strain of dealing with his two high-spirited female travel companions. He was glad to have some solo time now while Vic and Sasha rested below.

He settled into a padded deck chair, punched on the TV, and watched CNN until Rosie arrived with coffee, orange juice, and pastries.

"Mr. Blackwell," she said, "your friend Mr. Witherspoon is here to see you."

He tossed the remote noisily onto the table and scowled at

her. "Oh, all right. Go get him, Rosie."

The smiling CIA spook joined Cliff before he had a chance to taste his coffee.

"Glad to see you back in one piece, Cliff," Witherspoon said, eyeing the retreating steward.

Cliff nodded and tried to look pleasant. "Thanks for that military escort last night. I wasn't looking forward to entering Cuban airspace even with proper clearance."

The agent made a throwaway gesture. "No problem. Didn't want those nervous flyboys to shoot down a friendly aircraft."

Cliff chuckled. "Leaving was tense enough."

"Speaking of which," Witherspoon said, "we got Badalamente out of here."

"Good." Cliff didn't want to ask how.

Witherspoon settled into a nearby chair and declined a cup of coffee. "So how was your trip?"

"Productive. Anything interesting happen while I was gone?"

"You could say that."

"Oh?"

"Saw my boss yesterday. He flew down here for a quick meeting with me and then went to see President Vivo."

Cliff took a sip of coffee and tried to look relaxed. "And?"

"Wanted to give me some firsthand information they got from British intelligence on the Russians. Nothing really new. Just a little concerned about British involvement. Politics, you know. And a little professional jealousy."

"Ah, yes."

"I went to see Toti," Witherspoon said. "Filled him in a little."

"Toti's pretty well connected, isn't he?" Cliff knew that the Cuban had become a trusted friend and a good extra pair of eyes and ears, which made Witherspoon's job in Cuba a lot easier.

The agent shrugged. "I updated him on the Russians, and next thing I know he's flying out the door, mumbling something about the inaugural party at the presidential palace. Just grabbed his beret and left."

"What the hell was that all about?"

An electronic buzzer sounded. Witherspoon swept his jacket back and grabbed a phone.

Cliff got up and slipped inside to give the agent some privacy and to ask Rosie to rustle up some chow for everybody. Then he went to the master suite to alert Victoria to Witherspoon's presence and ask her to join them for breakfast in a few minutes if she wanted some. Sasha, too. She said she'd be right there.

On the way back he stopped in his study and retrieved a tiny digital recorder from his desk. He thought that something interesting could come up during breakfast, something that could be relevant to Sasha's new mission and keep her on top of any developments concerning the Russians.

Topside again, he found Witherspoon pacing along the rail, still on the phone, oblivious to him. He spoke too quietly for Cliff to catch anything, but strain showed in Witherspoon's features when he glanced at him. Finally he clapped the phone shut and pocketed it.

"Everything all right?" Cliff asked, resuming his seat.

Witherspoon faced him, no longer smiling. "That was Danforth. The president spoke to Pasov." He patted his pockets in search of a cigarette.

"What's up?"

Witherspoon paused in his search. "The Russian government is absolutely not trying to invade Cuba."

Watching Witherspoon's now-familiar pantomime made Cliff sigh wearily. "I guess that's a relief."

Witherspoon agreed with a thoughtful nod, then resumed his search and his caged-leopard pacing. "But with Pasov," he said, "how does anyone know for sure?" He finally found his pack of Marlboros, tore out a single cigarette, and fumbled with it.

"What about the sub?" Cliff asked, casually handling his recording device. It looked like an expensive fountain pen. He twisted the top to get it running, then clipped it into the pocket of his sport shirt.

"Still on its way." Witherspoon popped the cigarette between his lips and pulled out a shiny gold Zippo lighter. "But the Russians say it's absolutely not them."

"Then who is it?"

Witherspoon lit his smoke, took a quick drag, and clacked the lighter shut. "Two troublemakers," he said, speaking through exhaled smoke. He described the pair to Cliff as he stumped about, his rubber-soled shoes making little sound on the teak decking. Occasionally he jabbed the air with his cigarette to emphasize a word.

"They sound dangerous," Cliff said, playing dumb. "This guy you call the Gold Man—" He poured coffee into his empty cup. "Who exactly is he?"

"Jonathan Edwards the third," Witherspoon said. "Controlling shareholder of Consolidated Global Exploration Limited in South Africa." The smoke he blew into the freshening breeze dissipated quickly.

Cliff nodded. "The largest gold producer in the world. I have some of their stock."

"That's the guy. He's a complete whack job, Cliff. He's been personally involved in some forms of genocide. Has delusions of controlling the world someday."

Cliff smirked. "Global domination? Who's he think he is, Goldfinger? And let me guess. We're his number-one target."

Witherspoon replied with a sour grin. "You don't know him. Get this. He occasionally sponsors a big-game hunt, on a remote island that he owns near Madagascar. Solicits only the best hunters from around the world, and they all have to be exceptional physical specimens themselves." He stopped and turned when the door opened behind him. "Not that he is, mind you," he finished quickly.

Victoria and Sasha appeared on the afterdeck, Sasha's gaze fixed on Witherspoon. Cliff couldn't read her expression, but something had flickered across her face.

"*Buenos días*, gentlemen," Victoria said.

"We meet again," Sasha said, taking Witherspoon's hand.

Cliff began to make introductions, but the CIA man's strange expression stopped him. "Don?" Cliff asked.

"I'll be damned," the agent said, staring at Sasha. He looked as if he'd stopped breathing.

"This is Sasha Volga, Don."

Witherspoon dropped her hand like a hot rock and stepped back. "Yes," he said. "I know. What is she doing here?"

"We picked her up, so to speak, on our trip. Why?"

Sasha eyed Witherspoon and said, "You were speaking of the infamous Gold Man?"

Witherspoon just nodded.

"To complete the story," said Sasha in her precise Oxford accent, "the invited guest hunter shows up, all excited about a rare private safari in a remote, exotic locale. Once-in-a-lifetime, you know." She raked her mop of red hair away from her face. "Then he discovers he's the only participant. And, even worse, that he's the trophy— the prey." She grinned wickedly.

Witherspoon shook his head slowly, his gaze riveted on Sasha. "You sure can steal a punch line."

Sasha sobered. "Sorry to spoil your fun." They looked at each other with slitted eyes.

Cliff said, "I guess you two know each other already."

"Something like that," Sasha said.

Victoria said, "Well, since we're all friends now, how about if we all sit down. Cliff says breakfast is on the way."

"What'd you do, Cliff," Witherspoon said, "buy her from the British government?"

"You guessed it. I wanted to keep abreast of things."

Witherspoon gave him a cool look. "And just what do you think I've been doing?"

"Look, Don, we appreciate everything you've done. We just

hope you appreciate our efforts, too."

"Of course, Cliff, but—"

"I can't afford to be the last to know," Cliff said.

Witherspoon raised his hands, palms up. "Okay, okay. Here I am, bright and early, bringing you up to date, almost right after you get off the friggin' plane!"

"And you look so radiant, too," Sasha said.

Witherspoon gave her a frosty stare, then turned back to Cliff. "How did you get onto an MI6 agent, Cliff? A search on the Internet? Or did you just have her number in your goddamn little black book?"

"Bingo!" Cliff said. "We used to date."

Witherspoon's face flushed.

"Just like you and I did," Sasha said to Witherspoon. She flashed a look at Cliff. "Later."

Cliff grinned at Witherspoon. "Small world."

Witherspoon flicked his cigarette butt overboard and said, "Look, there's a conflict of interest here, and that's not amusing."

"I wondered about that on the flight to London," Victoria said.

"Victoria," said Sasha, "I'm here because the two of you stalked me all the way to Istanbul. Now I'm here on official business."

Victoria narrowed her eyes. "Let's hope it stays that way."

"Ouch!" Sasha scowled at Victoria, then turned to Witherspoon. "As for you, Donald, you are absolutely mistaken."

Witherspoon whirled on Cliff. "We can't have her getting in the way."

"She won't be in anyone's way, Don."

"That's what you think. She's already caused trouble."

Cliff sighed with exasperation. "What the hell's eating you, Don? And you, Vic? Both of you sound like children."

Victoria was still glaring at Sasha.

Witherspoon gazed toward the Havana skyline for a moment,

then turned back to Cliff and said, "All right, but you're disappointing me, Cliff."

"Let's just sit down and have some breakfast," Cliff said. "That is, if you can all get along for five minutes."

Cliff called the galley on the intercom, and before long they were all dining busily, heads down, concentrating on their food. The chilly atmosphere in the group gradually warmed as Rosie's culinary creations worked their magic. Nothing like a full stomach, Cliff thought, to improve human relations.

Finally Witherspoon pushed himself away from the table and patted his pockets for his cigarettes. "Umm, that was wonderful. I was famished. Thanks, Cliff."

The two women added their own appreciative noises and actually exchanged a tentative smile.

Cliff looked at each of them and smiled privately at the change in their demeanor.

Witherspoon pinched a cigarette from the crumpled pack. "We've all got to work together on this, Cliff. This is a critical time."

Cliff agreed. Vic and Sasha nodded at the CIA man.

"These two psychopaths," Witherspoon said, stabbing the air with his unlit cigarette, "can seriously mess things up, even without Russian sponsorship. We need to get to them first."

"I understand," said Cliff, eyeing Witherspoon's cigarette. "You ever tried dropping that nasty habit?"

Witherspoon gave him a weary look.

Sasha said, "All right, Donald. So the Russians will be here soon. Is that right?"

Witherspoon turned her way, looking reluctant to include her in the conversation. Finally he said, "That's right. And we're prepared. At first we thought they'd be here days ago."

"What about the inaugural party?" Victoria asked.

"Right now the place is crawling with U.S. Marines and special ops teams. Shouldn't be any problems there." He pulled out the Zippo again and lit up.

"You think the party is still on?" Victoria asked.

Witherspoon took a drag and blew smoke straight up. "Sure. They won't cancel now. Too many plans. Don't want to alarm the public."

"That could be a big mistake, Donald," Sasha said.

"I'll be there," he said. "The CIA's stepped up activity here in the past few days." He gazed coolly at Sasha. "As you know, the island is quarantined." He looked at Cliff. "So don't ask me for any more passes to leave here. You got back just in time, Cliff."

"Tell me," said Sasha, "where are they now?"

Witherspoon looked at her. "Who?"

"The nuke sub."

"We don't have any hard evidence."

"What about the Godfather and the Gold Man?"

"You know about Penkovsky, too, huh? Well, we think they might be here already."

"I doubt that," she said.

His jaw muscles worked. "Why do you say that?"

She cleared her throat and gave him a hard stare. "Because yesterday I intercepted a conversation of theirs by satellite. They were in Malta."

Witherspoon cocked his head. "Really? How did you get your Limey mitts on an STU?"

"My secret."

"Oh, yeah?" Witherspoon glared at her while color rose on his neck. "And what else did you learn in this conversation of theirs?"

"They made plans to come here," she said. "Very soon."

"Do me a favor, Sasha," he said.

"Name it."

He gave her a long look, then said, "Just keep me informed, will you?"

"Of course, Donald. And I expect the same from you."

"Of course."

Victoria said, "Listen, Cliff. In the bedroom earlier I heard on CNN that President Van Buren is going to make a televised announcement in a couple of hours."

Cliff was relieved to have the conversation change course. "Oh?"

"It'll be on CNN. Then President Vivo will address the Cuban people."

Cliff shook his head. "Incredible developments, folks." He got to his feet. "If you'll excuse me now, I think I'll go stretch my legs."

Witherspoon stood, too, looking serious. "I need to get going myself." He looked directly at Cliff. "Things could change any minute now. Expect anything." He turned and walked inside.

When the glass door slid shut behind him, Cliff turned to the women, who both looked concerned. "Hell of a turn of events," he told them. They both nodded gravely, each obviously lost in thoughts of her own.

That afternoon Cliff busied himself in his private study, thinking about everything and reviewing his pending business in Havana while Victoria directed the staff in preparations for dinner and accommodations for their newest guest on the *Havana Royale*. Now he was surrounded by a peaceful silence, his thoughts, and his things. His mind swam with the latest developments. The renegade nuclear submarine. His old love, Sasha. And Witherspoon, that dog—talk about *small* world. Then the promise of an intriguing dinner and a festive and historic inauguration party. And over it all, the inevitable threat of doom.

He scanned another file with blind eyes while his mind wandered to his friend Andre Martinez and their lunch together on election day. Since then Andre had probably been helping his friends Diego and Ernest Vivo make the transition into public office.

He tossed the file aside, grabbed the phone, and dialed Andre's cell number. The attorney answered on the first ring.

"How've you been, Andre? Your hands must be full."

"Apologies, Cliff. It's been an incredible week. Too much to do, and to top it off, something is cooking. Something big."

"Yes, I know. The party's still on, isn't it?"

"Reluctantly, yes. We don't want the people to panic. We have to portray calm now, they tell me. But I hear from Sydney Russo that the groundbreaking ceremony was canceled."

"Good. I'm looking forward to seeing you there tomorrow night."

"Excellent, my friend. Give Victoria my greetings."

After Cliff hung up he tried again to focus on paperwork, but soon pushed the pages aside. He didn't want to slow Sydney Russo's projects, but in a way, he didn't really give a damn. Their last meeting still felt like a bad omen, and all their carefully orchestrated plans could become pipe dreams if Havana suddenly turned into a Caribbean Beirut.

All at once a loud shriek ripped the air above the yacht. Cliff jumped to his feet, thinking that it had to be a military jet. He rushed through the starboard office door onto the deck to check the sky. A thundering sonic boom stopped him before he reached the rail.

"What was that?" Victoria said behind him. Farther down the deck some of the staff crowded outside and huddled by the rail, squinting into the bright sky.

"They're busy today," Cliff said, echoing his thoughts aloud.

"Who?"

"U.S. Air Force."

Victoria gripped his arm. "Have you heard any reports?"

He scanned the sky. "No. Been in the study working. What's Sasha doing?"

Victoria tossed her mane of blonde hair. "Who knows? Let's check the TV."

When they entered the main salon the staff eyed them furtively while they made the motions of returning to their tasks. Cliff knew that his crew had to be just as worried as he and Victoria were. The telephone rang just as Victoria punched on CNN. He stared at the TV as he answered the phone. Sydney Russo's familiar voice greeted him.

"You heard the explosion?" the old man asked.

"Couldn't miss it."

Victoria said, "Cliff, I think somebody just made an important announcement. They're giving a summary now."

Cliff held up a finger at her and said, "Sydney, I met with our friends this morning. Now there's something happening on CNN."

Victoria looked upset. Cliff covered the mouthpiece and said, "Go get Sasha."

She looked peeved by his imperative tone, but she got up and left anyway.

Keeping an eye on the TV screen, Cliff said, "They've quarantined the island, Sydney. No getting off now."

"I'm not going anywhere." His old voice sounded resigned and almost gentle. "I'll ride this one out."

"I hear Badalamente left."

"You heard right."

"Good. No more problems—okay, Sydney?"

"Not to worry, Cliff."

"Look, Sydney. I want to be there for the big payday, sure. But more importantly, I do not want trouble."

"Listen, Cliff. Things'll go real smooth if you let me run my business and you keep your nose out of it. *Capisce?*"

A chill coursed through Cliff, and then a spark of anger flared in his gut. "Oh, is that right?"

"You heard me, Cliff."

Cliff struggled to control his emotions and get on with business. "Those contracts we discussed, Sydney? They're ready for you and your, ah, group, to sign."

"Great. Send them over."

Cliff said that he would and ended the conversation, not feeling encouraged by the cold hand that squeezed his heart. Victoria returned, plopped onto the floor like a schoolgirl, and stared at the TV. He struggled to shake the feeling, to put it into a back closet for now.

"Sasha?" he asked, forcing himself to sound normal.

"She'll be here in a minute."

"So what's CNN have to say?"

She glanced at him and pointed at the screen. "It's coming down just like Don said, Cliff. Look at that."

Cliff studied a live aerial shot of Cuban waters, where, the CNN reporter said, U.S. ships had been deployed from Cuban ports and were scouring the surrounding sea while aircraft patrolled the skies.

Cliff said, "Probably tough looking for a submerged submarine around a six-hundred-mile island."

Victoria glanced at him and nodded.

"The crew knows something's up, of course. Maybe you could speak with them, Vic. Give 'em a break to watch the news. Tell 'em no one's allowed off this island now, but not to worry. For us it's still business as usual."

Victoria stood. "I'll do that."

"And remind them about our important guest."

She gave him a mock salute. "Aye-aye, Cap'n."

He smiled at her. "Say we'll all just have to wait and see."

"I'll reiterate our privacy act, too."

"Good thinking, Vic."

She made no move to leave the salon. "Was that Sydney on the phone?"

He looked at the carpet and nodded slowly.

"Trouble?"

He shrugged to hide a shiver of fear. "No . . . not at the moment."

Victoria hugged herself. "I can't wait to get out of Cuba."

"That makes two of us."

When Victoria had left the salon, the phone rang again. Cliff grabbed it and immediately recognized Virgil's voice. "Hey, Virg, where are you?"

"Nassau, of course. Are you and Victoria all right?"

"Yeah, we're okay. We had advance notice. Nothing came as a surprise."

"Wish you'd told me, Cliff. I'm a basket case watching the news."

"Don't get all wigged out, man. I couldn't say anything before. Security reasons."

"Yeah, I understand." Virgil said that everything was going fine there, but he didn't sound very convincing.

"What the hell's happening, Cliff?"

That sounded like Virgil, all right. The designated worrier. "Don't get your shorts all twisted up, Virg. Everything's okay. Although I can think of some safer places to be right now—the West Bank, maybe, or Somalia. Somewhere like that."

"You're not making me feel any better, Cliff. What about the business with the Chicago people?"

"Just a few glitches. No big deal."

"You're having problems with them again, aren't you?"

Cliff didn't know what to say.

"Dammit, Cliff! I thought so. You know, I think about Max all the time, and I don't want to be thinking about you like that someday."

Cliff was both warmed and startled by his friend's words. "Virgil, please don't worry. That'll never happen."

"It better not. Otherwise, I'd have to kill you myself."

Cliff chuckled. "Relax, man. Business is going fine. Really."

Cliff's phone made a call-waiting beep. He told Virgil he had to go, but he'd talk to him again soon. When Cliff pushed the button for the new call, he was pleased to hear the voice of Victoria's father.

"Just called to ask how you're doing down there," Grant Love said.

"You and everybody else. We're all fine here, at least for now. You hear the president's address?"

Grant said that he had. "Cliff, I must say that it's frightening. Bad enough if you're in the States, but—"

"Don't worry, Grant." Cliff was beginning to feel like a guy putting out a lot of little brush fires. "Victoria's fine, and Washington's keeping us up to date, if you know what I mean."

"Okay, Cliff, but you know how much I trust those bastards."

"Yeah, I know we have our reasons to be suspicious. Hopefully they'll find that damn sub soon."

"Puts a crimp in your style, doesn't it?"

"You could say that. And to make matters worse, they've quarantined the island."

Grant said, "I heard." And then he lowered his voice. "Cliff, please promise me. Protect Victoria. She's everything to us. If anything happens to her, her mother and I would just die." Then he chuckled. "And we both know what a little hotshot she can be."

Cliff considered his response for a moment. "Grant, you know how grateful I am to you for everything you've done for me. If I'd ever guessed we'd find ourselves in a situation like this, we wouldn't have come. The government gave me the green light after you-know-what happened, when it seemed safe."

"I understand," said Grant. "You've been thrown a curve ball."

"I'll protect her with my life, Grant. You can take that to the bank."

"Thank you, Cliff. You're a good man. Now can I speak to the hotshot, if she's around?"

Cliff turned and bumped right into Victoria.

She looked at him expectantly. "Is it Daddy?"

He placed his hand over the mouthpiece and nodded. "Listen, Vic, no mention of our meeting tonight—or, for that matter, anything people can't see on the news."

She nodded and took the receiver, her eyes alight. After listening to her father for a while, she replied, "Don't worry, Daddy. We've been busy. Cliff's working, and I've been practicing with the helicopter." She turned toward Cliff. "You know it's never boring around Cliff." She beamed at him.

Cliff could tell that she was doing a good job of diverting her father's attention and masking her real feelings. He left the salon on that note. This seemed like a good time to hit the gym and work off some stress.

As dusk began to gather its shadows around the *Havana Royale*, Victoria took a brisk walk around the deck. She breathed deeply of the cooling salt air and gradually shed the tensions of the day. Maybe she was just enjoying the calm before the storm, but she decided not to think about that now and concentrate on all the good things that had made her days so exciting and so special.

She knew that her life had run on a privileged fast track before she met Cliff, but she also realized that she had gotten lost on a deeper level after losing her husband to pancreatic cancer a few years before. In Cliff she had found a man with the depth of character and the heart of someone whom she feared would never be hers again—and something more. Since they'd been together he'd also danced her through some fascinating times. Now here she was at the very center of a wonderfully frightening place in history. She shivered as she gazed across the darkening water toward some distant lights that winked near the blurred conjunction of sea and sky.

Her thoughts turned to Sasha, whose motives and passions seemed as indistinct as the murky horizon. The woman could be a threat to her, perhaps, but maybe she had been too hard on Cliff. Hadn't he sworn to her father to protect her with his life? After overhearing that, she felt guilty, felt as if she had been acting like one of those bitchy soap-opera queens. Maybe she needed to ease up on Cliff and try to make nice with Sasha. After all, these new

developments really were scary, and she was grateful to have a
new team member who might be of help.

On the other hand, she knew that she couldn't take this
woman lightly. Sasha was something special. And she and Cliff had
a history—an intimate history. Victoria couldn't help but feel
something ominous every time they were together, speaking and
laughing with animation the way they did or talking seriously about
world events and their current situation. Cliff and Sasha seemed to
share a special knowledge that excluded her—and would always
exclude her—no matter how close she was to Cliff.

As if that wasn't maddening enough, the thought of being
stuck in Cuba in such a goddamned dicey situation really fried her.
What is it with Cliff? she wondered. God, he can make me crazy,
and the funny thing is, it's not entirely his fault. Damn it all, maybe
I should've never gone to Nassau in the first place. Look what I
got myself into. They all seemed to be caught in a current of
events over which they had no control, and the potential for loss
seemed to be way too high for her liking. But what else could she
do now but ride it out?

The automatic deck lights blinked on to dispel the darkness.
Her vigorous rounds had winded her. She pushed all her worri-
some thoughts aside, took a moment to catch her breath, and
headed inside, thinking about a long, cool shower. After that, she
thought, things would look better.

Cliff settled into his favorite club chair in the main salon with
the *International Herald Tribune* and a vodka martini, hoping to calm
his nerves. He found that if he could lose himself in reading that
he could relax here almost as he used to, before the world had
been whacked off kilter. He opened the paper, tasted his drink,
and absorbed himself in the news of other people and places.

He had just started into the arts and books section when the
sound of a doorbell startled him. A moment later Victoria glided

in wearing a puzzled look. "Doorbell?" she said. "I didn't even know we had a doorbell."

Cliff shook his head. "You and me both."

"Who could it be?"

Chauncy, the butler, soon appeared behind Victoria and announced the arrival of a Mr. Witherspoon. Cliff smiled at the man. He was glad that Chauncy was still part of the staff. He and his wife, who was head of domestics, had worked at his home in Tahoe before Cliff sold it. They had served him well for many years.

"Show him in, Chauncy," Cliff said. While the butler was gone, Cliff unpocketed his pen-shaped recorder, switched it on, and placed it on the coffee table.

Witherspoon breezed in a minute later, looking distracted, followed by a dark-haired female steward.

Victoria offered refreshments. They all ordered drinks, and the steward left to fetch them.

The CIA man unbuttoned his rumpled gray suit jacket, but remained on his feet. "Where's Ms. Volga, Cliff?"

Cliff grinned. "'Ms. Volga'? My, aren't we formal all of a sudden."

Witherspoon tried to work up a smile but failed.

Cliff glanced at his watch, enjoying the agent's discomfort, and then at Victoria, who covered her grin with one hand. "She should be along soon. Glad you didn't decide to cancel on us."

"Busy day. But I told you I'd keep in touch."

"Looks like the military's been busy, too."

"You'll see a lot more of that soon."

Victoria smiled grimly. "Always good to see you, Don. You're just full of good news, as usual."

"Sorry. Actually, some of my news is good."

"Like what?" said Cliff.

"We now have the support and cooperation of the Russian government. Pasov made an announcement today, too. Made it crystal clear to the world that his government is not behind this action." He looked directly at Cliff. "Of course, Washington was relieved to hear that."

"Wonderful," said Cliff, rubbing his forehead. "Wish I felt the same way."

Victoria agreed.

"We've got a real PR management situation going on now," said Witherspoon, sounding defensive. "Everybody's hammering the White House."

The steward returned with the drinks and served them. When she left, Victoria said, "Where's the submarine?"

Witherspoon sat down and took a drink. "No one knows yet."

"That's reassuring," Victoria said. "Maybe they forgot to turn left at Florida and got lost."

Witherspoon didn't seem to appreciate her sense of humor. "Don't worry, they'll intercept it. One carrier group has been sitting offshore for the last few days, and the second group will be on station before the weekend is over."

"You sure about that?" Cliff asked, picking up his fresh drink. "To me the situation has become even more iffy. Normally we could threaten the Russians on their own turf, but who do we point our guns at now?"

Witherspoon nodded.

Victoria said, "Why are you so sure it's nuclear?" Her eyes had turned dark and serious, and her drink sat untouched.

Witherspoon leaned toward her, looking just as concerned. "Another MI6 agent stumbled across that little piece of information. It's an Oscar-class sub. Nuclear-powered, nuclear warheads. And today Pasov learned how they got it. Right out of the old Russian military arsenal. A real bargain at only a hundred and fifty million on the black market. Pasov decided to cooperate when he confirmed that."

"Good Lord!" Victoria said. "Unbelievable."

Witherspoon said, "You have enough money and you know

the right people, you can get damn near anything these days. Usually it involves the Russian Mafia. A lot of 'em are former KGB and politburo big shots. The ones minding the store turn their heads and put their hands out. The corruption runs deep. Pasov's looking into it."

Cliff rubbed his eyes with both hands. "A lot of help that is now."

"I know," Witherspoon said. "This is Pasov's most embarrassing moment, but not the first. When they get those bastards, though, they'll pay with blood."

Cliff said, "Who's operating the sub?"

"Former Russian servicemen, highly trained people, all hired by the Mob."

"Wouldn't that be expensive? How many men are we talking about in the sub's crew?"

"They're big boats. Maybe a hundred, a hundred and twenty. But that's not a problem for those Russky gangsters. They can easily pay a helluva lot more than the military—something like five hundred bucks a month per man, I hear."

Cliff and Victoria exchanged a concerned look.

Just then Sasha marched into the room.

Witherspoon looked up and frowned at her. "Ah, the spy who came to dinner."

"Speak for yourself, Donald," Sasha said flatly. She plunked herself into a chair next to Cliff's and smiled at him brightly. She looked quite stunning, he thought, in tailored black leather slacks and jacket.

Looking glum, Witherspoon shook his head. "Oh, boy," he said. "This should be an interesting evening."

16

The Finest Hour

THE NEXT EVENING CLIFF AND VICTORIA CLIMBED OUT of their hired limo and stood alone for a moment under the lofty porte cochere in front of the Presidential Palace. Other newly arrived guests mingled in excited talk and laughter a few steps above them in the long arcade. While Victoria clung to his arm, Cliff took a deep breath and looked around. The place was a swarm of formally attired VIPs, men in uniform, and dark-suited security people with walkie-talkies and earphones. The fresh evening air carried hints of flowers, expensive perfume, and the hydrocarbons emitted by an armada of fancy cars all crowding the street and the driveway. Horns blared, and drivers shouted just as they always did on the streets of Havana. He had taken a long look at the grand old building when they arrived, the vast facade an eclectic blend of Cuban baroque and other effusive styles, its row of tall windows and domed roof all aglow under the flood-lights. Until only recently the monumental place had housed Castro's Museum of the Revolution, but now it was the home of Cuba's president once again.

Everything had changed so quickly here, Cliff thought, and

now he and everyone else occupied a unique moment in history. They were about to attend the inaugural gala of the first democratically elected Cuban president ever, thanks, in part, to his own efforts. That thought gave him an unexpected frisson of pride but also a certain amount of trepidation. Nevertheless, he was glad to be here and pleased to share this special occasion with Vic.

Several liveried doormen, a squad of U.S. Marines in full dress uniform—with M-16s—and a platoon of security men protected the entrance. But Cliff and Victoria had the right paperwork, so they were soon admitted to the spacious, circular foyer, with the grand staircase sweeping upward before them. Cliff followed Victoria's gaze to admire the mosaic dome that arched high above. The soaring space echoed with voices. A Moorish fountain splashed nearby, and sparkling crystal chandeliers lit everything with a cheery glow.

"Good evening sir, madam," said a young Cuban man dressed in the khaki uniform of some kind of a guard. He escorted them to a long, marble-topped table. "If you'll just sign in here, please."

Once again they presented their passports and invitations and waited while two officials checked separate lists, then smiled and handed them passes, name tags, and a program. Their escort handed them off to a serious-faced guard who led them to a line of guests waiting near what Cliff recognized as a Swiss-made metal detector. When they had passed that test, another guard directed them down the hallway to the ballroom.

Again they found U.S. Marines standing guard at the entrance and checking everyone's pass. Inside, more armed Marines stood at stony attention along the walls of the vast room, eyeing the milling throng.

Cliff recalled the clusters of military vehicles and soldiers that he had seen outside. Smiling to himself, he thought of Camp Pendleton and how glad he was to be out of the service. The scene sure had all the trappings of a major historical event, by God, and he and Vic were part of it. He also knew that an affair like this was vulnerable, but security as tight as this made him feel better. He smiled at Victoria and ushered her into the midst of the much-awaited cocktail party, the kickoff of the evening's events.

Lively Latin music and the animated babble of the glittering crowd filled the room. Cliff snagged two flutes of champagne from a server and handed one to Victoria with a wide grin. He hoped that his outward appearance looked more relaxed than he felt inside. She smiled at him, her face flushed and her aquamarine eyes flashing with excitement. The red dress that she had poured herself into revealed a daring amount of décolletage. In a room full of dark and stunning women, he thought she was the most delectable eye-candy around.

A heavy hand closed on Cliff's elbow. He wheeled to see Andre beaming at him, his florid face glossy with perspiration. He gathered Cliff into a bear hug.

"Cliff! Victoria! Can you believe this?" the attorney exclaimed above the din.

"I didn't expect to see so many people," said Cliff. "Change seems to be welcome."

Andre's eyes went wide. "Welcome? It is a marvel to see this." He spread his arms. "Cliff, you are an instrument of freedom."

Cliff examined the shiny black toes of his shoes and shook his head. "I think this could've happened just fine without me."

"I'm afraid I must disagree with you this time, Cliff. When you two came to Miami in November for your new yacht, I knew in my heart that change was coming for my country."

"We had no idea," Cliff said. "Must have been destiny calling."

Still smiling, Andre eyed him doubtfully. "Well, no matter what you say, I'm proud of you both. Also my dear friend Diego. As vice president he will be a loyal public servant of the people."

"Here, here!" Victoria said, lifting her glass.

Cliff threw an arm across Andre's wide shoulders. "You know, you've been an instrument of change, too. Let's hope this latest business we discussed on the phone plays out quickly."

Andre's face clouded. "*Dios mio*, let it be so, Cliff."

Victoria whispered into Cliff's ear. "Look over there. It's Witherspoon."

Cliff glanced at Andre, who had turned away politely, pretending to inspect the crowd. "Don't look now, Andre, but here comes the man from U.N.C.L.E.—the one who put in the good word for me with Diego."

"Oh, yes?" Andre gazed with interest at the approaching man.

Witherspoon greeted them curtly, keeping a professional eye on the crowd.

"Hello, Don," said Cliff. "Haven't seen you in ages."

The agent hung around just long enough to be introduced to Andre. He said that he had seen Sasha Volga in the wings, then hurried away, shouldering a path through the multitude.

Cliff shook his head. "That's our man from the spy shop."

Andre shepherded Cliff and Victoria around the room, introducing them to a variety of men and women, all of whom, he said, would "lead Cuba into the twenty-first century." An hour later he interrupted Cliff's conversation with a university president to say that dinner would be served soon. Many guests were already moving toward the door.

"Our seats are near the front," Andre said. "Diego arranged it so."

Cliff was pleased to hear that.

The three of them shuffled along with the herd to a spacious corridor that had been turned into a makeshift dining area. It was crowded with round tables, all draped with gleaming white linen and shimmering with silverware and crystal, each table marked with a number. A stage and podium occupied the front of the space, where workers scurried around with last-minute preparations, including a screeching sound check. Draperies on the tall windows that overlooked the courtyard had been drawn against outside distractions. Cliff took a deep breath as he surveyed the room, thinking, *The stage is set for Cuba's finest hour.* A chill of anticipation shivered through him.

"Over here," Andre said when he found their table. "This is your spot, Cliff, at my side, with Victoria on your other side."

Cliff had a perfect view of the podium. Newsmen shouldered big video cameras and gestured at their sound men on either side of the stage. Before long, Witherspoon returned and settled in across from him, still surveilling the room.

Victoria nudged Cliff and pointed. "Look—Dan Rather."

"Oh, yeah. This'll get some major coverage."

She squeezed his leg. "And check out all the big shots over there. Must be American delegates."

"Yes," said Andre, turning back to them. "That portly one there, he is the new American ambassador to Cuba."

Witherspoon looked at the man, too, then continued to survey the room with keen eyes.

Before long, an unsmiling Sasha appeared, sat down next to Witherspoon, and adjusted the spaghetti straps of her simple black dress. She drew curious looks from all the men and women who sat nearby. Cliff stared, too, but tried not to. He thought she looked hot enough to wilt the exotic floral centerpiece on their table. Witherspoon bent close to her and said something that was lost in the chatter. She thumbed back a wing of flaming hair, displaying nails painted a shocking scarlet. Victoria had told Cliff once, with a laugh, that the color was known as "Joan Crawford come-fuck-me red."

"Good job with your protective coloration," Witherspoon said to her.

Sasha gave him a pointed look. "That's not all I'm good at."

The CIA man looked away and fingered his tie.

Victoria squeezed Cliff's knee so hard it made him flinch.

A regiment of servers, all dressed in starched black and white, filed into the room and threaded among the tables to serve the first course. The volume of conversation dropped noticeably as the guests turned their attention to the food.

Between the main course and dessert, a balding master of ceremonies in an undersized tux took over the podium and kicked off a program of speakers interspersed with feeble topical jokes that drew only polite laughter. One speaker, though, a professor from an American Ivy League university, caught Cliff's attention.

"The whole world is watching us here tonight," the bespectacled man said. "In a relatively short period of time this country has shifted smoothly from the dictatorship of Fidel Castro to the inspired interim leadership of President Diego Perez to that of our president-elect, Ernesto Vivo, who has taken the helm through a democratic election process. This is a resounding victory for freedom."

He allowed those words to hang in the room for a while as he gazed at the audience. A few people clapped, and then more, and finally everyone joined in the applause. When he finished his optimistic remarks, the assembly buzzed with conversation, and a giddy energy filled the hall in anticipation of the final speaker, President Ernesto Vivo himself.

A few minutes later, after a long-winded introduction by the overinflated emcee, President Vivo marched to the podium. Instead of a tux, the president-elect wore a plainly cut black suit, white shirt, and a discreetly patterned red power tie. Everyone stood and greeted him with cheers and thunderous applause. Vivo beamed and waved to the crowd for what Cliff guessed to be a full two minutes before he bowed deeply and then motioned for quiet. Finally the new leader of Cuba launched into a long and emotional speech that reviewed Cuba's past, expressed his hopes and plans for the future, and addressed the troubling issues shouted in recent headlines. By the time he finished he had mesmerized the audience into a hushed silence. Then the crowd burst into shouts of *"Viva Cuba!"* and *"Viva la libertad!"* and an ovation that seemed to rock the palace.

Cliff was impressed with Vivo's reception, with his thoughtful speech, and with the crowd's enthusiastic reaction to it.

Vivo stepped away from the podium, raised both arms high,

and waved to the crowd. The image reminded Cliff of President Nixon, although Vivo was heavier and had more of the look of a statesman and patriarch.

"Ladies and gentlemen! Ladies and gentlemen!" the emcee shouted into the microphone, trying to quiet the crowd.

Vivo returned to the podium and blew kisses while the noise abated.

"We have one more special guest," the master of ceremonies announced. He introduced the new U.S. ambassador to Cuba, George Marley, who promptly strode to the podium, shook hands with Vivo, and took over the microphone.

"Mr. President," Marley said, "it is indeed an honor to present to you this evening a token of our high esteem." He gestured toward the nearest set of draperies, which opened on cue to reveal the floodlit courtyard outside. Most of the murmuring audience, including Cliff and his party, stood to peer out the tall windows to see a glistening black stretch Cadillac limousine frozen in the dazzle of unseen spotlights.

Everyone made appropriate noises in response to the sight. Marley had to raise his voice to be heard. "Mr. President," he intoned, "the United States hopes that you will accept this small gift as a symbol of democracy, freedom, and the future prosperity of the Cuban people."

The ambassador and the president-elect shook hands again amid another wave of applause. Vivo leaned into the microphone to express his thanks. Marley patted him on the back and invited him to take a closer look at the limo.

"Of course, of course!" Vivo said effusively. "But only if you and all these honored guests join me."

With that agreed, the crowd clapped and cheered again until the uniformed guards threw open the courtyard doors. While the two gentlemen strolled from the stage, the emcee, looking slightly deflated, dutifully invited everyone to visit the open bar. Everybody ignored him.

Cliff returned to his seat next to Victoria and smiled at his companions. Witherspoon and Sasha sat with their heads together in serious conversation, both of them looking twitchy. Victoria excused herself for a trip to the ladies' room. Andre stood beside him, watching streams of partygoers funneling into the courtyard.

Cliff tugged on Andre's sleeve to get him seated again. "When Victoria comes back," he said, "let's go outside and say hello to Diego."

"Excellent idea! He will be pleased to see you again. And he can introduce you to the president."

Suddenly Toti appeared out of nowhere, dressed in a khaki jumpsuit and beret, and collapsed into the chair next to Witherspoon. "*Dios mio, hombre!* I have been looking everywhere for you."

Cliff leaned across the table, and Sasha crowded closer to the Cuban operative, gluing her pneumatic chest to Witherspoon's shoulder.

"What's up?" the CIA man said, frowning.

"*Mierda!* It cost me fifteen minutes just to get inside, even with my ID." He glanced down and smiled crookedly. "But then I suppose I am not dressed for—"

"Chrissake, man! What is it?"

Toti caught his breath and said, "I picked up a rumor. I have been checking it out with help from my brothers, in Havana and in Miami."

"What kind of rumor?"

"A very bad thing. It is about the limousine that—"

A thunderclap jarred the marble floor beneath Cliff's feet and toppled all the glassware on the table. He whirled just in time to glimpse the draperies balloon into spinnakers swollen by a gale of broken glass from the shattered windows, and then he dived for cover. Chairs and tables, china, cutlery, and glassware crashed to the floor all around him as a dirty cloud of smoke and debris boiled through the openings. A shower of glass pelted Cliff's head and back. Screams and shouts filled the bruised vacuum that followed the concussion.

When he lifted his head again, the room looked like the inside of one of those glass balls that you shake to create an artificial snowstorm. He turned to crawl away toward his companions, but found himself blocked by a young Cuban woman who was sprawled on her back with her sequined party dress hiked to her sturdy, café-au-lait thighs and her bare heels thumping the cold marble spasmodically. She clutched her slender throat with both hands and made choking sounds as she tried to stem the pulsing flow of arterial blood that fountained from the side of her neck, where a triangular shard of glass had imbedded itself.

Cliff crabbed his way around her and found Toti sitting on the floor and squinting at his fat wristwatch.

"Mother of God!" he cried. "I have to get out of here. I cannot be too late again." He scrambled to his feet and lurched away through the wreckage, pushing dazed people aside like a drunken fullback rambling toward the end zone.

Cliff had no idea what the hell he was talking about. But he didn't like the haunted look that he had seen in the man's eyes.

His heart galloping, Toti made a mad dash through the bedlam of soldiers and security men at the entrance to the Presidential Palace. They all seemed to be shouting orders and running in circles. *A classic Chinese fire drill,* he thought. He flew down the front steps and darted straight to the next car that pulled up. When the valet got out, Toti slapped a twenty-dollar bill into his hand and dived into the driver's seat. "Keep the change," he said with a grin and a quick tip of his beret. He smoked the tires all the way down the driveway, braked hard at the street, and cranked the wheel just in time to avoid a wildly swerving taxi. He burned rubber again and raced down the dimly lit street. *The park at the waterfront. I've got to get there in time.*

Tires screamed as he whipped around another corner into the

blinding headlights of an oncoming car. When he swerved violently to miss it, he sideswiped a parked car and sheared off chrome
trim and a side mirror. He strangled his steering wheel with sweaty
hands to regain control. *Go! Go! Go!*

Two more shrieking turns and the park came into sight, most
of it lost in darkness except for a few pools of weak yellow light
cast by the lampposts. He stood on the brakes and shuddered to a
stop near the departure dock. The area looked deserted. *Where is
the little shit?* He tried to catch his breath as he probed the darkness and fought a rising sense of panic. Sirens yowled in the distance. He scanned the trees and the shrubbery. Across the park a
small rubber boat hunkered darkly on the sand near the water, all
but invisible. *Thank God!* But no sign of the Count anywhere.

Then a small, dark figure broke away from the shadow of a
distant cabbage palm and scurried across the patchy lawn, stubby
legs churning madly, heading for the boat. *Dios mio*, that little
fenomeno can run! Toti knew he had no chance to catch him on
foot.

He stomped the accelerator pedal, and the engine roared.
The rear tires whirred and kicked up shreds of turf. He surged
ahead until the trees grew large in his windshield. He yanked the
wheel to miss them and close the distance to the little man, who
stumbled and stopped just long enough to glance at him. Toti
whipped the wheel around again to clear a tree. The tires lost their
grip on the slick grass, and the car slewed sideways, not respond-
ing to the wheel, until it slammed into a fat date palm. Toti's head
smacked the door frame painfully.

"*Mierda!*" he cried, watching the little *bastardo* scuttling away
toward the beach. Toti cranked the wheel, hit the gas, and dis-
lodged the car with a howl of metal and the rattle of broken glass.

Toti bore down on his quarry. At another place and time, he
thought, the image would be comical, like a midget clown in a
circus. When the tiny figure arrived at the beach, he got bogged
down in the sand. That's where Toti finally caught him. The right

front fender clipped him smartly and sent him tumbling over and over until he came to rest curled into a fetal position.

Toti ploughed to a hard stop, jumped from the car, and legged it toward the balled shape on the dark sand.

He stopped a few feet away and drew his Colt Python. The Count was tiny, but he was always dangerous. Toti edged closer, pointing the gun, and squinted. Damn! Had he killed the little monster?

The midget groaned. Then he rolled over, coughed, and spit sand. He looked at Toti and said, "You asshole!"

Toti breathed a sigh of relief. "Asshole?" he replied. "That is a most unkind thing to say, comrade." He grabbed a handful of the Count's thin, greasy hair and forced the shiny barrel of the Colt into his puckered little mouth. "If I push this a little farther down your throat and pull the trigger, do you know what will happen? You will have a new asshole, my friend. Then you won't be calling people dirty names like this, I think."

The little man flailed his stumpy arms and snorted.

Toti said, "The only way to avoid this bad thing is to tell me where to meet Penkovsky's sub—now!"

"Go fug yousef!" said the Count, unable to access a number of useful consonants.

Toti shoved the gun barrel in further and cocked the hammer. The count choked and goggled at him.

"You have only moments left to live, comrade."

Barely able to suck air, the Count bucked and kicked up sand with his diminutive cowboy boots.

Toti grinned at that sight and said, "Your life ends in five seconds, my little *caballero*."

The Count gasped and said, "Way! Way! Don' shoo!" Cold terror flashed in his eyes.

Toti yanked the gun barrel free, bringing a tiny set of dental plates with it—another amusement. "Your time is up. Talk quickly."

The midget spat into the sand. "The coordinates. On the

memo pad . . . of my GPS." He raised one arm.

Toti skinned back the Count's coat sleeve, unbuckled the device, and peered at the screen. "Which button?"

"Green one, you pig."

Toti lifted the Colt reflexively and flicked the barrel across the Count's nose. The midget yelped and clapped his pudgy little mitts to his face. Blood streamed darkly into his mouth and across his chin.

Toti pushed the green button. Numbers appeared on the tiny illuminated screen. "What next?"

The Count just moaned. Toti showed him the gun.

"Push the Auto button," he said quickly, his voice muffled by his hands.

Toti did that. "What else?"

"Nothing. The readings, they change as you get closer to the coordinates of the sub. They will flash across that grid." He coughed a spray of blood into the sand.

"When will the sub get here?"

The Count considered him with weary eyes. "At eleven-thirty. You will never make it."

Toti checked his watch. It was just after eleven.

The Count pawed blood from his chin and groaned again. "I have told you all I know. Pinky will kill me. Let me go."

"One moment, comrade." Toti grabbed the Count and frisked him, feeling revulsion at touching the freakish body.

"Ow!" the little man wailed. "I think I broke something."

Toti removed what looked like an explosive device from the count's waistband. "What the hell is this?"

"Just what it looks like."

"Ah, and I believe this must be a firearm," Toti said as he withdrew a slim automatic pistol. He stuffed it into his pants. "What else do you have?"

"Nothing. Now let me get out of here." The Count struggled in Toti's grasp.

Toti jammed the muzzle of the Colt against his temple. "I don' thin' so, little buddy. You come with me."

Toti jerked the Count to his feet and prodded him across the sand to the rubber boat, a black Zodiac with an outboard motor, keeping the Colt on him. "Get in. Start it."

The Count struggled into the boat, complaining all the way. Toti pushed the boat into the water and climbed in after him, still pointing the gun. One pull got the outboard motor going.

"Take us to the spot, and don't try anything funny, Sergei. If you do, you will be the first one to die."

The Count backed the boat away from the beach, shifted gears, and got them turned around and heading offshore. "What do you think you will gain by your stupid heroics?" he said. "When Pinky's submarine surfaces, you will be a dead man."

"Shut up and watch where you are going," Toti said, keeping one eye on the disgusting little *bastardo* and the other on the screen of the GPS. "Go faster!"

The motor growled with the increased RPMs and pushed the boat bouncing across the light chop. Cold sea water sprayed Toti's back. He glanced around. No life jackets, no oars, no spare gas. *Mierda* Precious minutes evaporated in the salty breeze.

He checked the time—eleven twenty-five—and the GPS display. Almost there.

The Count swiveled his head like a radar dish, looking worried. He should be, Toti thought.

Something caught Toti's eye. He waggled a hand at the Count and shouted at him to cut the motor. The silence deepened as he scanned the black water. Soon a storm of bubbles broke the surface about ten meters away, as if from a great exhalation, and then the dark sea heaved, reminding Toti of one of those idiotic Japanese monster films—*Godzilla*, probably. Finally an eerie apparition appeared, slowly at first and then more rapidly, its long, black shape a little darker than the sea. As the water boiled around it, the submarine rose until it eclipsed the dim horizon and wallowed there, limned by the faint light of the moon.

Toti shivered, then turned to his captive pilot, gun in hand. "Crank up that motor and get us over there."

The Count did as he was told.

Their rubber boat bumped the pregnant swell of the side of the small sub a minute later. Toti shivered again as he looked at the ominous thing. No sign of life anywhere. He tied a line to the nearest cleat, then pointed the Colt at the Count again. "Put that motor in neutral and get your ass up there."

The little man looked up and then back at Toti. "That is something I cannot do. That should be obvious."

Toti cocked the gun. "Tonight, you wretched little freak, you will test your limitations. Please do not test mine." He gestured with the Colt. "Get up there and open the hatch. I will follow."

"You are completely insane."

"Go!"

The midget said something again, but the wind and the burbling purr of the outboard carried the words out to sea. Finally he stood unsteadily, climbed out of the Zodiac, and pulled himself up the glistening side of the sub. His child-sized cowboy boots scraped on the metal hull.

Toti trailed him. When they reached the grated iron deck, they both stood looking at the watertight hatch, trying to keep their balance. It had a simple wheel. One must only turn it to open the hatch, Toti reasoned. Probably counterclockwise. He shifted the Colt to his left hand, grasped the wet, slippery wheel with his right, and tugged as he kept the gun trained on the Count, who had sat down to keep from falling overboard. At first the wheel wouldn't budge, but then it creaked and gave way. Toti spun the wheel, then pulled the hatch open.

Toti let out his breath and looked at the Count. "Get in."

The little man scowled at him but got to his feet, maneuvered himself into the hatch, and started down the ladder while Toti watched him closely.

The Count called out something in Russian. A big, muscular sailor in white pants and T-shirt appeared below them and looked up with an expression of puzzled surprise on his pockmarked face. He shouted something to the Count in the same language.

"So sorry, my friends," Toti said, aiming the Colt down the ladder. The discharge sounded like a bomb in the hollow space. The round caught the sailor high in the chest and sent him sprawling onto the metal deck. He bellowed something else, and shouting voices answered him. The Count clung to the dripping ladder with tiny white fingers, frozen in place, goggling at Toti, mouth agape, wearing the look that a man must wear under the blindfold when he stands before a firing squad, Toti thought. He had seen that look before when blindfolds were in short supply. He took aim again, and the Colt bucked in his wet hand. The Count's undersized head split like a cantaloupe. His doll's hands lost their grip, and he tumbled backward. One leg got hung up between the rungs, which left him hanging upside-down, bumping against the ladder.

Toti was quite familiar with the type of explosive device that he had taken from the Count. He activated it now, dropped it into the hatch, and secured the cover. He rode his butt down the side of the sub into the rubber boat. His heart thumping wildly, he tugged the quick-release knot loose, then scrambled to the outboard and threw it into gear. He twisted the throttle as far as it would go and roared away—not fast enough, he thought—holding his breath.

Before his time as a jet jockey, during those days in the mountains with a little guerilla band, sometimes they had to live off the land. If they thought it was safe enough, they would lob hand grenades into a river, then gather the stunned fish. He remembered the muffled sound of the explosions—a deep-throated whump! that you could feel under your feet. The sound that rocked his world now was a lot like that, but much louder, and it contained a clanging note—a hollow metallic ring.

The sea needed little time to swallow that heavy sound, leaving only a brief, salty shower and a shock wave that whitecapped just before it lifted the rubber boat. Toti clung to the seat and rode it out. When he looked back, only a moonlit haze of rising smoke remained.

The sea, he thought, knows how to hide its secrets.

17

Thimblerig

CLIFF AWOKE WITH A VAGUE SENSE OF ALARM and a head full of roiling images like the remnants of a bad dream. The stateroom was dim and quiet behind the blackout draperies. He rolled onto his side and touched Victoria's shoulder.

She made a low, languorous moan, turned to him, and threw a lazy arm across his waist. He kissed her lightly on her parted lips and wondered again how she managed to avoid the dreaded dragon breath of morning. Lifelong dental care, he supposed, and good oral hygiene.

That was the last coherent thought that swam through his mind before she snugged the long, warm length of herself against him and made one of her patented purring sounds. He responded immediately, and all the nightmare outtakes evaporated in the grassy scent of her tumbled hair. They clung and curled into the practiced rhythms that had yet to dull his ardor for this extraordinary woman, her scalding lips on his face and neck and her deft hands guiding him to their mutual satisfaction.

Afterward, they both lay limp on the damp tangle of Egyptian cotton sheets, panting in the darkness. At such times he wished for the long-abandoned sin of a cigarette. Eventually he roused himself enough to squint at the bedside clock.

Victoria yawned and mumbled, "Whutimezit?"

"Just after one—in the afternoon."

"Oh, Gawd . . . Which day—and which planet?"

Cliff chuckled. "Same planet, different day."

She bolted upright and gaped at him in alarm. "Cliff . . . Last night . . ."

"I know, Vic."

"I can't believe . . ."

"Neither can I." He placed a gentle hand on her naked thigh. "But we better get moving and see what's happening."

While Victoria got the shower going, he called Rosie and requested brunch on the afterdeck in fifteen minutes. He also spoke briefly with Karen, his secretary. Then he joined Victoria under the steaming spray. As they bathed she managed a brave smile and a brief giggle, but this time their soapy games lacked their usual lighthearted enthusiasm.

"Karen says the whole world has been trying to reach us," he told her. "Looks like the rest of the day's all downhill from here."

Victoria made a face and turned to rinse her hair.

After a hurried meal, they plunked themselves onto the big couch in the main salon and flipped through channels on the big-screen plasma TV. Everyone was talking about the explosion at the Presidential Palace. Eighteen people had been killed in the blast, including George Marley, the American ambassador, who had been standing next to President Vivo, and Vivo himself. Dozens more had been injured. Fortunately, Dr. Diego Perez had not been harmed. That meant Perez would remain as the interim leader of Cuba. *The Russian badniks have to be behind this,* Cliff thought grimly. *Maybe they aren't done yet.*

They continued to absorb all the bad news until Cliff said,

"You know, I'm sure glad you left for the ladies' room last night."

She raised a quizzical eyebrow at him.

"Andre and I were waiting for you before we went outside to see Diego and the president. If we hadn't waited, we'd be dead, too."

Victoria's eyes looked haunted. "Cliff, I—"

"Luck of the draw, I guess. But I'd say you're my lady luck."

She threw herself into his arms and tried to stifle a sob.

Karen entered the salon timidly, as usual, and excused herself. Cliff told her to come in. She handed him a fistful of pink phone message slips. He sighed when he took them and asked her if she had seen Sasha.

"According to the security monitor," she said, "she came in about four this morning. She asked Rosie for a bite to eat around nine and then disappeared."

"You think she's still on board?"

"I wouldn't know, sir."

Cliff pulled away from Victoria and said, "Maybe we should go look for her."

Victoria quickly stowed her linen hanky and nodded.

They found Sasha perched on the edge of a chaise lounge on the sun deck, toying with her STU. Behind her the Bell 407 chopper hunkered on the helipad, its sleek blue-and-silver hide winking in the sun.

Sasha looked up wearing a frown, but greeted them cheerily enough.

"You getting anything on that gizmo?" Cliff asked.

"Not what I want, I daresay. So far just Spanish news channels and a soccer game from Brazil." She kept pushing buttons.

"How about the Godfather or the Gold Man?"

"Indeed!" Sasha said, brightening. "We located Penkovsky."

"Where?"

"In Cuba. Holed up in an old KGB retreat in the mountains near near Gorga, about six hundred and seventy kilometers southeast of here."

"And the Gold Man?"

"I'm working on Dr. Edwards now," Sasha said. "He's supposed to be headed this way."

Cliff nearly gagged at the thought of the Gold Man operating right under their noses. If the intelligence agencies of Great Britain and the U.S. combined couldn't pin him down, no wonder those maniacs had been able to hit the World Trade Center.

Sasha looked at him as if she were reading his mind and continued to fiddle with the STU. "Sorry, mates. Sometimes this bloody thing just won't—"

Suddenly the holographic screen appeared in midair like magic. "Here we go!" Sasha cried. She handed Cliff and Victoria a pair of the special lenses, then returned to the controls.

Victoria leaned close to Sasha. "Wow, I can't get over this thing. The picture's so detailed."

"What are we seeing?" Cliff asked.

"Looks like a polo game," Sasha said. "I'll zoom in."

"Another sports channel?" asked Victoria.

Sasha sharpened the image. "No, this is the Gold Man's ranch in Pretoria, South Africa—one of the places I wanted to check out."

Cliff squinted at the airborne movie. "Is that a soccer ball?"

"I'm afraid not," Sasha said. "That's some poor bloke's head."

Victoria covered her face with her hands and turned away.

Sasha looked at her and snorted.

"That's a sport?" Cliff asked.

Sasha shrugged. "Revenge, torture, murder, sport. It's all the same to the Gold Man."

Cliff kept watching until the picture flickered and began to break up.

"Damn!" Sasha said. "On the bloody blink again."

Victoria had recovered enough to say, "Who were those people playing polo with that . . . that *thing*?"

"Friends," Sasha said. "Likely other members of an organization based at the ranch that the Gold Man helps to fund."

"What's that?" Cliff asked.

Victoria looked at Cliff. "Not the Red Cross."

"No, indeed," Sasha said. "It's called SAFRA—South African Revolutionaries and Assassins."

"Lovely," Victoria said.

The STU beeped, and the 3-D movie dissolved.

"Just as well," Cliff said. "I think we've seen enough." He turned away and leaned on the rail, feeling thoroughly disgusted. A distant movement caught his attention. Three Cuban patrol boats sliced through the swells near the harbor. His gaze panned to the bright western sky, where several military jets circled like seabirds over a shoal of bait fish. That sense of dread stirred in him again. He wished he knew what the hell was going on.

He turned to the two women and said, "If you ladies will excuse me, I think I'll check the news again. Vic, don't forget to return that call from your parents."

CNN kept rehashing the same reports on the TV in the main salon. Cliff clicked through the channels, ignoring Fox News, an outlet he scorned for its biased reporting, and finally paused on MSNBC and hoped for the best. Their talking heads babbled more of the same. The bombing. The death of President Vivo. The innocent victims. The rampant, shouting crowds in the streets. The hunt for the Soviet nuclear sub. The lack of new information forced the reporters to repeat obvious questions and suspicions. Who had engineered the assassination? The Russian Mafia? Cuban anarchists? The mysterious Gold Man?

How did they dig up that name? Cliff wondered. The powerful but obscure Dr. Jonathan Edwards III had appeared on the international radar as quickly as Osama Bin Laden after 9/11.

What would become of Cuba now? That was the question on everyone's lips, the anchorman said. Was the world on the brink of a nuclear incident? Cliff didn't want to speculate on that subject. Outside, the sound of shrilling jet engines increased as more aircraft streaked over the *Havana Royale* at mission speed. One thing was certain, he thought. Whatever happened, the U.S. would have to maintain a strong military presence in Cuba until things could be stabilized. And that could mean another blow to American taxpayers, many of whom were already drowning in the multibillion-dollar debt forced upon them by the occupation of Iraq and Afghanistan.

Cliff mulled over a few questions of his own. Would a nuclear blast turn Havana into another Hiroshima? If the city was spared that horror show, could Sydney Russo and his people get their casinos ramped up soon enough in the midst of all this chaos? Could they still attract foreign investors? Would the gambling crowd come in sufficient numbers for them to turn a profit? Or would Russo's backers say the hell with it and pull out? Beyond that, was gaming the golden goose that would help Cuba's new capitalist economy to take flight?

Too goddamned many questions, he thought. And too many variables—a lot more than he usually determined to be an acceptable risk in any business venture. Why did he get himself involved in this mess? Maybe he had made a colossal error in judgment. Even worse, he knew that they could all pay for his mistake with their lives.

Cliff blew out a heavy sigh and scooped up his stack of phone messages. He saw that Witherspoon had called that morning and hoped that he would stop by with an update soon.

He placed a call to Andre and spoke with him briefly. Then he tried Sydney Russo's number. The old man answered on the first ring.

"Thank God you and Victoria are okay," he said, sounding

genuinely relieved.

"Thank you, Sydney. Car bombings seem to be very popular lately." Cliff listened to the silence on the line for what seemed like a long time. Maybe he shouldn't have hinted at the death of the hotel owner—a troubling incident that he couldn't bring himself to share with Victoria.

"A setback," Russo finally said in a voice that had gone flat. "As long as war doesn't break out, no problem."

"Glad to hear that, Sydney."

"Tony and I been right on top of things. Figure Washington'll stop these bastards somehow."

"Let's hope so."

"I got the contracts all ready for you to sign."

"Okay."

"We gotta look on the bright side, Clifford. Now our man will be president the next four years. He'll be good for business."

The old don's resilience amazed Cliff. Now in his eighties, Russo still managed to muster a young man's hunger for success —dreams that he might not live long enough to see and enjoy, especially with the way he was operating.

"The way things're going, you'll need the clout," Cliff said, surprised at his own loose tongue. His comment received only more arctic silence, so he decided to end the conversation.

"Let me get off the line, Sydney, so I can call Andre. I'll send him over to get the contracts."

Cliff called his trusty associate Virgil Carter in Nassau next, then got Andre on the line. They talked about the previous evening for a minute or two. Andre was obviously grieving for Ernesto Vivo and deeply concerned about the future of his beloved Cuba. Cliff let him voice his concerns for a while, but he wasn't in the mood to parse the deeper meanings of current events. He cut the conversation short by asking Andre to pick up the contracts at the Riviera. When Andre sounded alarmed by the request, Cliff assured him that he had his reasons. He also told him that he wanted to see him again soon and talk some more.

Just as Cliff ended the call, a steward popped his head through the forward salon door and announced that a Mr. Witherspoon was here to see him. The CIA man stepped into the room a minute later looking as if he had slept in his rumpled black suit. He probably had, Cliff thought. If he had slept at all.

"Is Sasha here?" he asked without even saying hello.

"No, Vic said she left about an hour ago to look for you."

"Damn! I need to talk to her." He dropped into an overstuffed chair. "I hope to God she's made some progress."

"I hope you have, too," Cliff said. "We're really in the dark here, so tell me something good."

Witherspoon let out a deep breath. "I've talked to Washington a few times. And to Toti. He was quite informative."

Cliff pulled the pen from the pocket of his guayabera shirt and casually clicked on the recorder. He used it to scribble a note on a message slip, then stowed both pen and note in the same pocket. "Is he okay?"

"Yeah," Witherspoon said. "He was a busy boy last night. And he got lucky. Seems that a Russian hit man, a guy known as 'the Count,' was working for the Russian kingpin in Miami who set up this hit—a scumbag named Boris Forostenko."

"Any connection to the guy in Moscow?"

"Yep. The Count was supposed to arrive with the new presidential limousine."

"And Forostenko was working with the Godfather?"

"Correct. They're tight. Makes things tough on everybody. Taking down the Russian mob is like getting rid of crab grass. Makes the Italians look like a tea party."

"I'm not sure I'm following you," Cliff said.

"Okay. Let me skip to the part about Toti last night."

And he did.

"Like I told you," Witherspoon concluded, "Toti got lucky. Forostenko's old sub went down like a stone, and Toti got away with his hide still in one piece."

"Unbelievable," Cliff said. "But what about Forostenko?"

"Still in Miami. Business as usual." He dropped his head onto the back of the chair and closed his eyes. "Maybe we can nail his ass one of these days. But right now we gotta stop Penkovsky and Dr. Edwards."

"I think Sasha can help you there, ol' buddy. That's what she wanted to tell you. The Gold Man is still in Pretoria, and the God-father is right here in Cuba, hiding out at some old KGB retreat."

Witherspoon bolted upright. "No shit? Christ, I've gotta talk to Sasha. If we can take out those two, the Russian sub commander may get cold feet and abort."

"Any communication with the submarine?" Cliff asked.

"No. Admiral Phillip Dallenbach himself will captain the *U.S.S. George Washington* and was airlifted to the first carrier group two days ago. He's taking charge. The admiral and the Joint Chiefs of Staff had plenty of briefings with their advisors and strategists on the what-ifs of this situation. They have a battle plan, and con-tingency plans, too."

"That's good to hear."

Witherspoon dropped his face into his hands and rubbed his eyes. "I won't sugarcoat this for you, Cliff. This is as dicey as the Cuban Missile Crisis. Things could go to hell in a heartbeat."

Cliff nodded slowly. "I hope Van Buren can be as cool-headed as Kennedy was."

Witherspoon agreed. "The Russians timed all this well. You can bet they wanted to catch these two new presidents off balance."

"Fortunately," Cliff said, "from what you say, the Russian government isn't behind any of this. Otherwise, we'd have a hell of a fight on our hands."

Witherspoon didn't argue with that, either.

"One thing bothers me, Don. How do you know there's only one nuclear submarine?"

The agent gazed at him with weary eyes for a while and then

said, "Well, I guess we don't." He dragged himself to his feet and said he had to go. He turned at the door and said, "By the way, did you hear about the other two hotel owners?"

Cliff shook his head, unable to speak.

"Found one floating in Havana Bay and the other shot to death in his car, not far from here."

Cliff was glad Witherspoon left before he could read the look in his eyes.

18

Night Moves

AFTER A QUIET DINNER WITH VICTORIA, Cliff excused himself, mumbling about having some accounts to review, and shut himself in his private office. There he shuffled papers and wrestled with a host of unwelcome thoughts for an hour, until someone rapped sharply on his door.

"I'm sorry, sir," the steward said, looking flustered, "but these men insist on—"

Two men dressed in blue uniforms shouldered past the cowed steward and entered the room. "*Señor* Blackwell?" asked the taller man, looking stern.

Cliff excused the steward and admitted to his identity, although he wished he could be someone else just now. "Who do you think you are, barging in like this?" Cliff demanded. "This is a private yacht."

"We are from the *Policia Nacional de la Revolucion,*" the tall one said. He dug out his badge and flashed it at Cliff.

The shorter, darker man did the same thing. He sported a generous paunch that hid his belt buckle and, incongruously, a pair of dark sunglasses. "We want to have a word with you," he said. It didn't sound like a request.

Their accents were strong, but their English seemed good enough. He knew he had to play it cool, even if his chest had suddenly constricted. "All right," he said. "Have a seat."

Neither man made a move to sit down. Instead they both took their time looking around. "*Impressionante*," the potbellied cop said, nodding.

The tall man didn't look all that impressed. "Mr. Blackwell," he began, "we are here on official business." He seemed to be the leader. "What is it you do here in Cuba?"

Cliff took a deep breath and tried to let it out quietly. "I'm here on business, too. Just not official. Personal."

"What type of business?" the fat cop asked.

"Investments."

The tall one leaned toward Cliff. "What *type* of investments?"

Cliff was already tired of these two, but didn't want it to show. "Real estate, gaming," he replied with a shrug.

The two *policia* glanced at each other as if on cue, eyebrows raised.

"Why do you ask?"

The tall one raised three fingers—all the fingers he had on that hand. "Well, *señor*, we are investigating the murder of three men. Sad to say, but they all turned up *muy muerto* this week."

"My God," said Cliff, trying to assume a shocked expression. His chest tightened even more. "What does this have to do with me?"

"*No se*," said the tall cop. "You tell me."

Cliff shook his head. "I know nothing about any murders."

"That is what they always say," the tall one said, his eyes narrowing.

"I just told you I don't know anything."

The tall cop smacked his open palm on Cliff's big cherrywood desk and loomed over him. "Mr. Blackwell, we must have your cooperation, or we have to take you to PNR headquarters for interrogation."

Cliff jumped to his feet and said, "Back off! I'm happy to cooperate, but you're asking the wrong guy."

The fat cop said, "You are no aware of *Señor* Jimenez, the president of the Hotel Nacional group? Blown up in his Mercedes three mornings ago?"

Cliff took another deep breath and sat down. If he denied knowing the man and they found out that he knew him, he'd look guilty. If he admitted meeting with him recently, they'd assume his guilt anyway. A textbook dilemma. He was screwed either way.

"Yes," Cliff said, "I know who he is. I recently had a business meeting with him and a Mr. Sydney Russo. I consult with his group on various investments and financing."

"I see," said the tall one. "Now we get somewhere."

"Listen," Cliff said, "Mr. Russo's people were inquiring about the purchase of Mr. Jimenez's hotel. That's all. Just normal business, and—"

"Do you know a *Señor* Badalamente?" the tall guy said.

Cliff gulped at the name. *Jesus.* "I met him a couple years ago in the States on business, but I don't know him. Why?"

His interrogator crossed his arms and replied with a tight smile that was wryly victorious. "Just curious," he said. "We know he is an associate of Russo."

The questioning continued for another twenty minutes, until it seemed to be dying a natural death. Cliff decided to end it and stood up.

"I'm sorry to cut this short, gentlemen, but I have work to do. If you need me again, I'm at your service."

The tall cop cut a sidelong look at his partner, then said, "*Muy bien.* We will take the hint to go, but you will hear from us again."

Cliff opened the door for them.

The tall officer said, "*Señor,* we will conduct a background check on you. Like we did on your associates, *Señor* Russo and his *amigos.*"

"So far, we don't like what we find," the fat cop said. "Hopefully, we don't find nothing on you."

The tall one stopped in the doorway and turned. "Just one more thing, *Señor* Blackwell. You must not leave Cuba until we complete our investigation."

A chill tickled Cliff's neck. "How long will that be?"

The fat one took a threatening step toward him. "Why? You have some plan to leave our beautiful island?"

"No, no," Cliff said, trying to sound casual. "Just curious. I have business to attend to."

They had just started down the passageway when they ran into Victoria. The Cuban men stopped and ogled her. Cliff gave her a look and shook his head, hoping that she'd take the hint.

"Actually we *do* have plans to leave," Victoria said. "We're sick of this hellhole."

"Vic, please, *not now*," Cliff said.

She looked at him with alarm. "What's going on?"

"The police just had a few questions, Vic. Something about a murder."

Her eyes widened. "Murder?"

The tall officer took a step toward her with his hands clasped as if in prayer—or as if to keep them from pawing the lovely lady. "*Señorita?*" he said. "Do you know a Sydney Russo or a Johnnie Badalamente?"

Cliff's heart leaped. "For God's sake, that's enough of this inquisition," he said as he stepped between them.

Victoria clapped a hand over her mouth.

The fat cop said, "The *señorita* knows some things, I think."

Cliff was suddenly furious with Victoria, and he had to struggle to keep his anger hidden.

"Perhaps this is so," the tall one said. "If you cooperate, *señorita*, it will go easier for you."

What the hell is this, an old Edward G. Robinson film? Cliff thought.

Victoria stood frozen.

Cliff wagged a dismissive hand. "We'll both cooperate, of course. But let's call it a night, okay?"

The tall cop pursed his lips and considered both of them sternly. "*Bueno*," he said. "As you wish. For now."

"I'll get a steward to show you out."

The fat one shook his head. "Do not bother yourself, *señor*. We know the way."

The two men started to go, and then the tall one turned back to Cliff. "One thing more," he said, holding up a finger.

Shit, the guy thinks he's Columbo.

The cop said, "You know, we have more murders in Cuba this year than ever. All in a very short time. And all very important people. This is not a good thing."

Cliff's mind raced. "Do you think these murders have something to do with the Castros and Vivo?"

The swarthy men looked at each other and then back at Cliff. "Maybe."

"No way," Cliff said. "What would the odds of that be?"

"You are the one in the business of gambling, *Señor* Blackwell," the tall cop said. "You tell me what are the odds."

How'd they draw such a wild conclusion, and so quickly? Cliff wondered. "I wouldn't care to guess."

The officers exchanged another look, then regarded him smugly. They finally turned and plodded down the passageway, whispering in machine-gun Spanish and gesturing dramatically.

Victoria grabbed his arm and said, "What was that all about?" She didn't sound happy.

He whirled on her. "For Chrissake, Vic!"

"Whoa, cowboy. Why are you yelling at me?"

"You butt into a delicate, dangerous situation, then just about admit to knowing a couple of gangsters who probably *killed* some people around here!"

She took a step backward. "I didn't say that!"

"You didn't have to!" he cried with clenched fists raised. "Shit, we'll never get out of this stinking place now. They'll *bury* us."

Her face crumpled. She wheeled and marched off toward the salon, and Cliff hurried after her.

He nearly ran into her near the big couch when she braked suddenly and turned on him, her face contorted with anger. "I never wanted to come here in the first place! You and your crazy goddamned schemes!"

"My *schemes?*"

"You didn't have to go along with them. You just can't stop trying to make more money on crooked deals."

"I resent that."

"So what?"

Cliff felt as if he'd been poleaxed. "So now the truth comes out."

"Are you out of your mind? How do you think I should feel? These people are going to get us in a lot of trouble. We could go to jail—or get . . . *disappeared!*"

"*You're* the one who's going to get us in trouble."

Her furious gaze bored into him. "I'm leaving!"

"You can't do that!"

"Watch me." She spun, stomped out of the salon, and slammed the door.

"*Vic!*" he shouted. He couldn't believe what had just happened. "Shit!"

He took a minute to catch his breath and allow his heart to stop racing, then grabbed the phone and pushed a button to call Paul, his personal steward. He told him that Victoria had left the yacht alone and asked him to follow her. "We had an argument, and she's really upset. Please make sure she's safe, okay?"

"Roger that. Don't worry, sir."

Cliff was glad to have a man like Paul to handle such special duties.

Victoria's departure made the whole yacht seem deserted. Where the hell was everybody? Did they all take cover after the shouting match? At the moment he didn't care. He fixed himself a drink and wandered back to his study, shut the door, and turned on the banker's lamp on his desk.

He thought about the whole story, including Badalamente and the gangland-style murders, and about how expertly he had painted himself into a corner. If he revealed everything to Victoria now, she'd be incensed about his holding out on her. And that could confirm for her his guilt by association with Russo and Badalamente. The background check by the Cuban police must've lit a fire under them. My God, Chicago mobsters! What would they dig up on *him*? You didn't have to be a member of Mensa to put this puzzle together. He chuckled sourly. But what would it matter? Just doing business with the goddamned Mob could be a ticket to the slammer. Probably for Vic, too. And they'd face— what?—some Cuban idea of justice? How could he live with himself if *that* happened?

Christ, why did *Victoria* have to be so careless, so stupid? And why did I have to get so damned upset? What have I done to her —and to us? He hoped that Paul would keep a sharp eye on her, no matter what she was doing or planning to do.

He wondered about the two Cuban cops. Didn't they have better things to do? The Russians are about to blow the place off the map, and they want to work on a small investigation? Keep a private yacht from leaving the harbor? The tall cop sure had a weird sense of humor. Don't leave Cuba, he says. Ha ha. How could we do that?

The same thoughts chased one another around the inside of his skull for at least another hour until the phone on his desk buzzed. Andre had arrived.

The attorney apologized for his late arrival when he appeared at the office doorway. He looked at Cliff closely and asked him if he was all right.

Cliff told him not to worry. Everything was fine. Oh, sure it was.

Andre took a seat and said, "I understand now why you asked me to pick up these contracts."

"You heard about Badalamente?"

"Oh, yes, my friend. Bad news. Very bad news." He shook his head sadly. "Cliff, the things, they do not look well. I hope you keep a distance from these people."

"Good advice, Andre. Thank you."

"Here are the contracts, for whatever they are worth."

"What's wrong with them?"

"No, Cliff, the contracts, they are fine. I saw no red flags. You will, without doubt, do very well."

Cliff flipped through the pages without seeing the words. He should feel happy to have this paperwork in his hands, but he wasn't. The plan hadn't gone as smoothly as he had hoped. Now his conscience had kicked in, and his fears were threatening to take over. What could he do about Russo? Could he bail out now?

"You do not want to cross them, Cliff," Andre said as if he had read Cliff's mind. "And you do not want to test the Cuban j udicial system either."

Cliff thought about that for a while, until he remembered his mother's impermeable sense of justice. What had happened to right and wrong, black and white? Why was everything now painted in shades of gray? Could he have found another way to use the Mob to help the CIA, the United States, and the people of Cuba without getting his hands stained with blood? The answer eluded him.

"I appreciate your advice, Andre, as I always do. I promise I'll sleep on what you said. And I'll get these contracts back to you as soon as I can."

He and Andre had a drink together and rehashed the news. Andre seemed to be as distressed as he was, but the attorney was also sad for the plight of his homeland. Would Cuba's troubles never end? Cliff let him vent his emotions. He didn't tell Andre about the visit from the police or Victoria's departure. Doing so, he thought, might spawn the reality of his worst fears. When Andre bade him a good night, Cliff promised to call him the next day.

Although visiting with Andre had been a pleasant distraction, Cliff felt the weight of his troubling thoughts even more when his old friend left the *Havana Royale*. If he didn't hear anything from Paul about Victoria, he knew that answers wouldn't be the only thing to elude him tonight. Sleep would be out of the question. He decided to break one of his old rules and have another drink.

Cliff often thought of life and business—two sides of the same coin for him, he had to admit—as a chess game, so he spent the next hour writing notes at his desk, playing with a variety of what-ifs and making a list of moves and countermoves, of gambits and responses. When he was considering a business deal, this exercise was a regular part of his due diligence process. He scribbled away until a sickening thought stung him like a serpent's bite—he had not played the what-if game before getting involved with the Mob and the CIA in Cuba.

He threw down his pen in disgust and shambled to the minibar to build himself another drink—a stiffer one this time—and then slumped over his desk, head in hands, and cursed himself for a fool. That lapse in his standard operating procedure, he knew, could cost him dearly.

A soft knock on the door startled him. He yanked the door open, hoping to find Paul standing there, or maybe Victoria herself. Instead, he found himself staring into the grave face of Sasha. She looked slightly out of focus.

"It's nearly midnight," she said. "Are you quite all right?"

"Oh, sure. Never better." He reluctantly motioned her inside and closed the door.

Sasha perched a shapely haunch on the corner of his desk and eyed him sharply. Her short black leather skirt revealed entirely too much tanned leg. Even at the end of a long day she was still quite a picture—the fashionable tangle of flaming red hair, the crackling blue eyes. "Something's wrong," she said. "You aren't glad to see me."

He didn't want to take that bait.

"Oh, dear," she said. "You lose a bundle on Cuban cigar futures?"

"That's not funny."

"Romantic problems, perhaps?"

"That's none of your goddamn business!"

Sasha replied with a wicked smile and a knowing nod. "*Bin*-go!" she sang. "Has our dashing playboy of the western world gotten a taste of his own medicine?"

"For Chrissake, Sasha! Give it a rest, will you?"

"I'm sorry, love."

"Sure you are."

This time her brief smile was inscrutable. She slipped off his desk and said, "I don't know about you, but my mind's reeling. Thought I'd have a shower in my lovely little WC and then have a go at the pool table. Care to join me?"

Cliff took a deep breath. The alcohol was muddling his thoughts. "I guess I could use a little billiards therapy myself. And I'd like a chance to kick your butt."

"You're on," she said brightly and headed for the door. "See you there in fifteen. Then we'll see whose butt gets kicked."

Sasha appeared right on time at the billiards room and posed dramatically in the doorway, caught in the warm glow of the indirect lighting, looking like a model from Victoria's Secret. Her lace-trimmed white satin nightgown fell almost to her bare feet and clung to every curve. The look she cast at him was more challenge than coyness. Lord knows that she never bothered to play the coquette, Cliff thought, feeling both repelled by and attracted to this exceptional specimen of femininity. The drinks had made his head feel muzzy, but he was familiar with Sasha's games. He'd have to be careful.

He returned his attention to racking the balls and said, "Do you always dress like this to play pool?"

"Only with you, love."

Ignoring that remark, he plucked the pen recorder from his shirt pocket and tossed it to her. She had to break her pose to catch it.

"What's this? You making me sign a hold-harmless agreement?"

"You're a riot, Sasha." He told her about his covert recording sessions with Donald Witherspoon. "You might find something interesting on there."

Looking pleased, she said, "Good show, Clifford! This could come in handy sometime."

When? he thought. *At my congressional hearing?*

Sasha took her time choosing a cue stick and looked around the room as she chalked the tip. "Interesting decor, old love," she said. "Rather like a cross between early Inquisition and late Graceland. I love the medieval armor."

"You've been to Graceland?"

"Of course. I'm a huge Elvis fan."

"Part of your dark side, no doubt."

Sasha gave him an indulgent smile and moved on to inspect a large glass display case that contained a beautifully detailed replica of J.P. Morgan's famous yacht, the *Corsair*. She also examined a framed collection of antique cigar bands from around the world. "My, aren't we the collector?" she said.

Cliff broke to get the game going and said, "I appreciate rare and beautiful things, sure."

The colorful balls clattered sharply in the quiet room and scattered across the red felt. When he turned, Sasha glided against him, placed one hand on his shoulder and one on his cue stick, and tilted her head to gaze into his eyes. Her body felt soft and hard at the same time.

"Just like you collect beautiful women, I suppose?" she whispered. Her breath felt warm on his cheek.

"Sasha, this—"

She placed one finger over his lips and tugged on his cue stick. He allowed her to pull it from his hand. It hit the carpeted floor with a muffled *thump*. The pressure of her body increased. Her perfume was like some rare and heady incense.

Cliff closed his weary eyes and braced the back of his thighs against the pool table to take her weight. His clamoring thoughts spun into a whirlpool when his hands found the impossible smoothness of warm satin. And when she guided his hand to a bare breast he arched his back and thrust his hips into her. She responded with steamy, panting breaths against his neck.

"You know you want me, Cliff," she said, her voice soft and husky. "Like you always have." She crushed her moist lips against his.

Cliff heard nothing then except an airy rushing sound, like a great turbine whirring. His whole world tipped over the edge and slid down a long, dark pipeline. He made no effort to stop himself.

Just when he had trailed his lips to the pliant surprise of her milky breast, the billiard room door exploded open. He and Sasha flew apart just in time for Cliff to see a rifle butt arcing toward his head. An exquisite pain flared along his whole jawline to the crown of his skull. His eyes went blind, and the carpet rushed up to thud his face. A display of pyrotechnics worthy of the Fourth of July in Boston bloomed behind his eyes. Cliff sucked air and dimly thought that was a good sign. At least he wasn't out cold.

A moment later, or an hour—Cliff couldn't tell—he struggled onto all fours, shook his head, and spat blood like a boxer knocked to the canvas. He shifted his weight, rolled, and propped himself against a built-in cabinet. With that monumental task accomplished, he tried to focus on the two figures that circled the pool table like wolves vying for the alpha role. A thick-faced man who looked like a Bulgarian weight lifter shouted guttural curses and orders in a heavily accented voice as he jabbed his assault rifle at Sasha. Crouching, she backpedaled slowly away from him with a cue stick in her hands held at port arms. Cliff desperately wanted to do something to interrupt this grim minuet, but just now he felt as if his body had been constructed of tissue paper and spit.

When Sasha and the intruder had completed their second circuit, she allowed him to close the distance between them, and he took the bait. He bulled toward her with the gun thrust ahead. Quick as a whippet, she sidestepped the charge, and the cue stick blurred in her hands and smacked against the short, blued-steel barrel. The gun stuttered, its voice violently loud in the small room, spewing rounds that ripped into the teak wainscoting and exploded the glass case containing the *Corsair*. When the muzzle drifted away from her, Sasha twirled the stick and whipped the heavy end against the man's left ear. He took a stumbling step to one side, his eyes gone vacant, and tried to recover. Before he did, Sasha speared him savagely in his beefy gut and then broke the stick over his head. He went down like a sack of bricks and lay still. Blood seeped from his furrowed skull onto the carpet, adding a new shade of red to the design. Sasha snatched the gun away and stood over the hulk, ready for more. She wasn't even breathing hard.

Cliff struggled onto quivering legs and leaned on the edge of the pool table, his head spinning. Sasha rushed to support him with one hand, still holding the gun.

"Cliff, are you okay? You look like shit."

"Thanks. That's reassuring. I think my jaw's broken." He peered at the supine man who was soiling his favorite Persian carpet. "What about him?"

Sasha knelt and pressed a finger under the angle of the thug's stubbled jaw. "He won't be crashing any more parties, I daresay."

Wearing black cargo pants and a black muscle shirt that looked too small for his barrel chest, their unexpected guest was grossly underdressed for a party on the *Havana Royale*, Cliff decided. But he assumed that the man's costume matched his deadly assignment. Thank heaven for Sasha.

"Who the hell is this gorilla?" Cliff asked.

"See the picture on his forearm?"

The tattoo, all but hidden by the matted black hair, looked like some kind of primitive bird. Cliff nodded.

"That's a bird from Madagascar. Rahonavis. A raptor," Sasha explained.

"A meat-eater."

"Exactly. It's the symbol used by SAFRA."

"Oh, shit . . ."

"Quite right, old boy. He's one of the Gold Man's goons."

More bad news, Cliff thought. *When a deal goes sour, things sure go to hell in a hurry.* He shuffled to the nearest chair and eased himself into it like an arthritic old man. "That means we're all in danger, big-time." Words now felt like smooth, oiled stones in his mouth. The whole left side of his face had begun to swell.

Sasha agreed.

He thought about Victoria running around out there somewhere and shivered. Maybe he was going into shock. "How do you think he found us?"

She prodded the dead man's heavy body absently with a bare toe. "Maybe the Gold Man intercepted the signal from my STU, got a reverse bearing on us. Could be why the reception was so poor. I remember seeing him mucking around with something on his wrist."

"Great," Cliff said, holding his throbbing jaw. "Now we—"

Sasha whirled in a practiced crouch and pointed the gun at the entrance, where the mahogany door hung drunkenly on one bent hinge.

Victoria stood there gripping the jamb and gulping for air, her eyes wide. "What's . . . going on? Are you . . . all right? I heard shots!" She puffed like an Olympic sprinter.

Cliff pointed at the dead man. "We had a visitor."

"Oh, my God!" Her face paled. "Who is he?"

Cliff felt vastly relieved to see her—and more than glad that she hadn't returned before King Kong arrived—but he had no strength for conversation. He let Sasha tell Victoria what little they could guess. Victoria's gaze volleyed back and forth between him and Sasha. Her look of growing realization made Cliff turn away. He grabbed a monogrammed hand towel that hung from the billiards table and mopped the blood from his mouth.

At last Sasha looked at him and said, "We better get Don over here. Tell him to bring some help. You'll require security now. And he can get rid of the body."

Her words echoed in Cliff's aching head. *Get rid of the body . . .* An image of the Cuban cop holding up his three fingers appeared before his mind's eye. The cop leered at him, displaying a gold tooth.

"Cliff, we need to talk," Victoria said with calm authority.

"Victoria," said Sasha, "You don't—"

"*Shut up!*" She took a quick step toward Sasha, her hands balled into fists, ignoring the gun. "I'll deal with you later."

"Vic, please!" Cliff cried as he jumped to his feet. That was a mistake. A new pain burst behind his eyes.

She glowered at him.

"All right," Sasha said. She handed the automatic rifle to Cliff and headed for the door, giving Victoria a wide berth. "I'm off. I'll find Don and get him to send us some help straightaway."

"Good idea," Victoria said. "That should keep you out of trouble."

Sasha shot Cliff a look of grim dismay before she ducked out the door.

19

Don't Blink on the Brink

EARLY THE NEXT MORNING, CLIFF POKED ABSENTLY at a plate of eggs and glanced furtively at Victoria and Sasha, who sat as far away from him and each other as they could at the dining room table. They both looked as sleep-deprived as he was. Nobody spoke. He knew that he needed some food, but he had lost his appetite, and his painfully swollen jaw didn't make things any easier.

Witherspoon had done damage control late the night before by making the body of their unexpected guest disappear. Cliff didn't ask for the details. They had stayed up most of the night running interference for Witherspoon and reassuring the crew. Cliff demanded that Witherspoon make sure the local police didn't get wind of this latest incident. That was all Witherspoon needed to hear. Now rotating pairs of U.S. Marines were keeping a twenty-four-hour watch on the *Havana Royale*. But Cliff's gut told him that the cops would be back sooner or later.

Cliff knew they were in deep shit now and well past the point of no return. Thanks to him, the CIA had gotten what it wanted, and so had Sydney and Tony. He would need a lot of luck to reap any real reward from his questionable gambit in Havana now that

the risks had doubled, at least. More than ever, he knew that failure could mean jail time for him and Victoria, or worse. And part
of that worst-case scenario included the unthinkable—a nuclear
incident.

The music of Henry Mancini crooned softly from hidden
speakers. Cliff thought that was odd. The usual musical fare was
smooth jazz. Rosie's choice this morning, he guessed. Was she
hinting about recent events? That would be Rosie's style. Subtle as
a train wreck.

Cliff regarded his silent companions as they continued to
feign interest in their food. When the first notes of "The Pink Pan-
ther" theme floated from the sound system, both women froze
and then gazed at him inscrutably. Then, as the lighthearted musical riff continued, they both smiled in spite of themselves.

Cliff was smiling, too—as best as he could—when Rosie
entered the room and inspected their plates.

"Something wrong with the food?" she said.

Cliff shook his head. "No, no, Rosie, everything's fine."

"We like the music, too," Sasha said.

Victoria stifled a giggle.

"I guess you're right, Rosie," Cliff said. "We're living in a
Blake Edwards film." Victoria and Sasha grinned at him.

Hands on her wide hips, Rosie regarded them without amusement, shaking her head. She rolled her eyes, then turned and bustled away.

Sasha stood and said, "To hell with breakfast. I've got to find
those two scoundrels." She threw her linen napkin onto the table
and headed for the door.

"I have things to do myself," Victoria said, following Sasha.
"See you later."

Cliff soon abandoned his cold eggs and drifted to the main
salon to check the news. The CNN reporters kept up a steady
chatter, but they didn't have anything new to say.

He went topside to inspect the new day from the afterdeck.

No military aircraft streaked across the brittle blue sky. He paced in the warm sun and peered at the hazy outlines of Havana. Few people moved about on the quay besides the two Marine guards.

He felt edgy and impotent. Witherspoon and Sasha had things to do, but he didn't. He considered various courses of action all the way to his study, where he found the contracts still awaiting his final review. He frowned at them. Just now they looked like a covenant with the devil. Near them a little placard caught his attention. It read, "Invest in the future. Buy a cave."

Not a bad idea, he thought.

"God-*damn*-it!" shouted President Van Buren as he banged a fist onto his Oval Office desktop. "This situation has gone to hell!"

General Wesley Chalmers, sitting ramrod-straight in an armless, striped satin chair nearby, barely blinked. He had weathered the histrionics of three presidents before this one and more than his share of combat in Vietnam and the Gulf War, so a little executive temper tantrum was just a minor annoyance.

He almost felt sorry for the guy. Van Buren was a wet-behind-the-ears president who was saddled with too much too soon. The assassination of Castro had dropped a bunker-busting bomb on the White House. Since then his staff hadn't done much but run around in circles crying, "The sky is falling!" What a cluster-fuck. The media were camped just beyond the White House gates with all their satellite trucks, and the pressure was getting to Van Buren. That was obvious.

The United States was on the goddamnned brink, so he knew that somebody needed to be cool. Right now that somebody had to be him. Every branch of the armed forces was waiting for orders from its Commander-in-Chief. Russian President Pasov was waiting for their next move, too, the old commie bastard. He'd play nice only if he had to, Chalmers knew, and he'd do anything to save his own ass. He'd laugh, too, if Cuba got nuked, especially if prevailing winds blew northward. Shit, sometimes Chalmers felt nostalgic for the good old Cold War days. Havana gets blown off the map, then do the same to Moscow, just for drill. Fuck 'em.

The president stood swaying behind his desk, wringing his hands and looking like just what he was, General Chalmers thought—a prime example of the Peter Principle. "Wes, how are we doing?" he asked. "What's your take on this mess?"

The general said, "Sir, I've been in constant communication with Admiral Dallenbach. As you know, he's ramrodding the search for the Russian sub. With help from Captain John Heidrick of the carrier *George Washington* and her battle group." Chalmers set his coffee cup on a side table. "We also have Commander Jake Hamilton on the *Miami,* one of our best attack subs. I'm pleased to report that at approximately oh-ten-hundred hours our time"—he glanced at his Breitling Navitimer watch—"fourteen minutes ago, sir, the *Miami* identified the enemy by her acoustic signature."

The president sank into his chair and heaved a sigh. "Is it an Oscar-class sub, like Pasov says?"

"Their readings are consistent with that, yes, according to Commander Hamilton. Means it's well armed, probably with nuke warheads."

The president got to his feet wearily, drifted to the window, and studied the gray view, gazing in the general direction of Cuba as if he could see it.

Finally he turned back to General Chalmers and said, "I talked with President Pasov for a long time today. I don't think the Russian government is behind this. But I don't trust the son of a bitch."

Maybe Van Buren wasn't as stupid as he looked, Chalmers thought. "My people think it's a rogue op run by the Russian Mafia. He say anything about that, sir?"

"That's what he claims. Said they tracked down the people behind this and where they got the boat—at the sub base in Severodvinsk, near the Kola Peninsula." The president shook his head. "And Homeland says our port security sucks. Unbelievable."

"He could be lying."

The president nodded. "Could be—and might be." He sat down again, planted his elbows on the desk, and propped his chin in his hands. "But that man's voice was full of sincerity. He speaks good English. Apologized a dozen times, offered his help."

Right. And Stalin was a nice guy. "I guess that counts for something," the general said.

"I hope so. Said he plans to get to the bottom of this. Sounds like some heads will roll."

The general crossed his legs and folded his hands in his lap. "So whose orders are they following?"

The president pronounced the names. Penkovsky and Edwards. The general had a fat dossier on both of them, but he nodded as if this was new intel. "MI6 and our people are tailing them now," the president said. Chalmers knew all about that, too.

"Men like Commander Hamilton and Captain Heidrick have spent a lifetime training for something like this, Mr. President. We'll stop those bastards, sir. Don't worry."

Van Buren regarded him hopefully. "Thanks, Wes. I hope you're right. What happens next?"

"Right now Captain Heidrick is keeping the fleet at a distance. More backup's on the way. Two more subs. Guided-missile frigates, some of our fastest destroyers. Air support, of course, with sub-hunters and bombers. Plus Marine expeditionary forces and airborne troops. As you know, several hundred ex-Soviet soldiers have deployed in Cuba, so we need more boots on the ground there. All you have to do is say the word and everything moves."

The president managed to look both stunned and pleased with the enormity of that idea.

"It's all set, Mr. President. The Pentagon, the Joint Chiefs, the intel agencies, Dallenbach, Heidrick, and Hamilton are all hot-linked and ready to rock 'n' roll."

Van Buren's only response was a look of uncertainty. Chalmers wanted to lean across his glossy desktop and slap it off his face, but he resumed his steely control. "What's wrong, sir? Do you know something I don't?"

"No, it's just that I'm not sure if all the other chiefs are on board with this. Then we have Congress and the U.N. to think about. I don't want the world to see this as an excuse to make arbitrary war on another nation."

For Christ's sake! General Chalmers thought. What does this pussy need, a Russian torpedo up his ass? He longed for a President Bush—either one of them—in the Oval Office. They didn't need much of an excuse to play Commander-in-Chief and kick some butt when they had the chance.

The general forced himself to remain calm and diplomatic. "Forgive me, Mr. President, if I seem blunt. I don't think this is a time to split political hairs. If we don't take out that sub and get control of Cuba soon, you'll be worried about more than a second term."

Van Buren looked shocked momentarily and started to say something, then regained his composure. "That's blunt, all right, General, but I appreciate your candor. Okay, the hell with Congress and the U.N. and every-damn-body else. You've got the green light. But do it by the book, and keep me informed. If you don't, by God I'll have your stars."

"Now you're talkin', Mr. President. I'll pass the word." With that, General Chalmers jumped to his feet, saluted his Commander-in-Chief with a smile, and turned on his heel, thinking, *Mission accomplished.*

Later that morning Cliff tossed the contracts onto the desk in his study and sighed wearily. He was tired of reading legal-speak. In fact, he felt just plain tired all the way down to his bones. But he had finished reviewing the papers and had asked Andre to pick them up later. He stood and stretched, then left his study and wandered into the main salon. Victoria sat on the couch with her bare feet on the cushions, flipping through a magazine.

She glanced at him and said, "I wondered when you'd come out of there."

"Been that long?"

"Over two hours."

"Where's our friend?"

Victoria made a face. "She took off. Said she had to see somebody named Toti." Her tone was chilly.

Toti? That surprised Cliff. Witherspoon must've put her on to him. "I wonder what our favorite CIA agent's up to."

She dropped the magazine and stood up. "Who knows? He seems to run his own show. Maybe that's why the CIA likes to keep him around." She hugged herself and stared at the carpet. "I wish something good would happen. Anything. Soon."

"We could go make something good happen."

She didn't look up. "I already worked up a sweat once today in the gym."

That remark annoyed him, but he decided not to give up yet. "Oh-kay. Then how about a relaxing soak in the spa and a hot shower afterwards?"

"No thanks," she said and strolled out.

Cliff stared at the empty doorway and suddenly felt like the Lone Ranger, minus Tonto.

Cliff sat nose-deep in the spa an hour or so later, licking his wounds. The warm water massaged his aching jaw, which still throbbed in time with his heartbeat. He had decided that if it was fractured, then he'd just have to live with it. He didn't want to raise a red flag by making a visit to the hospital for X-rays. The steady pain made his solitude even more intolerable.

The buzz of the intercom derailed his miserable thoughts. He pressed the button and listened to Rosie announce Witherspoon's return. He told her to let him in and climbed out of the swirling water.

He pulled on a terry cloth robe, slipped his feet into his Tods, and scuffed toward the main salon. Witherspoon lounged on the big couch when he got there.

The agent grinned and said, "Am I interrupting anything, Cliff? You look like you're dressed for the pool"—he tipped Cliff a bawdy wink—"or something."

"Your impertinence is exceeded only by your vulgarity," Cliff said with an indulgent smile. He looked around for Rosie. "What do you want to drink?"

Witherspoon returned the smile. "Tempt me. I'm more than ready."

"How about one of Hemingway's favorites? A tall, cool daiquiri."

"A *mojito*, right?"

"You've done your homework, Don."

Rosie appeared right on cue.

"Make it a pitcher of Papa's Special," Cliff told her, thinking that he was ready for a drink, too, or maybe a lot of them.

Rosie nodded and bustled away.

Witherspoon said, "This whole thing started out simple enough." He patted his pockets. "Snuff the old revolutionary, install a democratic government."

"Yeah, it all sounded so easy at the time."

"We get all our ducks lined up, and then these bad guys want to crash the party. Par for the course when you play at nation-building, I guess. Look at what happened in 'Nam—and the disaster in Iraq."

Cliff nodded. "If you wrestle with a pig, they say, you both get dirty, and the pig likes it."

The agent grinned. "Exactly."

"Let's take a walk," Cliff said. "Rosie'll find us." He led Witherspoon into the shade of the half-covered after deck. The sea breeze did little to lessen the afternoon heat.

Witherspoon pirouetted slowly, taking in the view.

"By the way, thanks for sending the Marines," Cliff said.

"Not a problem."

"So what's new?"

The agent told him that the *Miami* had located and ID'd the Russian sub and that the president had given the nod to the Pentagon. "He's let all the dogs out now," Witherspoon said. "This should be some show."

The hairs on the back of Cliff's neck stiffened against the Havana heat.

A steward delivered a frosty pitcher of the pale green concoction, a silver tray holding a selection of cigars, and a heavy crystal ashtray. Cliff thanked him and sent him on his way.

Cliff stripped the wrapper from one of the cigars and said, "I almost forgot about these."

"What kind are they?"

"Don't know. I got a whole box for a few bucks at a little shop in Old Havana. Homemade, I guess." He clipped off the end neatly. "Want one?"

"No thanks," said Witherspoon. "I'll stick with my good old American coffin nails."

Cliff lit up and puffed away, enjoying the aroma of the no-name corona. Then, like a magician's trick, the cloud of smoke parted to reveal Victoria, looking fresh and radiant in a fluid summer dress.

"Hi, honey," he said. "Glad you could join us. Care for a *mojito*?"

"Sure," she said, then smiled at their guest. "Well, if it isn't the Havana vice."

Witherspoon grinned good-naturedly and almost lapsed into the aw-shucks mode, as he always did in her presence.

"So what's up, guys?"

Witherspoon briefed her while she poured herself a drink and settled into a chair next to Cliff.

"Sounds like all hell's about to break loose," she said when he finished.

"You can't blink on the brink," Witherspoon said as he lifted his glass.

Victoria eyed him sharply. "What does that mean?"

Cliff said, "It's like when you have a Mexican standoff. The first one that blinks loses."

"You got it," said Witherspoon, lighting a cigarette.

She shook her head, raised her glass, and swallowed a third of her drink.

"There's another saying," Witherspoon told them. He gestured with his cigarette while he paced. "Whoever gets there firstest with the mostest usually wins."

Cliff thought about that one. The U.S. military certainly had the mostest, but could they strike first?

The CIA man stopped and said, "Hey, where's our Limey spy?"

"Out looking for Toti is what I hear," Cliff said.

"Okay, good," said Witherspoon. "He may be able to help." He stubbed out his cigarette in the chunky ashtray. "I better get going. I figured you'd want another update."

"Thanks, Don," Victoria said. "I feel so much better now."

She had nothing more to say after Witherspoon left, so Cliff filled the awkward silence by scanning the latest issue of the *Financial Times*. He snapped the pink pages against the breeze and drew the paper closer to scrutinize an economic report on the American financial scene. It was full of surprisingly encouraging news.

"Man, the market sure is hot," he remarked casually, hoping to draw Victoria into conversation.

"Yeah?" she replied with little interest. She had killed half of her second *mojito*.

"Uh-huh. But I get nervous when the corporate astrologers paint such a rosy picture."

" 'Corporate astrologers'?"

"You know, the economists and analysts. They're worse than listening to a weather forecast. And the investment gurus, those self-serving you-know-whats."

"I guess I know what you mean."

"The *Farmer's Almanac* could predict economic turns more accurately. What goes up—"

"Must come down."

"Exactly." He was glad to get a few words out of her, but her enthusiasm was underwhelming.

"A lot of people want to get rich quick," she said.

Cliff agreed and then glanced at the date on his watch. "The news about the Russians should be released any time now. That'll jolt everyone back to reality." He snatched his sat phone from the table.

Victoria finally looked at him directly and said, "Don't you remember what Don said?"

"About what?"

"No outside communications."

He shrugged, then punched some numbers. He waited and listened as the telephone rang on the other end. "God, this could trigger a whole cascade of events. Mostly bad ones."

Virgil finally answered. Cliff gave him some sell orders and asked him to stay up late and execute them through Zurich.

When he was done, Victoria regarded him icily and said, "I hope that wasn't the *mojitos* talking."

"No. I've been thinking about selling some shares for a while now. Gonna short a few of 'em just for fun." The thought of making a quick killing tickled him.

Victoria stood and adjusted her dress. "I'm so glad you're having a good time. I'm not." She grabbed her drink and flounced off, mumbling something about playing a fiddle while Rome burned.

Victoria was still off somewhere, probably in the galley giving Rosie three kinds of grief, while Cliff waited for dinner in the main salon, drinking to pass the time. He had polished off the pitcher of *mojitos* and switched to a thirty-year-old scotch that tempted him now and then—an old companion for those times when he was alone and grappling with too many slippery thoughts. He didn't want to think about much of anything just then, because he felt like hammered shit despite the numbing effect of the alcohol. Less pain, but no real gain. Maybe he'd feel better if he stopped drinking, he wondered sourly. Or maybe not. The whole world was about to go down the toilet, and Victoria was icing the cake with her jealous bitch routine. Ain't that a bitch? he thought. *Bitch, bitch, bitch* . . .

When the forward door flew open he straightened involuntarily, expecting to see Victoria—or maybe the cops—but it was Sasha.

"How good of you to join us," he said. "Have a drink. Join the party."

She approached his chair and eyed him closely. "I don't see any party, and I dare say you've had more than you can handle. You're absolutely pissed, old boy."

"No way, Sasha, my dear. I'm just getting started."

"Blimey! I was afraid this might happen. You better get some black coffee into you straightaway and sober up fast. Because the shit, as you colorful Yanks say, is about to hit the fan."

"What?"

"You dear old sod, don't you remember? The end of the world and all that? Sound familiar?"

Cliff shook his head and tried to think.

"Look at me, Clifford. I spent the afternoon with our friend Toti. And I talked with my superiors in London. We can't waste any more time. I must get to that retreat. Looks like that's their base of operations."

"Retreat?" Cliff said.

"Bloody hell!" Sasha grabbed him by the shoulders and shook him like a rag doll.

That made the pain flare again in his swollen jaw, and the

agony burned away some of the fog in his brain.

"Cliff, I need your help! And Victoria's. We have to move on this, and I need that bloody beautiful helicopter of hers."

"The chopper?" Cliff said. "Vic can really fly that thing. You should see her."

Sasha released her grip on him. "That's precisely what I want. I'm a licensed pilot, but I can't fly a helicopter. I need Victoria to take me to that retreat."

"The old KGB compound, right?"

"Yes!"

Cliff scrubbed his face with both hands and took a deep breath. The pain was doing its job. All the pieces of reality were falling into place again, and Sasha's words had begun to sink in.

"Okay, Sasha, okay. I get the picture. Need to find Victoria. We can talk. I'll start in the galley. Get some food. Have 'em make a fresh pot of coffee." He heaved himself to his feet and lurched toward the door.

"Make that two pots of coffee," Sasha said. "I think we're all going to need it."

"That chopper of yours," Sasha said. "It's a Bell 407, isn't it?"

Victoria nodded, still chewing a mouthful of Greek salad and bread. They had canceled a sit-down dinner and opted to forage in the galley instead so they could talk and eat at the same time in Cliff's office.

Sasha said, "Good. Then it should give us the necess'ry range and speed."

"She's powered by a pair of Rolls-Royce 250 C47B engines," Victoria said. "Cruises at one-sixty and can maintain that speed for over four hundred miles."

Sasha nodded slowly, obviously making some quick mental calculations. She had told them that London had contacted her through her STU on her way to the *Havana Royale* and told her the same things that Witherspoon had reported. More important, they had confirmed Penkovsky's location in Cuba by intercepting his communications with the sub. Her orders were to go there immediately and eliminate him "at all hazards."

Victoria had listened quietly and taken in Sasha's news soberly, although Cliff knew that she had been drinking, too. The glazed look in her eyes always gave her away. She was tracking everything well now, he could see, and he thought that the food and the coffee would help her as much as it was helping him.

"I know how important this is," Cliff told Sasha, "but aren't they asking you to do too much for Queen and Country?"

Sasha smiled grimly. "I'm not a fool, Cliff. I know this is a suicide mission. I'm sure they're sending other people to get Penkovsky, but they could be too late. I'm already here, and I'm expendable, so they have to give it a go."

"You'd risk your life for this?" Victoria asked.

"Of course, dear girl. I knew the rules when I signed up. In MI6, when you're authorized to take lives, you have to be prepared to give up your own."

"That may be fine for you," Victoria said, "but why should I risk getting killed?"

Sasha swallowed a bite of cheese and said, "I'm asking for your help because you're my only option just now. No one can get to Penkovsky any faster than we can with that chopper. And I'm not asking you to risk your life, just give me a ride to Gorga. You can drop me and dust off straightaway, if you want to."

Cliff looked at Victoria, who returned her attention to the salad in her lap.

"Somebody has to stop Penkovsky," Sasha said. "He's the one directing the Russian sub. And that boat's fully armed with missiles that can hit Washington."

"Penkovsky wouldn't go that far, would he?" Cliff said.

"Actually, I think he would," Sasha said. "And if he does, the Americans are certain to retaliate. Then we have Armageddon."

Cliff had been born after the Cuban missile crisis in '62, but now he knew how everyone must've felt then.

Victoria surprised Cliff when she looked at Sasha and said, "When do you want to leave?"

Sasha tossed her hair and smiled. "As soon as poss—"

They all jumped at a heavy knock on the door. Cliff got up and opened the door just far enough to see the pink and sweaty face of Donald Witherspoon.

"Sorry," the agent said, gulping for air. "No time for formalities."

Cliff swung the door and let Witherspoon bump his way into the room. He dropped two black carrying cases onto the carpet and shrugged a lumpy knapsack off his back. He had traded his rumpled suit and scuffed slip-ons for fatigues and boots.

"Good grief, Donald," Sasha said. "Whatever are you doing here?"

"Same thing you are, Miz Bond. I'll bet we both know about Penkovsky now. And I'll bet we both have the same idea about Victoria's helicopter."

Sasha maintained a straight face.

"Okay, don't say anything. I don't care. I'm going with you."

"Donald, I'm not authorized—"

"Don't give me that MI6 crap. You can't go in there alone."

"I agree," Cliff said. "That's why I'm going, too."

Sasha jumped to her feet to protest, but Cliff cut her off. "Here's the deal," he said. "Either we all go, or nobody goes."

Victoria stared at him slack-jawed.

Cliff returned her gaze and said, "What? You thought I was planning to stay behind?"

Witherspoon plunked himself into a chair. "Okay," he said. "It's your funeral."

20

From Hell to Havana

THE PHONE NEXT TO GENERAL CHALMERS' BED BUZZED and flashed a red light at him. The sound made him flinch, even though he hadn't been asleep. He had tried to catch some Zs in his temporary room at the White House, but couldn't. He checked the clock—12:36 A.M.

His aging joints popped when he twisted abruptly to snatch up the receiver. He recognized the familiar voice of Admiral Bankhead at once, and he braced himself for more bad news. His mind raced as he listened to the admiral's terse message.

"Christ on a crutch!" He threw the phone down, whipped the covers back, and jumped from the bed. He yanked on a robe as he barreled out the door and loped barefoot down the hallway. When he rounded a corner he nearly ran into a pair of Secret Service agents.

"Wake up the president!" he shouted into their startled faces. "We've got a situation."

The dark-suited agents trotted away from him, spitting words into their lapel mics.

He paced the hallway, animated by adrenaline, his thoughts

popping like rockets from an old hedgehog launcher. He finally halted, took a deep breath, and ordered himself to settle down.

Moments later President Van Buren jogged down the hall with his silk robe fluttering behind him, escorted by a posse of Secret Service men.

"What is it, Wes?" the president said, short of breath. His face still wore the slackness of sleep.

General Chalmers repeated the same words that he had shouted at the agents.

"My office," said the president and hustled away.

The general followed Van Buren to the Oval Office. When they were alone inside, they both sat on the edge of a long sofa. The president peered at him, looking ill.

"This could be our worst nightmare," General Chalmers said, forcing himself to be calm and professional. "It's the *George Washington*, sir. Hit by a goddamned Russian torpedo."

Van Buren dropped his head into his hands. "Who told you this?"

"Captain Dallenbach spoke with Admiral Bankhead at the Pentagon, and Bankhead just called me."

"What's the situation on the *George Washington*?"

"She's a big carrier. Still afloat but crippled. Minimally operational."

"Casualties?"

"No more than fifty dead, they think."

The president shook his head sadly. "Stupid bastards! We gotta take out that sub."

Chalmers agreed. "We can do that, Mr. President, but if we try we could make a bad situation even worse."

"What do you mean?"

"That sub's carrying nuclear warheads. Maybe a couple dozen. Two-hundred-kilo size. Thirteen-hundred-mile range. They could do a lot of damage before we stop them."

The president looked pale. "How far is Washington from

where they are?"

The general bowed his head. "A thousand miles. A little more."

The president nodded thoughtfully and said, "All right. What do you suggest?"

The phone on the president's desk shrilled. Van Buren gave him the look of a stunned sheep before he got up and answered it. The president listened and nodded for a while and then replied quietly, with one hand cupping the mouthpiece.

Van Buren returned to the sofa and said, "Crazy son of a bitch Penkovsky," his voice a harsh whisper. "He's demanding we pull out of Cuba, or else."

The general's guts tightened instinctively. "I think we better get you down to the Presidential Emergency Ops center."

The president ignored that. "So he wants to play nuclear blackmail?" He smacked a fist into his open palm. "I can play that game, too!"

Ivan Penkovsky clapped his cell phone shut and leaped to his feet, feeling immensely pleased with himself. He raised his arms and snapped his fingers as he turned slowly, shuffling his feet in a clumsy celebratory dance. Everything was going precisely according to plan. Everything was in motion now. This was his time, and he was right where he needed to be. He had a secure command center here at the old KGB compound in the mountains, his communications network was fully operational, and he had a well-stocked backup armory nearby. Perfect. He whirled and swooped around the room until he felt dizzy, then collapsed into a creaky old office chair.

He had fired off volleys of orders to all of his cells in every corner of the island, all of them manned by well-trained ex-military personnel from the ranks of the Soviet army. Now hundreds of them were swinging into action, and all of it just for him! He considered that for a moment with a raging satisfaction. That made him feel as high as a fucking kite, more alive than he had ever felt before.

He had just received an ELF, an extremely low frequency radio transmission, from Captain Vasili Golubev, the commander of the Oscar. The encrypted message contained only a brief update, but what exciting news it was! Penkovsky clapped his hands as he read it again. The *George Washington* torpedoed! What a glorious time!

He must send the captain his congratulations immediately. He scribbled a note that praised the submarine captain and crew and said, "No second strike without my orders. Waiting for response from Americans. Confirm." He gave the message to his radio shack runner and danced some more while he waited for the reply. Thirty minutes later he was celebrating with a glass of vodka when the runner returned. The slip of paper contained just one word—Confirmed.

Now we wait and see what foolish thing you will do next, Mr. President Van Buren. Do you perhaps play chess? I doubt it. Make the wrong move, and soon I will be dancing on your grave.

He knew they were out there, hunting him like a pack of wolves. And he knew that the most dangerous one would be a boat a lot like his but probably quieter and faster. Another submarine captain was standing in his attack center, doing everything he could to locate and destroy the sub that had torpedoed the American carrier.

Captain Vasili Golubev hovered near his sonarman, waiting for any sign of his pursuers. They hadn't picked up anything for more than an hour now. Time maybe to resume his heading to Havana.

He excused himself to his first officer and ducked out of the sonar room, then navigated the tight passageways to his private quarters. He dropped onto his narrow bunk and took a couple of deep breaths, which led to a fit of coughing. When the spasms subsided, he collapsed onto his back and tried to catch his breath. His chest ached, and his face felt flushed and hot. Lying down felt good. He hadn't slept for more than two hours at a time for the last three days. Sleep was a luxury that he couldn't afford now.

He thought about the night before, when the crew had surprised him with an impromptu party to celebrate his fiftieth birthday. He had felt too tired and ill for such things, but the crew, they were good boys, all of them, and they were all taking part in an adventure of a lifetime. They knew the risks involved in their mission, and they were doing a fine job. They deserved to have a little fun.

He had issued terse orders to break out some special supplies, and soon all of them, officers and men, laughed and sang together while they feasted on caviar, brown bread, pickles, and quail eggs, with plenty of good Russian vodka to go around. He had not enjoyed such camaraderie in a long time.

His thoughts drifted to the attack. A beautiful thing—a fantasy that had played out in his mind many times with little hope of coming true. But they had done it. One quick strike and then run. The hunter had wounded his prey. But now they were the hunted one.

He sat up and keyed the lock of a small cabinet and removed the bottle. He filled a shot glass and threw it back, the fire of it warming his stomach while he took a few deep breaths. He checked his watch. Twelve forty-six American. Why wait any longer? He inhaled again. Hell, why run to Havana like a kicked dog and wait for orders from that barbarian Penkovsky?

He got to his feet and took a step to the little metal sink and splashed his face with water, then leaned on the sink and examined his dripping reflection in the mirror. Yes, why do you wait, Vasili? The man he saw in the mirror looked old—too old for his years. A man who had spent a lifetime waiting for the orders of others. The Americans would expect him to run. They wouldn't expect him to circle back and bite their ass again, would they?

He stood there for a few seconds in thought, then quickly

dried his face, retrieved the bottle, and let the liquid fire burn his throat again. He didn't feel so tired now.

He stepped from his tiny cabin and hurried to the attack center, with more energy in his stocky legs. When he entered that space, his first officer quickly answered his unspoken question. All had remained quiet. No sign of the American ships.

Captain Golubev acknowledged that with a nod and said, "Take her up. Periscope depth. I need targeting data."

The first officer looked startled for only a moment before he smiled and began barking orders.

"Slowly," Golubev told him. He prayed that they would have the few minutes needed to raise their data line mast and link up with RORSAT, the Russian Radar Ocean Reconnaissance Satellite. Then he'd have all the information he needed.

Although his Oscar was a quiet boat, he knew their move could be detected. They would have to be quick. Get the intel they needed, crash dive, and make straight for the enemy—the hunted turned hunter again. The thrill of danger rekindled the fire in his gut. Dangerous, yes. This was very dangerous. But it was much better than waiting.

Victoria squirmed in the pilot's seat, her whole body filled with the vibration of the chopper's idling engines, and ticked off the last items on her flight checklist. Beside her, Sasha adjusted a courtesy light over the map spread across her thighs. Victoria stowed her clipboard and leaned close to the map. Near the top it was marked "CIA Low Altitude Chart/Cuba."

"This map is brilliant," Sasha said.

"Yeah, lots of detail." Victoria settled into her seat and envisioned their course. They had already studied the map thoroughly, the four of them. By now she thought she could locate their target blindfolded. She tested all the controls, noting the impatience in her jerky motions. Or was it fear? Once they had all agreed to do this together, she wanted to get on with it, but Witherspoon and Sasha had to argue about every detail, and once they were satisfied with their plan they went over it again and again, making everyone recite his part in it word for word.

Then they had brainstormed equipment. What else did they need to bring? What other weapons could they add to Witherspoon's arsenal, which included an AK-74 and who knows what? She had begged a compact Walther PPK automatic from Cliff and had it tucked into the waistband of her Bloomingdale's camouflage pants now. They had to scrounge an old seabag to contain all the extra stuff. All the talking and planning had taken a long time. No wonder she was feeling anxious now. Sunrise was only a few hours away, and they had to get there by dawn.

Victoria turned when Sasha put a hand on her arm. The Brit agent had a funny look in her eyes, Victoria thought—a mixture of sadness and sheepish regret. Sasha spoke her name, lifting her voice over the engine noise and the whupping sound of the rotors.

"I have to tell you something," Sasha said. She retrieved her hand, but did her best to maintain eye contact.

Movement on the dark helipad distracted Victoria. Cliff ducked under the whirling airfoils, dumped his duffel bag, and duckwalked to a tie-down cable. She returned her gaze to Sasha's face—a pale mask in the light of the instrument cluster—and waited.

"You were right," Sasha said. "I did make a play for Cliff." She shook her head and frowned as if from a twinge of pain. "Bloody hell! My life is so crazy. I do foolish things. Maybe because I get so lonely sometimes." She gave Victoria a tearful look. "I don't know what I was thinking. Cliff and I—Well, what we had was over a long time ago. And he was never really mine. We didn't have what you two have. We—"

"Sasha," Victoria said, "you don't—"

"No, let me finish. I dare say I did my best to take him away from you. But he refused me. Literally pushed me away. He said he already found the love he was looking for—you."

Victoria's vision blurred with tears.

Sasha bowed her head. "I was wrong, Vic. Dead wrong. And I owe you a huge apology. I hope you'll accept it." She gave Victoria an imploring look. "You're lucky, Vic. So is Cliff. And I'm lucky to know you both. I hope we can get past this and be friends. I'm sorry."

Victoria gathered Sasha's hands into her own and thanked her. "I know that wasn't easy for you. Let's forget the whole thing. It's over now. You're an amazing woman, Sasha, and I'm proud to know you. I want to be your friend, too, and even more than that. Like sisters. What do you say?"

Sasha swiped away tears and said, "That would be . . . bloody wonderful, Vic." She smiled bravely.

"Okay. Let's get on with it. We have some work to do, right?"

Sasha nodded vigorously. "Damn right we do!"

Victoria glimpsed Cliff nearby as he bent to release the tie-down on the port side. Then Witherspoon hefted his bags of gear onto the helipad and followed them, stooping under the rotors. The hard wash of air flattened his clothes against him. Moments later, Cliff pulled the rear door open. The men hoisted their bags inside and climbed into the back seat.

"You ready to get this bird in the air, Captain Vic?" Witherspoon said.

"Just waiting for you slowpokes," she said.

"Good! We gotta make this happen, people. Langley just buzzed me. That goddamn Russian sub torpedoed an aircraft carrier."

Commander John Hamilton did his best to cloak his growing sense of exhilaration. Arms crossed, he stood in the middle of the attack center of the *U.S.S. Miami* and rotated slowly, monitoring his men as they concentrated on their various tasks. He felt as if he'd been doing nothing but standing and waiting for hours, and he guessed he had been.

His sonarman, a first-class petty officer named Fisher, appropriately enough, stirred in his seat and then shot him a glance over his shoulder. "Sir," he said, "take a look at this."

Hamilton bent and squinted at the BSY-1 sonar display. The sonarman pointed to a white frequency line and said, "See that? The power plant of an Oscar. I'd know it anywhere."

"All right! It's about time."

The sonarman grinned, and everyone else muttered excitedly.

As he tried to contain his own excitement, Commander Hamilton issued a string of orders to his men to get the Oscar's range, heading, and speed. He wanted to maneuver the *Miami* within twenty thousand yards of the Russian boat. He knew they had a slight advantage. They had spotted their quarry first, for one thing, and they had a quieter boat. With a little luck they could maintain the element of surprise while they closed in for the kill.

His heart thudded.

Victoria checked all her gauges again—altitude, air speed, trim, fuel—moving her gaze in a clockwise direction, and glanced at the occasional lights that slid by in the darkness below. So far so good. They were making good time with a slight tailwind, and fuel consumption looked optimal. Her passengers had remained mostly silent for the last hour. Probably too tired to make the effort of shouted conversation. Witherspoon just mumbled as he rummaged through the equipment bags, apparently sorting and repacking things.

Sasha rattled the map and touched her arm. "How long till we get there?" she asked.

"Hour and a half, tops."

Commander Hamilton's skin prickled. After thirty-five minutes of slow and stealthy maneuvering, he had positioned his 688I submarine within range of the Russian boat. No pings. The Oscar still hadn't detected them. Damn lucky. Now he could make the next move in this game of cat and mouse. Launch two wire-guided MK-48 ADCAP torpedoes. They would motor slowly through the depths, sending back information to the *Miami* as they went. Then, when the moment was right, he'd order them full speed ahead to their target.

Make it five more minutes. That's all he needed. Just five more minutes.

The vodka felt like a hot coal in Captain Golubev's stomach. Goddammit, he had to remember to eat at mealtime. But no time now for food. He had to concentrate on finding the American submarine. Where the hell was that son of a bitch? It had to be out there. He could feel it. But all the instruments here in his attack center reported nothing. Nothing. He used his damp, red handkerchief to mop his face again.

He had to find and destroy the American boat. Then the god-damn Amerikansky navy would take him seriously. They'd back off and give him time to make his next move. King takes queen. Checkmate. And then he could do something that he had dreamed about for thirty years—launch his missiles at Washington. After that, his name would appear in every history book ever printed.

Commander Hamilton massaged the back of his neck. His excitement had resolved itself into a dull headache during the last few crucial minutes. He had studied the BS4-1 system network and reviewed the Target Motion Analysis himself, and now he had an operative fire control solution.

A fire control technician stared at him over his shoulder. The young submariner knew the drill as well as he did. "Set up a pair of ADCAPS," he told him.

Giving that order punched the button on the commander's mental stopwatch. Everything had to go by the numbers. A few more seconds ticked by. "Make tubes ready," he said with more volume and authority. The fire control tech passed the order along. Hamilton pictured the men in the torpedo room jumping to their task, moving quickly and efficiently.

He drew a deep breath and said, "Firing point procedure."

The final seconds of the firing sequence tripped away. This was it. Showtime. He rocked forward on the balls of his feet, lifted a fist, and said, "Match bearings and fire!"

The weapons officer thumbed the Fire button. A few seconds later he reported that the fish were away and on course.

Commander Hamilton let out his breath and allowed his boys to punch the air and pump their fists in silent celebration, thinking, This one's for the *George Washington*.

"Sir, two torpedoes incoming!" cried Captain Golubev's sonarman.

The captain cursed under his breath. "Range and speed?"

"Nineteen hundred meters. Closing slowly to port. They must be ADCAPS, sir."

"Deploy countermeasures!" Captain Golubev shouted hoarsely. "Come about ninety! Match bearings and fire!" The attack center became a blur of frenzied activity. Mother of God, did they have enough time? They already had armed torpedoes in every tube, fore and aft, but . . .

Long seconds dragged by as the captain's heart boomed against his ribs. Finally, his weapons officer looked at him and said, "Two fish away, sir!"

"Dive! Dive! Dive!" Captain Golubev bawled. He stared at the sonar screens while some of his men cursed as they fought to maneuver their lumbering giant into the depths. His XO and a few others stood or sat at their consoles as if frozen, their expressions pained.

Captain Golubev shifted his gaze to the overhead—the closest he could get to the heavens just then—and muttered a prayer. A moment later a thunderous explosion jarred the Oscar. Every man who wore headphones cried out in pain and ripped them off. Other men screamed and shouted in panic. The captain spread his feet and found a handhold as the boat shuddered like a wounded beast. Then a second explosion shook the boat and made it rock from port to starboard and back again. Every unsecured item in the attack center clattered to the deck.

"Damage report!" the captain bellowed.

Nobody replied.

The lights flickered as the big boat wallowed and then began to nose downward.

Captain Golubev repeated his prayer aloud, but his words were lost in the tumult of groaning metal, hysterical screams, and rushing water.

"Strike one!" cried the weapons technician. "Strike two!" Everyone in the attack center of the *Miami* whooped and cheered.

Commander Hamilton let out a long breath.

"Wait!" the sonarman yelled. Everyone fell silent. "We got two incoming!"

Christ! Hamilton barked orders. Then he moved from station to station, speaking encouraging words to his young sailors as the submarine descended. A mixture of anxiety and fear became a palpable odor. The almost-forgotten words of the Lord's Prayer chanted in his mind.

Suddenly the *Miami* recoiled as if from the weight of a great fist, and the muted roar of a violent explosion drowned his words. He got on the horn to Damage Control and braced himself for the second shock. The seconds ticked by.

Nothing.

Hamilton bent to his sonarman, gripped his shoulders, and

stared at the screen.

"Missed!" the sonarman said quietly. "It's going for the countermeasures, sir."

Thank God!

He spent the next few minutes quickly assessing the damage reports. They were hurt badly but still operational. "Okay," he said, "send a report to CINCLANT. Then let's see if we can take this baby up."

Twenty minutes later, the *Miami* rocked gently on the white-capped surface. The boat listed slightly to starboard, but it remained afloat, and, as the latest report had told him, they could make headway. Commander Hamilton said a silent prayer of thanks, then ordered a new heading, hoping they could make it to the fleet.

Victoria held the stick steady and hugged the contours of the hilly countryside as she urged the chopper toward the southwest. Some details of the landscape appeared here and there as the first blush of dawn limned the horizon. Her stomach grumbled, begging for food, but she ignored it.

She glanced at Sasha, who peered steadily through the windshield. "Let's take a look at that chart again."

Sasha opened the map, spread it over her knees, and studied it for a while, then held it up.

"It's right here, Vic," she said, pointing to a town identified as Guaimaro.

Witherspoon stuck his head between the seats and said, "Where are we now?"

Victoria checked the instruments on the glowing panel and then looked at the clock. "About eighty-five miles out," she said. "Be there in thirty minutes."

* * *

Sasha worked with her STU, trying to pinpoint the exact location of the old KGB retreat, as they roared into a lush valley. The first light of a rosy sunrise unveiled the geometric outlines of sugar cane fields and small buildings and the silhouettes of tall palm trees. Victoria had grown weary from remaining too tense at the controls. She took a deep breath and forced herself to relax as much as possible, thinking, It won't be long now.

"We should be getting close," Sasha said, studying her device. "Follow that range of low hills just to the south, Vic."

Victoria nodded and adjusted the course.

Witherspoon appeared between them and said, "How're we doing?"

Sasha said, "Precisely on track." Then she turned to Victoria and said, "You know what to look for." She pointed. "Should be just over that ridge."

"Roger," Victoria said, suddenly wondering what the hell she was doing here.

The vague, green landscape flowed past them below. When they had topped the next ridge, Sasha sat forward and jabbed a finger in the air. "There we go!"

Victoria's heart jumped when she spotted the cluster of low buildings that squatted in a small, palm-studded clearing about the size of a baseball field.

"Shit, yeah!" Witherspoon cried. "That's it! Vic, you're amazing!"

Sasha pointed and said, "Head over that way, Vic. Behind the ridge. Find a place to set 'er down."

That was the next problem. Victoria wondered if they could find a flat spot big enough in this overgrown botanical garden.

Witherspoon tapped Victoria's shoulder and stuck out a finger. "How about down there?"

Victoria squinted into the semidarkness below. Hard to see clearly. Not far away the darker jungle ended abruptly, revealing a nearly level meadow of tall grass. Part of an old, abandoned farm, perhaps. Maybe three acres or so. Not much, she thought, but it would have to do. She gave Witherspoon a thumbs-up and nodded.

Victoria throttled down and picked her spot, then slowly lowered the chopper. The wash from the rotors flattened the tall grass, reminding her of film she had seen of Cobra gunships setting down on a landing zone in Vietnam. When they had bumped to a stop and settled down, Victoria cut the power.

As the engines spooled down, Witherspoon said, "Okay, people. You all got a quick look at the compound. I hope you remember the layout."

"How could we forget?" Sasha said. Witherspoon had made them pore over a sheaf of CIA satellite photos back on the *Havana Royale*.

Witherspoon turned to Cliff and said, "And don't forget, you're just backup. Only Sasha and I go in. We'll find a good spot for you on the ridge. You cover us the best you can. And if everything goes to shit, you haul ass back to the chopper and dust off."

"Yeah, yeah," Cliff said. "You only told me that a hundred times."

"Just so you don't forget. I don't want you playin' Rambo on me."

Cliff gave the CIA man a crooked smile and saluted.

"Same goes for you, Vic," Sasha said, touching her arm. "Any trouble, you get out fast."

Victoria pulled Sasha into a clumsy hug and said, "We're all going to leave together, that's what I'm planning. Be careful, and good luck."

Cliff and Witherspoon were already on the ground, shrugging into their backpacks beneath the slowly turning blades. Sasha gave Victoria a quick kiss on the cheek and piled out.

"Let's go! Let's go!" Witherspoon shouted. "Daylight's coming fast."

Cliff pulled open Victoria's door and grabbed her. She clung to him and cried, "Oh, Cliff . . ."

"Don't worry, honey," he said. "I'll be okay."

"How did I ever get hooked up with you, Clifford Black-well? This is insane. If you get hurt I'll kill you!"

Cliff laughed and pulled away.

Witherspoon stepped up and took her hand. "Thanks a lot, Vic. You're an ace."

She hugged his neck and told him to bring his dumb ass back in one piece.

Witherspoon smiled shyly and said he'd do his best.

"I'm ready," Sasha said as she joined the group. "Looks like you've decided to travel light, Don." Witherspoon had a back-pack, his AK-74, and a .45 holstered on his hip.

"Yep," Witherspoon said. "And I suggest you do the same. We have to move fast."

"Okay, Don," she said. "But just remember one thing. Pen-kovsky's mine."

Cliff's knapsack felt too heavy as he followed Sasha and Witherspoon through the dense brush toward the top of the ridge, and so did the SIG 550 assault rifle that was slung over his shoulder and banging into his ribs. This overgrown backbone of land hadn't looked like much from a distance, but now, after slog-ging up the ridge for fifteen minutes, he was winded, and his legs were quivering with fatigue. He made a mental note to spend more time in the gym on the *Havana Royale* and then wished that he were there now.

When they finally neared the crest, Sasha and Witherspoon slowed and crept forward in a crouch. Cliff did the same. Wither-spoon reached the top first. He motioned for them to stay low, then bobbed his head and shoulders to take three quick peeks at the other side. He pointed over the ridge top, nodded emphatically, and made a thumbs-up sign. Then he motioned Cliff forward.

"Right up here," he whispered, indicating a thick bush. "On

your stomach. You can see the whole compound."

Cliff unslung his rifle and followed orders.

"I hope you know how to use that thing if you have to," the CIA agent said.

Cliff gave him the finger.

Witherspoon grinned, turned toward Sasha, and made more hand signals. She blew a kiss at Cliff, and Witherspoon threw him a salute, then they crouched away slowly in opposite directions, following the ridge line.

Cliff raised his head just far enough to get a good look at the complex in the growing daylight. He thought it looked like a half-baked terrorist camp, smaller than he had expected, even after studying the photos. Just a scrubby, sunburned little clearing with a scatter of small buildings, some of them wood with faded beige paint and some with oxidized corrugated tin. All of it fenced with sagging chain-link and barbed wire. Your basic shoestring, Soviet-era installation, he assumed. The ragged jungle had encroached since its heyday, with clumps of it crowding the bases of the tall, stately palms that offered some shade and camouflage to the place. A flock of birds greeted the new day with raucous calls and flitted between the cockades of the palms, making rustling sounds in the long, nodding fronds.

Nothing else moved. He dug out his pair of opera glasses to take a closer look. The little building there with the antennas had to be the radio shack. Beyond that a long, low structure with a rusted tin roof. The barracks. To the right of that a rust-streaked Quonset hut—the motor pool—with a big, open shed next to it that sheltered a burly, canvas-topped truck—a Soviet personnel carrier—an American army Jeep, and a four-wheeled trailer. A storage building. The mess hall. And on the opposite side of the camp a weedy, rock-lined path led from the narrow, unpaved main street to the front door of a more substantial-looking structure with a tin-roofed addition tacked on to the back—the command post and officers' quarters, they had decided.

That's where Penkovsky would be.

Cliff knew the plan as well as they did. They'd cut the fence and enter the compound from different directions—Witherspoon first—and he'd signal the start of the assault by blowing the radio shack. Then he and Sasha would hit the barracks. Take out the soldiers, then go for the Godfather.

He was relieved to see no one moving about, but, God, they'd need a lot of luck to pull this one off. They had the element of surprise, but how many soldiers were stationed here? That was the wild card.

Cliff observed the compound for what seemed like a long time while everything grew lighter around him and the birds continued their morning chatter. He tasted bile from his empty stomach, and his jaw ached dully. An insect bit his sweaty neck.

The force of the explosion made a seismic shudder beneath him. He threw his glasses to his eyes in time to see a mushroom of white smoke billow from the place where the radio shack had been. Birds exploded from the palm heads, and dark scraps of the building arced through the air with contrails of darker smoke. Seconds later, a few bits of shrapnel pattered into the bushes around him.

Cliff quickly panned the binoculars and refocused on the barracks building. No sign of life yet. He thought he caught a glimpse of movement to the right. Witherspoon? Then the door of the barracks burst open, and a hulk of a man appeared holding an AK-47 and dressed only in fatigue pants. He cranked his square head back and forth, searching the compound. The skin of his broad, hairy chest shown pale in the morning light. Soon he was joined by another soldier, this one dressed only in combat boots and white skivvies. They crouched and took a few tentative steps in opposite directions. A half dozen soldiers crowded through the doorway behind them, shouting and gesturing with their assault rifles.

The Russian soldiers ducked as one when an automatic weapon chattered. One right after the other, three of the men bumped into their comrades and fell hard onto the dirt. The big soldier shouted orders and swung his arm, then sprinted to the left, toward the command building. He covered no more than ten yards before he stumbled, spun, and sprawled in the weeds. Those who had followed him froze, then whirled and fled the other way, shouting and firing their weapons wildly. They didn't get far.

Witherspoon and Sasha had done what they had wanted to do—set up a crossfire. Cliff was excited to see how well it was working, but he was shocked by the violence. The two of them were blasting away with controlled bursts now, enfilading the muddle of panicked soldiers from concealed positions. They cut them down in ones and twos as stray rounds ripped wood and shattered glass along the front of the barracks. A few of the men retreated to the door, firing blindly as they went, until all but one of the survivors disappeared inside. That man clawed his way across the threshold on his stomach and collapsed.

The gunfire stopped. Cliff caught some movement again, just to the right. Witherspoon. He had emerged from cover as he dug into his backpack. He removed something, fiddled with it, then stepped to one side and made a roundhouse throw. Seconds later, another blast buckled the tin roof of the barracks and exploded what remained of its front windows. Smoke boiled into the sky.

Whoo-yah! Just like in the movies!

Witherspoon snatched up his pack and scuttled around the back of the storage building, heading for the command post.

Cliff dropped his binoculars and took in the whole scene. The radio shack damn near atomized, the barracks wrecked—and now it was burning, too. Flames licked from the front windows. Cliff put his glasses on the building again. A soldier stuck his head from a side window and looked around, then tumbled out. Six or seven more men followed him. They scrambled to their feet and raced toward the vehicle shed, pumping their strapped AK-47s. Cliff could almost hear their clumping boots and panting breath.

No gunfire stopped them. They piled into the big truck, cranked the engine, and backed out of the shed. The driver wrenched the steering wheel, and soon the truck lumbered down the rutted main street, its laboring engine growling as the driver accelerated through the gears, making for the gate. The men in back ducked under the canvas and fired madly from both sides as they roared along. If Sasha or Witherspoon returned fire, Cliff couldn't tell.

The truck bucketed along, building a good head of steam, and then crashed through the gate with a sharp clang of metal. Top-heavy, it slewed onto the dirt access road and jounced out of sight between the palm trees.

Cliff nearly whooped for joy. Not a retreat, he thought. A "tactical withdrawal." Fewer guns meant fewer bullets that could harm his friends.

He swept the compound with his glasses again, straining to see through the smoke. Nobody in sight, thank God. Maybe Witherspoon had reached the command building by now. Sasha, too. He knew how badly she wanted to get to Penkovsky first. Goddammit, why couldn't she wait for Witherspoon? Why did she always have to be the best? That could get her killed this time.

Witherspoon appeared in Cliff's glasses again, this time humping from the mess hall to the side of the command building, staying low, his pack swinging in one hand. He crouched at a door they hadn't seen in the sat photos, removed a pry bar from his pack, and went to work on the latch. Soon the door popped open, and Witherspoon disappeared inside.

When Cliff lowered his glasses, another running figure caught his attention. Sasha? No, much too tall—and in uniform. A sentry, maybe, attracted by all the noise. Cliff thought the soldier would follow Witherspoon into the building, but he didn't. Instead, he crept to the bushy base of a tall palm about ten yards away and hunkered there, watching the broken door.

An ambush. The soldier was too smart—or too cowardly—to go in after the intruder. He'd just wait for somebody to come out, and if that person was an enemy, he'd open fire.

Cliff didn't like the odds. If either one or both of his friends walked out of there, they wouldn't have a prayer. He knew about games of chance. Throw a single unexpected element into the mix, and the odds could change dramatically. He quickly decided that he had to be that ingredient.

Victoria turned to stone when she saw the man. He had broken cover like an animal fleeing a forest fire, maybe fifty feet away, but when he saw the helicopter sitting there in the middle of the meadow, he skidded to a stop and goggled as if he had stumbled upon an alien spacecraft. He was dressed in a sweat-darkened khaki uniform, a tall, rangy guy who was no longer a young man —and not a Cuban, either. Gradually, as he gawked at her, a smile twisted his angular face. He slowly unsnapped the holster on his hip, extracted a handgun, and stalked forward, looking wary.

Seeing the gun restored Victoria's motor skills. She tore her gaze from the soldier to the instrument cluster and started flipping switches. When she hit the starter the engines coughed heavily, then caught, whining as they spooled up. The drooping rotors quivered and then began to turn with a leaden sluggishness, the way her legs moved in a nightmare of escape and pursuit. The shadow of one blade crawled across the bright windshield. Oh, God, too slow! No way she could get this thing off the ground in time.

She glanced through the side window. The man was only about forty feet away now. She clawed the little automatic from her waistband and thumbed the safety off. Then she yanked the door handle, stood awkwardly, and rested both forearms on the top edge of the door. The Walther trembled in her hands as she tried to take aim, her eyes watering in the downdraft of the four accelerating rotors.

The soldier froze and stared at her, looking surprised. Then he lifted his gun. Victoria squeezed off a round. The man fired at almost the same moment. He staggered, took a step backward, and let his gun hand drop. He clapped his other hand to his neck and then whipped it away, bright with blood. He stared at his hand for a moment, and when he looked at Victoria again he displayed that same wolfish grin.

She fired again. Missed. His smile widened. He didn't seem to be impressed by the pop of her small-caliber weapon. Ignoring his leaking wound, he lowered his head and plodded forward. Victoria pulled the trigger again, and . . . the gun jammed.

She flopped into her seat, slammed the door, and tossed her gun aside. She caught the stick in a death-grip, swiped at her tearing eyes, and quickly scanned the gauges. The muscular engines full-throated now, making their reassuring whistling growl, and the blades whumping steadily, still accelerating. RPMs almost up to the takeoff line. She shot a glance at the soldier. He was closing in and pointing his gun again.

The gunshots made a dull, cracking sound under the roar of the engines. One bullet cracked the windshield before it ricocheted away, and another round starred the plexiglass no more than six inches from her face.

Fuck this! I'm outta here! She planted her feet firmly on the pedals and worked the stick. The chopper shuddered, and the twin engines complained, but it started to struggle upward. A hot dart of adrenaline punctured the pit of her stomach when the tail slewed around and the nose dipped, but she kicked the pedal and adjusted the stick and corrected the pitch just in time to stare straight into the soldier's leering face. He aimed his gun at her carefully.

Nothing happened.

But she had reacted by jerking the stick, and now the chopper rocked drunkenly as it spun only a few feet from the ground. The man disappeared and reappeared twice before she got the machine under control and fought for altitude. The last time she saw him he had his arms raised, empty-handed, as if waving her good-bye.

The meadow slowly dropped away, the tall grass thrashing in the urgent wind from the rotors, but the chopper yawed to the left. Victoria choked for air when she realized what had happened —and what could happen next. The crazy son of a bitch had latched on to the port skid. And if he was as athletic as he looked, he could climb onto the skid, pull open her door and— God, that could tear it. They'd struggle, she'd lose control, and they'd augur in for sure.

No fuckin' way, José! But she had to act quickly. She cast a glance below. They were hovering over land crowded with low bushes and palms at maybe two hundred feet above the deck. She looked around, picked her target, and dropped the nose, then headed down at close to full throttle. When the altimeter read fifty feet, she pulled the chopper up so hard she thought she'd lose the rotors. But the sturdy Bell 407, like its Cobra cousins, held itself together somehow. When they were straight and level again, she clamped her jaws, took aim, and gunned it.

The big fronds made a terrible shrieking sound as they raked across the belly and struts of the chopper when she flew into the top of the palm tree, but her baby took that punishment, too, with only a modest shock, and roared on, air speed near seventy-five and no longer listing to port. Victoria banked hard to the left and circled back. She stopped at the damaged palm tree and hovered at no more than thirty feet and searched the bushes.

There he was, sprawled on his back, looking up. She was close enough to see that he wasn't smiling now. With luck, maybe he had broken his back—or something just as important. She was disappointed when he rolled onto all fours, labored to his feet, and stumbled away from her. She took a deep breath and wiped her hands on her thighs. Okay . . .

She dropped even lower and caught up with him in less than thirty seconds. Maneuvering the chopper carefully, she took aim once again and swooped down. The man turned a bloody, terrified face up to her, then continued to lurch away, limping awkwardly.

She felt the sudden bump when the port skid struck him. She flew on by, throttled up a bit, and turned the aircraft to take a look. The soldier lay on his side, clutching his crotch with both hands, his mouth torn open in a silent howl. Hard to see what had happened, exactly, but she guessed that she had come in a little too low, and the curved end of the skid had caught him between the legs and flipped him like a matador from a bull's horn.

Olé!

Time to finish it now.

Victoria lined up the left skid with the writhing soldier and dropped the helicopter onto him, all 2,600 pounds of it. The impact jarred her. Testing the highly touted ruggedness of the 407 again, she lifted off and peered down. He looked broken, but he was still moving. She let the chopper slam him into the ground again. And again. When she hovered to take another look, he wasn't moving anymore, and she didn't like what she saw.

She urged the chopper up and pointed it toward the landing zone in the meadow, her whole body trembling uncontrollably with the shock of what had happened in the past—what?—ten minutes or so? Only a few minutes, but she knew they had changed her life forever. She forced herself to concentrate on maintaining a steady course as she fought back the tears.

I'm not going to cry. . . . Goddammit, I'm not going to cry! Not until I get Cliff and Don and Sasha into this bird again and we're back on the *Havana Royale*.

Staying low, Cliff crept through the broken gate, making sure that he stayed out of the sight line of the soldier who waited in ambush. He placed each foot carefully as he picked his way through the litter of dead, brown palm fronds, angling slightly away from the man and behind him. He froze at the distant popping sounds of small-arms fire behind him, beyond the ridge. A few shots, spaced apart. All from the same gun? Victoria . . . Then a short, muffled burst of heavy gunfire from the command building made him turn again, and when more than one automatic weapon replied, a hidden instinct made Cliff scuttle for his objective—the fat bole of a palm tree—while the noise covered his movement.

Cliff caught his breath and peeked around the trunk while startled birds squawked in the fronds overhead. The soldier stood almost upright with the AK-47 at his shoulder, obviously riveted on the side door, completely exposed to Cliff. He was a chunky guy with broad shoulders and short, sturdy legs. Sweat stained the back of his taut, khaki fatigue shirt in the vague shape of Africa.

Cliff looked up the ridge again. No more gunfire over there. All right, he decided. First things first.

Fighting off an attack of the shakes, Cliff raised his SIG, slipped a damp finger onto the trigger, and lined up the sights on the Dark Continent, knowing what he had to do. He took a deep breath and held it. But when he tried to work his trigger finger, he found that it was locked in place. Sweet Jesus! All his fingers worked just fine. He knew that. He just didn't want to kill a man, especially if he had to shoot him in the back.

The front sight trembled on the target, and then the Swiss assault rifle shook in his grip as if from palsy. He made another maddening attempt to aim and fire, but it was no good. He lowered his weapon, and the air trapped in his burning lungs burst free. The whooshing sound made the soldier whirl, and as soon as he saw Cliff he loosed a staccato blast.

Cliff ducked behind the tree and hugged it as bits of foliage and hairy palm trunk jumped into the air. He squatted and shifted the gun to his right hand, rolled onto his knees, and counted to three. Then he pointed the gun around the trunk and fired it blindly. Two quick bursts of .223 Remingtons at close to twelve rounds a second. Rolled back the other way and did it again.

After that, silence. What was left in the SIG's thirty-round magazine? Can't dig out a new one now. Cliff peered around the ragged palm trunk. The guy wasn't standing there anymore. He was on his back, immobile, with his arms extended like a referee signaling a touchdown and one leg crooked under the other. Cliff scurried to him, found his AK-47, and dragged it away. He couldn't see a mark on the soldier. Then he forced himself to take a look at his slack-jawed face. One hooded brown eye looked sleepy. The other one had drowned in the dark blood that made a little pond in his deep eye socket.

Spray and pray, as the instructor at the gun range had put it. Sometimes your prayers are answered.

Cliff turned away from the dead man, then squatted and studied the command building. No movement. Everything quiet. Good news or bad news? He didn't want to guess. He took a fresh clip of ammo from his bag and reloaded.

After making a quick survey of the compound, Cliff jogged to the main building and slipped through the jimmied side door. A long, dim hallway stacked with cardboard boxes along one side stretched before him. It smelled damp and moldy. Halfway down, faint ambient light showed a connecting passage to left and right. The one on the right, Cliff figured, should lead to a front office or squad room, and the one on the left to the space added on to the back of the building—to private quarters, he assumed.

Somebody moaned.

Holding his weapon ready, he tiptoed down the hallway until he reached the next corridor. A quick glance to the right showed him part of an old gray metal desk and a few wooden chairs. Ten feet down the hall in the other direction, a man slumped against the plywood paneling, grunting as he stuffed a wad of white material under his shirt. Witherspoon! Twenty feet beyond him, past several closed doors, the dark, humped shapes of two prone soldiers blocked the hallway where it turned to the right. Neither one moved or made a sound.

Cliff hurried to his CIA friend. Witherspoon glanced at him and dove for his AK. Cliff knocked the gun aside and whispered, "No, Don! It's me!"

Witherspoon goggled at him. "Goddammit, Cliff!" he said in a harsh murmur. "I told you—"

"Shuddup! I'm here, and I'm going to help. How bad are you hit?"

"Little fucker . . . got me. Broken collar bone, I think." He grunted with pain. "Blew out . . . my shoulder. Tryin' to stop . . . bleeding."

"Take it easy, man."

"Go in . . . my pack."

Cliff found more dressings. As gently as possible he pulled the wad of bloody material from Witherspoon's shirt—not as much blood as he had expected to see, thank God—and stuffed in the fresh bandages, then rebuttoned the shirt and combat jacket over them.

"Where's Sasha? And Penkovsky?" Cliff asked.

As if to answer him, a woman shrieked.

Sasha!

Witherspoon lifted a bloody hand and pointed toward the end of the hall. He didn't look good. His pale face glistened with perspiration, and his breath came in rapid, shallow gasps. Shock. But Cliff knew he couldn't do anything more for him now.

Cliff retrieved his rifle and said, "I'll be right back. You stay here."

Witherspoon grimaced and said, "I think I will."

Cliff stepped over the dead soldiers and peeked around the corner. A closed door just a few feet away. Then another glass-shattering female scream, followed by a string of shrill curses mixed with deep, male laughter. Cliff scuttled to the door and pressed his back against the wall next to it as sounds of a struggle continued in the room. He carefully turned the doorknob. Locked.

Okay . . . Just like on the cop shows. Stay low, slam through the door, roll, and come up firing. Piece of cake. He sucked in two deep breaths and counted, One . . . two . . . three!

The flimsy door splintered open. Cliff's momentum carried

him well into the room, and when he tried to lower one shoulder and roll, he tripped on his own feet and dived like a runner sliding into home plate, his gun clattering away. He scrambled after his weapon and tried to get his bearings at the same time.

One quick image, caught in a freeze-frame. Sasha with a bloody face, on her back across a desk, her knees up and her hands clawed, her jacket and tattered shirt torn away, and the paleness of her exposed breasts, a constellation of freckles between them. Those milky, well-remembered breasts . . . Holding her down, a hulk of a man in an ice-cream suit, one hand clamping her throat, the other balled into a hammy fist, poised to strike again.

When the film resumed, Cliff found himself turned to a statue on hands and knees, mesmerized by the tableau of man and woman, his weapon still well out of reach.

After a glance his way, Penkovsky cocked his arm and hammered his fist into Sasha's cheek, and she went slack. Two seconds later he stood over Cliff with the muzzle of an ugly, black, blunt-looking automatic pointed at him.

Penkovsky bellowed a burst of happy laughter—a laugh like that of Zorba the Greek breaking dinner plates. "Oh, ho!" he said. "So another amateur has come to join our little party. Welcome, my foolish little friend!" He beamed at Cliff and waggled the muzzle of his gun at him—a Glock, Cliff thought dully.

The Godfather of the Russian mob made another gesture with his gun and ordered Cliff to his feet. "I do not want to shoot you like a dog," he said, still smiling broadly. "I want you standing up so I can cut you down like a tree."

"Fuck you!" Cliff said. "You can kill me, but your game is over."

Penkovsky boomed a laugh. "You think you have ruined all my plans? Ha! You are mistaken, my friend. Your silly little attack is just a minor inconvenience." He motioned with the gun and said, "Your comrade out there, he is—how do you say—a dead duck. And the woman will be soon, when I am done with her."

Cliff's body remained rigid while his mind screamed with warning lights and sirens. Only seconds left before a bullet erased all his yesterdays and canceled all his tomorrows. He had to say something, at least. Try to distract Penkovsky, maybe. Buy some time.

"Think you're some kind of mastermind, don't you? Think you know everything. You better think again. My friend out there isn't dead. And right now he's got a gun pointed at your big, fat head."

Penkovsky's leer dissolved, and he couldn't resist the urge to cut his eyes from Cliff to the door. Then his eyes went wide. Cliff followed his gaze and gaped at what he saw.

Looking like death, Witherspoon sprawled in the doorway, aiming his AK unsteadily at Penkovsky. The Godfather lurched backward and swung his gun hand. The muzzle of Witherspoon's gun jumped, filling the small room with a sound like four-by-fours dropped onto a wooden dock. Rounds whacked into the big Russian's meaty torso with a terrible sound, stitching him from his right hip to his left shoulder and hammering him into the wall with a thud as stray bullets bit into the plywood all the way to the exposed tin ceiling. Penkovsky's chin hit his chest, where blossoms of bright blood appeared on his creamy suit, and when his legs gave out he dropped the Glock and collapsed like a building. His big, square head cracked into the corner of the desk where Sasha lay moaning before he crashed to the floor.

Cliff's ears rang in the silence that followed. When he could move again, he crawled to Witherspoon, hugged him, and kissed the top of his head. The agent's gun clunked to the floor as he passed out.

Ten minutes later, all of Cliff's arms and legs were working well again, and Sasha was sitting up and speaking coherently as she blotted her swollen face with a wet towel that he had given her. Most of what she had to say, though, couldn't be repeated in polite company.

Cliff worked on Witherspoon with another damp towel. He had retrieved the last of the dressings from the agent's backpack and replaced the bloody ones. The bleeding hadn't stopped, but Cliff was glad to see that it seemed to be under control.

Witherspoon groaned and whispered, "Did I get him?"

"You got him good, ol' buddy," Cliff said with a smile. "I owe you a big one."

"Sasha?"

"She's okay."

Witherspoon's lips twisted into something like a smile. "Get outta here," he said hoarsely, regarding Cliff with glazed eyes.

Cradling the agent's head, Cliff said, "That's exactly what we're going to do. You just take it easy for a while."

"Have to carry him," Sasha said. She was leaning on the desk and holding the towel to her jaw. Her left eye was already purpling with a bruise.

"Not sure if I can do that alone."

Sasha spat another curse. "Don't worry, love. I may feel like I've been run over by a lorry, but I'm not done in yet." She shuffled across the room, stooped beside them, and patted Witherspoon's blanched face with her own towel.

Witherspoon opened his eyes, found her face, and gave her a hoarse but cheery hello.

She kissed his forehead. "Oh, Don, why did you have to go and get yourself shot?" Her eyes brimmed with tears.

Witherspoon smiled weakly and said, "Why, Sasha, I didn't think you cared."

"Oh, you great, bloody oaf!"

"Now I'm an oaf," Witherspoon said, turning to Cliff. "Rhymes with loaf. Ain't that sweet?"

"If we drag him," Cliff said, "he could bleed to death."

Sasha swiped away a tear and said, "We'll use the door. Make a litter."

Cliff eyed the office door lying nearby. He had ripped it from its hinges and torn off the knob and lock, and it was dented in the middle. But it was still in one piece. A cheap hollow-core door. It would be light. Could work.

He nodded at Sasha and said, "Okay. Let's do it."

They were ready to go a few minutes later. Sasha had punched two holes near the top of the door, one on either side, threaded telephone cord through the holes, and tied that into double-stranded loops. She had Cliff tear one of the old, threadbare towels into strips, which she used to wrap the cords. They hooked Cliff's belt to the carrying straps from three AKs to secure Witherspoon to the door.

"Tally ho, Clifford, old man," she said finally. "Time for you to do some real work for a change."

Cliff cheerfully told her to bugger off and grabbed a loop of wire.

Horsing Witherspoon and the litter out of the building was slow and awkward work, but they made better time on flat ground. They were both puffing with the effort when they stopped for a break at the foot of the ridge.

Cliff looked up the brushy slope and said, "Now comes the hard part."

"Not to worry, old boy. Only about thirty meters to the top. After that," she said with a wry smile, "it's all downhill."

"Brilliant," Cliff said. "Ten thousand comedians out of work, and you're trying to be funny. Let's go. I'm worried about Vic."

When she saw them coming, Victoria bolted from the chopper, pitched onto her hands and knees, then jumped up and charged at them through the tall grass. She practically tackled Cliff. "Oh, my God, are you all right?" She hung on his neck and kissed him. "Sasha? Don? What happened to Don?"

Cliff held her at arm's length and quickly gave her the *Reader's Digest* version. "He's lost a lot of blood, and he's unconscious again. Fire up that chopper, baby. We gotta get him back to Havana fast."

While she did a minimal preflight and got the engines started, Cliff and Sasha unstrapped Witherspoon from the door and hoisted him into the back. Good thing they had plenty of room back there. She dug out a first-aid kit and handed it to Cliff. When they were airborne, she pointed the blunt nose of the 407 north-east, checked her heading, and throttled up, determined to coax the last mile per hour from the twin Rolls-Royce engines.

Cliff squeezed her shoulder and said, "You okay, Vic?"

"I am now."

"What do you mean?"

"It's a long story. Tell you later. I'm in kind of a hurry right now."

He patted her shoulder.

Tears blurred her vision. She wiped them away impatiently. Goddammit, I'm not going to cry! She found her aviator's shades and hooked them over her ears. Bright sunlight burned through the windshield. The land below was a blur of dark green shot with shades of brown.

Victoria craned her neck and shouted, "Penkovsky—did you get him?"

Sasha said, "Yes, love, we got 'im."

Victoria nodded gravely, keeping her thoughts to herself. She had never felt glad about anyone's death before, but she did now. Elated was more like it. Maybe that horrible man's death made everything worth the risk of losing the love of her life and maybe losing Don Witherspoon, too. And maybe that somehow balanced the cosmic scales for what she had done. But she didn't want to think about that now. They had all done what they had to do. They had made a day-trip to hell. But now they were going home.

Epilogue

DONALD WITHERSPOON KNEW HE WAS GOING TO LEAVE Cuba with a helluva sunburn, but he didn't care. For the moment he was just glad to be alive and soaking up the bright August sunshine while he lounged beside the aquamarine glare of a freeform pool—one of six swimming pools, the guest relations girl had told him, scattered around the lushly landscaped grounds of the brand-new Palace of Fortune in Havana. This particular pool featured a swim-up bar under a thatched palm roof, a disappearing waterfall, and an obscene number of lovely young women displaying a remarkable amount of toffee-colored skin.

The warm, tropical breeze was filled with the buzz of conversation, laughter, and tinkling island music, all sweetened with the perfume of flowers and suntan lotion. The atmosphere seemed to be especially gay and animated, probably because this was the grand opening day for the lavish casino resort. Witherspoon thought the place had a slightly overwrought, Disneyesque feel, but what did he care? If Cliff and his Chicago buddies wanted to blow $700 million on a Caribbean fantasy of a gambling house, that was okay with him. And so was the free two-week stay that they had comped him, including ten grand in pocket money to keep himself amused.

When he reached for his daiquiri, a familiar figure caught his attention. His colleague John MacGregor sauntered toward him along the pool deck, a tall, sloshing drink in his hand, ogling every attractive female stretched on the long line of chaise lounges. His Hawaiian-print trunks were too big, and his freckled skin was nearly as white as his own. Together, Witherspoon thought, they might blind somebody. MacGregor threw him a cheery wave and a big, fox-in-the-henhouse grin.

His fellow spook dropped onto a recliner next to him, shook his hand, and said, "Is this place too much, or what? If I'm not careful, I could die of acute priapism."

"I know what you mean," Witherspoon said with a smile.

As if to reinforce that idea, a tall Cuban girl with oiled, café-au-lait skin slinked up to them wearing a hot-pink, knitted bikini that was almost big enough to cover MacGregor's appreciative leer. "Another drink, gentlemen?"

Her dazzling smile and charming Cuban accent rendered Witherspoon speechless.

"Hi, darlin'," MacGregor answered for them. "Bring us margaritas. A pitcher of 'em!"

She smiled and glided away. MacGregor looked hypnotized as he watched her go.

"Careful, John," Witherspoon said. "You might hurt yourself."

MacGregor chuckled, picked up his half-empty glass, and turned a serious face to him. "I'm damn glad to see you in one piece, Don. To be honest, I didn't think you'd make it."

"Yeah, I screwed up. Been a long time since I had to run any wet ops."

"How's that shoulder?"

Witherspoon's attempt at a casual shrug made him wince. "Can't complain. One more surgery to go. But I think it turned me into a desk jockey."

"No way, Don. The old man'll keep you in the field, you show him you're still up for it."

"He gives me a chance, I will."

MacGregor downed the rest of his drink. "You talked to Blackwell lately?"

Witherspoon nodded. "He's okay. Came out smelling like a rose."

"Lucky bastard."

"In more ways than one." Witherspoon mopped his face with a fluffy white towel. "Gotta give him credit. He stayed cool through the whole thing."

"Not to mention saving your ass there at the compound— not that you didn't pay him back about five minutes later."

Witherspoon smiled, feeling the irony. "It was the least I could do."

"Charmed life, that Blackwell," MacGregor said. "And he sure knows how to live in style."

Witherspoon chuckled. "Yeah, and get this. When I called to ask about the grand opening—you know, get a reservation? The clerk heard my name and put me right through to Russo's office." He told his partner all about the comp package deal and said that it included him, too.

MacGregor was still grinning about that when the girl in the pink bikini returned with their order. Witherspoon signed the tab as she filled the two shallow glasses. MacGregor's attention was focused on more anatomical matters.

They enjoyed their drinks in silence for a while. Witherspoon let his gaze travel across the crowded beach and past the shifting whitecaps and the jet-skiers all the way to the dim horizon. His thoughts drifted back to the early days of their Cuban op. Hard to believe that seven months had passed since that day in the mountains, taking out Penkovsky's hideout—and the Godfather himself, the sick bastard. All of them almost buying it, too. That was a hot one. Too damn hot. Maybe he was getting too old for shit like that. A desk job was sounding better all the time.

"A penny for your thoughts?" MacGregor said.

"I was thinking about that Russian sub we sank. If our guys

hadn't stopped them, I'd say that Washington'd be toast now, and Havana, too."

"You think so?"

Witherspoon nodded vigorously.

"And if you hadn't taken out Penkovsky . . . That was great work, Don. Really above and beyond."

Witherspoon smiled modestly and said, "With a little help from my friends. Too bad you were over there chasing those rag-heads when I really needed you. You missed all the fun."

MacGregor laughed and said, "Yeah, right. We got some good press out of it, too. I loved hearing the president singing the agency's praises for a change."

"Yeah, that was a switch. And we both got a pretty citation stuck in our file. Should be good for a sweet retirement bonus."

MacGregor grinned as he poured himself another drink. "So what's up with our heroic Mr. Blackwell and that babe he's married to?"

Witherspoon dug out a smoke and lit up. "Still on a cruise, I guess. They took that damned love boat of theirs and got the hell out of here as soon as they could."

"Oh? I heard the local *federales* were leaning on him pretty hard."

"Uh-huh, until Sydney Russo had a little chat with the chief of police."

"Made him an offer he couldn't refuse, eh?"

"Something like that. Cliff and Russo are also tight with President Diego. That doesn't hurt."

MacGregor grinned and said, "So where did the Blackwells go when they left Havana?"

"Some kinda world cruise. In the South Pacific, last I heard."

"Tough life."

Witherspoon sat upright suddenly and tapped MacGregor on the knee. "Hey! Don't look now."

"What?" MacGregor followed his gaze.

"Speak of the devil."

"No shit?"

"The one and only."

MacGregor whistled softly. "And that has to be Queen Victoria."

Witherspoon felt slightly offended. He had gotten to know a different Victoria Blackwell. She and Cliff waded through the sand, heading toward the pool apron, looking like a picture in a magazine ad. He stood up and waved at them. Cliff halted, said something to Victoria, and they both looked at him and grinned.

MacGregor got to his feet when they drew near.

Cliff laughed and said, "My God, look what the cat dragged in! Man, I'm awfully glad to see you looking so chipper, Don."

Witherspoon felt genuinely happy to see them. He shook Cliff's hand and said, "The prodigal returns. I had no idea you two were here." He introduced Victoria to MacGregor.

"You must be Don's better half," she said with a wry smile.

Ignoring that, Witherspoon said, "I thought you were in the South Pacific."

"We were," said Cliff, "but we decided to spend some time at Vic's ranch in Nevada."

Victoria smiled. "I wanted to see my horses."

MacGregor gaped at her as if he were in a trance. "Horses?" he asked finally.

"Thoroughbreds and German Trakehners," she said. "Race 'em, show 'em, and breed 'em."

MacGregor just shook his head thoughtfully.

Cliff said, "And of course, we couldn't miss the grand opening of our dream casino."

Everyone exchanged smiles.

Victoria squeezed Cliff's bicep with both hands. "Cliff's been working on an interesting project, too. Right, Cliff?"

"Really?" Witherspoon said.

Cliff and Victoria exchanged glances, then Cliff said, "I'll tell you about it sometime, Don, I promise."

"I can't wait," he said.

"I've been meaning to call you, Don, and discuss a few things."

"Like what?"

Cliff glanced at MacGregor, then regarded him seriously. "Like the Gold Man. I can't seem to get him off my mind. What happened to him?"

Witherspoon asked if they had time to sit down, and everyone found a seat on the lounge chairs. "Turns out he never came to Cuba," he said. "Funny you should ask about him, though. We just heard something about him."

Cliff's eyes narrowed. "And what might that be?"

"He's hooked into some international deals with a woman they call the Dragon Lady."

"Bad news," said Victoria. "That guy's the worst kind of creep."

Witherspoon gave her a nod. "We've been onto her, too. But we thought she died in a car accident in Hong Kong. She's the only one who survived."

"Interesting," said Cliff. "Any news about Sasha?"

"Not much," Witherspoon said, smiling shyly. "But I have a new assignment if I'm a hundred percent again soon enough. A top-secret mission of mutual interest to the U.S. and Great Britain. I'd be working with her."

Cliff and Victoria gave him a wide grin. "That sounds even more interesting," Victoria said. "But dangerous, no doubt."

MacGregor laughed. "Hey, sounds like fun to me." He punched Witherspoon on the shoulder. "And all I get is another assignment in the Balkans."

"Must be karma," said Cliff, smiling. "Payback for taking me on that long ride in the desert."

MacGregor looked down and shuffled his feet. "I'm sorry about that, man."

"It's all right, John. Everything worked out."

"I guess it did," Witherspoon said, gesturing around him.

"This place looks like an instant success."

Cliff nodded. "All of our other Cuba operations, too." He snickered. "And get this. The media's praising Tony Carlo right and left. 'A true visionary,' blah, blah, blah. Tony loves it."

"And the stock's doing well," Victoria said, "in spite of the lousy economy."

"Congratulations," Witherspoon said. He sat there for a moment and took it all in—the dazzling beach, the pools and tiki bars, the milling guests, and the casino-hotel rising like a digitally created sandcastle beside the turquoise sea. It all seemed surreal, like a dream. And it seemed like only yesterday since that crazy car ride with Cliff in the desert.

MacGregor said, "Good thing we got everything stabilized in Cuba so quickly. All the drama down here really shook up the world. But the president scored a lot of points with our allies for his decisive action."

"Yeah, even with France," Witherspoon said.

They all laughed.

Cliff said, "But I guess things aren't so good with Russia now."

MacGregor shook his head sadly. "Diplomatic relations have gone to hell."

"Why, exactly?" Victoria asked.

"Simple," Witherspoon said. "The Iranians keep supporting terrorists, like the Hezbollah and the Palestinians, and the Russians keep supporting Iran."

"That'll do it," Victoria said.

MacGregor appraised her with unconcealed appreciation. "Because of that and our missile defense initiative, they stepped up their spying efforts against us." He shivered theatrically. "Brrr," he said. "Feels like another cold war coming on."

"Good for job security," Witherspoon said, smiling.

MacGregor said, "We've already thrown fifty-one Russian diplomats off American soil."

"They must be unhappy," Victoria said.

"They're not the only ones," said Witherspoon. "The Chinese have beefed up their submarine fleet. Now they can move nuclear missiles within range of the U.S."

Cliff and Victoria regarded him keenly.

MacGregor said, "When you got back, maybe you noticed the high gasoline prices. That's because OPEC retaliated by reducing oil supplies to us." He shrugged. "Of course, the Russians have plenty of oil, but now they ain't selling any to us."

"Destabilize the region," Cliff said, shooting Witherspoon a look. "One of the reasons we invaded Iraq—again. So what's the real situation with the war on terrorism?"

A cold wind blew through Witherspoon's thoughts, chilling the festive atmosphere. "Not so good. Things are worse with Iran and North Korea than they're admitting. Pakistan's a loose cannon, too. And the occupation of Iraq has created more terrorists than we've eliminated already. Then there's the problem with the Mexican border. We think terrorists are planning to smuggle nuclear material and components into Mexico, then sneak it into the U.S."

"The good news is," MacGregor said, "the gloves are off now, thanks to the Cuban crisis. Congress and the American people are finally standing behind the president again, even more than after nine-eleven. He's damn near got carte blanche to do whatever he thinks best."

Witherspoon nodded. "Which means we have the green light to do what we think is necessary. Now our black ops don't have to be so clandestine."

"Whew!" Victoria said. "You guys are a barrel of laughs. That's why it's always so good to see you." She gave them her most venomously charming smile.

Cliff looped an arm around her waist. "Actually, it *is* good to see you guys, and I genuinely appreciate your frankness."

Witherspoon said, "We know we can trust you now, Cliff—you and Victoria."

"Well, in the immortal words of Ringo Starr," Cliff replied,

"I'm glad we passed the audition."

Witherspoon had to grin at that one. "There's some good news, too. Gold stocks are up."

"Then the Gold Man's in luck," Cliff said.

They all chuckled.

Cliff told them that they had to run now. Dinner with the management. Everyone stood, and they shook hands all around.

"Enjoy your vacation, Don," Cliff said. "You've earned it. You, too, John." He took Victoria's arm, and they strolled away toward the hotel.

For some reason Witherspoon hated to see them go. He took a step in their direction and called, "Hey, Cliff! You have a name yet for your new project?"

Cliff smiled and waved the question away. "Some other time, Don." He said something to Victoria, kissed her, and guided her along, his other hand still waving goodbye, their laughter drifting back to him on the scented breeze.